ROYAL CALEVA

Luis

NANCY
HERKNESS

Dedicated to my amazing children, Rebecca and Loukas

In my heart, you are royalty.

Author's Note

Royal Caleva: Luis contains spoilers for *Royal Caleva: Gabriel* (Book 1 in the Royal Caleva series). If you wish to enjoy the suspense in *Royal Caleva: Gabriel,* I strongly recommend you read it before you read this book. If you hate surprises, go ahead and read Luis's story first.

CHAPTER 1

"Ten minutes until start time, *Su Majestad.*"

Luis Dragón, King of Caleva, nodded to the young woman wearing a dark suit. She curtsied before scurrying out of the private chamber where the king, his son, Prince Raul, and his assistant, Bruno, waited. Luis was here to preside over the annual opening of the new session of the two legislative *consejos* that helped govern Caleva.

He treasured this particular ceremony because each year he used it to set forth his hopes, dreams, and plans for the country he both led and served, the country he loved to the marrow of his bones. This fresh beginning gave him the chance to rise above the daily responsibilities of being the head of state to express his larger vision for Caleva, with the goal of inspiring others to join him in it.

He glanced around the *salón* reserved for royalty when they visited the Palacio de la Ley, the building where the legislature had met for three centuries. It was in the oldest part of the original government structure and had rough stone walls, carved wooden beams in the vaulted ceiling, and heavy oak furniture with Calevan green velvet cushions trimmed in gold.

"I have your speech here." Bruno held up the black leather folder embossed with the Calevan coat of arms, as though Luis had been searching for it in his survey of the

1

room. Bruno would place the folder on the podium just before Luis arrived there, so no one could sneak a peek at its contents.

"Gracias." Luis walked to an ornate gilded mirror to make sure his medals were still neatly lined up on his deep-red uniform jacket. He had long ago stopped wearing the crown and cape for this ceremony, but every other embellishment of gold braid and regal embroidery was on display.

The royal uniform reminded the members of both councils that Luis's power came from a different source than theirs. They were voted into and out of office at the whim of their public.

After the election, Luis would still be king.

"You look magnificent, Pater," Raul said.

"You look equally resplendent," Luis said with a smile.

Raul was also dressed in full royal regalia, although with fewer medals and less gold braid. When he looked at Raul, Luis saw himself at the age of thirty, with the same dark brown hair, pale blue eyes, high-angled cheekbones, and lean, athletic build. Raul had an easier smile and a more relaxed charm, but behind those surface attributes burned the same intensity and devotion to the crown that Luis felt.

Of course, now Luis's hair and beard were salt-and-pepper, a sign of maturity he blamed more on being king than on his fifty-odd years of age. Running a small but wealthy and strategically important country required a constant balancing act on both the domestic and international fronts.

Raul tugged at his high, gold-encrusted collar. "You could use one of these jackets as an implement of torture."

Luis had been king for almost three decades, so he barely noticed the discomfort. Raul had been born just before Luis was crowned and therefore was less practiced.

"The collars are meant to force you to stand straight," Luis said. "To impress your loyal subjects with your strong backbone and authority."

"And your ability to endure strangulation." Raul made a comical face.

Despite the joking complaint, Luis was struck by how much his son had matured in the last couple of years. Guilt over his cousin Gabriel's kidnapping had toughened Raul, even though he bore no blame for the terrible crime. As a father, Luis wished Raul had not been forced to learn in such a harsh way about the burden of being the heir to the throne. The position he was born into meant that people would put themselves in harm's way for him, as Gabriel had, whether Raul wished them to or not.

As the king, Luis appreciated the fact that Raul was now better prepared for his future. In fact, his son was already taking on some of Luis's lesser duties and excelling at them. He was ready for more.

The door opened again. "Five minutes," the same young woman said with another curtsy before she dashed away.

Sparks of energy fizzed through Luis's blood.

"Let's go give them hell." Raul reached for the doorknob, but the door swung open before he could grasp it.

"*Su Alteza Real, Su Majestad.*" Mikel Silva, the behind-the-scenes head of security for the royal family, bowed to Raul and more deeply to Luis. The man somehow managed to make his formal greetings both respectful and ironic. As always, he was dressed in a dark suit, white shirt, and sober red tie. "My apologies for disturbing you at a critical moment, but we have an urgent situation."

"I have an important speech to give," Luis pointed out, although Mikel knew that, of course.

"Yes, *Señor,*" Mikel said. "However, you need to read this." He held out a plain white envelope.

"What is it?" Luis asked as he accepted the envelope.

"A letter from Odette Fontaine."

Luis hated only three people in the world, a surprisingly small number, given how long he had been king.

Odette Fontaine was number one on his list because she had orchestrated the kidnapping and maiming of his nephew and had tried to murder his son.

Cold fury at the woman whipped through him. "What the hell does Odette want?"

"Read the letter, *Señor,*" Mikel said. "I have already and would recommend you do so in private."

The only other people in the room were Raul and Bruno, two men Luis trusted with his life. If Mikel felt they should be excluded, the letter must be explosive.

"Will you excuse us?" Luis said.

Although Raul stiffened, he and Bruno took Luis's request for the command it was and exited the *salón.*

The envelope was not sealed. Luis yanked the single page of paper out and unfolded it.

He recognized Odette's slanted handwriting. Twenty-nine years before, after his wife's death, Luis had made the mistake of having a six-month relationship with the French-woman. Disgust at his stupidity fanned his anger.

My dearest Luis,

Remember the drive back to the palace after le Duc de Montagne's ball? There were consequences. One consequence, at any rate. You have a child.

4

We need to discuss this immediately, or I will release the news to the media within one hour of the time I hand this letter to the prison warden. He is aware of its urgency.

Your ever devoted,
Odette

He reached back into his memories of that turbulent time. The ball had been a private celebration, not a state occasion, so he had taken Odette as his partner. She had worn a dark blue dress that clung to every curve, which meant she could wear no undergarments underneath it, a fact she reminded him of in a throaty whisper at every opportunity. She also had spent the evening touching him and dancing as close to him as possible, while he had drunk more wine than was prudent.

It had been late when they climbed into the royal limousine for the hour-long drive back to Castillo Draconago. The screen between the driver and the passenger compartment had already been closed.

Odette had yanked her dress up to her waist and straddled him on the seat, unzipping his trousers, pushing aside his briefs, and impaling herself on his already erect cock in one swift movement. Enflamed by her hours-long seduction, he had fucked her.

Without a condom.

Could Odette have gotten pregnant?

No. She had wanted to be queen. If she had carried his child after that encounter, she would have used that as leverage to force him to marry her.

He crumpled the letter in his fist. "She's lying, as always." A cruel lie, since she knew how much he had longed for more children.

"She says she has proof." Mikel's expression was tight with frustration. "Proof that will be released to the media if you don't go to the prison to meet with her."

"*Joder!*" Luis swore. He did not believe in her proof, but the media would still run with the story. It was too juicy. "She's in a maximum security prison. How can she get information out to the press?"

Mikel's jaw tightened. "She is allowed visitors, all carefully screened. She has had only three. A work colleague, her lawyer, and her cousin. None of them are reporters, but any of them could have this proof somewhere outside the prison. Any conversation with the lawyer is confidential and therefore not recorded, so she could be the conduit...or it could be someone outside the prison." He shook his head. "It doesn't matter. We don't have time to track down the source."

"She could have done this at any time in the last year, since all she has to do is stare at her cell walls," Luis said.

"She knows you are giving your annual speech to open the *consejos*," Mikel said. "She wants to force you to cancel it."

Luis started to swear again before a thought struck him. When he was Raul's age, he had already been king for several years. "Bring Raul and Bruno back in."

Mikel gave him a questioning look but opened the door and called to the two men waiting outside.

Once the door was closed behind them, Luis turned to Raul. "I have no choice but to go deal with Odette immediately. She threatens to release highly sensitive information if I do not go now." He gestured to the leather folder in Bruno's hands, the gold-embossed Calevan coat of arms catching a gleam of light. "You know this speech as well as I do because you helped write it. You will deliver it in my place."

Excitement and fear tightened Raul's face as he glanced at the folder. "I…I'm not the king. My words will not carry the same weight."

"You will *make* them carry the same weight," Luis said. "You are *el Príncipe de los Lirios.*"

His son straightened, his shoulders square. "I will not disappoint you." His voice was thick with emotion.

"Of course you won't, *hijo mío.*" Luis softened his tone as he squeezed his son's shoulder, feeling the solid muscle under the wool and gold braid. "Nothing you do could ever disappoint me." He shifted his gaze to Bruno. "I leave you with the task of coming up with a good excuse for my absence."

His assistant didn't flinch. "Of course, *Señor.*"

Luis turned to Mikel. "You will accompany me to the prison."

"Would you like to change your clothes first?" Mikel asked.

"No. Let Odette see that she has dragged me away from my duties, as she intended," Luis said.

"She forgets that you have a worthy stand-in," Mikel said.

Luis looked at Raul, pride expanding in his chest at his son's outward composure. Luis was asking a lot of his son, but he had no doubt that Raul could handle it.

The door opened again, this time to admit the Portavoz del Consejo who would officially announce the king to the *consejos.* "*Su Majestad, Su Alteza Real,* it is time to go."

"There's been a change of plans," Luis said. "I've been called away. *El Príncipe* Raul will deliver the opening address."

"But, *Señor*, the *ciudadanos* are expecting the king." The official was aghast.

Luis leveled his gaze at the man. "*El príncipe* speaks for me. His words are my words."

♛

Luis sat in the big leather chair behind the warden's desk in CárcelMax, Caleva's maximum security prison, as he waited for Odette Fontaine. He forced himself to sit still, despite the anger boiling inside him. Mikel had finished sweeping the area for any kind of surveillance and then set up a jamming device to add another layer of privacy. Bodyguards were stationed at every door into the warden's office. Not Luis's personal ones. They were too recognizable. Mikel had brought in his own private security team, anonymous men and women dressed in prison guard uniforms.

Still, Luis would be alone with the woman he hated most in this world.

The woman who had nearly destroyed Luis's beloved nephew, Gabriel. For a moment, he was back in those terrible days after Gabriel's kidnappers had sent Luis his nephew's severed ear. He had wondered then what other mutilations his abductors would subject their victim to as time ticked away. Thank God Mikel had been there to negotiate Gabriel's release before anything worse could occur. Luis banished the gut-wrenching fear to its dark place in his memories. He could not allow emotion to cloud his thinking when dealing with Odette.

Despite his resolution, when the door swung open, he dug his fingers into the upholstered arms of the chair as his hatred surged.

The bodyguards ushered Odette through the doorway, the chains that joined her hand and ankle cuffs clanking as she shuffled across the carpet.

She looked old and drawn, the glaring yellow of her shapeless shirt and trousers giving her pale skin a jaundiced tint. Her reddish-brown hair was yanked back in a messy ponytail. A flare of satisfaction warmed him.

Luis gestured to the straight-backed metal chair in front of the desk, and the bodyguards moved her to it.

"Sit," Luis said.

Instead, Odette raised her hands as far as she could before the chain stopped her. "Really? Do you feel these are necessary?" Incredibly, her voice held amused condescension.

"Sit down," Luis repeated, his tone like granite.

She shrugged and sat, resting her clanking wrists on her thighs.

"You may go." Luis nodded to the bodyguards.

"You're not afraid I'll try to wrap the chains around your neck and strangle you?" Odette's eyebrows were raised.

Luis and the bodyguards ignored her.

As soon as the door clicked shut, Odette smiled, her gaze skimming over Luis's uniform. "Did I drag you away from another engagement?" she drawled.

"As you are well aware, you did. Fortunately, Raul was prepared to take my place." He kept his tone neutral.

Satisfaction flashed across her face. "You sent a boy to deliver a king's speech?"

"Raul is a *prince*." Luis leaned back in the chair. "What is this new lie you have manufactured?"

"You don't fool me," Odette scoffed. "You dropped everything and came running when you read the letter."

"I came because you claim to have evidence of this ridiculous story. What is it?"

The short silence pulsed with her angry frustration.

"Our daughter lives in Iowa," Odette said. "I went to see her."

A tiny crack of doubt worked its way into his certainty that Odette was lying. Her trip to Iowa had been the last unresolved thread in the investigation into Gabriel's kidnapping. No one could figure out why she would go there.

Yet her actions still made no sense to him.

"If you truly had carried my child, you would have used her as leverage long ago," he said. "You wanted to be queen."

"*Va te faire foutre, connard!*" Spit droplets sprayed from her mouth as she cursed him. "You dumped me like a sack of trash. You did not deserve to have me as your queen, and I was not going to give you the happiness of having a child. I gave birth and tossed her away like you did me." She leaned forward. "And now—now that you have been deprived of holding her as a child, of grooming her to be a perfect princess, of being loved by her as her father—now I reveal her to you. This is my revenge on you, one I have waited almost three decades to take."

If she had really had a daughter and cast her off, she was even more monstrous than he could fathom. Yet her words about not being able to hold his daughter, of not having her love him as a father, struck at him like knives. Odette was right about how effective her revenge would be...if it was true.

"What did your daughter say when you met her in Iowa?" Luis couldn't imagine the reunion had been a happy one.

"Nothing. I didn't speak to her. I *saw* her." Odette's face twisted with disgust. "She wore no makeup. She was dressed in jeans and a shapeless sweatshirt. I overheard her voice. She sounds like *un péquenaud*, an uneducated yokel. I could not bear it, so I left. That was not *my* daughter."

"You made her that way by refusing to accept your responsibility as her mother." His voice was harsh. "I do not understand how seeing your daughter incited your desire to kidnap Raul."

"Because instead of being *un péquenaud*, *my* daughter should have been a princess. She should have been raised in a palace by me as the queen." Odette's mouth twisted in fury. "You did not deserve to have a perfect prince of a son. Your child needed to be ruined like mine. You needed to suffer the way I did when I looked at my daughter. Too bad those incompetents took Gabriel instead of Raul."

"You find wearing blue jeans and speaking with a Midwestern American accent comparable to slicing off a young man's ear?" He had met many unstable people in his reign, but this went far beyond that. He would not remind her that he loved Gabriel like a son. That the torment had almost been worse because his nephew had not been the real target.

"Oh, come now," Odette said. "It was not so terrible. I made sure one of the world's best ear surgeons performed the surgery to ensure the reconstruction would be easy. No one can tell that Gabriel's ear is not the one he was born with."

His vision went red as he imagined wrapping his fingers around her throat and feeling her struggle to breathe while he squeezed.

After the mutilation, Gabriel had believed he could no longer hear music properly. He had nearly given up his passion for playing flamenco guitar. If he hadn't met Quinn, he might have done so, depriving the world of a brilliant talent and, even worse, extinguishing his own radiant spirit.

Luis clenched his fingers into fists so tight his fingernails bit into his skin. When he finally had control of himself again, he asked, "How do you expect me to believe that this long-lost child is really mine and not a creation of your twisted need to punish me?"

"I put your name—Luis Dragón—on the birth certificate as her father. That was to needle you when I decided to tell you about her. There it was, the truth of her parentage, but no one in the U.S. would ever believe it was you, the King of Caleva, even if they connected you with the name. They would think I was delusional...or joking." Odette laughed, a sound of smug satisfaction. "And my secret would be safe because you didn't know she existed so you wouldn't look for her."

"That is not proof that she is mine," Luis said.

Odette waved that away before her expression turned calculating. "I have her DNA analysis from a blood sample taken when she was born. It was entered into a private genetic databank."

At last, something that could be confirmed or denied. His nephew's fiancée, Quinn, was an expert at tracking information in databases. She could find the DNA analysis and confirm or disprove its validity.

"That is the extent of your so-called evidence?" Luis put unalloyed scorn in his voice, but the crack of doubt in his mind widened.

"It will be enough to stir up a storm in the media." Odette sneered. "The noble, widowed king has a bastard child. Quite a blot on the escutcheon."

"Our affair was never a secret, and it is now ancient history," Luis said. "The media has already had its fun with it."

"Ah, but a child! In line to inherit the Dragon Throne. *That* will pique the media's interest," Odette said.

"The media isn't going to run a story based on an old DNA record in an unofficial database. All that *might* prove is that a baby you delivered nearly thirty years ago was related to me." Luis sat back in a pose of unconcern. "You have no evidence that the young woman in Iowa is my child. If the media claims she is, it will be met with a denial and the threat of a lawsuit from the palace, not to mention whatever legal action the girl's family might take to protect her."

In fact, his press office would quietly put out the word that this story had come from a psychopathic criminal bent on revenge and had no basis in fact. No respectable media outlet would touch it after that. He didn't care about the tabloids.

Odette leaned forward, her eyes gleaming with sly cunning. "But you always wanted more children. How can you brush off the possibility that you might have a grown-up daughter who is alive and well and living in Iowa?"

He couldn't. Even worse, he could feel the bud of hope beginning to unfurl in his chest. Odette wanted to make him suffer, and she had found a brilliant new way to do it. "Tell me how to access the databank record."

"Oh, no. You will have to get your minions to do that. But I will give you a gift," Odette said. "Your daughter's name is Grace. Grace Howard."

It was a poisoned gift, and Odette knew that. Instead of an anonymous woman, he now had a name for the fresh-faced, jeans-clad young lady who *might* be his daughter. "What do you want?"

"I want to be acknowledged as the mother of the bastard princess, of course. It is my due." Odette's smile held smug triumph. "Think of it. Your child's mother is a convicted criminal, locked up in prison. What a blow that will be to your much-vaunted honor! The perfect King of Caleva has a hideous skeleton rattling around in his palace closet."

Luis didn't care about a blow to his own reputation. He would, though, be concerned for the unknown young woman's feelings. If she existed. Until he could confirm that, there was no point in further discussion with this madwoman.

"This conversation is finished." He rose to his feet. "*If* I have a daughter, I will find her myself."

He pushed a button on the warden's desk phone, and the door opened instantly to admit Mikel. "You may remove the prisoner," Luis said.

CHAPTER 2

In the SUV, Luis yanked off his brimmed hat before he shrugged out of the drab brown coat Mikel had used to disguise him as an unidentifiable prison visitor. The clink of his medals reminded him of Odette's shackles, which brought him a grim satisfaction.

"How did the meeting go?" Mikel asked from the seat beside Luis. There was no inflection in his voice.

"We won't have to worry about the press. Yet," Luis said, but he had another concern to address first. "Before we discuss what Odette said, I need to check in with Francisco. We will decide if my presence is needed at the Palacio de la Ley."

Mikel pulled a cell phone from the inside pocket of his suit jacket and handed it to Luis.

"*Gracias,*" Luis said, hitting the speed dial for his most trusted political advisor, Francisco Vargas. "Francisco, what is the situation?"

"*Un momento.* I will go to the guest office where our conversation will be private." Luis could hear voices in the background, a click, and then silence. "*El Príncipe* Raul created quite a stir." Francisco's voice held satisfaction. "He delivered the speech with a great deal of emphasis."

Luis understood that to mean that Raul's delivery had

been more fiery than Luis had planned. The same words could sound very different depending on the tone in which they were spoken. "Is that a problem?" he asked.

Francisco gave it a moment of thought. "Had *Su Majestad* done so, it would have been considered heavy-handed. *El príncipe*, though, is young, so it was appropriate."

"And the response?"

"Nothing unexpected yet. We will find out when the action begins behind the scenes."

"Where is Raul now?" Luis asked.

"On his way back to Castillo Draconago. He made a most dramatic and regal exit before the *consejeros* could get organized to lobby him. We agreed that it would be wisest not to be dragged into conversation with one faction or another." Francisco's tone became more personal. "You can be very proud of *el príncipe*, *Señor*. He spoke and acted like a future king."

His words lit a glow of fatherly pride. Francisco was an exacting critic and did not compliment where it was not deserved. "I will return to the castle as well, then." He nodded to Mikel as he spoke so he could inform their driver of their destination.

"Do you wish me to meet you there?" Francisco asked.

"Only when you feel you have gathered all the useful information you can. Your instincts are invaluable."

"Gracias, Señor."

Luis handed the phone back to Mikel. "Raul did well. He exited before the *consejeros* could buttonhole him."

"I am sure he was excellent. He has learned from you."

Luis nodded and turned his mind back to his alleged daughter. A maelstrom of anticipation, disbelief, regret, fury, and yearning ripped through him with such power that he clamped his hands on his thighs to withstand the surge.

"According to Odette, there is a DNA record stored in a private databank that proves she gave birth to my daughter. That daughter's name is Grace Howard, and she lives in Iowa. That is why Odette traveled there two and a half years ago."

Luis wanted to go straight to the royal jet and fly to the U.S. to find out if Grace Howard was really his daughter.

"Odette is a manipulative, lying psychopath," Mikel said in a matter-of-fact way. "Is the DNA her only evidence of this claim?"

"Based on the rest of our discussion, I believe it is."

"Did she tell you where the databank is?"

"No, but I am sure Quinn can find it. Although I hate to ask her when she is dealing with wedding plans." The thought of Gabriel's happiness with his bride-to-be drained away some of Luis's fury at Odette. His nephew had weathered his trauma and come back from it stronger than before.

"I believe Quinn will be happy to have a valid reason to avoid some of the more tedious meetings," Mikel said. "But even if the DNA is authenticated, it does not prove that this particular woman, this Grace Howard, is your daughter. The DNA could have come from some other child."

Luis ran one hand over his face. "As I am aware. But if it *is* authenticated, it means that somewhere in the world, I have a child. DNA does not lie."

The hope he had been quelling with an iron control flickered to life again.

"I understand that family is of the utmost importance to you, *Señor*, but we must go slowly. If nothing else, there is the succession to consider, given that this child is illegitimate."

"Fortunately, my ancestors were not respectable citizens,

so they made provisions for heirs born out of wedlock," Luis said. "I can acknowledge her as mine, and she will be a princess."

"And next in line for the throne after Raul, a role she has no training for and may not wish to fulfill," Mikel pointed out.

"I understand the complications," Luis snapped.

Mikel merely nodded. "Please tell me everything that Odette said."

Luis repeated the conversation almost verbatim, a useful memory skill he had honed over his many years of being king. "Only five people should know of this. Outside this car, that includes Raul, Quinn, and Gabriel," Luis said. "Odette must be kept in solitary, with no visitors allowed, until we get ahead of this situation. I don't want her releasing any information to the media."

Mikel nodded before he said, "Remember that we are limited in how long we can keep a prisoner in solitary confinement without offering a valid reason."

"And she will know that, of course," Luis said with a snarl of anger.

"Indeed." Mikel's tone turned reflective. "One wonders why Odette chose this particular time to share such a bombshell with you."

"It is impossible to know what goes on in a mind that twisted," Luis said.

His hatred of Odette had intensified to the point where he wanted to return to the medieval way of punishment. He wanted to seize her with his own hands, hurl her off the highest point of Acantilado Alto, and watch her body smash onto the rocks below. He wanted her to survive, as legend said two others had, so that her broken, agonized body could be dragged back up to the pinnacle, where he could fling her off again. Then he would stand atop the high cliff and smile as the waves battered her body against the boulders until the sea sucked her under forever.

Since civilized kings no longer had that option, he would have to be satisfied with prolonging her miserable captivity.

An unpleasant thought struck Luis. "Grace may wish to meet her birth mother."

"It might be better if she didn't. Odette is not a mother to be proud of," Mikel said, his harsh tone surprising from a man so controlled.

"I believe it is important to know where you came from," Luis said. If Grace was truly who Odette said she was, his daughter should have the opportunity to make her own choice.

Mikel shook his head. "With respect, I disagree. There are times when the past should be buried as deeply as possible."

Luis wondered again where Mikel had come from—he'd arrived in Caleva with his young daughter eight years ago—but he refused to pry. Mikel would tell him when he was ready. Or when it became necessary.

"Mikel, my friend, today proves that the past refuses to stay buried, no matter how much dirt we heap on top of it."

"What did Odette want?" Raul started to stand as Luis entered his private office, but Luis waved him back to his seat in one of the armchairs. Raul's uniform jacket was tossed over the chair's arm, so he wore only a black cotton T-shirt with his dress trousers. A glass of water dangled from his fingers.

"First, how did the speech go?" Luis unfastened the high collar of his own jacket before he sat in the chair nearest to his son.

"I'm sure Francisco already reported to you about it," Raul said, but he grinned. "I was nervous as hell walking down the aisle to the podium, but once I got there and spotted some of the assholes who tried to grab the lily fields, I got pissed off. I enjoyed rubbing their noses in the fact that we defeated them. The speech just poured out of me after that."

"Anger can be useful if channeled in the right direction. I am proud of you, *hijo mío*. I am also grateful that you were there to step in for me."

"It was an honor to be entrusted with such an important job," Raul said, the grin gone as his tone turned formal. "Thank you for your confidence in me."

"Be careful," Luis warned. "You may find yourself shouldering my responsibilities more often."

"Pater, I am here anytime you need me. You know that," Raul said. "But the *consejeros* might not be so happy about the substitution."

"I already have half a dozen requests for private meetings," Luis acknowledged. "I will definitely drop some of those on you."

Raul nodded with a mischievous glint in his eye. "That will annoy them even more." Then he sobered. "Was what Odette had to say explosive enough to be worth missing the address?"

"It depends on whether it is true," Luis said.

Raul waited.

"She claims that I have a daughter, a half sister to you." Luis watched Raul's face. "Odette put her up for adoption right after the baby was born."

His son straightened abruptly, but his expression gave nothing away. "Do you believe her?"

"I believe her enough to ask Quinn to find the private databank where Odette claims her daughter's DNA analysis is stored."

"If anyone can find it, Quinn can." Raul hesitated before he spoke again. "Pater, I know how much it would mean to you to have another child," he said with care, "but Odette is a psychopath. She lies without compunction to cause you pain."

"Mikel said the same thing." Luis leaned forward and locked his gaze on Raul. "I do not need another child. I am honored to be your father every day. I love you with all my heart and soul."

"I do not doubt your feelings for me." Raul reached across the space between them, and Luis took his hand, savoring the strength of his son's grip. "You have been both a brilliant king and a wonderful father to me. That's amazing, because just one of those roles is demanding enough." Raul squeezed Luis's hand before releasing it. "What worries me is that *you* will be hurt when Odette's story turns out to be a complete falsehood."

"You are a very perceptive young man." No wonder Raul was not affected by suddenly acquiring a new sibling. His son did not believe Odette.

"You understand, though," Luis said, "that if there is even a small chance that I have another child, I must do everything in my power to find her." The image of a young woman in jeans and a sweatshirt flickered in his mind's eye for a moment.

"Do you know where she lives?" Raul asked.

"In Iowa."

Raul's eyes widened. "*That's* why Odette went to Iowa? To see her daughter?"

"To *see* her and nothing else. Odette did not speak to her." How could a mother be within reach of her daughter and not touch her? That was a level of coldheartedness Luis could not fathom. "She felt that Grace—her daughter's name—was not worthy to be her child because she wore blue jeans and spoke like a yokel. Odette's words."

"Why did that make her decide to kidnap and mutilate me?" Raul asked, his face tight with pain at what had happened to his cousin instead.

The horror of his ultimate responsibility for the abduction lanced through Luis again, but he kept his voice level. "Since she perceived her daughter as being damaged, she wished to damage my child. To cause me the same level of pain. She was lashing out at me for what she had done in the past. She knew what would cause me the maximum amount of agony."

"*Madre de Dios*, she is a sick human being." Raul's eyes blazed with anger.

Luis had sensed something was off with Odette all those years ago. That was why he had broken off their relationship. Yet he had allowed her to remain friends with his brother's wife, Hélène, and to become a sort of honorary aunt to Raul and Gabriel. Guilt had warped his judgment, and Gabriel had paid for it. Luis would never forget or forgive his terrible decisions.

"And now?" Raul asked. "Even if the DNA proves Odette's claim, that doesn't mean this Grace in Iowa is the same person as the baby."

"One step at a time, *hijo mío*. One step at a time."

"There's something I don't understand," Raul said. "Why was it so urgent to meet with Odette about this when you were supposed to be giving a major speech?"

"She threatened to share the story with the media if I didn't arrive within an hour. She was proving that she could make me dance to her tune."

"It's a pretty juicy story," Raul said. "Are you sure she won't release it anyway?"

"Given the inconclusive evidence and Odette's attacks against us, I don't see any respectable media outlet picking it up without confirming the facts with the palace. Of course, we will dismiss the story as the fabrication of a criminal madwoman."

"Because it probably is," Raul agreed.

Luis nodded, but he would be tempted to hover over Quinn, urging her to work faster to find his child's DNA.

CHAPTER 3

With a great effort, Luis pulled his attention back to the discussion going on around the conference table. Four men—a *marqués* and a *conde* from the Consejo de los Señores and two citizens from the Consejo de los Ciudadanos—had presented a proposal to negotiate an increase in the amount the Americans paid to lease the property on which their military base was built. Luis was attending only to get a feel for the players and how committed they were to this issue. He had every intention of letting Raul handle subsequent meetings, which was why his son sat to his right.

The Marqués de Huarte passed black binders to Luis and Raul. "These reports show the costs the military base imposes on Caleva versus the amount the Americans pay for use of our land. I think you will see that their presence here has become less and less beneficial to us over time."

Luis tapped the folder without opening it. "Have you included the cost of building our own navy and air force if the Americans no longer protect us? Or the money the sailors pour into our economy when they leave the base to visit our cities and towns?"

"We have factored all that into our analysis, of course," Huarte said stiffly.

The two aristocrats were part of the same group who had tried to wrest control of the lily fields away from the crown a year before. Luis had fought them off then, and he would do it again. He just wondered who had whipped up this sudden hunger for more money within the *consejos*. In this case, the money from the military base's lease flowed into the national treasury. He assumed the councillors would promise their constituents tax cuts if the proposal was approved. At least that was less greedy than the nobles who had wanted the profits from the dementia-stopping lily sap for themselves.

Luis turned his gaze to the two representatives who did not hold titles. One had been an agitator in the Consejo de los Ciudadanos since his election seven years ago. He attached himself to any cause that brought publicity and strife. Felipe Camacho, though, was new to the *consejo* and an unknown quantity politically, according to Francisco's briefing. Camacho was in his early sixties, had a mane of white hair, and worked as a professor of mathematics at the national university.

"*Señor* Camacho, the military base is in your district," Luis said. "Do your constituents feel it is a burden economically? I would have thought the opposite."

"I am honored by your question, *Su Majestad*," Camacho said, tilting his head downward in a gesture of respect before he met Luis's gaze. "Our concerns are less about economics and more about interactions with our citizens. We have had some...friction with the military personnel recently."

"How will raising the rent ameliorate those issues?" Luis asked, his tone sharp.

"It will not, of course," Camacho conceded without hesitation. "I simply hoped to use this opportunity to bring these problems to your attention."

"Ah." The man might be new to politics, but he understood how to work the system. "That should be a separate report."

"I will be happy to submit it at your soonest convenience, *Señor.*" Camacho's words were polite, but Luis saw a flare of anger in the man's eyes.

Luis had no intention of getting involved in a local matter, but he nodded before turning to Huarte. "Don Pedro—"

A knock sounded, and the heavy oak door swung open. Mikel slipped into the room and glided to where Luis sat at the head of the conference table, his presence creating a ripple of uneasiness on the faces of the assembled *consejeros.*

Mikel bent to murmur beside Luis's ear. "You asked to be informed the moment Quinn found the DNA information. She is waiting for us in your office."

Luis nodded, keeping his expression neutral as a strange mix of excitement and anger pinwheeled in his chest.

"My apologies," he said to the group. "A pressing matter calls me away. *El Príncipe* Raul will continue this meeting in my stead."

Luis stood, and everyone at the table rose with him, bowing as he walked out of the room. Before Mikel closed the door, Luis saw Raul claim his chair at the head of the table with authority in every line of his posture. Having Raul give the opening address to the *consejos* had brought unexpected dividends in the seriousness with which the politicians regarded the prince.

Luis strode down the carpeted hallway with Mikel at his side but one step behind him. Neither of them spoke since this wing of Castillo Draconago was busy with staffers and other officials at this time of day. Mikel pressed his thumb to the pad beside the entrance to Luis's private office suite and held the door open for Luis to pass through.

Quinn had jumped to her feet and now curtsied, her black-rimmed glasses catching a glint of light and her brown braid bouncing with her motion.

Luis waved her back to her seat in front of his desk. "What did you find?"

"If you will be seated, *Su Majestad*," Mikel interjected. "We will share all the information we have gathered."

Luis tightened his lips in irritation but allowed his security chief to stage-manage the revelation for the time being. He moved behind his desk and sat in the leather chair. "Quinn?"

She pushed the glasses up on her nose. Despite all his efforts to ease their relationship, she was still nervous around him.

"Odette made it almost too easy," she said. "Of course, that was only true once we knew what to look for." She pulled two sheets of paper from the leather portfolio she held and slid them across the polished wood of Luis's desk.

On top was a New York State birth certificate for a baby named Marie Dupont. The mother's maiden name was Jeanne Dupont, the French equivalent of Jane Doe.

And the father was listed as Luis Dragón.

Seeing his name on the official document socked him in the gut, which was why Odette had done it. He looked up at Quinn. "And the DNA record?"

"That baby was definitely yours," she said, her voice growing more confident.

Luis rocked back in his chair and closed his eyes, releasing the emotions he had shoved into a box and slammed the lid on. His hatred for Odette flared a moment before he was swamped by joy at the knowledge that he had a daughter. He snapped his eyelids open. "What do you mean 'that baby was'?"

"The next page is the amended birth certificate that was issued when Marie Dupont was adopted, the day she was born," Quinn said.

Luis flipped the page to find a similar document, except on this one, the baby's name was Grace Howard, with parents Eve Beaumont Howard and Benjamin Howard. Luis ran his finger over Grace Howard's name as though he could conjure her up from the ink.

"The amended birth certificate appears legitimate," Mikel said. "But given the implications of acknowledging the child as yours—"

"We must test Grace Howard's DNA to confirm she is the same person as the baby named on this birth certificate." Luis did not need to be reminded of his duty to the crown. It was grafted onto his bones. He turned back to Quinn. "Have you found her?"

"Yes, we have." Quinn pulled a black binder from her portfolio and pushed it across the desk. "This is not a full report," she said. "I pulled it together quickly once I found the DNA and birth certificates. I will get you more soon."

Luis quelled his impatience long enough to smile at his nephew's fiancée. "You have done more than I could expect in such a short period of time. Thank you for this."

"It was an honor to be asked to work on such an important project," she said, her brown eyes glowing at his praise.

"We are keeping all this information off the palace servers," Mikel said, gesturing to the binder. "These pages reside only on the highest-security storage in my private office. I would recommend that you read this while we wait and return it to me so that I may destroy it."

"Of course," Luis said.

Mikel and Quinn stood, which reminded Luis of something. "Gabriel is traveling to recruit new talent for the next music festival, is he not?"

Quinn nodded. "I'll be joining him in a couple of days."

"I will not ask you to keep this information from him, because there should be no secrets between you and your betrothed," Luis said. "I will request that he not tell anyone else, though."

"I understand," she said, hesitating a moment before she added, "I hope this is really your daughter, *Señor*. I *want* her to be yours. She seems like someone I would like to know."

"I hope you will have the chance to do so," Luis said, touched by her sympathetic support.

"We will leave you to absorb the report in private," Mikel said. "Let me know when you would like me to return for it."

Mikel held the door for Quinn and closed it with a quiet click.

Luis opened the folder to see a full-page photograph of a beautiful red-haired young woman smiling directly at the camera. With his fingertip, Luis traced the strong, straight line of her nose, the clean-cut angle of her jaw, the slashing cheekbones, and dark, winged brows. He saw those features every day in the mirror. He saw them when he looked at Raul and Gabriel.

Her face was *his* face but softened into the female version.

A drop of water spattered onto the photo. Only then did he realize that tears were running down his cheeks.

Mikel must have seen the extraordinary resemblance, too, but the security expert would not let that sway him until he had incontrovertible proof. Nor could Luis.

Luis sat back, pulling a handkerchief out of a drawer to wipe the tears away. When he was a young man, he had looked forward to having a family of four or five children of his own. His brother, Lorenzo, had expected to do the same. They had envisioned the private wing of the palace filled with children's voices, unlike their own quiet, restrained childhood.

But life—and death—had changed their plans. As had Hélène. She had chosen Lorenzo instead of Luis, shocking both brothers.

Luis had believed his heart was shattered, but he had been young and only a prince then. With the arrogance of his youth, he had thought he had plenty of time to find a new love.

Then his father, *el Rey* Carlo, was diagnosed with brain cancer. He commanded Luis to wed before the cancer killed him. Luis had married the woman his father chose, a political marriage, and it had been a disaster in almost every way.

The only joy in that period of his life had been Raul's birth. When Luis had felt overwhelmed by the demands of his dying father, his fragile wife, and the thousands of decisions he felt unprepared to make, he would sneak off to the nursery and cradle his infant son in his arms. At first, the nurses had been flustered by his presence, but they became accustomed to his sudden appearance at all hours of the day and night and simply handed over Raul without question. The sweet, innocent scent of Raul's tiny head had soothed Luis's soul and given him the strength to face his challenges again.

When his father and wife died within six months of each other, and Luis was drowning in a maelstrom of pressure, self-blame, and loneliness, Odette Fontaine had come to visit Hélène in Caleva. Odette had seemed to be everything his dead wife was not. Strong. Confident. Independent. Adventurous in bed. He had ignored all the red flags and plunged into a mad affair with her.

Until one too many red flags had snapped in the breeze, and he had broken off the relationship. To say Odette had taken it badly was an understatement.

He shook his head. If Grace Howard was truly his daughter, he could not entirely regret his lapse in judgment.

He leaned forward to devour the photo once again. He wanted to savor the knowledge that he was the father of *two* children.

He drank in the sweetness of Grace's smile, the intelligence that glinted in her ice-blue eyes that matched the color of his, and the way her thick auburn hair—Odette's genetic contribution—waved away from her temples.

There were several more photographs, taken from different angles. Luis lingered over each one.

Then he turned to the printed pages and began to read. He finished and closed the folder, his hand splayed over the cover protectively.

He pressed the button that summoned Mikel and sat back to think.

"*Su Majestad.*" Mikel bowed as he entered and closed the door behind him.

"First, Quinn did an excellent job," Luis said. "You were very smart to hire her despite the issues in her past."

Mikel gave a faint smile and bowed his head in acknowledgment. "She is a remarkable young woman in many ways."

"I am glad of that for Gabriel's sake." Luis turned back to the report. "I see that Eve Howard and her husband divorced when Grace was a baby and that Grace lives with her mother still," he said. "Is the ex-husband part of his adopted daughter's life at all?"

"As far as we were able to ascertain, he is not," Mikel said. "*Señora* Howard has carried all of the financial responsibility for Grace's education, which is substantial, given that veterinary school tuition is high. As you can see, Grace is in her fourth and last year now."

Luis frowned at the thought of a man who adopted a child and then abandoned her entirely. On the other hand, the fact that Grace had grown up without a father might leave more room for Luis in her life.

"I will approach her mother first." Eve Howard was a veterinary technician at Iowa State College of Veterinary Medicine's clinic, so she and her daughter were undoubtedly close. "I need to know everything you can find out about Eve Howard before I meet her."

Mikel looked pained. "It would be safer to confirm Grace Howard's parentage before you become involved personally."

Luis stabbed a finger on the closed binder. "You saw the photograph. Grace Howard looks exactly like a Dragón. Add Quinn's findings to that, and it seems almost certain that she is my daughter. I wish to meet her as soon as possible, but we will handle it through Grace's mother. She can buffer the fact that I am the king. I do not want Grace to feel overwhelmed by that aspect of the situation."

Mikel made a wry face. "The latter may be difficult."

"I will go as Luis Dragón, not as the King of Caleva." A private trip to the U.S. with no fanfare and as few people as possible informed of his presence there. Mikel would manage that.

"We can strip away the trappings of kingship, *Señor*," Mikel said. "But you are ever the king."

"After so many decades, it is difficult not to be." He had borne the weight of the crown for so long, he could no longer remember how it felt to be free of it.

He pushed the binder toward Mikel but kept his hand on top of it. "I want that first photo of Grace on my phone. Strip all identifiers, but get it onto my personal cell."

"Of course, *Su Majestad*."

The intercom on Luis's desk pinged, and Bruno said, "*Señor*, the delegation from the *consejeros* has departed. *El Príncipe* Raul is here in my office, ready to brief you on the conclusion of the meeting."

"*Gracias*, Bruno." Luis looked at Mikel. "Grace Howard is now your top priority."

Mikel bowed and started toward the door.

"Mikel!" Luis softened his tone. "I may need your advice about having a daughter. I've only ever dealt with young men."

His security chief hesitated before half turning. "Daughters seem so vulnerable that you want to build a ten-foot-high wall around them, yet they are as strong as the steel blade on one of your swords."

CHAPTER 4

Eve Howard stopped in front of the entrance to the local law office in Ames, Iowa, and tugged at the collar of her striped cotton blouse. She had gone home to change out of her scrubs after work. Something about the mysterious Mikel Silva's voice on the phone had made her suspect she needed some metaphorical armor for this meeting. She had twisted her hair into a low bun, applied mascara and lipstick, donned a navy skirt and the businesslike blouse, and shoved her tired feet into high-heeled black pumps.

Silva had refused to say much during his call to set up their meeting, but he had assured her that this was not a legal matter, that he was merely borrowing a colleague's office to give them privacy. Still, she couldn't shake the feeling that he had bad news of some kind.

She squared her shoulders and pulled open the glass-and-steel door to enter a small waiting room containing a few unoccupied chairs, a large potted Ficus shrub, and an oak desk behind which sat a young blond woman.

"May I help you?" the receptionist asked with a pleasant smile.

"I'm Eve Howard, here to see Mikel Silva."

"Of course, Ms. Howard." The receptionist rose, exuding a physical energy, as though she should be rock climbing, not sitting at a desk. "Follow me, please."

She led the way down a carpeted hallway lined with closed doors on both sides. The office was surprisingly quiet, even for the end of a workday. The lawyers in the firm must keep bankers' hours.

The receptionist stopped in front of a door with a brass nameplate, knocked, and opened it without waiting for a response. She gestured that Eve should go inside. "Mr. Silva is expecting you."

"Thank you." Eve stepped into the office, getting a quick impression of furniture that matched the blandness of the waiting room except for the photos of men holding up large fish arrayed over the walls.

"Ms. Howard, thank you for coming." A wiry, dark-haired man stood with his back to the window, so his face was in shadow. He started toward her with his hand held out. "I'm Mikel Silva. It is a pleasure to meet you."

The way he moved reminded her of a hunting cat, attention laser-focused, muscles coiled to spring in any direction. He wore a charcoal suit, white shirt, and maroon tie, all precisely fitted but not attention-catching.

As he came away from the backlighting of the window, she could see that his smile reached his eyes, making their pale blue look almost warm. She judged him to be in his forties. When he shook her hand, his grip was firm but unthreatening. Yet she had the sense that—like the receptionist—he was tamping down his real strength. "Nice to meet you too," she said.

"Please." He gestured toward a seating area holding a beige love seat, glass-topped coffee table, and two chairs upholstered in rust-colored fabric. On the coffee table sat a tray with two carafes, a pitcher of water, mugs, and glasses. "May I offer you tea, coffee, or water?"

She caught a faint accent in his voice. Spanish, she guessed, given his name.

"No, thank you." She seated herself on one chair, tucking her skirt over her knees. "I'd like to know why you wanted to talk with me, Mr. Silva." *And who the hell you are.*

"Mikel, please." Humor glinted in his eyes. "This is why I enjoy Americans. They get straight to the point." He filled two glasses with water before he sat back on the love seat. "I have come here on behalf of someone else. He is a prominent person and feels it would be less...overwhelming if I speak with you first."

The nebulous sense of dread dragged at her breathing. She nodded.

Mikel clasped his hands on his knees and locked his gaze with hers. "Ms. Howard, I come to you because the person whom I represent has recently discovered that he has a daughter. We believe that child to be your adopted daughter, Grace."

The dread forced itself out in a gasp as shock tightened her chest. She had always wondered if this day would come.

"As you can imagine," Mikel continued, "her father would very much like to meet your daughter. However, he feels strongly that he should speak with you first. You will know how best to approach your daughter so she is not upset by the revelation."

"I appreciate his tact." She did, but at the moment, Eve was the upset one. She had been Grace's only parent for so many years, trying to fill the place of both mother and father after the divorce, fighting to give her daughter everything she deserved on a vet tech's salary and the tiny amount of child support her ex had grudgingly paid. Now a total stranger wanted to waltz into Grace's life after Eve had raised her beautiful, brilliant daughter almost entirely on her own. *Who the hell does he think he is?*

"All I know is that the father's name listed on the birth certificate is Luis Dragón, but I always thought the birth mother made that up," Eve said. "I'm pretty sure she didn't use her real name either."

"His name is the one thing the birth mother did not lie about," Mikel said.

"Who is he, then? Where does he live? Why didn't he know about Grace before?" So many questions that she needed answers to. Since Mikel had that slight accent, perhaps Grace's biological father was from another country.

"It would be best if he answers those questions himself," Mikel said. "There is also the issue of confirming that Grace is truly his daughter. Because of his prominent position, it is necessary to perform a DNA test."

He didn't shift a millimeter, but Eve could tell he was watching her reaction as she tried to sort through how she felt about such an intrusive request. Why did Grace need to prove anything to her father? Silva had sought out Grace, not the other way around. The burden of proof should fall on *him*. "How did he find out about Grace in the first place?"

"Grace's birth mother told him, but only recently."

Why had Grace's birth mother kept that a secret? Was the father a criminal? Abusive? An addict of some sort? Had the mother been protecting her infant daughter? Fear clenched a fist in her throat. Eve had handled rabid dogs. She could face down a mere human, even if he had some high-level position in the world.

Eve picked up a glass of water and swallowed a mouthful to loosen up her throat. "And why do you doubt the biological mother's word about Grace's father?"

Mikel's face tightened. "She is not a reliable source." He seemed to make a decision. "Would you be open to meeting Grace's father? He will be able to both explain his position and reassure you."

"I—" Who could this highly important person be? "Yes, of course." For Grace's sake, she needed to gauge what kind of man this Luis was. Not that she could stop him from contacting Grace if he wished to. Grace was an adult.

"He would very much like to meet you as well," Mikel said. "He is waiting in the office next door. I know this must be something of a shock. If you need a few minutes…"

Putting it off would only wind the anxiety tighter. She shook her head. "Let's get this done."

Although Grace was an adult now, Eve found she didn't want to make room for another person in her daughter's life. A selfish impulse. She should be happy that Grace would have the option to know her biological father. Depending on what kind of person he was, of course. The next few minutes would tell her. Maybe. After Ben's desertion, she wasn't sure how good a judge of men she was.

Mikel nodded before he stood and left her in the office alone. Eve took another gulp of water and then wiped her damp palm on the sofa cushion. Stand or sit? She decided to stand, dodging around the coffee table to stop beside one of the chairs and face the door. Although she was only of average height, her heels added a couple of extra inches, so she felt taller. That might give her more confidence in facing the person who claimed to be Grace's father.

She took a deep breath and braced herself to face whoever came through the door. He would be a factor in her life going forward. She would have to deal with him, whether it was to accept him or to protect Grace from him.

The door opened. The man who entered somehow projected his presence into every corner of the office, not with arrogance but with power. He was tall and lean with a short, neatly trimmed beard and salt-and-pepper hair combed back from his temples. He wore gray trousers and a pale blue dress shirt, open at the neck, casual clothing that did not look in any way casual on him. His smile was so potent that she nearly backed up a step.

"Ms. Howard? I'm Luis Dragón." He strode forward with his hand outstretched. "It is a pleasure and an honor to meet you."

"Please call me Eve," she said as his long fingers wrapped around her hand. His handshake was as firm as Mikel's but somehow warmer. As she examined his face, she felt a tug of recognition. She knew him from somewhere. Or maybe it was just that she could see in him a more mature and very masculine version of her daughter's face. She swallowed her impulse to say how much he looked like Grace. Better not to give away too much at the outset.

"Eve. Thank you. And I am Luis." He had a smooth baritone voice and, like Mikel, a slight Spanish accent. "I appreciate your willingness to meet with me on short notice. I know this must be something of a shock to you." His smile took on a rueful cast. "It was a shock to me as well, but of the most miraculous kind. Shall we sit?"

He swept his hand toward the seating area, and something about the gesture gave her that nag of familiarity again. Yet she was sure she had never met him before.

Who is he?

Mikel Silva had said Luis was a prominent person, so maybe she had seen him in the media. She snuck a sideways glance at him as she sank onto the sofa again, trying to chase down his identity.

He waited until she had settled before he seated himself in a chair, his back ramrod straight and his hands resting on the arms as though he sat on a throne rather than an ugly orange chair.

A throne.

"Holy shit," she whispered. "You're the King of Caleva."

He had been in the news recently because of the wildly successful music festival in his country. Grace's favorite rock star, Kyran Redda, had been the headliner, so they—and Redda's millions of other fans around the world—had watched the festival on television. The king had introduced Redda at the concert, and Eve had commented to Grace that Caleva's ruler was a sexy silver fox. The cameras had loved him, too, because they had often panned to show him sitting in his box, applauding Redda's performance.

She realized what she had said out loud and embarrassment scorched her cheeks. "Oh my God, I shouldn't have…"

Now she understood Silva's secrecy and the DNA test. She also understood that she was dealing with a man way out of her league.

Did he expect her to stand and curtsy? That would seem weird and awkward, especially since she had never curtsied before in her life. But maybe it was required when one met a king.

"Please. Here, now, I am just Luis Dragón." He looked…resigned, his smile slipping a bit. "A man who is overjoyed to discover that he has a daughter he did not know existed."

"But you're the King of Caleva. How... Why... I don't understand." Confusion took away coherent speech as she tried to connect Grace with Caleva's monarch. "I mean...I don't know where to start."

Was this some kind of elaborate prank? Did this man just *look* like the King of Caleva? But why would anyone go to all this trouble to prank *her*?

Or maybe it was a scam of some kind. But she had no money—only debt—so why would anyone bother to set up such an elaborate plot? If anything, it should go the other way around, where *she* would try to claim Grace was the king's daughter to get some of his vast fortune from *him*. Which would be so far-fetched no one would consider doing such a thing.

"I understand that it seems strange that my infant daughter found her way to Iowa," Luis said. "From what I have learned, though, she was very fortunate that you adopted her."

The compliment sounded sincere. "She was a gift to me, but thank you." Eve shook her head, trying to settle her whirling thoughts. "How did this happen?"

"It is not a pretty story." For a moment, he stared out the window, obviously not seeing anything but the past. He brought his gaze back to her. It was daunting to have those ice-blue eyes locked on her with utter focus. "When I was in my twenties, my father, King Carlo, was diagnosed with glioblastoma. Knowing he had only a short time to live, he asked me to marry, which I did. It was a political marriage, and my wife was emotionally...fragile in ways I didn't understand until too late." Sorrow dragged at the corners of his mouth. "Sofia became pregnant and gave birth to my son, Raul, but she struggled with postpartum depression. My father died shortly after Raul's birth, so Sofia also had to endure the weight of a state funeral and a coronation. Six months later, the car she was driving went off a cliff in what was ruled an accident."

Wow. He was almost admitting that his wife committed suicide. Why? To manipulate her into feeling pity for him?

"I'm so sorry," she said.

He waved one hand in a way that was both acceptance and dismissal. "It was a long time ago. I have learned to live with my responsibility."

He meant it. He felt responsible for his wife's death. She couldn't help feeling a little sad for him.

"Time dulls pain but doesn't erase it." She knew that from her own experience.

He gave a small nod. "It was a difficult time. That is my only excuse for the poor judgment I showed when I chose to have an affair with the woman who is Grace's mother."

He became father, king, and widower in one short period of time. That could excuse a lot. It was strange to feel sympathy for this powerful man, but she did.

"We all make mistakes," she said, thinking of her own failed marriage.

His smile held no humor. "My mistakes reverberate."

She nodded as though she understood his issues, but she was more concerned about Grace's. "This woman got pregnant and didn't tell you? That seems strange since you certainly had the means to take care of a child."

This was the crux of his story. *Why?*

Before he could answer, an ugly thought struck Eve. He was a *king.* "Was it because Grace was illegitimate? Would you not have wanted her because she couldn't inherit the throne? Or because she would be a public relations problem?" She couldn't keep the accusation out of her voice.

Luis's features tightened as though she had slapped him. "I am here because I want her," he said harshly. "I would *always* want my child, no matter what the circumstances of her birth were." He snapped his mouth shut and took a breath before he said in a softer tone, "My apologies. Your questions were quite reasonable, given the circumstances."

"Yes, they were." She kept her voice firm.

He gave her a rueful half smile. "My ancestors were not a respectable bunch. Children born out of royal wedlock are always considered part of the family, if they wish to be. Grace's legitimacy would not be an issue for me or for the people of Caleva."

Luis might feel he could ignore the lack of a marriage license between Grace's biological parents—he was a king—but Eve wasn't convinced that the people of Caleva would be as unconcerned.

He locked his eyes with Eve's. "I broke off the relationship before she realized she was pregnant. I did not handle the ending well, and she was very angry." His hands clenched on the chair arms. "I terminated the affair because I sensed a lack of mental stability that worried me, especially after my experience with my wife." His gaze did not plead, but rather hoped for understanding. "Her revenge was to withhold knowledge of my child from me until now." His voice dropped to a near whisper. "It was quite effective."

She thought of her smart, beautiful daughter having to accept the limitations of Eve's financial situation in the schools she attended and the few places she had been able to travel. If Grace had been raised by the king, she could have studied anywhere in the world and been to exotic locales many times over.

Maybe, though, Grace would not have been loved in the all-encompassing way that Eve loved her. Weren't the children of royalty often raised by nannies? Could Grace's birth mother have been worried about that?

Although, if she had been concerned about Grace not receiving a parent's love, why would she put her baby up for adoption? Had she worried that Luis would figure out who the child was if she had kept her?

The whole scenario made Eve's head spin. "I don't understand why she would deprive her child of the advantages you could give her."

Sorrow shadowed Luis's face. "Odette is a very troubled woman."

"Why did your ex-lover decide to tell you now?" Eve asked, suspicion making her question sharp.

"The story gets even uglier in the present," Luis said. "Odette Fontaine is currently in prison for life in Caleva. She masterminded my nephew's kidnapping two years ago."

"Oh, dear God, I remember that! His ear was cut off." Horror clawed at Eve's gut as she recalled the tragic story. The American media had reported on the attention-grabbing details with relish: A handsome royal duke's brilliant talent had been destroyed by the horrible mutilation his kidnappers had inflicted on him. Even at the vet clinic, everyone had talked about it.

Grace's mother was a monster.

"Yes, Gabriel suffered terribly." His words were filled with pain. "The victim was supposed to have been my son, but my nephew convinced the abductors that he was the prince, so they took him instead."

For a fleeting moment, he sagged in the chair. But then his spine straightened, and she wondered if she had imagined his slump.

"That's horrendous," she said, but her real distress was for *her* child. Terrible things might happen to Grace because she was the king's daughter. Eve suppressed a shudder.

"My only consolation is that every single person involved has been punished." His eyes blazed with a satisfied fury that was almost frightening. "But Odette reached out from her prison cell in an attempt to torment me further." The fury died. "She miscalculated, because this news was pure joy. I had hoped to have many children, but..." He shrugged.

Why hadn't he married again? Women would have lined up to have him father their children. But that wasn't a question she could ask a king.

So now he wanted *her* daughter, which could put Grace in danger too.

"It seems to me that this Odette would lie if she thought it would hurt you," Eve said, choosing her words with care. "Mr. Silva mentioned that you want to have a DNA test done."

"Mikel is being very cautious, but I believe more and more that Grace is my daughter." He held up both hands to frame his face. "Do you not see me in her?" He pulled a cell phone from his back pocket, tapped at it, and then held it out to her, a glow of love in his eyes. "My son, Raul. They are clearly siblings."

She took the phone, feeling the warmth of his body on it. *Royal body heat.*

The young man who smiled from the phone looked like a younger version of his father, but also almost like a twin brother to her Grace. His hair was brown streaked with blond, while Grace's was a deep auburn, but the angle of the jawline, the strong cheekbones, the curve of his lips, and the shape of his face all matched her daughter's to a stunning degree.

She wondered if Raul shared Grace's integrity, dedication, and persistence.

Handing the phone back, she said, "People can look alike but not be related."

"I have some proof already. Odette had her baby's DNA stored in a databank. It has been confirmed that I am the father. Mikel has, of course, pointed out the remote possibility that Grace isn't the same child that the DNA was taken from." Luis sighed. "Asking for a DNA test is an awkward way to begin a relationship."

A startling thought struck her. "If she's proven to be your daughter, then would Grace be a *princess?*"

The irony almost made her laugh. All of Grace's little girlfriends had dressed up as princesses every chance they had gotten. Grace had preferred to be a unicorn, a puppy, or a cat.

"If she wishes to be. There are various technical options involving her royal standing, all of which we can discuss later." Luis sat forward. "I would be overjoyed to acknowledge her as my daughter, but she already has a mother. Perhaps she does not need to have a father as well."

His words jabbed like daggers. He had more legal rights than Eve did, and she hated that. Grace was *hers!* Eve had changed her diapers, wiped her tears when her boyfriend dumped her, edited her essays for college and grad school, and *loved* her for all of Grace's life.

She swallowed her outrage. Grace deserved to have a father. She especially deserved to have one who could offer her the advantages Luis could. His resources made Eve's look downright pitiful. Grace didn't crave material things, but Luis could send her on journeys anywhere in the world or pay for advanced degrees at the finest universities. Jealousy reared its ugly head before Eve could smack it down.

"If I acknowledge Grace, I must be honest with you." Luis gave a half grimace. "She would need a certain amount of security."

Because the king's relatives could be targets for kidnapping and, dear God, mutilation. Fear wrapped icy fingers around her heart and squeezed.

"Or I can be a beneficent uncle with no acknowledged blood ties, but with a very strong interest in being part of her life in some way," he offered with a noticeable lack of enthusiasm. "We could keep it very private."

"You already have an heir," Eve said, wanting to protect her child from potential kidnappers. "Why would you even need to claim Grace as your child?"

His face sharpened with something she could only call hunger. "If she is my daughter, she is of my blood."

Another slash at Eve's heart. Grace was *not* of Eve's blood.

"I would have her honored as she deserves," Luis continued. "Even more, I would wish to be a father to her in whatever way she—and you—will allow." The angles of his face softened. "I have missed so many years of her life. I want to make up for that."

Another unwelcome thought charged in. "If you acknowledged her, would you expect her to move to Caleva?"

He spread his hands in an admission of uncertainty. "She is an adult. She will make her own decisions about where to live."

But a father and a palace could be very tempting. If Grace moved, Eve would have to move to be near her. A small bubble of panic lodged in her throat. She coughed once to clear it. "All of this is up to her, of course. I appreciate your courtesy in letting me know first."

"I thought you could help her in navigating this surprising situation," he said. "If something of this magnitude had happened to Raul, I would wish to know so I could assist him."

He was not only a king, but a father. He had some understanding of how this would upend Grace's world. He was also a parent who was desperate to meet the young woman who might be his child. That resonated in Eve's heart, and she found herself softening toward him.

The final decision, though, was Grace's.

"I assume you want me to be your envoy," she said.

"I thought it would be best for her to learn the news from you, but if you don't feel comfortable..." He lifted a hand to indicate he would handle it.

He wanted her to put her seal of approval on the DNA test and their meeting. That would smooth his way. It was to his credit that he didn't just swoop down on Grace from his throne, assuming his daughter would be thrilled to be a princess. Eve respected his restraint. Of course, as a king, he must have had a lot of practice dealing with touchy situations.

"I'm happy to start the ball rolling with Grace, but she has a mind of her own. I can't guarantee how she'll respond."

"I understand." For a moment, he looked stricken, and her heart cracked open a little more for him.

"Knowing Grace, she'll want to meet you. Beyond that, I can't predict."

"If you persuade her to give me that one chance, I will accept whatever comes." His smile held the confidence that he would convince Grace to let him into her life.

He was probably right.

"When will you speak with her about this?" he asked.

Right. He was a king. He had responsibilities that didn't allow him to hang around in Ames, Iowa. Besides, there was no good reason to delay telling Grace such important news. She glanced at her watch. It was six o'clock. Nearly dinnertime, yet her usually healthy appetite had deserted her. "I'll tell her tonight."

A fleeting look of relief crossed his face. "Thank you."

She started to stand, then sat again. "I don't know how this works. Do I need your permission to leave?"

He pressed his hand against his chest. "Here, I am only a man who begs your help. My crown was left outside the door."

She considered the confident tilt of his head, the authoritative set of his shoulders, and the way his presence filled the room. "You don't need a crown to be a king." She stood.

In a surge of graceful power, he came to his feet as well. "You have Mikel's number. Please contact him anytime, day or night, and he will reach me."

"What exactly does Mikel do?" she asked.

"Mikel is in charge of my personal security, as well as being a trusted advisor." Luis spoke with sudden intensity. "He came to me after Gabriel's kidnapping and was instrumental in arranging his release."

"Ah." Whoever had been in charge of security when his nephew was kidnapped probably was not working for the king any longer.

She went around the table and held out her hand. "No curtsy either, right?"

He nodded and folded his fingers around hers, laying his other hand on top. "It has been a great pleasure to meet you. I know it is not necessary, but I would like to thank you again for being such a wonderful mother to Grace."

All she could focus on were the sparks flickering up her arm from where his skin touched hers. His grip was strong, yet protective.

When he released her hand, she mentally shook herself and tucked her hand into her skirt pocket. Luis had said something nice to her, hadn't he? "Thank you," she said. "But I'm the lucky one. Grace is an amazing person."

He walked beside her to the door. She was aware of his long stride and of a faint scent that evoked fresh air. When he reached for the doorknob, she felt the tiny brush of his shirt-sleeve against the fabric of her blouse. What was wrong with her?

She stepped through the door to put some distance between them before she pivoted. "I'll be in touch as soon as I speak with Grace."

He lowered his chin, almost in a bow. "I am in your debt."

The receptionist was standing partway down the hall. As soon as Eve reached her, the woman smiled and turned to accompany her.

In the lobby, Eve looked around the silent, empty space and realized something. The lawyers in the office weren't lazy—they and their clients had been cleared out for this meeting.

"You're not really a receptionist, are you?" Eve said to the young woman. "You're with the king, right?"

The woman unlocked and opened the front door for her. "I am part of *el Rey* Luis's security team."

Right. He traveled with his own personal security.

Grace's father could claim all he wanted that he was just Luis Dragón, but Eve understood who he really was.

Luis watched from the window as Eve Howard headed down the sidewalk to her car, her steps slow, as though she was lost in thought. Not surprising, given their meeting.

A knock sounded on the office door.

"Come in, Mikel," Luis called.

His security chief entered in his silent way and gave a slight bow. "May I ask how the conversation went, *Señor*?"

With some difficulty, Luis separated his anticipation of connecting with his daughter from his objective evaluation of how Eve Howard had responded to his revelations. "On balance, it went well. *Señora* Howard seemed sure that Grace would choose to meet with me. That is the outcome I hoped for."

"And the DNA test?"

"She understood the necessity for it, given who I am." Luis frowned. Eve had not commented on whether she thought Grace would be willing to take the test.

"Does she know who Grace's birth mother is?" Mikel asked in a neutral tone.

"It was unavoidable." Luis grimaced. "I told her as little as possible about Gabriel's kidnapping, but it was impossible not to explain the reason Odette is in prison."

"*Señora* Howard strikes me as an intelligent woman who would understand some of the less positive implications of her daughter's relationship with you," Mikel said.

"Yes, she will conclude that being related to me could put her daughter in danger. I even told her that some security would be necessary if Grace allows me to acknowledge her as my daughter."

Mikel nodded.

"You, too, have a daughter, one you love deeply," Luis said. "Would you refuse to include her in your life because it might put her in harm's way?"

A haunted expression flickered across Mikel's face. Luis knew Mikel carried a dark past, but the man was loyal to the core, and that was all Luis asked.

"Our positions in life are very different," Mikel said. "In my case, I took Serena away from a dangerous environment."

"Whereas you feel I am leading Grace *into* a dangerous environment?" Luis put a warning in his voice.

"You are bringing her into a *complicated* environment, especially for someone who did not grow up in it." Mikel did not intimidate easily.

"If she is mine, it is her birthright!"

Mikel gave him a level look. "Have you not sometimes wished to lay down your crown? She may not wish to pick up hers."

Worry overwhelmed the anger, and Luis sat in a nearby chair, briefly closing his eyes against Mikel's relentless gaze. "She would not be the heir. She would not face as much pressure."

"*Señor*, I sympathize with your desire to hold your child close, but she is from this small town in the midst of Iowa.

She may not understand what you are offering her. And if she does, she may not want it."

Luis pictured the alarm on Eve Howard's face when he had mentioned Grace needing security. The woman had grasped the problem immediately, and he had regretted bringing up the subject so early in the conversation. "Grace did not have all the advantages I could have given her, but she was raised by a smart, capable woman. Eve Howard will guide her daughter with wisdom."

"Assuming she understands how drastic the changes in her daughter's life will be," Mikel said. "And her own."

Luis waved a hand in both acceptance and dismissal of Mikel's words.

In fact, Eve had shown an impressive composure even after she realized who he was. There had been no apparent calculation of what benefits *she* might derive from the relationship, which surprised him. Too often, Luis had seen the avarice in people's eyes as they angled for his attention. Eve might have a real claim on his resources, yet she didn't seem to care about that. Perhaps the shock hadn't worn off enough for her to consider her possibly advantageous position yet.

He could only hope that Eve was the exception to his previous experience with significant women in his life. He needed her as an ally until Grace took the DNA test. Once Grace was confirmed as his daughter, he would not hesitate to go around Eve, if necessary.

CHAPTER 5

Eve paced over the braided rug in the living room, listening for the sound of Grace's car in the driveway. Her daughter had worked late with classmates doing charts, as she often did. Eve had spent those hours composing and discarding ways of delivering the stunning news about the man who might be Grace's father.

Might be. A strange glimmer of hope arose. Maybe all this agonizing would be over nothing. The DNA test might prove that Grace was *not* the king's daughter. Then Eve and Grace could go back to their familiar, comfortable lives and laugh over this bizarre memory.

She grimaced at her wishful thinking. The King of Caleva and his very intense head of security would not have trekked all the way to Ames, Iowa, and cleared out an entire law firm if they weren't pretty certain Grace was his child.

Eve went back to pacing and trying to figure out how to ease into telling Grace about her potential parentage.

There was no way to make the words less shocking. All Eve could do was be there to help her daughter through it.

When the dogs barked and jumped off the couch at the sound of the old Honda rattling up the drive, Eve took a deep breath and went to greet her daughter at the kitchen door.

As Grace trotted up the wooden steps, Eve traced the resemblance to Luis in her daughter's striking features. It was impossible not to see it now that she knew what to look for.

"Hey, Mom." Grace gave her a peck on the cheek before she unslung the backpack from her slim shoulders and bent to greet Trace, Eve's three-legged golden retriever, and Army, Grace's rescued marshmallow of a pit bull. "I'm starving. Have you got any leftovers of last night's lasagna?"

"Of course!" Eve was half-relieved and half-anxious about postponing the upcoming revelation.

Grace grabbed a fork before she dropped into one of the antique Windsor chairs at the round oak table. "Dr. Young is such an asshole. He made us redo our charts for the third time this week."

"What did he claim was the problem now?" Eve asked as she put a generously heaped plate of lasagna in the microwave.

"Nothing of any importance. He was just nitpicking."

Since she worked as a veterinary technician in the school's clinic, Eve knew most of the teaching veterinarians. Evan Young was a prissy, rigid, stick-in-the-mud. None of the vet techs liked working with him.

"Don't take it personally. He's like that with everyone. At least you don't have much longer on your rotation with him." Eve pulled salad greens out of the fridge, added some sliced vegetables, and tossed them with a balsamic dressing. As the microwave dinged, she set the salad on the table before she fetched the lasagna. "Here you go. How about some Chianti?"

Grace looked surprised. "No, thanks, but you go ahead and have some."

Eve debated before grabbing a glass and twisting the cap off the cheap Italian wine. A quick gulp eased the tightness in her throat a little. Grace gave her a curious glance before digging into her chunk of lasagna.

Eve had drunk her entire glass of wine before Grace finished eating. The Chianti had done nothing to dissolve her tension.

Grace leaned back in the chair with a satisfied sigh. "Okay, Mom, what's up? You never drink on weeknights."

Of course, Grace would notice.

"Let me clear off the table, and then we'll go in the living room to talk," Eve said, standing.

"Now you're scaring me." Grace's brows lowered in a frown of concern. "Did you get bad news from a doctor? Just tell me before I freak out."

"I'm fine, but I have something…significant to tell you." Eve rinsed the plates and stuck them in the dishwasher. Then she poured herself more wine.

"Maybe I'll have a glass after all," Grace said. "It feels like I might need it."

Eve filled another goblet and handed it to her daughter before leading the way across the creaky wooden floor to the living room. She gestured Grace toward the blanket-covered sofa, figuring she might need room to join her if the conversation grew emotional. As soon as her daughter sat, Army jumped up beside her and curled up against her thigh.

Grace stroked the dog's head absently. "Okay, tell me," she said. "I can't handle the suspense."

Eve sat in one of the roll-armed chairs, also covered by a blanket to protect it from pet stains. She watched Grace closely as she said, "Sweetheart, your biological father wants to meet you."

Grace opened her mouth, closed it, and finally said, "I have so many questions I don't know where to start." She twisted the wineglass in her hands. "Is his name really Luis Dragón, like it says on my birth certificate? What about my birth mother? Are they not together anymore?"

Eve set her glass on the occasional table beside her chair and leaned forward. "Yes, his name is really Luis Dragón. In fact, I met him today."

"Why did he show up now?" And the unspoken question in her daughter's eyes: *Why did he not want me for all these years?*

"He didn't know you existed until very recently," Eve said. "Then he needed time to find out where you were. He came here as soon as he could track you down."

"That means he's not with my biological mother." A little of the sadness left Grace's gaze at hearing that her birth father hadn't deliberately abandoned her. "What's he like?"

Eve recalled the room-filling power that Luis Dragón projected and the intensity of his desire to connect with his daughter.

"He's—" *Regal. Imposing. Charismatic. Crazy attractive.* Eve shoved that last thought away. "Right. Here's the thing that's going to be hard to wrap your mind around." She paused. "Luis Dragón is the King of Caleva."

Grace stared at her, ignoring Army when he headbutted her hand because she had stopped petting him. "What?"

"He's the King of Caleva. We saw him on television during their big music festival, remember? He introduced Kyran Redda at the main concert because Kyran was staying at the palace. Everyone thought that was kind of funny. That's how I recognized the king."

"I know you wouldn't joke about this, but…" Grace shook her head in bewilderment. "I don't understand. Caleva is an island in the Atlantic Ocean, off the coast of Spain. We're in the middle of Iowa."

"I'm in shock, too, but here's what…Luis told me." She felt awkward calling a king by his first name. "His wife died in a car accident soon after their son, Prince Raul, was born. We saw the prince on television too." The prince who might be Grace's half brother. "The king, Luis, was, er, upset and lonely. He had an affair with your biological mother but broke it off before either of them knew she was pregnant. Evidently, she was angry at being dumped and punished him by not telling him about you."

"Holy crap," Grace muttered, massaging her temples as though she had a headache. "This can't be real."

Eve thought of the emptied-out law office, the bodyguard masquerading as a receptionist, the slightly sinister Mikel Silva, and the compelling presence of Luis Dragón. "What I've told you is real, but because Luis is a king, the proof of your relationship has to be undeniable before you meet him. They need to do a DNA test to make sure you are really his daughter. The only evidence they have right now is DNA taken when you were a baby, and they need to confirm you are the same person as that infant."

"Then it's possible that I'm *not* the King of Caleva's child?" Grace said slowly.

"Possible, but I would say unlikely. He has gone to a lot of trouble to find you and come here."

"Then let's get it done, because there's no point in getting worked up about it if I'm not related to him," Grace said. "How soon can I take the test?" That was so typical of her daughter—cut right to the heart of the matter.

Eve wanted to slow things down, because once Luis's paternity was confirmed, he would turn their world upside down just by being who he was.

"Are you sure you don't want to take more time to absorb such overwhelming news?" Eve asked.

"I feel like I'm in limbo right now." Grace swirled her wine in her glass. "I need to know the truth."

"I can call the king's…assistant, Mikel, and ask him about the test," Eve said.

Grace glanced at her watch. "Isn't it kind of late?"

Eve could picture Luis pacing his room, wherever it was, trying to will the phone to ring. He would be accustomed to getting things done when he wanted them done. "He said to call anytime, day or night."

Grace took a deep breath and let it out again. "Go for it."

Eve retrieved her phone from the kitchen and called the number for Mikel. The man answered on the first ring. "Good evening, *señora*. How may I help you?"

"I've spoken with my daughter. She would like to take the DNA test as soon as possible."

"That is good news," Mikel said. "Could I come to your home to take the samples in half an hour?"

So soon. Events were spiraling out of Eve's ability to control them. But Grace was driving this, too, and Eve had to respect that.

"Let me check with her." Eve muted the phone. "The king's assistant can be here in half an hour. Are you okay with that?"

Grace stroked Army's big square head as she hesitated, her eyes still wide with shock. To give her time, Eve put the call on speaker. "What is involved in the test?" Eve asked Mikel.

"Just a cheek swab," Mikel said. "I will be bringing some legal forms giving consent for the test. If you feel uncomfortable signing them without a lawyer's review, we can delay the procedure until tomorrow."

Eve glanced at Grace. "As medical professionals, I think we can interpret legal permissions ourselves. Will the king be coming too?"

Grace shook her head frantically.

But Mikel was already on the same page. "I believe it would be better if he and your daughter met only after any question about their biological relationship has been laid to rest. Then it can be a joyful occasion without reservations."

That protected both Grace and Luis. "We support that plan," Eve said.

"Shall I come in half an hour?" Mikel repeated.

Eve hit the mute button. "It's perfectly reasonable to delay the test until tomorrow."

Grace was silent for a moment before she sat up straighter. "There's no point in waiting. It won't change anything."

Eve reached out to squeeze her daughter's hand as she unmuted the phone. "Grace will be ready."

"Very good. Please ask your daughter not to eat or drink anything from now until the samples are taken," Mikel said before he disconnected.

"I'm glad the king isn't coming," Grace said, a quaver in her voice. "It would be too uncomfortable not knowing whether our relationship is real or not."

Eve thought of Luis's almost overwhelming presence and agreed. "I'm going to put the dogs out in the yard so they won't bother Mr. Silva. Remember not to drink any more of that wine."

"Wine is not nearly strong enough for how I'm feeling right now," Grace said.

Eve herded Army and Trace outside. When she came back into the living room, her daughter wore a worried frown.

"Mom, how do you feel about all this? I mean, having my father walk into my life and having him be a king, for God's sake. It's going to change a lot…if it's true."

Eve's heart clenched, both at how right Grace was and at how sweet she was to think of her mother's concerns. She sat beside Grace on the sofa. "I'm okay with anything you want to do. All I care about is that you're happy."

Tears brimmed in Grace's eyes before they overflowed down her cheeks. "I don't know what I'm feeling right now. Maybe happy, but also like I'm in an alternate reality."

Eve stroked her daughter's hair. "You look like your father, except for your hair color. I guess that came from your mother."

"*I* look like the King of Caleva?" Grace pulled her phone out of her jeans pocket and tapped at the screen.

Eve peered over her shoulder to see a gallery of images of Luis Dragón. Some showed him in an elaborate uniform at various state occasions. Most showed him in perfectly tailored suits, standing beside or shaking hands with world leaders. Grace scrolled past those before she stopped at a photo of the king when his hair was still dark brown and he was clean-shaven.

"I do look kind of like him," she murmured.

The resemblance was also in the way Grace held herself. She stood exactly the way her father did—straight-backed, shoulders squared, chin lifted. Maybe royal genes affected posture too.

Grace flicked the screen to display more photos. Eve's attention snagged on one—clearly taken by a paparazzo with a long lens—in which the king was walking up the steps of a swimming pool on what appeared to be a yacht. Water glistened on well-defined shoulder and chest muscles and an abdomen carved like a Michelangelo statue.

He was one hot royal.

She jerked her gaze away and banished the thought to a dark corner of her brain.

"Find photos of Prince Raul," Eve said. "You look even more like him."

"I have a half brother." Grace's voice was filled with wonder. Then she turned to Eve with doubt in her eyes. "Do you think he'll be glad to have a half sister? After all, he's been the only child of a king all his life. That has to be a pretty privileged position."

"If he's not happy to have you as his half sister, he's an idiot."

"Thanks, Mom." Grace gave her a strained smile and went back to scrolling, this time pulling up pictures of the crown prince. She went into the entrance hall and stood in front of the gilt-framed wall mirror that had belonged to Eve's grandmother. Holding up the phone, she studied her own face next to the prince's.

"I look even more like Raul." She shook her head and declared, "My father is the King of Caleva," as though trying to convince herself.

She shook her head again before returning to the sofa. Huffing out a breath, she locked her gaze on Eve. "What about my birth mother? What did he say about her?"

Eve couldn't bring herself to weigh down Grace's shoulders with such an ugly revelation yet. Maybe Luis could find a way to soften the blow of what her birth mother had done. He should be an expert at diplomacy, after all.

"We discussed the past more than the present," Eve said, which was true in its own way. "I was very focused on who your father was since he was standing in front of me. If the test comes back positive, you could ask him about your birth mother."

"Anyone would be a little overwhelmed by meeting a king." Grace looked down at her hands twisted together in her lap. "I'm overwhelmed at the idea too."

Eve covered her daughter's hands with a gentle touch. "He said not to think of him as a king. He wants you to see him as just Luis Dragón, a man who is overjoyed to learn he might have a wonderful daughter."

Grace turned one hand over to grip Eve's. "I guess I shouldn't miss my rotation tomorrow, but it's going to be hard to concentrate."

"Just remind yourself that if Dr. Young gets annoying, you could have him beheaded," Eve joked.

Grace's laughter might have a slightly hysterical edge, but the sound of it sent a wave of relief through Eve.

When the doorbell rang, they both jumped. If a king wanted something done, it got done at high speed.

Eve gestured for Grace to wait in the living room while she opened the door. Mikel stood in a pool of light on the front porch, holding a silver metal briefcase. Behind him stood the young woman from the lawyer's office.

"Come in." Eve held the door open.

Mikel smiled and stepped inside, followed by the woman. "Eve, you met Bridget earlier today."

Eve nodded to Bridget and ushered them both into the living room, where Grace stood tall, her gaze shifting between their two visitors. Only the clenched fists at her sides gave away her nervousness.

"Mikel, Bridget, this is my daughter, Grace," Eve said, pride in her voice.

"Nice to meet you." Grace took a step forward with her hand held out.

Mikel covered the distance between them, took her hand, and bowed over it. "It is an honor to meet you," he said.

Grace looked at Eve with a startled expression. All Eve could do was shrug. Then Bridget curtsied to Grace.

"Really, you don't have to do that," Grace blurted. "I mean, it's not even confirmed yet."

Eve figured Mikel and Bridget didn't want to risk offending even a potential princess. "Why don't we go to the dining room?" she said. "We can sign the forms there."

After they sat, Mikel opened his briefcase and pulled out a folder, passing papers to Grace and Eve. "These are the consent forms. I think you'll find them straightforward. If you would please sign both copies, Grace."

Eve read through the legalese. As Mikel said, there was nothing worrisome about the form. She turned to Grace. "Are you comfortable signing this?"

"It seems fine." Her daughter's voice was tentative.

"I don't see any problems," Eve said, injecting reassurance into her voice.

Grace accepted the pen Mikel held out to her, signing her name so it was clear and legible on both pages.

Mikel tucked the forms back into the folder before he pulled out a white plastic box. "With your permission, Bridget will administer the test. She is trained as an EMT."

"What do I have to do?" Grace asked as Bridget opened the box and took out a couple of long swabs in sterile packages, along with two plastic vials.

"You just let me swab the inside of each cheek for forty seconds," Bridget said. "May I wash my hands?"

"Of course," Eve said. "Go right in the kitchen."

"His Majesty asked me to convey his gratitude for allowing us to administer the test so quickly," Mikel said to Grace. "He looks forward to meeting you once the results are confirmed."

Grace nodded but said nothing. Eve suspected her daughter's throat was tight with nerves.

When Bridget returned, she unscrewed the top of one of the vials and tore open a swab's envelope. "Would you mind standing up? It will be more comfortable for you."

Grace stood and opened her mouth so Bridget could twirl the swab against the inside of her right cheek. Mikel started a timer on his phone. The room grew very silent as they watched Bridget roll the swab to gather Grace's saliva. The timer chimed, and Bridget withdrew the swab, inserting the absorbent end into the vial.

Bridget repeated the procedure on Grace's left cheek and packed the vials into another plastic box, this one smaller and flatter, before she handed it to Mikel. He laid three labels in front of Grace. "Would you sign these as well? I will use them to seal the box. It will not be opened again until it is in the testing lab, but the labels will prove your DNA has not been tampered with."

"How long will it take to get the results?" Grace asked as she wrote her name on the labels.

"We will have the answer by tomorrow morning." Mikel stuck one label over each seam of the box.

For a moment, Eve's gaze rested on the box. It seemed so small and unassuming to bear the weight of her daughter's future.

"I will transport this to the lab personally." Mikel placed the box in the briefcase. He closed the lid and then pressed his thumb against the locking mechanism. "The lab is a private one, and Grace's identity will not be anywhere in their records. Once the test is completed, her samples will be destroyed under my supervision."

Not just for Grace's benefit, but for the king's. He wouldn't want any extraneous royal DNA floating around.

Mikel picked up the briefcase. "We will not impose upon you any longer."

"Please call me as soon as you have the results," Eve said. "No matter what time it is."

"I will be in touch immediately after I inform the king," Mikel said, but a gleam of understanding showed in his eyes. "He also wishes to hear the moment the analysis is complete."

Eve nodded as they all stood and went to the front door.

Once again, Mikel bowed. Grace eyed him for a moment. "Are you going to bow every time you see me?"

His lips quirked into a half smile. "On official occasions, yes. It is your due as the daughter of my king. If you prefer to dispense with the gesture in less formal settings, I will follow your wishes."

"Good." Grace nodded. "Let's do that."

As soon as the door closed behind them, Grace burst into tears.

"Oh, sweetheart, it's okay." Eve wrapped her arms around her sobbing daughter.

Grace burrowed into her. "It's…it's insane! People are bowing to me! My father might be a king, and I might be some kind of princess! I don't know what to do with all that."

Eve let her daughter wail a little longer before she drew her to the sofa. Grabbing a box of tissues with one hand, she set it beside Grace. "Let's wait for the DNA test results before we plunge into the princess issue."

"Wait, Luis wasn't married to my mother, so I'm illegitimate. Even with a DNA match, I might not be a princess," Grace said, mopping the tears off her face. "Except that Bridget curtsied, and Mikel bowed. By the way, is it just me, or is Mikel a little scary?"

Eve heaved an inner sigh of relief. If Grace was trying to analyze the ramifications of her birth, she had gotten past the emotional overload…for now.

"Mr. Silva is the king's head of security," Eve said, "so it's probably an occupational requirement that he strike fear into the hearts of evildoers. As for you being illegitimate, it seems that there have been other royals born without benefit of married parents who were still considered full members of the royal family."

"Huh." Grace twisted around to face Eve. "I'm never going to be able to sleep tonight. There's too much spinning around in my brain."

"You and me both, kiddo," Eve said, brushing a tear-dampened strand of hair away from her daughter's face. "But we need to try. Tomorrow could be a doozy of a day."

"Can I sleep in your bed?" Grace asked. "When they call with the DNA results, we can hear them together."

"Of course you can, sweetheart." It was like the old days, when Grace had been sick or sad. They would share Eve's bed, wrapped in the double wedding ring quilt her grandmother had handstitched.

If her daughter was living in a castle, that probably wouldn't happen ever again. A terrible sorrow jabbed at Eve.

CHAPTER 6

Luis sat alone on the second-story porch of the rented house, the late-night fall sky huge and star-spackled above the flat horizon. A coffee mug threw up a ribbon of steam from the table beside him while his cell phone lay stubbornly silent on his thigh.

He could not sleep, an unusual problem for him. Government matters never disturbed his rest. Only family could do that. The last time he had stayed awake all night had been when Gabriel had been kidnapped.

Luis scooped up his phone and launched himself out of the chair to pace across the porch, the light spilling through the door of his bedroom illuminating his path.

What the hell was taking so long?

Once he had collected Grace's samples, Mikel had driven to Des Moines, then flown to Chicago on the royal jet. From there, he had traveled to the private DNA lab where a team of experts awaited the DNA samples from both Luis and Grace.

The phone rang, and he nearly dropped it in his haste to answer.

"Su Majestad," Mikel said, his voice solemn, "I am honored to tell you that Grace Howard is your daughter. The

DNA demonstrates a ninety-nine point nine percent match. It also matches the genetic record from her birth."

An explosion of joy and pain sucked the breath out of Luis's lungs. He had to grab the porch railing to brace himself against the geyser of emotions Mikel's words released.

"Gracias, mi amigo," he managed to gasp.

"The lab personnel and I will swear under oath that the test is accurate and valid." Mikel's voice softened. "I congratulate you on gaining a daughter. She will bring you great joy. And also great worry."

Luis recognized that Mikel spoke from his own experience of being father to a young woman. "Your good wishes are accepted with gratitude, especially given all you've done to bring about this happy conclusion so swiftly."

"Do you wish to share the news with Eve and Grace yourself?" Mikel asked.

Luis wanted to trumpet the news to his daughter, but... "No, it will be easier for them to hear it from you." They would need time to absorb the impact, and he wanted his first interaction with Grace to be as relaxed and uncomplicated as possible.

The complications would pile on soon enough.

"I will call them as soon as we finish speaking," Mikel said.

"Please tell them how elated I am to have Grace as my daughter," Luis said, "and that I cannot wait to meet her."

"Por supuesto, Señor," Mikel said.

The call ended, and Luis paced the porch boards once again, but for a different reason. Now he vibrated with the anticipation of meeting his daughter face-to-face.

His brain spun plans for when to call Raul, how to get Grace to Caleva, how to introduce her to their family, how to present her choices about her legal relationship with him, how to handle the media…and then he stopped the scheming.

Right now, this moment was for savoring the wonderful, astonishing fact that he had another child. A precious addition to the family he treasured. A daughter he could embrace in his heart.

He leaned on the railing, letting the delight of that soak into his bones. Pulling out his phone, he scrolled to the photo of Grace so he could trace the family lineage in the slant of her cheekbones, the angle of her jaw, and the ice blue of her eyes. He basked in the beauty and sweetness of her smile.

My daughter. Hija mía.

When he looked up from the phone, the edge of the sun glowed just above the horizon, painting faint pink brushstrokes across the lightening sky.

A new day. Luis stretched his arms out wide to welcome it with exultation.

Eve started when the phone lying on her chest vibrated. She glanced out the window to see a pale rosy glow signaling early dawn. Grabbing the phone, she pushed herself upright in the bed and shook Grace's shoulder. Her daughter had fallen asleep a few hours before, but Eve had lain on her back, staring at the ceiling as she tried to decide whether she wanted the DNA test to be positive or negative.

"What?" Grace muttered sleepily.

"It's Mikel," Eve said as the phone vibrated again.

Grace bolted into a sitting position. "Oh my God!"

"Ready?" Eve asked, her finger poised over the screen.

Grace nodded, her hair catching a crimson gleam from the soft dawn light.

Eve took a deep breath as she swiped to answer. "Hello, Mikel. I'm going to put you on speaker so Grace can hear the news from you too."

"Let me know as soon as you are ready." Mikel's voice was kind with understanding.

Eve hit the speaker symbol and looked at Grace again. Her daughter sat sideways on the bed so she was facing the phone in Eve's hand as though it were Mikel himself. Her shoulders were squared, and her jaw was tight. Eve gave Grace's knee a squeeze. "Go ahead, Mikel."

"I am honored to inform you that Grace is *el Rey* Luis's daughter. The DNA matched at ninety-nine point nine percent." Mikel's voice rang with conviction. "The king asked me to convey how elated he is about this news. He looks forward to meeting Grace as soon as possible."

Grace's eyes were wide, and she flattened her palms against her cheeks, mouthing, "Holy crap!" without making a sound.

"That's…quite something," Eve said. "I guess I'm not surprised after seeing the family resemblance." However, the results were shocking. Until this confirmation, some part of her had believed the story was all a crazy lie the evil Odette had fabricated to upset Luis. "But it's still hard to absorb."

An understatement. Panic and happiness danced a tango in her chest. Happiness because Grace had a father at long last, a father who truly wanted his daughter. But this man would disrupt their lives down to the very foundations. He lived in—no, he ruled—a foreign country. Luis might sweep Grace off to Caleva, where Eve would become just a visitor.

Eve could almost feel Grace slipping away from her, and the panic intensified.

"I understand." Something in his tone told her he did, and that steadied her.

She had to focus on Grace in the here and now.

"We'd like to invite Luis to dinner..." She glanced at the clock. "Tonight, at seven." She and Grace had discussed it earlier as they lay talking in the big bed together. Eve wanted to make the first meeting between father and daughter as smooth as possible. Having it on Grace's home turf would give her daughter one less thing to be nervous about.

Grace had been dubious. "Do you think our house is grand enough for a king?"

"I think it's grand enough for your father. That's how you should think of him," Eve had said.

Now Eve wondered if her daughter was right about the house...and the food she would have to prepare. She would be cooking for a *king*. Nerves butterflied in her stomach, but it was too late now.

"Perhaps you would like to issue the invitation yourself?" Mikel said. "I will text you his direct number. Please do not attach his name to it in your contacts."

"No, of course not." She was getting a direct line to a king. How bizarre was that? At least she could have some fun with deciding what his pseudonym should be.

She heard the ping as Luis's number arrived as a text.

"By the way, he is awake, so feel free to call at any time," Mikel said. *"Buenos días."*

Eve set the phone on the bed and took several deep breaths to settle herself. "How do you feel, sweetheart?"

Grace sat cross-legged in her T-shirt and pajama shorts, her hair in tangled waves around her shoulders, a dazed expression on her face. "I—I don't know. It's too far out of my ballpark, this whole royalty thing."

Eve took Grace's hands in her own. "Let's forget the princess part. Instead, think about meeting your birth father. How do you feel about that?"

"Excited, I think." Grace's eyes lost their stunned blankness as she nodded. "Especially because now I know he didn't abandon me back then." ,

"I think you'll like him a lot." Eve wanted this encounter to be nothing but positive for Grace. "He will certainly like you."

"You think so?" Grace asked.

Eve cupped Grace's smooth cheek. "You're brilliant, hardworking, compassionate, funny, warm, and you look just like him. No father could resist that combination."

"And you're not biased at all." But Grace smiled for a moment before she grew serious again. "Mom, I don't need any parent except you. You're the most wonderful mother—and father—anyone could want. That's not why I want to meet...Luis. Or whatever I should call him."

"Oh, sweetheart, I understand." Eve leaned in to wrap Grace in a hug. "You want answers about where you came from. It's natural." Grace's answers just happened to have major baggage attached.

Luis Dragón wanted his daughter. A man like that had a lot of ways to pressure anyone standing in his path. Eve would just have to find the strength to stand up to him, if necessary.

"I have a whole history I know nothing about." Grace returned the hug, and they sat entwined with each other in silence for a long, sweet moment. Grace tightened her embrace. "I love you, Mom, so, so much."

"Right back at you, sweetheart." Tears welled in Eve's eyes, and she buried her face in the silky, citrus-scented fall of Grace's hair, soaking up this precious calm before the coming storm whirled them up in its maelstrom.

Eve waited for Grace to loosen her hold before sitting back and picking up the phone. "Do you want to make the call to invite your dad for dinner?"

Grace stared down at the phone before shaking her head. "No. I want our first contact to be in person."

Eve tapped the secret phone number and raised the phone to her ear, trying to swallow down her nerves. Who the heck was she—a vet tech from Ames, Iowa—to host a king for dinner at her house?

"Eve, I'm so glad to hear from you." Luis's deep, rich baritone seemed to pour into her ear and radiate through her veins. "You have heard the happy news!" She also heard the elation in his voice.

She had to swallow again. "Yes. Mikel called us."

"What does Grace think about her new father?" An undercurrent of worry came through the phone.

Eve looked at her daughter, who was listening avidly to Eve's side of the conversation. "She very much wants to meet you. We would like you to come to our house for dinner tonight at seven."

"I hoped…of course. I would be honored." She could hear his impatience being curbed as he accepted the invitation.

"She's on a rotation in her specialty, so she can't take the day off. Her supervisor could penalize her for it." Especially since he was the obnoxious Dr. Young.

"Of course. Please let me know what I can do to help you. May my chef provide some part of the meal?"

She had a vision of the king coming in her front door holding a casserole dish and almost laughed out loud. "I'm all set." Although the offer was very tempting. She wouldn't have to sweat over what dishes to fix for a king. "Do you have any food allergies I should know about?"

"I have eaten some bizarre meals in my travels, so I am sure that nothing you prepare will bother my stomach." His amusement sent a wave of warmth tingling through her. "Not that I expect your cooking to be anything other than delicious."

Ha! Another thought struck her. "How many people should I cook for? Will you have bodyguards? Is Mikel coming?"

"Only I will be dining with you. Although"—his tone turned apologetic—"Mikel will need to discuss some security measures with you ahead of time. What time would be convenient for him to come by to review those?"

Were there going to be armed guards surrounding her house? Would a security inspection be required every time *Grace* visited someone's home? Eve's hand tightened around the phone until it dug into her fingers.

Nope, she wouldn't think about what had happened to the king's nephew. Doing a quick mental review of what she needed to accomplish, she asked, "Would two o'clock work?"

"He will be there at two. And I will be counting the minutes until seven. *Hasta luego!*" Luis disconnected.

His voice was even sexier when he spoke Spanish. Oh dear God, she had to stop thinking such inappropriate thoughts.

As she lowered the phone, Grace said, "Bodyguards? Mikel? How many people are coming to this dinner?"

"Only Luis is eating with us, although Mikel is coming by at two for a security inspection." Eve tried to ease Grace into the realization of what being a king's daughter might mean. "Your father is a very powerful, important man. That can make him a target."

Eve had said that so calmly. She was impressed with herself.

"Right." Grace was silent a moment. "You told him about my rotation." There was a question in her voice.

"Because I got the impression that he wanted to meet you sooner." Eve wrapped her arms around her daughter. "One thing I am sure of—your biological father cares about you already."

If only that was all that mattered.

CHAPTER 7

At one forty-five that afternoon, Eve surveyed her living room, trying to imagine what a king—or in about fifteen minutes, his head of security—would think of it. All the furniture-protecting blankets had been whipped off the sofa and chairs after the three cats had been confined to a bedroom upstairs, and the dogs had been banished to the backyard. She had vacuumed every surface in the room twice. Hopefully, the King of Caleva was not allergic to pets since it was impossible to remove every last hair.

Her gaze skimmed over the braided rug of faded blues and greens, the brick fireplace filled with neatly laid logs, and the framed landscapes painted by her great-uncle, an amateur artist. The Victorian oak coffee table gleamed with furniture polish and held a nosegay of red roses and yellow gerbera daisies in a teal glass vase, a combination that paid tribute to the colors of Caleva's flag. She had not included lilies, the Calevan national flower, because they were deadly poisonous to cats. She didn't want to take the chance that one of her not-so-bright kitties would eat the flowers before she tossed them out. A matching bouquet was ready to go on the dining room table.

She snorted as she compared her old Iowa farmhouse with the online photos of Castillo Draconago's grand *salóns*.

Last night, before they lay down to sleep, Grace had brought her laptop to the bed to search the internet for information about her biological father, his family, and the land he ruled.

Caleva was a dramatically beautiful country with its spine of soaring volcanic mountains and miles of glittering white and black sand beaches. Brilliantly colored flowering vines climbed the dark gray basalt walls of historic houses and churches. She and Grace had oohed and aahed over the fields of deep red medicinal lilies shrouded in mists of geothermal steam and the giant teal lizards called Calevan dragons.

The royal family was equally dramatic, strikingly handsome like Luis, with the features and coloring that spoke of their descent from a Spanish pirate king. Evidently, the pirate had stumbled upon the island eight hundred miles off the coast of Spain when his galleon had been blown there in a storm. He had returned to declare himself king and take the last name of Dragón.

As she had sat beside Grace, Eve had made appropriately interested comments, even as she had agonized about what the future held for her daughter and herself.

Why couldn't Luis Dragón have been a doctor…or a chef…or a taxi driver? Even a CEO of a multinational corporation would have been easier to deal with than a frickin' *king*.

And now she had to cook for him. Her early morning had been spent racing around to the limited selection of food stores in Ames. After Mikel finished his inspection, she would plunge into cooking the menu of Iowan specialties and Spanish tapas she had cobbled together, in the forlorn hope that something would appeal to Luis's royal taste buds.

The doorbell rang, and she marched to the front door, bracing herself in case a battalion of heavily armed guards was about to invade her home.

When she opened the door, Mikel stood on the porch, flanked by the pleasant young woman who had played receptionist and DNA collector yesterday and a tall, muscular man with short brown hair and no expression on his face. They all wore jeans and T-shirts in various subdued solid colors and carried black duffel bags.

Only three people. That wasn't so intimidating. Her tension eased a little.

"Good afternoon, *Señora* Howard," Mikel said. "Bridget and Ivan will be assisting me today."

"Please call me Eve," she said to all three.

Bridget smiled. Ivan nodded.

"Come in," Eve said. "I should warn you that my cats are confined in a bedroom upstairs."

"We will make sure not to allow them to escape," Mikel said.

"The dogs are out in the yard," Eve said, closing the door. "I can leash them, if you prefer."

"Only if they're likely to bite us," Mikel said with a half smile.

She shook her head. "They might bark at you, but then they'll sniff your pockets for treats."

"In that case, would you provide us with some treats to offer them?" Mikel's eyes held a disarming glint of humor. "Making friends with the locals is always a good idea."

Maybe he wasn't as scary as she had thought. "Follow me."

The security team trailed behind her to the kitchen, waiting as she pulled the tin out of the cabinet. When she turned to hand them the canine goodies, she caught them looking around the room with focused intensity. So Mikel's charm was just a façade.

Mikel distributed the treats to his team. "With your permission, Ivan and I will begin inside, while Bridget introduces herself to your dogs."

"Whatever you need to do. I've never had a king visit before." Eve gave them a nervous smile. "Shall I show you around?"

"I am sure you are very busy, so we are happy to work on our own," Mikel said.

And keep her out of their way while they did their top secret stuff. "That's fine with me." She needed to start food prep, anyway.

"First, I need to ask you a couple of questions," Mikel said. "Please be honest. We have no intention of reporting anything you say to the authorities."

Eve frowned in utter bafflement. "Go ahead."

"This is standard procedure," Mikel said before fixing his gaze on her face like a laser. "Do you have any firearms in the house, whether modern or antique?"

"I don't think so," Eve said, still confused. "Unless there's one in the old trunks in the attic."

"We will check there," Mikel said. "Do you have any controlled substances in the house?"

"Controlled...you mean illegal drugs?" Eve was insulted, even as she understood why the questions were being asked. "Of course not." The closest she had was the Prozac prescribed for one of the cats.

"Has anyone other than you and your daughter been in this house in the last twenty-four hours?" Mikel continued.

"No," Eve said as she mentally reviewed the last two days. "Certainly not since I met with you and your...boss at the law office."

"Thank you," Mikel said. "My apologies. I meant no offense." He sounded neither grateful nor apologetic, but that didn't surprise Eve.

She was relieved when he and his colleagues removed themselves from her kitchen. Leaning back against the countertop, Eve tried to shake off the unpleasant sensation of enduring the Spanish Inquisition. This was the dark side of Grace's newly revealed heritage, and Eve was glad her daughter hadn't seen it.

Glancing up at the kitchen clock, Eve gasped. She opened the refrigerator and pulled out the ingredients for the Iowa sweet corn soup. While she cleaned the leeks and carrots, she watched out the window as Bridget made friends with her three-legged golden retriever and Grace's pit bull, handing out treats and ear scratches until the dogs stared up at her with adoring expressions.

Footsteps sounded over her head while she chopped the vegetables. She wondered what they were doing up there, prowling through the four bedrooms—one of which she and Grace used as an office/study space—and two bathrooms. She heard the telltale metallic protest as someone opened the retractable stairs to the attic space. They were being thorough, that was for sure.

By the time Eve added the chicken stock and sweet corn to the garlicky sauteed vegetables and turned them down to simmer, Bridget had disappeared from her view.

As Eve lined up the dessert ingredients, Mikel and Ivan vanished down the cellar stairs. Eve didn't mind because she kept the basement clean, as well as stocked with emergency supplies, since it was also a tornado shelter.

She was carefully stirring the Rice Krispies into the corn syrup and peanut butter mixture when Mikel returned to the kitchen. "That's a nice setup you have down there."

Eve poured the gooey mixture into the baking pan and patted it down. "My grandmother believed in being prepared for the worst."

Mikel peered at the contents of the pan. "That smells...sweet."

"Oh, it is, but it gets even better when I add the melted chocolate and butterscotch chips on top. They're called Scotcheroos, Iowa's signature sweet treat for every potluck, picnic, and bake sale." She grinned. "Don't worry. I made plenty for you and your team."

"I also smell garlic and...onions?"

"Leeks, but close. That's the sweet corn soup. There's also more than enough to share."

He smiled. "You are very generous, but my team will have eaten before the king arrives. However, I don't think they would turn down some...Scotcheroos to take back to the house with them."

"The house?"

"We have rented a house for the king to use during his visit." He obviously wasn't going to tell her the address.

"Ah, I wondered where a king would stay in Ames, Iowa." She dumped chocolate and butterscotch chips into a bowl and put it in the microwave without turning it on. "Probably wherever he wants to," she said.

Mikel chuckled politely. "I would like to introduce you to the people who will be stationed around your house until the king departs. Is now a good time for you to come outside to meet them?"

There were *more* security guards, and they would be *stationed?*

"How many more people are there?"

"Eight, plus Bridget, Ivan, and myself," Mikel said. "We have kept the number small in order to avoid attracting attention."

Eleven people, and he considered that a low number. Her property wasn't that large, about half an acre that had been retained around the house when the farmland had been sold off by her grandmother. Most of it was taken up by the fenced backyard where the dogs roamed.

If eleven people were barely enough to keep the king safe on a secret visit to Ames, Iowa, how many guards would it take to keep Grace safe? A cold chill ran through her.

She was glad that Mikel Silva took his job very seriously.

"Okay, let's go meet your guards." She rinsed off her hands and followed Mikel out her back door, where the dogs greeted them. Mikel pulled treats out of his pocket and earned Trace's and Army's undying devotion. "They're terrible watchdogs, aren't they?" she said with a grimace.

Useless for keeping a king or princess safe.

He ruffled Trace's floppy ears. "If I attacked you, I'm willing to bet they would act to protect you."

Eve looked at Trace's blissfully goofy face. "Maybe Army would."

Mikel led her to a clump of tall shrubs at the corner of her house. A wiry young man with light brown hair and a charming smile stepped out of the shadows, startling her.

"Ms. Howard, this is Pierre," Mikel said.

"A pleasure," he said as they shook hands.

They visited seven more guards in their places of concealment among the trees and shrubs around her house—

four men and three women, all very fit, all dressed in jeans, dark shirts, and jackets. She was pretty sure they all had guns hidden under their outerwear, but it wasn't obvious. She was grateful for the overgrown hedges on either side of the property, blocking the next-door neighbors' views of her house with its lurking guards.

After the tour to meet the security guards, Mikel accompanied her to the back door. "Once the king arrives, Bridget will also be outside, while Ivan and I will be upstairs."

In case she or Grace tried to attack Luis? "You're very thorough."

"Do you have any questions for me, *señora?*" Mikel asked.

So many questions, and none of them happy ones.

"I'm good for now." Such a lie.

Mikel nodded. "I will leave you to your preparations."

He left so swiftly that she barely had time to call out a goodbye.

She stared blankly at the door, stunned by the number of armed guards arrayed around her creaky, old farmhouse. This was just the tip of the iceberg when it came to all the changes Grace's new father would wreak in their lives. What else did she have no idea was headed for them like the *Titanic* at full speed?

Her phone sounded an alarm she had set earlier as a reminder to start the next phase of prep. Time to kick into high gear.

CHAPTER 8

Fifteen minutes before the King of Caleva—no, he was Luis here—was due to arrive, Eve and Grace stood in the archway that separated the living room from the dining room, nervous tension vibrating around them. Mikel and Ivan had arrived half an hour before and glided up the stairs to the second floor.

She and Grace had tried out curtsying and decided they looked awkward. They were going to take Luis at his word and pretend that he was not a king.

"You made the dining table look lovely," Eve said.

"It helps that Nana Nelle gave you her Victorian sterling flatware," Grace responded.

Eve had dug all the good stuff out of storage in the basement, but the slightly yellowed antique lace tablecloth, the gleaming silver, and Eve's wedding crystal looked elegant under the light of the brass chandelier. The faint scent of melted chocolate and butterscotch still threaded the air. It might not be castle-level, but it looked—and smelled—darned nice.

"I'm so nervous, Mom," her usually unflappable daughter admitted. "Do I look okay?"

Grace had decided to wear her "interview outfit." The dark plum dress with its narrow black belt and box-pleated skirt projected poise and self-confidence. Grace had brushed her hair into smooth, shining waves and finished the ensemble with black box-heeled suede pumps. In the V-neckline of the dress, she had fastened the necklace Eve had given her when she got into veterinary school, a pair of tiny gold wings on a slender chain. Grace fiddled with it now.

Eve felt tears pooling in her eyes as she took in the luminous beauty of the young woman she had raised. Her daughter stood tall and strong in the face of meeting a king—and her father—for the first time. "Your father will be knocked sideways by how extraordinary his daughter is."

"I don't know about that." Grace's voice quavered a bit. "Kings are surrounded by extraordinary people."

"Sweetheart, no one is more incredible than you are."

"I think we established that you're biased." Grace managed a shaky smile. "You look beautiful too. Very elegant with your hair in that sleek do."

Eve touched the hair she had swirled into a low bun. "I stuck every bobby pin I possess into it to keep it up." Eve had tried on all three of the dresses that she owned before choosing the royal blue silk sheath. She had accessorized the dress with a gold rope chain, also inherited from Nana Nelle, and gold ear-hugging hoops that Grace had given her to match the chain. After doing her makeup with painstaking care, she had spritzed on Chanel No. 5.

Maybe the whole effect would fool the king—and Grace—into thinking she was calm and self-assured when her insides were quaking like jelly.

"The weird thing is that we could be having dinner with a king a lot in the future," Grace said.

"You should think of him as your father, not a king." The thought of future dinners with Luis added another knot to Eve's stomach.

Grace opened her arms. "Hug for luck."

Eve wrapped her arms around her daughter and dropped a kiss on her silky hair before she gave Grace a squeeze and eased away. Despite the nerves, excitement sparkled in her daughter's light blue eyes.

Reassured, Eve stepped back and swept her gaze around the living room. A small plate of Iowan pickle wraps and another of miniature Iowa ham balls sat on the coffee table. To make the king feel at home, she had raided the only gourmet food store in Ames for a bowl of Spanish olives, a wedge of Manchego cheese, and some crusty sliced bread. Looking at her basic offerings, she wondered if she should have bought more of everything.

She had to stop herself from wiping her damp palms on her dress, because that would definitely spot the silk. Instead, she shifted a throw pillow by an inch and surreptitiously dried her sweaty hands on the cotton fabric.

"This is really crazy, isn't it?" Grace said, fidgeting with her necklace again.

"It sure is, but we can handle it." Grace's anxiety counteracted Eve's because she had to be strong for her child.

"We can handle anything together." Her daughter's voice held a conviction that made Eve want to weep.

She tried to will it to be true.

Grace looked at her watch just as the old wooden wall clock began to chime seven. On the third peal, the doorbell rang.

Eve lifted her eyebrows in a question. Grace took a deep breath and nodded. Together, they walked into the front hall. Eve stepped forward to swing the door open.

The evening sunbeams slanting across the porch painted Luis in a glow of gold, warming the silver in his hair and softening the aristocratic angles of his jaw and cheekbones while it lit up his ice-blue eyes. The same light gilded his navy blazer, blue shirt, and gray trousers along with the huge vase of lavender-colored blossoms he held.

He smiled, and she felt the power of it blaze through her body.

"Eve, it is so lovely of you to welcome me to your home," he said.

"It's my pleasure." That was all she could manage.

He held out the vase. "I brought flowers from Caleva. Our *raho* hibiscus are known for their fragrance."

He had brought them all the way from his country. For his daughter. "They're beautiful." Eve accepted the flowers, their exotic scent enveloping her, and stepped back. "Please come in."

Luis strode through the door, politely stopping only a few feet inside while his gaze swept past her, seeking Grace.

Eve put the flowers on the hall table and moved to stand beside her daughter. "Grace, this is Luis. Your father."

Luis felt Eve's last two words vibrate in his soul as he drank in the beautiful young woman who stood before him. *My daughter.* He wanted to shout with joy. He wanted to wrap his arms around her. He wanted to sweep her away to Caleva to live in his palace so he could know and love her as he did Raul.

He held out his hand. "It is my greatest happiness to meet you at last."

"I'm glad to meet you too." Her grip held a strength that surprised him. He covered the top of her small, firm hand with his left, savoring this first tactile connection between them.

He stood still, feeling her gaze as it roamed over his face. Her shoulders were stiff with wariness, but she left her hand in his double clasp, the warmth of her skin radiating against his. The angles of her jaw, cheekbones, and brows were his and Raul's, but somehow made strikingly feminine. Only the russet of her hair spoke of Odette.

"What should I call you?" she asked with the same Midwestern accent as her mother's.

"You may call me whatever feels most comfortable to you at this moment," he said, releasing her hand. "Raul calls me Pater because I insisted that he study Latin."

A faint smile tugged up the corners of her mouth. "I took Latin because I'm terrible at speaking foreign languages. For now, would Luis be all right?"

"Of course." A pang of disappointment jarred him, even though he could not expect her to call him Father in any language yet.

"Come in and get comfortable," Eve said, waving toward an archway that led to a cozy living room. "Would you like red wine, Scotch, or water?"

She had obviously checked with Mikel about what Luis usually drank. "Wine, thank you."

Eve walked to a console table that held bottles and glasses. For a moment, his attention was distracted by the way her dress touched the curves of her body, promising sensual beauty underneath.

But his focus swung back to his daughter. Once again, they simply looked at each other as they stood among the homey furniture. He read a fierce intelligence in her eyes, as well as pride in the upward tilt of her chin.

He did not need the proof of the DNA test. He felt their bond in his heart.

"You are studying to be a veterinarian," he said. "What type of animals do you most like working with?"

As he had hoped, the familiar topic eased the stiff set of her shoulders. "The small, furry ones. Dogs. Cats. An occasional bunny or ferret. I love horses, but I would rather ride them than fix them. They're fragile creatures."

"Have you studied reptiles at all? We have an endangered species of large, frilled lizards known as Calevan dragons."

She nodded. "There's one on your coat of arms. Is that where your surname comes from?"

"It does." Luis gave her a mock grimace. "I suspect my ancestors adopted it in order to sound intimidating."

Eve gave each of them a glass of ruby-colored wine, her hands around the glasses small like Grace's, with short, unpolished nails. A working woman's hands, appealing in their simplicity.

He waited until she fetched her own glass before lifting his toward the two women. "A traditional Calevan toast. *Salud, amor, pesetas y tiempo para disfrutarlos!* Health, love, money, and time to enjoy them!"

"That covers it all," Eve said, returning his salute before she took a sip. "Please, let's sit. Have some tapas." She threw him a glance as she said the last word. "I've included some Iowan specialties as well."

He waited as Eve settled on the sofa and Grace sat beside her, a united front in the face of his incursion into their lives.

He sat in a green corduroy armchair and took another sip of his wine before setting it on a side table. It was a surprisingly good rioja. "You must have many questions for me. Please ask them."

His daughter visibly squared her shoulders. "I don't understand how I got from Caleva to Iowa. Mom said you would be able to explain better than she could. Who is my biological mother?"

Eve gave Luis credit. His relaxed but attentive posture, as he sat in the ugly green chair, did not shift by a millimeter.

"That is a complicated story," he said. "And it does not do me any credit."

Eve wanted to throw her arms around Grace to offer protection from the answer. But she could not ward off this blow, only hope that Luis softened it as much as possible.

Now he sat forward, his brows drawn down with regret. "Your biological mother and I had a brief affair after my wife died. When I broke it off, your birth mother punished me by not revealing that she was pregnant." He looked down at his elegant hands, which were clasped together on his thighs. "She felt—quite accurately—that hiding your existence from me would be the best revenge for my temerity in ending our relationship."

He lifted his head. Sorrow etched lines around his eyes and mouth that made him look older.

"But who is she?" Grace persisted.

Eve held her breath.

"Her name is Odette Fontaine," Luis continued. "She is in prison on Caleva because she instigated the kidnapping of my nephew, Gabriel."

"*She's* my birth mother?" Grace reached for Eve's hand. "I remember that from the news. The kidnappers cut off Gabriel's ear!"

"I believe Odette knew that she had profound psychological issues and would not be a fit parent for you," Luis said. "You are fortunate that she found such a wonderful mother to take her place."

Eve wanted to hug Luis for finding the most generous interpretation of his crazy ex-lover's actions.

"That's more than an *issue*." Grace's voice had gone up in pitch. "That's psychopathic. I'm the biological daughter of a psychopath."

Eve tugged her hand loose and put her arm around her daughter's shoulders, pulling her against her side.

"You are *my* daughter," Luis said with all the regal authority of his position. "And you are *Eve's* daughter. Odette merely gave birth to you."

Grace took a deep, shuddering breath. "But I have her genes."

Eve wanted to strangle Odette Fontaine with her bare hands. She wasn't a whole lot happier with Luis, who had dumped all this emotional baggage in Grace's lap.

"I've known you for nearly twenty-nine years," Eve said, giving Grace's shoulders a tiny shake. "Trust me, I would be aware if you had any tendencies in that direction. You can't bear to kill a spider, even though you hate them."

Luis's chair creaked. Eve glanced over to see his mouth tightening into a grim line. "I am sorry to be the bearer of this news," he said. "But I want our relationship to be based on honesty from the beginning."

Grace gave a little whimper, but she moved out of Eve's embrace. "It was a shock. An even bigger one than finding out that my father is a king."

"You have had a great deal to absorb, *hija mía*." Luis's tone was soft with concern. "Perhaps we should talk of happier things. Why don't I tell you about your family in Caleva? You have your half brother, Raul; your uncle, Lorenzo, and his wife, Hélène; their son and Raul's first cousin, Gabriel, who is about to marry one of your countrymen. I think you'll like his fiancée, Quinn, very much."

"I saw Gabriel announce his engagement at DragonFest. It was very romantic," Grace said.

Luis's face lit up with pleasure. "You watched Dragon-Fest? We had hoped it would find its way all over the world."

"I'm a big fan of Kyran Redda," Grace confessed. "And now of Gabriel. His guitar-playing is fantastic."

"He is brilliantly talented," Luis agreed.

"Tell me about Raul. What does a prince do?" Grace asked.

"Since Raul will be king someday, he is involved with governing our country. Fortunately, he has a passion for it. And if you ever heard him sing, you would find out that Gabriel got all the musical talent in the family," Luis said with a sly smile.

He was a charmer, that Luis. Eve found herself leaning in to bask in the glow of his charisma as Grace peppered him with questions about her royal relatives. It was hard to tell if her daughter was just curious about her new family members or if she was trying to figure out how she would fit into her new role. Perhaps both.

Having an extended family would be a new experience for Grace. Eve was the only child of an only child, so Grace had no close cousins. After the divorce, Ben had quickly remarried. Once his new wife had a baby, he'd made it clear that his new family was no longer Eve's…or Grace's.

The cruelty of her ex-husband's actions still twisted a knife between her ribs. Even if he hadn't been able to face her, he should have continued to include Grace in his life. But Grace reminded him of his failure to have a baby with Eve, and that struck at Ben's manhood.

The welcome music of Grace's laughter pulled her out of her ugly memories.

"Try an Iowa ham ball," Grace said, holding out the plate. "Mom's always get eaten first at potlucks."

Her daughter's compliment made her chest swell a little. Maybe Luis wouldn't be too disappointed by his dinner.

"Potlucks?" Luis asked as he jabbed a toothpick into a miniature ham ball.

"Those are meals where a whole bunch of people get together and bring whatever food they make really well," Grace explained. "Mom's specialties are Iowa ham balls and Scotcheroos. We're having those for dessert tonight."

With a flash of white teeth, Luis bit the ham ball off the toothpick and chewed. "Superb. I cannot wait to taste the Scotcheroos." He nodded at Eve with a warm glint of appreciation in his eyes.

His enthusiasm for her food sent pleasure shimmering through her. Although she wondered—did he really enjoy her basic cooking, or was he being nice to ingratiate himself with Grace?

As he began to ask Grace questions about her studies, Eve stood. "I'm going to get dinner going now."

"May I help in any way?" Luis asked.

Eve almost laughed as she tried to picture him with his elegant hands encased in her ratty quilted hot gloves while he bent to pull a pan of rolls out of the oven. "No, you two keep chatting."

She listened to the give-and-take of the conversation while she seared the filets, nearly scorching the butter when she got distracted by Luis's velvety baritone. As she ladled out bowls of sweet corn soup, she splashed a few drops onto her dress and bit back a curse. Of course, the wet splotches stood out on the blue silk. All she could do was blot at them with a clean dish towel and hope Luis didn't notice.

Although he seemed to notice everything, his gaze intense to the point of an almost physical touch.

She had to stop thinking about him that way.

Giving herself a mental shake, she shifted the steaks to the warming oven and returned to the living room.

"Dinner is served," she said, not letting her gaze rest on the too-attractive man sitting in her ugly corduroy chair.

"The aroma is delicious," Luis said as he gestured for Grace to precede him into the dining room.

"It's a classic Iowan menu," Eve said. She had decided not to try to compete with all the gourmet meals a king must eat. "Corn, meat, and salad."

"And Scotcheroos," Luis added, his faint accent making the funny word sound exotic.

"You were paying attention," Eve said, her eyes inexorably drawn to him.

His blue eyes locked on her. "Always."

A not unpleasant shiver ran down her spine. "Why don't you sit there?" She indicated the chair between hers and Grace's at the round table.

"Permit me." He pulled out the chair Eve stood beside and waited.

"Oh." He wanted her to sit first. "Thank you." She plunked down with speed rather than grace.

Luis strode around to hold Grace's chair for her as well. For a moment, their faces were almost side by side, and the family resemblance was striking.

Her Grace was really the child of a king.

Eve shook her head as though that could ward off the gut-wrenching truth of it.

Dinner passed in a blur of candlelight and conversation. Eve tasted nothing that she ate as she fell under the spell Luis wove around the three of them. He asked questions about their lives in Iowa, listened to their answers with focused interest, and offered his own anecdotes of Caleva, painting a tantalizing picture of his home. He downplayed the fact that he lived in a castle and ruled a country so that Eve could almost relax and talk with him like any other dinner guest.

Grace was enthralled by her father. As the evening progressed, she teased him a few times and threw some occasional snark. In fact, she treated him the same way she did her friends' fathers, respectfully but with ease. Relief washed through Eve.

After Luis polished off his second Scotcheroo, he turned to Eve. "That was one of the best meals I have ever eaten."

Not for a moment did she believe him. "I suspect your pleasure had more to do with the company than the food." She glanced at Grace, whose fascinated gaze was locked on her father.

"A truly excellent meal is always more than the food." He swept his hand around. "It includes the beautiful table, the excellent wine, and most especially, the warmth and brilliance of my two lovely companions."

Eve shifted on her chair at his continued flattery. "Shall we move to the living room for coffee and brandy?"

"Por supuesto." He rose with a fluid motion and pulled out Eve's chair as she stood. When he bent close to her, she caught his faint, exotic scent that evoked fresh air and the sea. Her bare arm brushed against the soft cotton of his shirt, sending a flicker of delight across her skin.

She had to get a grip.

"Grace, will you pour the brandy while I prepare the coffee?" Eve asked, nearly bolting into the kitchen.

As she turned on the coffeemaker, Eve decided that her reaction was not so surprising. This whole evening had been a kind of seduction. Luis had exerted all his considerable charm to win over both Grace and her. He had made Caleva sound like an earthly paradise and his family seem close-knit and interesting. There had been no further mentions of kidnapping, mutilation, security teams, or DNA tests.

Eve sighed. As a ruler, Luis would be adept at manipulating people. She needed to keep that in mind.

But, gosh, the man was hard to resist. The spell that he wove threatened to swamp her Iowan common sense.

A few minutes later, she carried the coffee tray into the living room. Luis leaped up to take it from her, their fingers brushing with a delicious friction. She looked up to find his face alight with what looked like happiness. Being with Grace gave him pleasure, and she couldn't begrudge him that.

She smiled at him as she released the tray into his grasp. His gaze sharpened and heated in a way that sent a sensual flame licking through her. Thank goodness he was holding the tray because she would have dropped it.

He bent to carefully place the tray on the coffee table, and she watched the play of muscles under the fine cotton of his perfectly fitted shirt. She wanted to run her fingers over the swells and valleys of his shoulders. She averted her eyes and sat.

After she poured coffee for all of them, she decided it was her turn to ask the questions. It might keep her mind off his body. "Where are you staying while you're here in Ames?"

"At a house to the west of town," he said. "I would like to invite you to dinner there tomorrow night."

"We'd love to come," Grace said, her face bright with enthusiasm.

"*Muy bien.*" Luis nodded. "I will send a car to pick you up. Would cocktails at five thirty be agreeable? I would like to spend as much time with you as possible before I have to return to Caleva."

Grace's glow dimmed. "When do you have to leave?"

Luis frowned. "In two days. I wish I could stretch my visit a little longer." He leaned forward. "But you must come to Caleva! We will organize that as soon as possible."

"I'm on rotations at school, and I don't have scheduled time off for another two months," Grace said. "We can video chat, though, can't we?"

"Most definitely," Luis said, but he looked dissatisfied.

Eve relaxed a little. A couple of months of video chats would give her adequate time to talk with Grace about the more complex implications of her new identity.

Not that Eve could stop this train now that it was barreling down the tracks.

"May I request that you bring some of your Scotcheroos tomorrow?" Luis's eyes gleamed. "And perhaps share the recipe with my chef?"

Eve slanted him a skeptical glance but nodded. "I'm sending a batch back with Mikel for your team, so you can grab one of those if you get a craving."

Luis lifted his eyebrows at her. "Are you trying to subvert the loyalty of my staff? Because Scotcheroos might do it."

"I've used them to bribe a couple of professors," Grace volunteered. "Works every time."

Her daughter radiated delight as her gaze traveled from Eve to her father. Eve felt a flare of anger. This was what Grace should have had all her life—*two* parents to support and love her. Damn Ben for being a selfish, narcissistic jerk!

Grace cast an odd, apologetic look at Eve before turning to her father. "This might be too difficult to arrange, but would you like to come to my graduation ceremony?" Grace asked. "It would be fantastic to have you there."

His face blazed with joy, and Eve's heart melted.

"I would be honored to attend," he said. "Please tell me the date so I can make sure it is on my calendar."

"The date is engraved on my brain," Grace said. "I'll text it to you. Oh, wait, am I allowed to do that?"

For a moment, he looked uncomfortable. "As long as you use the secure cell phone Mikel brought you."

The king issue was starting to come to the fore...and Luis didn't want it to.

"Got it," Grace said, unbothered.

His smile held relief. He swallowed the last of his brandy and stood. "We all have to work tomorrow, so I will say goodbye. It has been the most pleasurable of evenings."

Grace and Eve rose as well.

"There's one thing I want to confirm," Eve said, her shoulders tight with tension. "I assume you won't announce the news concerning Grace until she has made decisions about her legal standing as your daughter?"

"Of course not." Luis looked offended, but his expression softened when he gazed at Grace. "Our relationship will be private until you wish to share it with the world. Then we will discuss the best way to handle the revelation together."

Eve felt a sense of reprieve, although she wished she could discuss this situation with one of her levelheaded friends. An outside perspective would be useful.

"I won't say anything either," Grace said with a nod.

Grace also wouldn't be able to lean on the support of her friends. Eve would have to try to view this crazy development in their lives from every possible angle and guide Grace to her decision solo, a daunting prospect. All the secrecy made her role even harder in many ways.

"You should know," Luis said, his face solemn, "that my heart wants me to stand on the highest tower of Castillo Draconago and shout to the entire world that you are my daughter."

Eve fell a little in love with the man right then because Grace's eyes brimmed with tears, even as a huge smile spread across her face. "Thank you," Grace said in a voice that quavered slightly.

As they started toward the door, Eve realized that Luis had left his blazer draped over the back of the dining room chair. "Let me get your jacket," she said, pivoting.

As she collected it, she marveled at the gloriously soft wool and caught again the distinctive scent that made her think of open water. She was tempted to rub the jacket's lapel against her cheek.

"*Muchas gracias,*" he said, taking it from her with a slight bow.

More Spanish words had crept into his speech as the night had gone on, perhaps as he had grown more comfortable with them. She liked that. Not to mention that his elegant baritone made the Spanish sound like music that rippled inside her.

When they entered the front hallway, Eve started at the sight of Mikel standing by the front door, holding the Scotcheroo-filled plastic container she had given him earlier. Somehow, he managed to make it look normal for the king's scary security chief to be carrying Tupperware.

But how had he known Luis was ready to leave? She shrugged internally. A king's security was beyond her.

Mikel nodded to her and opened the front door, the drift of air sending the fragrance of *vaho* hibiscus swirling around them from the vase on the table.

"Oh, that smells so good." Grace closed her eyes and inhaled.

"It is one of the trademarks of Caleva." Luis looked pleased. "You must experience it in its natural habitat."

Luis turned to Eve. "Thank you for a most memorable evening." He took the hand she offered before leaning in to barely brush his cheek against hers in a European air-kiss. Then he drew back before doing it beside her other cheek.

The scent of his skin, the silken tickle of his beard, and the heat of his body sent a rush of desire flooding through her body.

She stepped back abruptly.

What the hell is wrong with me? This was her daughter's father...and a king!

He repeated his European farewell with Grace.

And then he was gone, the door closing quietly behind him.

Grace did a little dance. "Mom, he's incredible! He's so down-to-earth that I almost forgot he's a king."

He had a different effect on Eve, but she could never admit that. "He's pretty impressive."

Grace broke off a hibiscus blossom, sniffed it, and then tucked it in her hair. "He loved your cooking too."

"Speaking of which, I'd better clean up." And forget about his praise of her meal. Eve started toward the dining room. "You're excused from clearing duty since you have school tomorrow."

"No way. I want to talk about…Luis." Grace was bubbling with excitement.

Eve picked up a couple of wineglasses while Grace began to collect the dessert plates from the table, talking all the while about various snippets of the evening's conversations. Eve interjected encouraging comments whenever necessary as the two of them worked like the smoothly functioning team they had melded into over the years.

A cloud of melancholy settled around Eve's heart. How many more times would she and Grace do this together? Yes, her daughter would be graduating later in the year—with her royal father in attendance—but Eve had expected to have these last months with Grace to savor and build memories from. Now Luis had changed the dynamic of her little family. Selfishly, Eve resented the intrusion into this last stretch of mother-daughter time before Grace struck out on her own, probably somewhere other than in Ames, Iowa.

As Eve handed the last scrubbed pot to Grace to dry, her daughter went still. All the light vanished from her face as she said, "Mom, I think there's something wrong with me."

"What? Do you feel sick?" Eve examined her daughter's face for flushing or paleness.

"No, not that kind of wrong." Grace's gaze shifted to the pot in her hand and then back up to Eve. "This sounds twisted, but I want to meet Odette Fontaine."

♚

Luis settled into the back seat of the SUV with a deep sense of satisfaction. "My daughter is an extraordinary young woman," he said to Mikel, who sat next to him. "I have found my lost child."

Luis had always felt his family was incomplete, but he had put it down to his frustrated desire for more children. Now he believed he had somehow felt the tug of Grace's presence in the world because she shared his Dragón blood.

"I truly celebrate for you," Mikel said, his voice warm. "You deserve this happiness."

"*Gracias, amigo mío,*" Luis said with satisfaction. "It is amazing how much she reminds me of Raul. They even have some of the same mannerisms." When Grace was considering an idea with seriousness, she narrowed her eyes slightly, just as his son did. She also had the same way of going from solemnity to charm with a sudden flash of a smile.

"Your genes are very strong," Mikel said.

Luis laughed, more as a way to release his buzzing excitement than because he was amused. "I take no credit. Those were bequeathed to me by my ancestors."

"And how soon will Grace be coming to Caleva?" Mikel asked.

"She is doing something called rotations that do not allow her any time off from her studies for two months. I cannot wait that long." Luis considered for a moment. "I think that Caleva needs to open a veterinary school in the near future to fill a glaring gap in our institutions of higher education. We will begin to develop our plans by polling a group of fourth-year students and their professors about what should be included in their educational experience. Why not start with the top five students from Iowa's well-regarded veterinary college...so Grace won't be singled out? All expenses paid, and with a sizable donation to Iowa State, of course. Bruno will work out the details."

Mikel sighed in resignation.

Luis reached over to squeeze his forearm. "I have missed my daughter's entire life until now. I cannot bear to miss more."

"I know that hurts you, *Señor.* Another cruelty to lay on Odette Fontaine's shoulders."

"Let us not talk about that viper on this joyous occasion." Luis released his grip on Mikel's arm, brushing against the plastic box resting on the seat between them. "Are those the Scotcheroos?"

"Yes. Eve wanted the security team to have a treat."

"Ah, Eve," Luis said, the image of her face gilded by candlelight rising in his mind's eye. "I will have to be careful with her."

"She seems like a sensible woman," Mikel said. "I don't see the problem."

"She and Grace are a tightly melded family unit. It will require finesse to become a significant part of Grace's life without upsetting that balance."

He faced an additional issue that he wouldn't share with Mikel. Every time he got near Eve, he felt the urge to wind his fingers into her glorious hair, tilt her head back, and taste her generously curving lips before he slid his mouth lower.

He wasn't sure what attracted him so strongly. She was not beautiful in the classic sense, but she had a warm sensuality that called to him. Perhaps it was also because once she had relaxed this evening, she had treated him like any other dinner guest. He had found himself at ease in a way he hadn't been for a long time. If she hadn't been the adoptive mother of his daughter, he would be tempted to begin a discreet affair with her.

He seized the plastic container of sweets and popped off the top before offering it to Mikel. "Have one. You'll be amazed at how delicious it is."

As delicious as the woman who had made it.

CHAPTER 9

"What is this bad news you have for me?" Luis asked.

The sun was barely peeking over the flat line of the horizon as he sat in front of a computer monitor on the desk in the rental house. He was discussing developments in Caleva with Raul, Bruno Sanz, and his top political advisor, Francisco Vargas, via video call.

"The group of *consejeros* who wants to renegotiate the Americans' lease is threatening to stage a protest right outside the military base if they don't get a meeting with you soon. The new one, Camacho, seems to be riling up the others." Raul's jaw was tight with frustration. "I am sorry that I failed to pacify them, Pater."

"*Joder!* You have nothing to apologize for, Raul. Those *gilipollas* just want my attention." Luis scowled at the computer monitor. "Why are these idiots trying to antagonize the Americans? The world is an unsettled place. We need their military presence now more than ever."

"I think they are making trouble like the Lily Cabal did with trying to take over the lily sap production," Raul said. "They got elected to the *consejos* by appealing to the voters' greed, so they have to make it look like they are trying to squeeze money out of the rich Americans. They'll claim they can use it to cut taxes."

"You would think the Lily Subsidy would be enough," Luis muttered at the screen.

"*Señor*, you know how sensitive the Americans are about their image in the international media," Francisco said. "They don't like friction with the local people. I think you need to meet with the *consejeros* before they organize the protest."

A strange reluctance to leave Iowa clogged Luis's throat. He wanted to be "just Luis" to Grace and Eve for a little longer. Once they came to Caleva and saw him amid the trappings of his position, he feared that he would never be "just Luis" again.

"I will be home by tomorrow morning." He would sleep on the overnight flight home. "Try to work with Camacho, win him over to our side. Since he's fresh to the *consejo*, he won't have entrenched loyalties yet. Did you read his report about the conflicts he claims have occurred between the Americans and the locals?"

"Yes, and I spoke with the *jefe de policía* in Camacho's district," Raul said. "He says the number of incidents has not increased in the past six years, as Camacho claims. Nor have they escalated in violence."

"Which person do the facts support?" Luis asked.

"Both, in a way," Raul said. "Camacho's report includes clashes—mostly in bars—where no one pressed charges on either side. Some of those have been confirmed by witnesses."

"What is your gut feeling on this?" Luis asked his son.

"Camacho feels strongly on the subject," Raul said. "I don't think it's a major issue, though."

Luis nodded. "Good work."

The tense set of Raul's shoulders eased, and they moved on to other matters, most of which did not require Luis's immediate attention. While he listened to the discussion, he wondered again what Grace thought of him. He glanced at the time in the corner of the computer screen. Much too early to call Eve to see if she would meet him for lunch. He could not interrupt Grace's rotation today, but he could develop his relationship with Eve. He also wanted to get her perspective on his daughter's reaction to her newfound father.

"That's all we have right now," Raul said, pulling Luis's full focus back to faces on the computer screen.

"*Excelente!*" Luis said. "Raul, would you give me a few more minutes of your time?" He had told Raul about the DNA test results the day before, sharing his excitement with his son while also making sure Raul knew this would change nothing in their own relationship.

"*Por supuesto.*" Raul waited until Bruno and Francisco had left the video call. "How did it go with Grace? Will I like my half sister?" He smiled, but Luis saw the wariness in his eyes.

"That is a question only you can answer, but I find her intelligent, engaged, passionate, and articulate. In short, she shares many of your finest qualities." Luis smiled at his son with all the pride he felt in both his children.

Raul laughed, relief in the sound. "Then she's not the country bumpkin Odette described."

"Not at all. Her adoptive mother has done a superb job of raising an impressive young woman."

"What's her mother like?" Raul asked.

"Down-to-earth, hardworking, and devoted to Grace." Luis kept his thoughts about Eve's other attractions to himself. "She is torn between wanting Grace to have her rightful position and wishing to protect her daughter from the…drawbacks of being a royal."

Eve probably worried about how her own life would change as well.

"They know Gabriel's story, of course. That was all over the international media," Raul said. "What about Odette's?"

"I've told Eve some of it. I gave Grace the barest outline. Not surprisingly, she was quite distressed by her birth mother's actions."

"I understand." Raul looked down with a grimace. "At least my mother tried to kill only herself, not others."

"*Hijo mío...*" Pain ripped through Luis's chest all over again. He had tried to shield his son from the knowledge of his mother's fragile psyche as much as possible, but as Raul had grown up, he'd heard the whispers about Sofia's attempted suicide after his birth. When a teenage Raul had finally confronted Luis about it, he had told him only as much of the truth as he'd thought was necessary, but had withheld his suspicions about the fatal auto accident.

"I am not like my mother." Raul's gaze returned to Luis. "I will try to help Grace understand the same is true about her and Odette."

Love overlaid the pain. "Your personal experience and insight will mean more to her than anything I can say."

"Pater, it may be hard for her to adjust to what her new...heritage will mean to her life," Raul said. "I will try to help with that as well."

Luis nodded. He understood all that his son had left unspoken. Luis had once been *el Príncipe de los Lirios*, the Crown Prince of Caleva, with all the honors and responsibilities it carried. Grace might now be second in line for the crown, which was not as heavy a position as Raul's, but it still brought its own burdens.

He had no doubt that Grace was capable of handling the position. The question that clawed at him was whether she would want it.

"When will I get to meet her?" Raul asked.

"Bruno is working on that. I hope it will be soon." Luis let his gaze rest on his son's beloved face on the monitor. "I cannot wait to see the two of you together. It will be one of the happiest days of my life."

"I look forward to it too, Pater," Raul said. "Having a sister… That will be a new experience."

Raul was undoubtedly feeling the absence of Gabriel. The duke had moved out of the palace once his relationship with his fiancée, Quinn, became public. In his role as cultural ambassador for Caleva, Gabriel traveled a great deal as well.

"I think Quinn will enjoy having a fellow American in the family," Luis said.

"And Quinn will help her adjust to being royalty." Raul grinned. "Although I'm not sure whether Quinn has adjusted herself."

Luis smiled too. "She's making progress. I must go, *hijo mío. Te quiero mucho.*"

"*Y yo también,*" Raul said. "It will be good to have you home."

After Raul's face disappeared from the screen, Luis dropped his head into his hands, wishing yet again that he had grasped the seriousness of his wife's emotional state all those years ago. He had been overwhelmed by inheriting the throne so suddenly, but he should have seen the severity of Sofia's pain and stopped her from destroying herself.

Still, he couldn't regret his affair with Odette, for all the horror she had caused his family. He would not have Grace now if he hadn't temporarily lost his sanity all those years ago.

He lifted his head and glanced at his watch. Too early to call, but he could text Eve about lunch. Picking up the secure cell phone from his desk, he thought a moment before typing.

I would very much like to meet you for lunch to discuss how Grace is feeling. Would you be able to join me at whatever time is convenient for you? Will send a car for you, and we will eat near your workplace.

He sent the text and set the phone on the desk, feeling a spark of anticipation at the thought of seeing Eve again.

He quashed it by plunging into the unending list of governmental matters requiring his attention.

Eve was sitting at the kitchen table, sipping her coffee, and watching the early morning sunbeams slide through the windows, when a text dinged on her new super-secure cell phone. It still boggled her mind that she and her daughter had a king on speed dial.

"Someone's up early," she muttered, swiping to the new message with a strange mixture of trepidation and excitement. "Oh, shit!" Her coffee mug hit the table with a thunk.

Lunch with the king!

Why did he want to see *her*? *Alone*? She pushed down the shock and considered the invitation rationally. He probably just wanted to know how Grace had reacted to meeting her father, as he'd said in the text.

Eve felt like she couldn't say no to him, but she barely got an hour to eat lunch and usually not even that. Leaving her coffee behind, she tiptoed upstairs to the bedroom-turned-office and flipped open her laptop to check the day's schedule.

It looked manageable. Both the vets and the other techs on duty for the day were competent. With a little help from her colleagues, she might swing an hour and ten minutes with Luis. Less than that might seem insulting to royalty.

Pulling her phone out of her pocket, she typed, Thank you for the invitation. I will be outside the clinic entrance at noon.

She stared at the barebones message before adding, I look forward to lunch.

Uninspired but polite.

His response was immediate.

Thank you for meeting me. I understand that I am disrupting your day, so I am grateful for your willingness to accommodate me.

That was ironic since he must have a much busier schedule than she did. How the heck did she respond to that?

I am happy to do so, she typed before she headed back toward the stairs. She didn't have time to trade inane messages, even with a king.

"Hey, Mom." Grace emerged from her room, yawning, her loose braid partially unraveled from sleep.

"Morning, sweetheart." Eve gave her daughter a hug. "Sleep well?"

"Not really. I kept thinking about Luis and Caleva and...everything." She yawned again.

"I had the same problem," Eve confessed. "It's a lot to wrap your mind around."

"I wish I could take the day off, but"—Grace shrugged—"at least I get to see my father at dinner."

Grace had called Luis her father.

Eve made a snap decision not to tell Grace she was meeting him for lunch until after the fact. She didn't want Grace worrying about what was being said while she was trying to focus on her rotation.

Her daughter shuffled toward the bathroom. "See you downstairs, Mom."

Eve had taken three steps down the staircase when she realized she was wearing scrubs. They happened to be her favorite purple ones, but she couldn't eat lunch with a king in scrubs, especially not ones that might be stained with blood and who knew what else once lunchtime rolled around.

She bolted back to her bedroom to shove her black heels and a lint roller into a small duffel bag. On top of those, she placed navy trousers and a carefully rolled ivory silk blouse. Swapping out her gold pawprint earrings for classic pearls, she decided that was the best she could manage. Luis knew what she did for a living.

At ten minutes before noon, Eve was in the clinic's restroom, ripping off the bloodstained scrubs as she toed off her sneakers. She yanked on the navy trousers and shoved her feet into the pumps. After buttoning the blouse, she unclipped her hair, ran a brush through it, and decided she looked respectable enough.

"Enjoy your date!" Her friend Pam Baker called out with a smile as Eve jogged past the break room where the veterinarian was eating.

Eve had decided it was easiest to explain her extended lunch hour by saying it was a date. When she came back, she would tell Pam it hadn't gone well and that she was swearing off men again. She hoped that would be the end of it. Since Eve hadn't been on a date in years, Pam still might see this an opening to try to fix her up with someone else.

She burst through the exit to find a long black limousine parked under the canopy. Ivan stood waiting and opened the rear door for her. As Eve bent to scoot inside, she hoped like heck no one from the clinic saw her get into the ostentatious vehicle, or there would be far too many questions to evade.

As she settled on the seat, she gasped. Luis sat in the limo facing her, his long legs in navy trousers stretched out diagonally so his polished black loafers almost touched the bench seat where she was perched.

"I'm sorry to startle you," he said with a contrite smile. "My rental house is so far from your clinic that it would take most of your lunch hour to get there and back. Instead, I thought we would have a light lunch in the car." He gestured to two green coolers sitting on the floor.

"That's fine with me." She could hardly confess that being alone with him in this small space was already sending an unsettling slide of heat deep inside her.

"I would prefer to sit outside on this beautiful day." Luis gave a shrug of apology. "Mikel did not feel comfortable with that, though, so we are going to park in some hidden corner nearby."

He leaned down to flip one cooler open, his head so close she could easily reach out to stroke his gleaming silver-gray hair.

Oh no! No touching this man!

"Would you like some sangria?" he asked, pulling out an insulated beverage flask with a built-in straw. "I know you have to return to work, so I wasn't sure you would drink at lunchtime."

She would love to gulp down some sangria to ease the tension in her shoulders, but she needed to stay sober for the job...and to keep her brain out of the gutter it kept jumping into. Meeting his eyes, she felt the sizzle of his blue gaze. "I have to keep my reflexes sharp so I don't get bitten. But please feel free to have some yourself."

"I don't have to avoid teeth, except of the metaphorical kind, but I, too, have to return to work after our meal." His rueful look invited her to consider them as equals in their obligations.

Damn, the man is charming on top of being sexy as hell.

"So, a dry lunch for us both." She somehow felt like she should be serving him and not vice versa. "Can I help you with the food?"

"As soon as we stop." He reached into the cooler again to bring out another insulated cup, this one clear. "In the meantime, water?"

There was no way not to brush against his long fingers when she took the cup, so she braced herself for the little thrill that shimmered through her. Flipping up the straw, she sucked in a long, cold gulp to counteract her reaction.

The limo glided to a stop.

"We seem to have arrived." Luis glanced out a window. "Not terribly scenic."

Eve peered out to find nothing but brick walls on either side of them. Mikel had found a very secure hiding place for them, probably between a couple of the university buildings.

"Let us eat," Luis said, leaning sideways to press a button. A tabletop unfolded from the limo's side console.

"Fancy," Eve said. "The limo must be imported from Des Moines."

"That is a joke, yes?" Luis asked in a quizzical tone before he pulled another bottle of water out of the cooler and set it on the tabletop.

"Only partly," Eve said. "I assume you didn't bring the car with you from Caleva."

He simply lifted an eyebrow at her.

She pulled the other cooler closer, noticing a coat of arms featuring a fierce-looking Calevan dragon imprinted in gold on the lid. Even the darn coolers were royal. Two plate-sized containers with lids labeled *ensalada mixta* sat on top, so she slid them onto the table. Luis neatly placed a set of silverware rolled into a teal linen napkin beside each plate.

It was such a prosaic action for someone so...regal that it disarmed her. And that was very dangerous.

She unlatched the cover and lifted it off her plate to find an artful arrangement of multihued greens, colorful vegetables, thinly sliced hard-boiled eggs, slices of cheese, and bite-size cubes of barely seared tuna. "It's so beautiful I hate to mess it up," she said.

"My chef would be disappointed if all you did was look at it," Luis said, unrolling his napkin.

As soon as she had swallowed one perfect morsel of fish, Luis said, "Since our time is limited, I will go straight to my main concern. How is Grace feeling about her meeting with me?"

"That's a big question." At least she was expecting it. "She's excited, and she paid you the great compliment of saying she forgot you were a king."

His face lit up. His care for his daughter's opinion warmed her heart and fanned the flare of attraction she was fighting.

"She looks forward to visiting Caleva and wishes she could go sooner." Eve defaulted to formality to cover her unwanted response to him.

"I am working on that," he said.

"What do you mean? She can't change her rotation schedule at this point. It's pretty much engraved in stone." It required death or a natural disaster to budge the school on that.

"There are ways to influence such things," he said cryptically.

She gave him a hard stare as her protective mother bear emerged. "I thought we agreed to keep her new identity quiet for now."

"Her new identity will not be revealed until she is ready." He locked his gaze with hers. "I promise you."

She searched his face—the jut of his jaw, the blaze of his ice-blue eyes, the arch of his dark brows—and decided she accepted his promise. "I'll trust you on this, but you shouldn't push Grace too hard. You're not the easiest father to get used to."

"You are fierce on her behalf." But he seemed impressed rather than annoyed by her warning. "Please believe me when I say that I wish only the best for her."

"The problem is figuring out what the best is," Eve pointed out.

Luis nodded and turned the conversation to simple questions about Grace's life growing up, giving Eve a chance to relax and enjoy her salad that tasted as though it had just been plucked from the garden.

Then Luis hit her with a new angle.

"I know that you have been divorced since Grace was nearly one year old," he said. "How involved has your ex-husband been in Grace's life? I wish to tread carefully so I do not threaten that relationship."

The thought of Ben stopped her lascivious thoughts cold.

"There is no relationship with my ex," she said. "He started a new family and made it clear that he wanted nothing to do with us."

The bastard. She had no intention of telling Ben about Grace's biological father. He could find out whenever the rest of the world did.

"Why would he adopt a child and leave her a year later?" Luis asked, his voice holding a thread of anger.

Eve stabbed viciously at a slice of egg. "We got married too young. We wanted children, but we both had issues that kept us from conceiving." The remembered despair at hearing the doctor's diagnosis could still hollow her out. "Ben was not as enthusiastic about adopting as I was, but he agreed to it. When we got the notification about Grace, I was so thrilled that I didn't notice that he was less excited." She shrugged. "I was self-centered, too, I suppose."

"He should not have gone forward if he had second thoughts about something so important," Luis said.

"Well, I was the moving force in our marriage. Ben kind of went along." She savaged a piece of cheese next. "At first, he seemed delighted with Grace. He changed diapers and took turns with me doing the night feedings."

Why was she sharing all these personal details with him? Maybe because he listened with such focused intensity. And because Luis saw Ben's actions in the same light she did—an abandonment of the daughter he had made a commitment to parent.

She should shut up now, but he had opened up to her about his wife's problems.

"After about six months, he stopped participating in her care. I had to ask him to do things for her. And for me." She had been hurt and bewildered by Ben's distance from both her and his baby daughter. "Grace was so adorable. I didn't understand why he would withdraw from her like that."

She looked down at the shredded food on her plate. "He had found another woman and gotten her pregnant."

"*Cabrón!*" Luis snapped.

She could take a guess at the meaning of that. His strong reaction on her behalf was weirdly satisfying.

"He was thrilled about it in a way he hadn't been about Grace." When Ben had smugly announced his girlfriend's pregnancy, she'd felt like he had punched her, since his implication had been that Eve was defective. "There was no point in trying to make him stay with me and Grace. He could only love a baby he had fathered himself."

"He must be a very stunted person." Luis's voice held an edge.

"You know, that's a good description of Ben." Except for cheating on her, her ex had led a life bound by narrow convention.

"He is also an idiot to let go of two women as extraordinary as you and Grace." His gaze was warm with admiration.

"You're very kind." Even though his compliment was really about Grace, a shiver of pleasure still skimmed over Eve. Maybe he noticed her as a woman after all.

"I am many things—some admirable, some not—but kind is not among them." His lips slanted into a sardonic smile.

Eve inclined her head stiffly, while she fought the desire to know in what ways he found her extraordinary.

"Although I am sorry for the pain it caused you and Grace, I am relieved that I will not be displacing her adoptive father," Luis said.

"It makes things less complicated on that front," Eve agreed. Which was a relief since every other part of this situation was extremely complicated...and getting more so.

"Thank you for your candor," Luis said. "You have helped me understand Grace's situation more fully."

Luis must have dossiers on all of them. Having watched Mikel Silva in action, she suspected those dossiers were quite thorough, and she couldn't help wondering what was in them. However, while their factual reporting might be accurate, the emotional nuances would be harder to uncover.

"Please, you must eat. I don't want you fainting from hunger on the job." Luis gestured to her half-eaten salad. "We have the dessert still to come."

Eve jabbed her fork into a cube of tuna. "You should have mentioned dessert sooner." She forced herself to eat more of the salad before she put down her fork. A tangle of emotions roiled in her gut, making it hard to swallow.

Luis gave her one of his penetrating looks before he also laid down his fork and latched the cover over his salad. She gratefully followed his lead and stacked their plates on the floor.

"If you check in that cooler, you should find the dessert churros," he said.

Sure enough, two smaller covered plates were nestled at the bottom of the cooler. She put them on the table to find that Luis had produced two mugs of fragrant coffee from his cooler. She uncovered the plates to find each held half a dozen little sugar-dusted, heart-shaped churros with a chocolate dipping sauce.

She dunked one in the sauce, bit into it, and hummed with delight at the combination of light-as-air dough and warm chocolate.

"You like the dessert," Luis said as he brushed sugar from his long, elegant fingers. And now she was imagining them stroking over her skin.

She nearly groaned at the sensations smoldering through her body.

"It would be hard not to." She polished off the churro and decided it was time to distract herself and warn Luis. "There's another issue that you should be aware of."

Luis waited, his posture one of concentration.

"Grace wants to meet her birth mother."

He sat back with a jerk and muttered something in Spanish that she suspected he would not translate for her.

"My daughter is an intensely curious person," Eve said. It was part of what would make her daughter a great vet. "Once she found out who her birth mother is, I knew she would wish to meet her face-to-face. The desire may be even stronger because she knows how...damaged Odette Fontaine is. Grace needs to make sure that she is not like her biological mother."

Anger flashed and died in Luis's eyes, leaving them dull with pain. "I would like to persuade her not to see Odette. Nothing good will come of it."

"It's better that she has a chance to look this particular monster in the eye," Eve said, even though she wished for the same thing. "It will allow her to ask all the questions she has bottled up inside."

"I don't know that Odette will answer them except to serve herself or to strike at me through Grace," Luis said. "She is a manipulative *bruja*—witch—even in prison."

"Sometimes asking has to be enough." Eve ripped a churro in half. "I want to be there when Grace meets Odette.

Not at the meeting, but in Caleva. Grace will need someone she loves and trusts to talk about it with."

"You will come to Caleva when Grace comes." Luis took a bite of churro as if that settled it.

"You know I have a job. It's not as important as yours, but people count on me to be there." Eve was irritated by his blithe dismissal of her obligations.

He lifted his eyebrows at her. "If I can arrange for Grace's rotation schedule to be changed, do you not think I can arrange for a substitute for you at the clinic?"

"I...I suppose you could." She just hadn't expected that he would think of it.

"There are *some* advantages to being a king." There was an undercurrent of humor in his voice.

She and Grace had done some research on King Luis IV of Caleva, but it was still hard to connect this living, breathing man with the larger-than-life figure in the photos and news stories. The man in this car worried about what his daughter thought of him, scarfed down ham balls, and rummaged around in coolers.

He glanced at his watch. "Unfortunately, we must end our fascinating conversation if you wish to be back at work on time." He looked at her with the dazzling smile that lit his eyes and eased the sharp angles of his face. The smile that made her traitorous body go liquid with longing.

"That was my promise to you," he said. "And I always keep my promises."

CHAPTER 10

That evening, Eve and Grace sat in the back of a black SUV piloted by Ivan, waiting for two starkly modern stainless-steel gates to swing open.

"Oh my God, did you know this place was here?" Grace asked.

Eve peered out the car window to see a long, curving drive ending in front of a mansion built of sheets of glass framed by steel girders. The late-day sun painted peach and gold reflections on the building's façade. "Nope. I'm pretty sure whoever lives here doesn't bring their pets into the clinic themselves."

As they cruised up the drive, she caught a glimpse of movement and saw a guard moving into position at the gates. How many more guards were concealed as they had been at her house? Since this was Luis's home away from home at the moment, probably a lot.

As they rolled onto the circular courtyard in the front of the house, she saw two more SUVs parked at odd angles. Then she realized they were positioned to make the fastest getaway possible in two different directions.

Ivan drove up directly under the steel-and-glass portico. He and Bridget jumped out to open the car doors and help Eve and Grace out of the SUV. Which was useful because

Eve's sheath dress—a black one this evening that zipped up the front to end in a V-neckline—made it tough to maneuver gracefully out of a high vehicle. Grace's moss-green silk dress had a fuller skirt, so she had less difficulty climbing out.

Two guards in black clothing stood on either side of the double doors. As she and Grace climbed the stone steps, one guard pulled a door open. "Welcome," he said with a brief smile.

They passed into a double-height entrance hall that showcased a huge kinetic sculpture hanging from a girder and a floating staircase rising from the slate floor.

"Not too shabby," Grace murmured.

"*Bienvenido!*" Luis strode toward them, his face aglow with pleasure. He wore tailored trousers in silver-gray and a flawlessly pressed black dress shirt. The muted palette somehow made his blue eyes more vivid while his hair glinted with silver highlights.

A familiar shimmer of attraction rippled through Eve. And then he took her hands in his, the warm, strong fingers closing around hers as he leaned in for an air-kiss. The press of his palms against hers, the barest brush of his beard against her cheek, the swirl of his sea-and-air scent around her, all seemed to glide down to ignite deep in her belly.

She practically yanked her hands out of his so she could back away. He gave her a questioning look before he turned to Grace, who skipped past his outstretched hands to give him a hug. The delight on his face as he hugged his daughter in return touched Eve's heart and helped her squelch her unwelcome reaction.

"Come!" Luis kept his arm around Grace's shoulders as he took them into a vaulted living room furnished with a mix of square modern sofas and chairs combined with antique rugs and accent pieces. A massive stone fireplace centered one wall with uniformly cut firewood stored in niches around it. It looked like the photos in a fancy home decorating magazine.

Luis handed Grace onto one of the sofas and waited as Eve sat next to her before he took a chair across from them. The coffee table between them was made of polished stone and held an array of tapas arranged like works of art.

"What would you like to drink?" Luis asked, gesturing to a young woman in a server's uniform who stood nearby.

Eve wanted an ice-cold beer to quench the internal flames Luis had lit—and she was sure his staff would conjure one up—but she thought that would be crass. "Red wine would be lovely," she said.

"The same for me," Grace said.

Luis nodded to the server, who vanished silently.

He turned back to them. "Since you treated me to Iowan specialties, I am offering you Calevan cuisine. We are surrounded by the ocean, so seafood features prominently." He waved an elegant hand at the coffee table.

The server appeared with a silver platter and handed them each an exquisitely thin wide-bowled crystal glass filled with deep-red wine.

Luis lifted his in a toast. "To finding new family! It brings me great happiness."

His voice rang with the truth of his words, and Grace looked as though she wanted to hug him again.

Eve wished she could hug him, too, but for entirely different reasons. Instead, she smiled and took a sip of the delicious wine.

"To the father I always hoped I had," Grace said, lifting her glass in return.

Eve looked at her daughter with respect. That was a graceful toast to come up with on the fly. She touched her glass to Grace's with an approving smile before she took a sip. Having her daughter living with her as a vet student sometimes made her forget that Grace was an adult with a mature confidence and sense of self. Not that it stopped Eve from wanting to protect Grace and help her navigate this crazy new future.

"I have some unfortunate news, but it is balanced by what I hope you will agree is good news," Luis said. "I must leave for Caleva right after our dinner tonight. A political matter needs my personal attention."

The beaming pleasure on Grace's face dimmed.

"On the other hand, my executive assistant, Bruno, has found a way to free you from your rotation schedule beginning next week." Luis shifted his gaze to Eve. "We have invited the top five fourth-year students to come to Caleva so we may get their input on what they would like to see in the new veterinary school we are building there." His smile held fatherly pride in Grace. "Your stellar academic record made it easy to manage this."

Grace met his smile with a grin. "I'm glad my GPA was useful."

And as he had promised, Grace wouldn't be singled out since she was among the top students in her class.

"You are invited to add your perspective as a veterinary technician," Luis said to Eve, his smile turning smug at his assistant's cleverness. "If you both are willing to travel at such short notice, of course."

He didn't fool her into thinking she had a choice. He knew damn well that Grace would jump at this and that Eve would never let her daughter go alone. The man had gotten exactly what he wanted. She narrowed her eyes at him for a moment to show she wasn't taken in. He raised his eyebrows in acknowledgment, but his smile remained.

"Are you actually building a veterinary school?" Eve asked.

"It is an important institution Caleva lacks." He took a sip of wine. "Perhaps Grace can head up the project."

Grace looked stunned and then eager. "That would be great, but I don't think I'm qualified."

"Perhaps not yet, but you will be soon," her father said. "You can also hire experts to assist you."

Shit! It was happening already. Grace was finding out how different her life could be if she lived in Caleva. Eve finished her wine in one gulp and wished she could go somewhere to cry. Yet she also felt a thrill for her daughter at the possibilities opening up for her.

Being a parent often meant suffering a severe case of emotional whiplash.

"Mom should be on the school start-up team too," Grace said. "She knows more about vet med than half my professors."

"I only have practical experience. The high-level stuff is beyond me," Eve said, although she felt a surge of gratification.

"Your diagnoses are never wrong," Grace said. "Half the time, you don't even need to look at a blood test or X-ray."

"I've been a vet tech for a long time, so I've seen it all," Eve demurred. "Although I do have some ideas about how to structure a clinic that makes the experience for the patients fear-free."

"Fear-free?" Luis asked.

"It's a concept of practicing vet med in a way that reduces the patients' anxiety and stress, which often improves the outcome of our treatments," Grace said. "We do a pretty good job of it at the school clinic, but to succeed fully, you need to start with the building itself. We could do that in Caleva, build it from the ground up and train all the students to do the same in their future practices." Grace's voice vibrated with enthusiasm.

Luis nodded, and Eve could see the satisfaction lurking in his eyes. He had hooked his daughter well and good with this bait.

More than that, Grace seemed to grow and change right before Eve's eyes, from a book-toting graduate student grinding through her studies to a visionary with the means to turn a dream into reality. Maybe having the blood of kings running in your veins gave you that kind of conviction that you could—and possibly should—make big things happen.

Eve had never felt that way. It had been all she could do to raise one child. Another thought pinched at her heart. Grace might never have reached her full potential if Luis hadn't found her.

"Mom?" Grace's voice pulled her out of her depressing thoughts.

"Sorry. Visions of fear-free waiting rooms were dancing in my head," Eve said.

"We will give your visions substance," Luis said. It was striking how much Luis and Grace sounded alike when they spoke about the imaginary vet school. "We have gotten ahead of ourselves, though," Luis said, smiling. "We must get you to Caleva first. Bruno will contact you about travel arrangements. Caleva is sponsoring the trip, so there will be no expense to anyone from the school."

Eve gave an internal sigh of relief, even though she had figured that Luis would underwrite the cost. With all of Grace's expenses for vet school, Eve didn't have extra money lying around for foreign travel.

"Who are the other people in the group?" Grace asked.

Luis picked up a tablet that was sitting on the coffee table and swiped a couple of times before handing it to Grace. She held it so Eve could read the list too.

Two of the students were friends of Grace's. The other two often joined them for exam prep. Two professors were listed as well, both of whom Eve had worked with and found bland but unobjectionable. The school must have chosen them because they weren't currently teaching any rotations.

Eve looked up. Luis lounged in his chair, long legs stretched out and crossed at the ankles, clearly waiting for their comments. Even his stillness held a coiled energy waiting to be unleashed.

"We know them all," Eve said.

"And you've included a reptile lover," Grace said. "He'll go crazy over your Calevan dragons."

"*Excelente!* Now let us enjoy dinner." Luis rose from his chair and gestured toward a wide archway. As they stood, he stepped forward to offer a crooked elbow to each of them. "If you will allow me?"

Grace stepped to one side of Luis and placed her hand on her father's arm with a smiling glance up at his face. Eve once again felt the solidity of the king's muscles as she followed suit. The cotton of his shirt was soft and warm against her palm and wrist. There was no point in pretending she didn't want to touch more of him and even feel his hands on her skin in return, but that was just a primitive response of her body. She could ignore it most of the time.

But, dear Lord, he smelled so good. Even better than the delicious aromas emanating from the door into the kitchen.

The rest of the evening passed with Luis weaving his spell of royal Calevan magic around them. Grace was ensnared by it, leaning toward her father as she drank in his every word. Eve fought the pull of his charisma, succeeding only because she recognized that he was glossing over the less pleasant aspects of royal life.

Sometime soon she would have to point that out to Grace, but for now, she let her daughter revel in her newfound father's warmth and charm.

They lingered over dessert and coffee because no one wanted to give up the cocoon of candlelight, excellent food, and one another's relaxed company. Finally, though, Eve said, "I'm sorry to be the party pooper, but it's getting late."

It was uncanny how identical the expressions of disappointment were from both Grace and Luis. Those Dragón genes were powerful.

They all stood, and Luis once again offered his elbows to his guests. Eve savored the last few moments of contact with his warmth and scent as they strolled to the front door.

"I hate to part," Luis said, "but we will be reunited very soon, and I will have the pleasure of showing you all the glories of Caleva."

Tears glittered in Grace's eyes, and she threw her arms around her father's neck. "I can't wait to see you again."

Luis's face blazed with jubilation as he returned the embrace. "*Hija mía*, I will be counting the minutes."

They released each other with obvious reluctance before Luis turned to Eve. He, too, had a liquid glint of emotion in his eyes. Taking both her hands in his strong grip, he did the double air-kiss, the brush of his beard sending another delicious flicker of sensation dancing over her skin. "Until we meet again," he said, his blue eyes locked on her in a way that made her feel like the only woman in the world. An illusion.

They were escorted to the car by Ivan and closed into the dark interior. As Ivan set the car in motion, Grace pulled her new cell phone out of her handbag and began to type madly.

"What are you doing?" Eve asked.

"Texting Luis to tell him how much I loved dinner," Grace said, her voice a little gruff.

"That will make him happy."

Grace's thumbs stilled, and she rested the phone on her thigh. "Did you have fun, Mom?"

"I sure did." Maybe too much fun.

Grace's phone dinged with an incoming text, and she checked it instantly. "He answered me!" She didn't read the message aloud, but in the dim moonlight, Eve could see the smile softening her face.

"Mom, we're going to Caleva!" Grace's voice vibrated with excitement. "Can you believe it?"

"I believe Luis can make almost anything happen," Eve said, a touch of dryness in her tone.

Luis looked up from his phone as Mikel came down the stairs to the front hallway. "Grace texted me"—he was unable to stop the upward curl of his lips—"about how much she enjoyed dinner."

Mikel surprised him by smiling in return. "You will receive many texts going forward. It is the preferred method of communication for that generation."

"Raul and Gabriel rarely text me," Luis pointed out.

"They were raised differently, they are male"—Mikel's expression turned enigmatic—"and you are their king."

"I like getting texts from my daughter." Luis slipped his phone into his shirt pocket.

"As do I," Mikel said. "Excuse me, *Señor*, I must complete our preparations for departure."

Luis waved a hand to indicate Mikel should do what he needed to, then wandered into the dining room. The table was already cleared, and the clink and water rush of dishes being washed emanated from the kitchen.

His mind roamed back to the pleasures of the evening. Grace leaning toward him, her face alive with interest and laughter as she asked a question about Caleva. Eve watching her daughter with pride and love glowing in her eyes more brightly than the candlelight.

He had not wanted the evening to end. Although he looked forward to showing Grace and Eve the beauties of Caleva, he knew their view of him would change once they arrived in his country. Here in the cornfields of Iowa, he could almost be an average person, particularly since he had instructed Mikel to keep the security measures as low-key as possible.

In Caleva, it would be impossible to hide the singularity of his position. He viewed the palace as simply home. A centuries-old suit of armor was no more extraordinary than a potted plant. Few people, though, shared his perspective.

Grace would take it in her stride because she had the delicious arrogance of a young Midwesterner who wasn't over-awed by royalty or history. Not to mention that she had royal blood in her veins, so she would feel that she had a right to be there.

Eve was another matter. She had recognized that he was painting a deliberately rosy picture of being royal, describing his family through the lens of his love for them, downplaying or ignoring the less relatable aspects of their lives. Eve had not called him on it, despite the skepticism that had flitted across her features.

Most of the time, though, Eve had listened and laughed along with Grace. Even she sometimes seemed to forget he was a king, treating him to the occasional blunt observation that was softened by her warmth. He could imagine her handling difficult pets and their even more difficult owners with her distinctive combination of compassion and no-nonsense good humor.

He would lose sight of that side of her in Caleva amid the bodyguards and staff and vast castle.

He could perhaps watch the candlelight play over the satin of her auburn hair and hear the throaty laugh that sent a tightening of arousal to his groin. But it would happen at a table filled with other people, not aimed just at him.

He wanted more of Eve, and that was a dangerous craving.

CHAPTER 11

"I can't believe he lives here," Grace murmured as their guide, Clara, led the group of vet students and their chaperones through a stone great hall decorated with heraldic banners and medieval weapons.

Their journey to Caleva had been marked by one amazing luxury after another. To start the trip, all eight of them had been picked up at the vet school and transported to the Des Moines airport by a private van. After the short flight to Chicago, they had been escorted to the first-class lounge, where they had dined and drunk champagne for free while they waited to depart for Caleva. The eight-hour flight on Calevan Airlines had been spent indulging in and exclaiming over all the amenities in first class.

At the San Ignacio airport earlier that morning, they had been met at the gate by Clara and whisked through Customs in a special line before boarding another elegant van. As they drove from the airport into San Ignacio and up the cliff to the castle, Clara had pointed out all the notable sights along the way. Eve caught glimpses of the lavender *vaho* hibiscus glowing against gray basalt walls, but the van windows were closed, so she couldn't smell it.

Now they were getting a brief tour of the castle on their way to being greeted by the minister of Agriculture. "We are in the oldest part of Castillo Draconago, which was built in about 1510," Clara said. "This hall is used for formal ceremonial events. Your welcome reception is in a newer and more hospitable wing built in the 1600s." She paused to let them gawk at the stone walls and vaulted wooden ceiling high above their heads.

As Clara marched them down another hallway, she explained that they were now in the wing of the castle that was Caleva's version of the White House, where King Luis and his ministers had their official offices. At the mention of his name, Eve's pulse gave a little leap, and Grace's eyes lit up as she gave her mother an excited smile. The air seemed to grow more vibrant at the thought that Luis was somewhere nearby.

Clara opened a door and gestured them through. "This is the Salón de los Lirios. Please help yourself to the food and beverages." She glanced at her watch. "The minister will be here in fifteen minutes. There is a bathroom through that door." She pointed to an oak door set in the paneled wall.

The *salón* featured tall arched windows, several comfortable seating areas delineated by vivid Persian rugs, and portraits of what Eve guessed were previous rulers on the walls. On one side of the room stood two long, carved wooden tables laden with elegantly arrayed food and drinks, behind which stood several servers wearing black trousers, white shirts, and teal vests and ties. The teal was a shade known as Calevan green, as she had learned on the flight over. It evoked the skin color of the native Calevan lizards.

Although they had all eaten on the plane, the students made a beeline for the food and drinks.

"I suppose we should make sure there's no alcohol over there," one of the veterinarians said with a worried look.

"Some of the students took full advantage of the free booze on the plane."

Eve watched the group piling their plates with food. "I think they're overawed enough by the castle to stay sober, but I'll check with the servers."

She strolled over to the beverage station and asked about the offerings and was assured that none contained alcohol. The server suggested she try a pineapple drink that was a Calevan specialty. She found it deliciously refreshing with subtle touches of mint and lime.

The students were clustered in one seating area, devouring their tapas, when the door swung open and a small brown-haired woman dressed in a burgundy pantsuit burst into the room. She was followed by a tall, thin young man in a gray suit.

"*Bonjour!* I am Adeline Arnaud, Caleva's minister of Agriculture," the woman said in a voice that made all the students jump to their feet. "This is my assistant, who will be your liaison during your stay." She smiled, and her stern face became beautiful. "We are excited to have you all here because a veterinary college in Caleva has always been a goal of ours. Now, I wish to meet you, so please come here and introduce yourselves."

Eve liked the woman's no-nonsense approach. Since the two vets looked taken aback, Eve shepherded the students over to meet the minister, introducing them one by one. The two vets joined them, and soon everyone was chatting in a single group.

The door opened again, and a gray-haired man, dressed in a dark suit, announced in an authoritative voice, "His Majesty King Luis!"

The room fell silent, and excitement fizzed through the air. Grace threw Eve a nervous look.

Luis strode into the room, dressed in a navy suit, pale blue shirt, and red tie, and as always took possession of every square inch of the space. His smile seemed to add extra megawatts of illumination as he said, "I wanted to welcome our delegation of veterinary education experts."

Eve suddenly realized that all the Calevans in the room had sunk into deep curtsies and bows. She quickly emulated them and gestured that her other compatriots should do the same.

"A pleasure to see you, *Ministre*," Luis said. "I heard that you were here with our new arrivals, so I took a few minutes to add my welcome to yours."

"We are honored, *Votre Majesté*," the minister said, looking stunned. She recovered quickly. "May I introduce them to you?"

His gaze swept the rapt faces turned toward him, but he gave no indication that he recognized Grace or Eve. "That would be delightful."

The minister marshaled them into an orderly line to make the introductions. Eve made sure she was at the beginning of the line so that she could demonstrate to her fellow Americans how to curtsy when meeting royalty. She mentally crossed her fingers that they would follow her lead. All of them had received instructions on proper Calevan etiquette, but she wasn't sure they would remember when dazzled by the king's presence.

"May I present Eve Howard, a veterinary technician at the university's clinic," the minister said, her memory impressing the heck out of Eve.

"Your Majesty," Eve said, curtsying before placing her hand in his to shake. That warm, strong grip felt so familiar and so delicious.

There was an intimate twinkle in Luis's eyes, and he gave her hand a slight squeeze. "Thank you for coming to advise my countrymen, *señora*," he said. "I hope you will find your stay here interesting and rewarding."

"We are happy to be here," she said.

And her turn was over.

The two veterinarians, both men, came next, and Eve was relieved to see that they made very creditable bows. If the students muffed their obeisances, they were young and would be forgiven.

She watched Luis as the students cycled through, suspecting that Grace also got the extra twinkle and squeeze because her polite smile widened a bit. Otherwise, he was clearly a king, warm and socially graceful, but with a profound distance between him and the others in the room.

Eve felt a quiver of unease. She had sensed his power in Iowa, but now it was on full display. Even the self-assured minister's manner changed to pure deference when addressing Luis. In the casual settings of their previous interactions with him, she and Grace had not grasped the full implications of his position. Now they were on his home turf, and Luis dominated it.

"My apologies, *Señor*." The man who had announced Luis's presence appeared at his side again. "We must depart for your next meeting."

Regret flashed across Luis's face as he said farewell to the starstruck group of grad students and vets. "We will meet again at the reception later this week," Luis said. "Until then, *adios*."

As the door closed behind him, Eve felt as though the lights dimmed and half the oxygen left the room. She would have been worried except everyone else looked like they felt the same way.

As the students chattered about meeting the king, the minister came to stand beside Eve and the two vets. "I am very encouraged that the king is taking an interest in this project," she said. "Your group's presence seems to have put it on the fast track."

Eve got the impression that the minister was mentally rearranging her schedule in order to attend the planning meetings now that the king had given the future vet school his personal attention. She hoped the minister wasn't disappointed when she found out the real reason behind this delegation's visit. Although Luis was waving the temptation of founding a school in front of Grace's nose, so maybe it would happen.

Clara appeared and rejoined the group. "If you would like to enjoy some more food, please go ahead. We'll be showing you to your rooms soon."

That seemed to be the signal for the minister to exit. The students revisited the catering tables before plunking down to eat and talk.

"I've never stayed in a castle before," Joe Murphy, one of the vets, said.

"Not to mention never meeting a king before," his colleague Ezra Keenan agreed.

Eve glanced around the antique-filled room. "It's pretty overwhelming, but it's only two nights here, and then we get to stay with normal human beings in normal surroundings."

Eve didn't share the fact that they were being scattered among Calevan households to give Luis, Raul, and Grace a chance to spend time together without being seen. She and Grace would be staying at a house Luis owned, and he would join them in the evenings. Exhilaration and nerves shimmied through Eve at the thought of seeing Luis again.

At the same time, she worried about the effect on Grace. Her daughter had a good, sensible head on her shoulders, but it was hard to withstand the barrage of enticements a king could conjure up. Hell, Eve was having a hard time resisting them, and they were only tangentially aimed at her.

She and Grace had talked about some of the implications of going public with her royal blood, but of course, neither of them had actual experience of what it would be like. All they could do was make intelligent guesses. Eve had encouraged Grace to talk with Prince Raul about his daily life. Assuming the prince embraced his half sister.

A few minutes later, the door opened again to admit three people dressed in the deep green that seemed to signify palace staff.

Clara stood. "You are now welcome to accompany your guides to your rooms."

A young woman stepped forward and called out two student names. When her charges joined her, she said, "Please follow me," and led them out of the room.

"I will escort you," Clara said to Eve and Grace. "We will wait just a little longer before we go."

Eve and Grace exchanged questioning looks, but Eve didn't ask why. This whole trip had been so carefully orchestrated that she assumed there was a good reason.

"I hope you are enjoying your visit so far," Clara said. "Tomorrow morning, you will have a tour that includes the lily fields and the research facility working on preserving our local fauna, in particular, the Calevan dragons. In the afternoon, you are scheduled to meet with various officials from the Ministry of Agriculture to begin discussions about the veterinary school. When that is done, you will be free to wander the streets of San Ignacio. If you would like a guide, text me, and I will arrange for one."

"That would be great," Grace said.

"We may go to your suite now," Clara said after everyone else had been escorted out.

She led them through so many corridors that Eve was thoroughly lost by the time they came to a halt in front of a carved oak door. Clara pulled two key cards out of her pocket and pressed one against the black pad on the door. The lock clicked, and she swung the door open, waving them through in front of her.

They entered a wood-paneled sitting room with three tall windows, furnished with rose velvet sofas and comfortable-looking armchairs upholstered in a floral fabric. Flames danced in a fireplace surrounded by burgundy-and-cream-painted tiles. A Persian rug lay on the polished wood planks of the floor, and a giant vase of *vaho* hibiscus stood on the desk between the windows, the fragrance wafting into Eve's nostrils.

Clara gestured to a basket sitting on the coffee table in front of the sofa. "You'll find tapas and *dulces* there and a bar in that cabinet, but you can ask the palace kitchen for anything else you would like. Your phones should have the intercom numbers programmed in them already. Just tap the castle icon."

She strolled to a doorway beside the fireplace. "One bedroom is in here. I believe we put Grace's luggage in this one, but feel free to swap." She crossed to the opposite side of the room to indicate a door near the window. "The other bedroom is here." She approached the desk. "You'll find paper copies of your schedules here, but they are also on your phones, of course."

Clara tapped the papers before she continued. "A palace staff member will be here to take you to dinner at seven. You do not need to dress up. You will be eating with each other in an informal dining room. We thought you might wish to relax after your long journey." She paused. "May I help you with anything else?"

Eve and Grace looked at each other and shook their heads.

Clara gave them a wide smile. "We are happy to have you here in Caleva." And then she was gone, the door closing behind her with a solid thump.

Grace spun around, taking in the elegance of the room. "Oh my God, this is amazing!" She dashed through the door into her bedroom. "Mom, you have to come see this bed!"

Eve followed her to find a canopy bed hung with billows of rose damask with flowers woven into the fabric. The two tall windows were layered with the same damask as well as swaths of floral-printed silk. "It's quite...spectacular," Eve said.

Grace laughed. "It's ridiculous, but I kind of love it. Let's see what your room looks like."

"Whoa! This is even crazier," Grace said, stopping in the doorway.

Eve's bed had a huge headboard carved with twining lilies, a canopy made of tapestry woven with more lilies, and draperies of rose velvet. The windows sported tapestry valances and moss-green velvet panels with cream silk undercurtains. Eve ran her hand over the quilted green velvet bedspread, finding it so soft to the touch that it had to be woven out of silk.

"Check this out," Grace said from the closet door she had pulled open. "Your clothes are already hung up in here." She closed the door and turned with a grin. "If we wanted to switch rooms, I bet they'd come up and move our clothes."

"Do you want to swap?" Eve asked.

"No, I was just imagining what would happen." Her grin disappeared, and she perched on one of the carved wooden chairs. "If I become a princess, I might have a suite like this here in the palace." She looked around. "It's not exactly cozy."

"You'd get used to it," Eve said, but she didn't feel like she belonged here either. These overwhelming rooms were Luis's first miscalculation in his efforts to win over his daughter.

"I'm not so sure," Grace said before she jumped up. "I need a real drink, and then I'm going to take a shower. Let's go raid the bar."

They had enjoyed a couple of glasses of excellent wine before trundling down to meet the rest of their group in a comfortable—and not overly formal—dining room. Everyone was exclaiming over their rooms, the palace, the food, and the incredible level of service. As Eve listened to the descriptions of the guest rooms, she realized that she and Grace were the only ones with an over-the-top suite. Neither she nor Grace shared that fact with their colleagues, of course. More wine flowed, and by the end of dinner, all of them were ready to go back to their rooms to sleep.

As Eve thanked their guide and closed the suite's door, she heard two pings, one from her phone and one from Grace's. Grace pulled hers out first and read something before she looked up with happiness dancing in her eyes. "Luis wants to know if he can stop by to see how we're doing. He sent the text to both of us." She didn't ask how Eve felt about it before typing something back. "I told him that would be great."

The exhaustion dragging on Eve evaporated at the thought of being able to see Luis without concealing their prior relationship. At the same time, she remembered the deep curtsies and bows of all the Calevans in the room when he had entered. The Luis she had gotten to know in Iowa now seemed to be someone beyond her reach.

Another message pinged, and Eve read it herself this time.

Luis wrote, I will be there in five minutes. Do not be surprised when a panel in the wall opposite the fireplace opens. Castles have convenient secret passages.

Grace dashed to the mirror by the door to smooth her hair. Eve barely stopped herself from doing the same. Her daughter turned away from the mirror with a twist to her smile. "Is it strange that I'm nervous about seeing him again? All that curtsying and bowing at the reception made me understand what a big deal he really is." She shrugged. "He was so *normal* back in Iowa. Now, he's the king."

"Oh, sweetie, I understand," Eve said. "He is still your father, though. No amount of pomp and circumstance can change that."

Yet she was glad that Grace was beginning to grasp what being the daughter of a king would mean to her life.

A loud click sounded from the side of the room, and the panel swung inward, revealing a dimly lit doorway. Luis stepped through, and the panel closed. He was dressed in the same clothes he had worn earlier, minus the suit jacket and tie.

"Grace, *hija mía!*" He opened his arms and strode to where Grace stood, enveloping her in a hug. "I wanted to do this the moment I saw you this afternoon. I am so happy to have you here." He skimmed his hands down to her shoulders to hold her away from him as he examined her face. "Have you been well taken care of?"

"We've been treated like royalty," Grace said with a sly grin.

Luis laughed, the deep, rich sound vibrating through the air. "I hope that's a good thing."

Damn the man, he knows exactly how to reel Grace in.

"And you, Eve." He turned to her. "It is a pleasure to welcome you to my home."

"It's a heck of a home," Eve said, waving at the opulent room.

Luis grimaced. "I am sorry about the overblown splendor. Since the secret passage connects this suite with my quarters, it allows me to visit without observers."

"I always wanted to live somewhere with a secret passage," Grace said. "It's very mysterious and romantic."

"Several of our early queens would not find it so romantic," Luis said. "This is where my long-ago predecessors would house attractive guests so that they could visit them clandestinely."

"Why two bedrooms?" Grace asked.

"Ah, the husband would be installed in one, and the wife in the other," Luis said.

"The husbands didn't mind?" Eve asked.

"In those days, they didn't have much choice if the king coveted their wife. Better to be cuckolded by royalty than tossed into the dungeon," Luis explained. "Some men even considered it a useful way to curry favor with the king."

Eve had a vision of Luis gliding into her candlelit bedroom, his long legs clad in tight breeches tucked into tall boots, his broad shoulders covered by a ruffled shirt open halfway down his chest, a long brocade dressing gown billowing out behind him. She was dressed in a translucent silk nightgown, her hair loose around her bare shoulders, waiting for him... A shimmer of heat sparkled through her body.

"What about the female guests?" Grace asked. "Did they have any say in the matter?"

"Probably even less than their husbands," Luis said.

Eve felt guilty about her sexual fantasy. Those women hadn't necessarily *wanted* to sleep with the king, not like she did.

"Please, let us sit." Luis gestured to the sofa in front of the fireplace.

"Would you like something to drink?" Eve asked, thinking she could use something to cool off her overheated imagination.

"Cold water would be most welcome," Luis said, settling into an armchair.

When Eve glanced at her daughter, Grace shook her head before she sat on the end of the sofa closest to her father.

"Tell me what you think of Caleva so far," Luis said, leaning toward his daughter.

Grace launched into an enthusiastic description of the sights they had seen, thanking her father for flying them there first class.

He waved a hand in dismissal, but it clearly pleased him that she had enjoyed it.

When Eve brought him a tall glass of water with ice, he accepted it with a warm smile of gratitude before his focus shifted back to his daughter. Eve was happy to let the two of them talk, so she snuggled into a wing chair, kicking off her shoes and curling her legs under her. The flickering fire, the music of Grace's soprano and Luis's baritone voices, and her exhaustion made her lean her head against the chair's high back in drowsy contentment.

"We are putting your mother to sleep." Luis's voice held a thread of apology. "I should leave you to rest from your journey."

Eve sat upright. "No, please don't go. It was so nice to sit here listening to the two of you talking."

Now that her eyes were open, she noticed that Luis had relaxed in his own chair, leaning back and stretching out his long legs, which he crossed at the ankles. He wore the shiniest wingtips she had ever seen. Of course, he had a valet to keep them that way.

"No, I am being selfish." He straightened his posture and folded his legs in to stand. "But before I go, I have a small gift for each of you." He reached into his trouser pocket and brought out a small velvet bag. "To welcome you to Caleva."

He unzipped the bag and poured something shiny into the palm of his hand. "For you, *hija mía*, in honor of your heritage." He pinched up a gold chain between thumb and forefinger to display the golden pendant dangling from it, a fiercely snarling Calevan dragon with glittering emerald eyes.

Grace stood and held the pendant against her palm to admire it. "He's the dragon on your coat of arms. I love it!"

"It is now your coat of arms as well," Luis said. "May I put it on you?"

"Yes, please." Grace turned and twisted her hair over her shoulder so Luis could lift the necklace over her head and fasten the catch behind her neck.

"It's perfect." Grace pivoted and kissed her father on the cheek. "I will treasure it always."

Luis kissed Grace on both cheeks in return, his eyes ablaze with happiness.

"And for you, Eve." Luis pulled out another pouch and tilted the contents into his hand. "A Calevan lily. Our miraculous flower that stops dementia."

He held up the necklace, and it sparkled in the firelight. The lily's dark red color was created by tiny rubies.

Oh God, he was going to want to put it around her neck. And she couldn't wait.

She uncurled her legs and stood. "It's lovely." And far too fancy for her, but she would keep it someplace safe.

He looked a question at her, and she mutely turned her back to him, flicking her hair out of the way as Grace had. His scent wrapped itself around her right before he brought the necklace in front of her. The temptation to lean back against his tall, strong body was overwhelming, but she kept herself from swaying.

Then his fingers were brushing against the sensitive skin of her nape, and electric desire zinged through her to coil between her legs. All too quickly, the clasp was closed, and his touch was gone.

She dropped her hair over the still-tingling spot and touched the lily as she turned. "Thank you for the beautiful gift."

He brushed his cheek against hers, which sent more heat skimming through her. "It is a joy to have you both here in my country."

Grace looked up from delighting in her necklace. "Will you come back here tomorrow night?"

"Wild horses could not keep me away," Luis said, and Eve heard the truth of it ring in his voice.

Grace linked her arm with her father's. "I'll walk you to the door."

Eve tracked them across the room. Grace had fallen for her father, hook, line, and sinker. To be fair, Luis was equally enamored of his daughter, but he had been inclined that way before he met her.

A pang of jealousy intertwined itself with the happiness in Eve's heart. She would be sharing Grace from now on, and not with just any father, but with one who commanded the resources of an entire country. She would have to stand strong to balance Luis's influence. She might even have to fight to have a significant role in Grace's life going forward.

She would also have to fight her insane attraction to Grace's father.

The secret panel closed Luis into the dimly lit corridor with its bare stone walls. He could hear Grace's voice through the wood, but he could not distinguish her words. She sounded happy, though. Almost as happy as he was to have her here. For a moment, he stood with his head thrown back and his eyes closed, basking in the knowledge that his daughter was here in Caleva. It felt as though his family was complete at last.

As soon as Grace and Eve moved to his cliff house, he would bring Raul to meet his half sister. They would have the time and privacy to get to know each other there. He was certain they would like each other because they were alike in so many ways. Responsible, hardworking, perhaps even driven, intelligent, and occasionally snarky. He smiled at the last, imagining them one-upping each other at the dinner table.

Now he had to persuade Grace and Eve to move from Iowa to Caleva. He did not fool himself that Grace would come to a distant country without her mother. They were a cohesive team, bound by a palpable love. He envied Eve that but hoped he could achieve almost as strong a relationship—albeit of a different quality—with Grace over time.

Which meant that he needed to control his problematic attraction to Eve. When she had curled up in the wing chair, with a sleepy smile and her head tilted against the side, he had been struck by a nearly overwhelming desire to kiss the exposed side of her neck, where the skin had been painted gold by the firelight. Even worse, he had wanted to scoop her out of the chair and carry her into the all-too-nearby bedroom to undress her and emulate his randy ancestors. Instead, he had limited himself to a single chaste air-kiss, although he had savored the warmth radiating from her skin and the delicious scent of woman combined with the citrus aroma wafting from her hair.

His history with women—other than the carefully vetted and very discreet liaisons he occasionally indulged in—was terrible, so he needed to stay away from Eve. He could not afford to alienate his daughter's adoptive mother. Grace would be upset and might feel the need to choose sides. Luis had no illusions about whom she would choose.

Yet he found himself imagining what Eve's glossy red hair would feel like if he buried his fingers in its curling mass. Thrusting his hands into his pockets, he forced himself to turn away from the suite that held so much that he wanted.

CHAPTER 12

Luis stopped himself from drumming his fingertips on the conference table as the Marqués de Huarte insisted yet again that the United States was underpaying them for having its military base in Caleva. Luis wouldn't have agreed to this meeting at all except that Francisco was concerned that they had come up with some new threat to upset the Americans.

"I thought we laid this matter to rest at our meeting last week when we averted the protest," Luis said. "You were promised a seat at the table when we renegotiate the lease with the Americans. Until then, I see no point to discussing this matter further."

The *marqués* looked as though Luis had slapped him, so perhaps his phrasing could have been more diplomatic. However, Luis was still irritated that their threat of a protest had forced him to leave Iowa early the week before. Furthermore, it was late, and he was impatient to finish so he could go see Grace and Eve.

"As you know from the report I submitted," Felipe Camacho said into the silence, "we feel that there are some nonmonetary issues with the base being on our land. Those still worry us."

"We continue to follow up on your report," Luis said, "although so far we have not been able to substantiate your claim that crimes committed by U.S. military personnel are underreported." He held up his hand as Camacho started to speak again. "We are researching the cases you included. What I do not see is how wringing more money from the Americans will fix that issue. Can you explain the connection to me?"

The *marqués* opened his mouth and closed it before he looked around at his fellow *consejeros* for support. There was none.

"Very well. We will consider the matter of increasing the annual lease fee closed. Yet again." He let his gaze rest on Camacho. "We will inform you of our conclusions about your issue as soon as they are available."

"Gracias, Su Majestad." Camacho gave him a respectful nod, but his posture was stiff.

Luis stood, forcing everyone else to rise. He was headed for the door with a sense of release, two of his aides trailing behind him, when Camacho stepped away from the table, a rectangular package wrapped in brown paper in his hand.

"Señor, I hope you will accept this gift in gratitude for your attention to my district's matter. It is a newly published history of fencing strategies, autographed by the author. I know that you enjoy the sport." The man bowed slightly as he offered the package.

Despite his impatience, Luis felt a spurt of interest. Knowing that security would have vetted the package before allowing Camacho to bring it into the palace, Luis had no fear of its proximity. "I am grateful for your generosity, but it is my job to attend to my countrymen's problems."

"And you never shirk your responsibilities," Camacho said in an obviously flattering tone. "I beg that you will accept this small token with my humble thanks."

"Do you fence yourself?" Luis asked. Establishing a personal connection could sometimes calm turbulent waters.

"No, I am not an athlete like you," Camacho said with an obsequious smile. "But I find the old ways worthy of preserving. We have lost much of morality and decency in the modern world. Fencing is a sport of honor." His voice had taken on a crusading tone. "It reminds us that order and respect are important to society."

Luis had heard the refrain before. How they should return to the glory days of yore when men were high-minded and noble, conveniently forgetting that Caleva had been founded by vicious, murderous pirates. He would be able to leave more quickly if he took the book, so he plucked it from Camacho's hand with a nod of acknowledgment before he started toward the door again.

"*Señor*, I believe you will find chapter eleven particularly interesting in its discussion of historical Egyptian dueling strategies." Camacho trotted alongside him, not taking the hint that the conversation was over. "Also, chapter fifteen, which traces the development of Greek fencing schools."

"*Gracias,*" Luis said, continuing to walk. "I will make special note of those chapters."

"I am honored, *Señor.*" Camacho finally stopped when they reached the doorway. "I hope you will find the book most enlightening."

As soon as he was outside the room, Luis handed the book to an aide. "After you record this gift, take that to my *habitación*. I would like to read it." In spite of Camacho's annoying persistence.

"*Por supuesto, Señor,*" the aide said.

Luis lengthened his stride as he headed in the direction of his palace quarters. He was in a hurry to see his guests, and a king in an obvious hurry was a king no one would bother. Mostly.

He made it to his suite of rooms, leaving his aides outside the door and unknotting his tie before he stripped off his suit jacket. A sandwich awaited him in the dining room. He carried it into his private office, where he could eat as he scrolled through the late-arriving emails his staff felt he should see. When he found nothing that needed to be addressed immediately, he polished off the sandwich in three large bites and shoved his chair back as anticipation fizzed through his chest.

He sent a text to let Grace and Eve know he would be arriving soon. Grace's enthusiastic response made him smile at his phone.

He took a few extra minutes to change into a pale blue polo shirt, tan trousers, and burgundy loafers. He had seen the slight distance of formality Eve had put between them after all the curtsying and bowing the afternoon before. He wanted to banish that, and casual clothing would help.

Then he was almost jogging along the secret passageway until he reached the panel. Knocking twice, he twisted the handle to swing it open.

Grace was waiting for him, her eyes bright with welcome. When she threw her arms around his neck, his heart twisted and lightened at the same time. "*Hija mía*, you are well?" he asked.

"I'm great," she said, almost dancing as she stepped away from him. "Today was a blast."

Delight coursed through his veins as he turned to find Eve standing by the drinks cabinet, wearing jeans that hugged her curves and a moss-green blouse, her beautiful hair clipped back in a ponytail. "Eve, I trust you enjoyed the day as much as Grace did."

He was relieved when she smiled. "Probably more. For the first time in history, someone gave the opinions of a vet tech just as much weight as those of a vet."

"That's not true. The vets always listen to you," Grace objected.

"The vet *students* do, but that's because they haven't had time to be brainwashed," Eve retorted.

"What were you discussing?" he asked.

"Mom's favorite topic—fear-free vet med," Grace said.

"I have a vested interest. Vet techs are the ones who get bitten and scratched when an animal is terrified," Eve pointed out.

"The fact is that reducing an animal's stress level makes it easier to diagnose and treat whatever is wrong with them," Grace said. "Everyone in vet med should have a vested interest in it. Your minister of Agriculture encouraged the discussion."

Grace looped her arm around Luis's and led him to the sofa in front of the fireplace. He couldn't resist covering the hand she rested on his forearm with his free one.

"Would you like a drink?" Eve asked, pouring wine into two glasses. "Grace and I are having some of this delicious rioja."

"Scotch, please, neat." He could relax here, and that felt good. "I am glad you were shown the respect you deserve."

Eve carried over a tumbler of Scotch that she handed to Luis, their fingers brushing in the transfer. He felt her touch flicker over his skin. *"Gracias, señora."*

"De nada," she said before returning to the bar to retrieve the glasses of wine.

Happiness sparked inside him at her response in Spanish. He hoped that meant Caleva was insinuating itself into her soul.

"Tell me what was so exciting about your day," Luis invited as he took a sip of his drink, enjoying the smooth burn of the golden liquor as it slid down his throat.

"We got to see your famous lilies," Grace said. "The way they grow in the valleys with all the geothermal steam rising around them is very atmospheric."

"Seeing the location in person makes you appreciate why they don't have the same dementia-curing qualities when grown anywhere else," Eve said. "There must be many variables in the environment, between the soil, the steam venting, the quality of light, and the mountains around them."

Luis nodded. "It has proven impossible to replicate, even though we have provided bulbs to any scientist interested in trying." He offered a rueful smile. "Of course, Caleva benefits economically from being the sole source of the valuable sap."

"But you don't charge as much as you could for the dementia medication, given that you have a monopoly on it," Grace said. "According to our guide, you keep the price reasonable in order to offer everyone access to it." She gave a decisive nod. "That's the right thing to do."

Luis felt a burst of pleasure at his daughter's endorsement.

"Of course, you make up for that with the price of those cosmetics made with the sap," Eve said with a smile. "Only the top one-percenters can afford that stuff. Not that I'm complaining, but I wondered, does it really make wrinkles vanish?"

A chill ran through Luis at the mention of the cosmetics. Archambeau Cosmetics, the beauty company Odette Fontaine had headed, still held the exclusive contract for the sap for another few months. He had instructed his sister-in-law, Hélène, their liaison with the beauty industry, to find a new company to sell the sap to, effective the moment the contract expired. He could not bear to deal with Archambeau again.

"I can't speak from personal experience because I've never tried it," Luis admitted. "Although I find it hard to believe that anyone would pay those exorbitant prices unless the formula had a significant effect."

"If they pay a lot for something, people can fool themselves into believing they look younger. It's the placebo effect," Eve said.

Luis made a mental note to have a jar of the expensive cream delivered to Eve the next day.

"We also saw the Calevan dragon research facility," Grace said. "Those lizards are spectacular. Josh, the reptile guy, was in heaven."

"Now you have the luck of the dragon for the day," Luis said.

"I do?" Grace said.

"Encountering a Calevan dragon is supposed to bring you luck," he explained.

"I'm not sure it counts if you see them in captivity," Eve said. "Have you run into them in the wild?"

"When I was younger and used to go horseback riding in the mountains. The dragons would sun themselves on the boulders at higher altitudes and flare out their frills if you got too close. It was quite a sight." Nostalgia swept through Luis at the memories. "Perhaps we could organize a trip into the mountains. Do you ride?"

Grace snorted. "We're from Iowa. Of course we ride."

He caught the warning glance Eve cast Grace, but he liked that his daughter spoke to him without constraint. "I haven't ridden into the mountains in far too long." Now he saw sympathy softening Eve's face. The demands of her life probably kept her from riding much herself. Another mental note got added to his list.

"What about you?" Grace asked Luis. "What did you do today?"

"Me?" He had not been asked that question in a long time. His family and his staff already knew what he did, since they often were involved. "I attended several meetings, read far too many reports and emails, and videoconferenced with several heads of state. In fact, the highlight of my day was greeting a delegation of brilliant veterinary experts from the United States."

Grace gave a gurgle of laughter while Eve raised a skeptical eyebrow.

"We may be brilliant, but we're not quite experts," Grace said with a grin.

A sense of contentment washed over Luis. To sit like this, being teased by his daughter, was pure bliss. He regretted only that Raul was not part of the family gathering.

He had included Eve in his image of "family." He tensed and then relaxed again. She was the mother of his daughter. Of course he would bring her into his inner circle.

He let his gaze roam over Eve as she sat in her usual wing chair. She had kicked off her shoes and curled her legs onto the seat of the chair, where he could see that her toenails were painted a vivid red. The sight sent a pleasant sizzle of arousal through him as he pictured her entire body bared above the sexy splash of color.

He watched her hands cup the wineglass as she brought it to her lips, no polish on the short nails. The light stain of wine on her lips and the way her hands cradled the glass sent his imagination into hyperdrive. When his attention drifted down to the swell of her breasts under the smooth green silk, he forced himself to look away.

What was it about this woman that shook his usual iron self-control? Perhaps she had gotten past his defenses because of her relationship with his daughter. Maybe it was because she treated him more as a man than as a king because she wanted Grace to see him that way. That spilled over into their interactions, and he liked it.

Grace cleared her throat. "I need to talk with you about something that you might not like." She met his gaze with her clear ice-blue eyes. "I want to meet Odette Fontaine."

With those words, she ripped away all his pleasure in the evening.

♚

Eve saw the flash of anguish in Luis's eyes and knew it for the pain a parent felt when they couldn't protect their child from grim reality.

Luis finished his Scotch in one swallow before setting it on the coffee table. "I would like to persuade you to change your mind," he said. "She is not sane, and she will say anything to cause damage to me. That includes hurting you."

Grace squared her shoulders and lifted her chin. "I feel like a puzzle with a piece missing. Now that I know where the piece is, I have to see it, to fit it into my idea of who I am."

"The piece is warped," Luis said with an edge in his voice. "It is not truly a part of who you are."

"Maybe," Grace said, "but I have the chance to face my birth mother, and I need to take it."

Luis sighed before he rubbed his hand over the back of his neck. "Of course, *hija mía*, but it is a delicate matter to arrange, and the timing is crucial." He sat forward to hold Grace's gaze. "The reason I know you exist is because Odette threatened to release your story to the media if I didn't...bend to her wishes. If she discovers that you are here in Caleva with me, and that my paternity has been confirmed, she could still release the story before we are ready."

"She can do that from prison?" Eve asked since Grace had gone quiet.

"We treat our prisoners humanely, whether they deserve it or not, which means she has some access to the world beyond the prison walls," Luis said. "Except when she is in solitary confinement, but that requires an official justification after a few days."

"When would be a good time for me to see her?" Grace asked, still focused on her father.

"After you have made some decisions about being part of the royal family," Luis said. "You should not rush, because your choices will change your life in ways you can't anticipate. I had hoped to give you time to know this country and all of my family before you decide."

Because he wanted to sway Grace in his favor, of course.

"It sounds like the longer I wait, the more likely news of my existence is to become public," Grace said.

"Yes." Luis's agreement was reluctant.

"You've said I have options when it comes to my position in your family. I'd like to know what they are," Grace said.

Grace was unflinching, even when dealing with a king. Luis caught Eve's gaze and nodded in acknowledgment of their daughter's strength.

"Before you reach any conclusions, I would ask that you speak with Raul," Luis said. "He will be joining us at the Casa en las Nubes tomorrow. He has been champing at the bit to meet you."

"What will he tell me?" Grace asked.

"I can't predict that," Luis said. "I have asked only that he answer your questions with honesty."

"That's fair," Grace said with a visible swallow. "But what are my options?"

Eve decided her daughter needed some support while Luis laid out her future, so she moved to sit beside Grace on the sofa. Grace reached for her hand and tucked hers inside it. Eve could feel a slight tremble in Grace's fingers and gave her daughter's hand a reassuring squeeze.

Luis straightened in his chair. "The first option is that you prefer not to have your relationship with me be acknowledged in any way." His tone was dispassionate, but shadows haunted his eyes. "I would ask to still be a part of your life, if I could, perhaps as a friend of the family or an honorary uncle."

Grace nodded.

"Second, I can acknowledge you as my daughter, but not as a member of the royal family." He still looked discontented. "You would have no title, no claim on the throne, and no duties or responsibilities."

"Got it," Grace said as Luis paused.

He glanced at Eve. "If it will not be a problem for you and your mother, I can officially proclaim that you are my fully recognized daughter. You will become a princess and be part of the royal family, next in line for the Dragon Throne after Raul. That would be my preference, of course, but I understand that it would be a major upheaval in your life."

"Would I have to live in Caleva if I chose that?" Grace asked, her face pale.

"There is no requirement for that, but it would be frowned upon if you didn't," Luis admitted. "Perhaps it could be arranged for you to live here only part of the time."

Eve's throat closed up in panic. This was what she had feared as soon as Luis had convinced her that he was Grace's father, that Grace would be lured away from her and into this world of luxury and privilege, and Eve wouldn't be a part of it.

Sensing Grace's misgivings, Luis hurried to speak again. "There is one more possibility. I can adopt you as my daughter, which will make you a princess and a member of the royal family, but I can remove you from the succession to the throne. It would be unusual, but there is a precedent from the past."

Grace's grip tightened convulsively. "It's a lot to think about."

"You must take as much time as you need, regardless of the concerns about the media," Luis said. "We have years of experience with handling reporters. We can weather any storm. Your mother will offer you her wisdom as well." Luis's eyes held a plea to Eve that he probably wasn't aware of.

Whether to become a princess or not wasn't a subject she had any experience with, so her "wisdom" would be fairly worthless.

Luis waited a moment before a look of regret shadowed his face. "I think I will say good night to give you time to absorb all this information."

Eve and Grace stood as he did. Despite all the tension, Eve still noticed the ripple of muscles in his shoulders as he pushed himself out of the chair. It was hard not to focus on him when his presence seemed to permeate the air around them.

He leaned over the coffee table to give Eve the usual tantalizing air-kiss, leaving a stir of sensation even with that small brush of the cheek.

"Come with me to the door," he said to Grace, holding out his arm.

Grace slipped her hand in the crook of his elbow, and he laid his other hand over it, leading her away from Eve. But he kept his voice at a volume she could easily hear as he said, "*Querida*, you will be my daughter no matter how you choose to be known to the outside world. Never doubt that I will cherish you in every way you will allow."

Grace nodded but said nothing. She was probably too choked up.

As they reached the secret panel, Luis turned to face his daughter, running his hands up to her shoulders to hold her as he placed a tender kiss on her forehead. "*Buenas noches, hija mía. Que sueñes con los angelitos.* I wish you sweet dreams."

Grace slid her arms under Luis's to hug him. "*Muchas gracias!* The same to you."

Luis smiled. "You are learning Spanish after all. *Bien hecho!* Well done!"

He released her and disappeared through the panel.

Grace turned and choked out a sob. Eve practically sprinted across the room to put her arms around her daughter. "Sweetheart, we'll figure this out."

Grace buried her face against Eve's shoulder, taking a couple of shuddering breaths before she lifted it again. "Why does he have to be a king? Why couldn't he just be a normal person?"

Eve had been asking herself that every day since she had met him.

CHAPTER 13

Eve pushed the button to bring the SUV's luxurious leather seat back to an upright position. She had caught a short nap as they drove because last night she and Grace had stayed up late, talking about her daughter's future.

Now they were headed to Luis's private home, whose name meant House in the Clouds. Bridget was driving, and Ivan rode shotgun. Eve winced at the term since he undoubtedly really had a gun. She was pretty sure that the SUV they seemed to be following was part of their security. There was probably one behind them as well. Was all the security because of Grace or because they were going to a house known to be owned by the king? Or both?

The other students and vets had been swept off to their respective guest homes in SUVs, too, so nothing about Eve and Grace's departure had seemed unusual. Their escort hadn't joined them until they were out of sight of the palace.

This morning, their Iowa delegation had met with several architects who specialized in medical facilities. They had brought some preliminary drafts of a veterinary school layout. Eve smiled at how they all felt like kids in a candy shop, since the architects added every item on their personal wish lists to the plans. Her smile faded as she remembered that the school was nothing but an elaborate ruse. No wonder there could be space for every fancy piece of equipment they wanted. It was all a pie in the sky. Still, it had been fun.

Afterward, they had been given a tour of the region of Caleva originally settled by French pirates, starting in St. Christophe and ending on one of the stunning beaches where the white sand literally glittered in the sunlight. Eve had fallen asleep on her lounge chair while the kids frolicked in the surf.

Now Grace would get to meet her half brother, the prince. Eve sucked in and blew out a long breath, reminding herself that Luis had raised Raul, so his son should have a strong loyalty to family. Still, sibling rivalry was real, and Grace was something of an interloper.

"Oh my God, Mom, look at this view!" Grace was staring out the window on her side of the car.

Eve leaned across to see that they were driving uphill along the edge of a cliff beyond which lay the endless ocean, a deep turquoise close to the island that shaded darker and darker as it reached the horizon. Below them, the surf crashed against glistening black boulders, throwing up wild sprays of water to sparkle in the sunlight. Being from land-locked Iowa, she found the sight mesmerizing. A glance at Grace's wide eyes and half-open mouth indicated that her daughter felt the same way.

Straightening, Eve looked out her window to see flat land covered with some sort of low-growing, pale green grass or moss dotted with pinpoint yellow flowers. An occasional small, wind-sculpted evergreen tree thrust up from what must be rocky soil. Far off in the distance, she could see the silhouette of Castillo Draconago rising from its own cliff above San Ignacio. A thrill ran through her because Luis was somewhere within those stone walls.

She needed to get a grip.

The SUV slowed and stopped. Peering through the windshield, Eve saw tall steel gates set in a high stone wall that extended away to either side of the road. A guard was speaking with the driver of the SUV in front of them, and the massive gates began to swing inward. Bridget opened her window to speak with the guard, and they were waved through.

They drove for another fifteen minutes before the SUVs swept through an archway into an enclosed courtyard, centered by an abstract bronze fountain and edged with beds of flowering trees and plants in a riot of colors.

Ivan leaped out of the car to open Eve's door while Bridget did the same for Grace. "Welcome to the House in the Clouds," Ivan said.

"Thank you," Eve said, but she was looking at the house with astonishment. It was boldly contemporary, constructed of vast sheets of glass, steel girders, and smooth basalt blocks.

"This is not what I expected," Grace said.

"Not a turret or gargoyle in sight," Eve agreed.

The front door flew open, and a short woman wearing a black dress appeared with outflung arms. Glints of silver shone in her dark hair. *"Bienvenido, señora, señorita,"* she cried. "Come in, come in! You must be exhausted from your day."

Eve and Grace exchanged a glance before going up the three wide steps to the door.

"I am Annamaria, *la mayordoma* of Casa en las Nubes," the woman said with obvious pride in her smile. "Anything that you need, I will provide for you. *El rey* and *el principe* will be arriving in an hour and a half, so I imagine you will want to freshen up. After that, I will be happy to take you on a tour of the house, if you wish."

"Muchas gracias," Grace said.

Annamaria beamed. "*Usted habla español!* You speak Spanish," she translated with a glance at Eve.

"*Un poco,*" Grace said. "It's good to practice."

"*Sí, sí! Muy bien!*" Annamaria agreed. "First, I will show you the view and then your rooms."

She led them through a double-height entrance with a large hanging red-and-black mobile that Eve guessed was by the American sculptor Alexander Calder. Beyond it lay a huge living space with multiple seating areas. That paled when compared with the vista outside the wall of glass. A stone terrace with an infinity pool extended from the sliding doors. The house was on the tip of a high peninsula, so the sea surrounded it on three sides. Right in the center of the view, a volcanic caldera erupted from the waves, its sloping sides covered with soft green vegetation. A break in the cone's wall showed a circular pool of brilliantly blue water cradled within. Seabirds wheeled in the skies around it, and a few boats bobbed near the pool's entrance.

"La Sorpresa de Los Piratas. The Pirates' Surprise," Annamaria said with a wave toward the island. "*El rey* will tell you the story of its name. It's one of his favorites." She said it with an affectionate familiarity that shifted Eve's view of Luis. In the palace, everyone had treated him as the King with a capital *K*. Annamaria seemed to look on him with less deference and more fondness.

"It looks like you can go to the volcano by boat," Grace said.

"Maybe we can work that into our trip," Eve said, knowing that Luis would make it happen if Grace expressed an interest.

"It is a national park," Annamaria said. "Only two hundred people are allowed there per day."

That wouldn't stop Luis.

The *mayordoma* shepherded them away from the spellbinding vista and through a bewildering array of rooms before entering a wide hallway. Stopping in front of a door, she beckoned Eve forward. "Put your thumb against this black pad, and it will know to open the door for you." She gave a shrug. "*Señor* Silva is security conscious even here."

Eve pressed her thumb against the black square and heard the click of the door unlocking.

"Would you like me to show you around your suite?" Annamaria asked.

"I can explore it on my own, but thank you," Eve said.

"If you need privacy from the outdoors, just say, 'Shades on,' and the glass will darken," Annamaria said. "You can also speak to the shower by saying, 'Shower on,' 'hotter,' 'colder,' and so on."

"The shower speaks English?" Eve joked.

"And ten other languages," Annamaria said with a straight face. She waved down the hall. "*Señorita* Howard's room is the second door down from yours. I will return in an hour to escort you back to the *sala*. Feel free to explore the house on your own, too, if you wish."

"Please call us Eve and Grace," Eve said. "We're Americans, so we prefer to be less formal."

"*Bien, Señora* Eve." Annamaria nodded.

Grace gave a muffled choke of laughter, but Eve just smiled. "*Gracias.*"

Pushing the door open, she found herself in a sitting room that included a desk and a gas fireplace along with a comfortable modern sofa and chairs in shades of taupe and blue. The outer wall offered the same view as the *sala*, except that the volcano was farther to the right.

Strolling through the open door to the bedroom, she found a king-size bed with multiple layers of exquisitely soft linens in soft creams and blues, another fireplace, and two armchairs set in front of the window wall. Exploring further, she discovered a palatial bathroom done entirely in gray-veined marble and a walk-in closet, where her clothing was already hung or folded into drawers.

She went back to the bedroom and stood, drinking in the incredible scene of sea, sky, and volcano. Then she remembered that Luis was coming...and Raul, of course. But the thrill of anticipation that zinged through her wasn't for the prince.

The scent of *vaho* hibiscus teased her nostrils, and she glanced around to see a vase of the lavender blossoms on the dresser. Beside it sat a square package wrapped in gold paper with teal and red ribbons tied around it. A cream-colored envelope with her name handwritten on it was propped behind the box.

Figuring that it was the kind of welcome note high-end hotels often offered their guests, she picked it up and pulled out the folded notepaper. It was embossed with a gold crown under which was engraved *Luis IV, King of Caleva*. Her pulse jumped. She opened it to find bold, flowing handwriting.

Dear Eve,

> *You do not need the aid of this gift, but you asked if it worked. You may draw your own conclusions by trying it for yourself.*

Warmest regards,
Luis

Like a silly teenager, she traced the slashing letters of his name, thinking of all the important documents he signed in the same way. This note was going in her box of special mementos, right alongside Grace's baby bracelet and first report card.

Placing the note carefully on the dresser, she tugged on the ribbons of the box before it dawned on her that this must be the anti-aging cream. She peeled back the paper to see a logo of a stylized lily and the words Vin de Lys—Wine of the Lilies—the name the French cosmetics firm had given its exclusive cream made from the sap of the Calevan lilies. Opening the box, she pulled out a cut crystal jar with a rose-gold lid, studded with wine-red crystals.

"Fancy packaging," she said, twisting off the top and removing the protective underlid to take a whiff. The white cream had barely any fragrance, probably for hypoallergenic reasons. She touched her fingertip to the surface and rubbed a tiny bit on her cheek, the cream like silk on her skin. A frisson of excitement ran through her. According to the hype, the lines on her face would disappear within a week.

Then she remembered the miracle cream was expensive. Curious, she turned the jar over to check the weight of its contents. *Baccarat* was etched in the crystal. "Of course," she muttered, pulling out her phone to look up the price.

"Holy shit!" she gasped. "Five thousand dollars! I can't accept this." She quickly replaced both lids. "Oh my God, I touched it already."

She stared at the jar in horror. Even if Luis got some kind of special discount, it still cost far too much. But she couldn't give it back after sticking her finger in it. Although who would know?

She would, and being a medical worker, she was all too aware of sterility issues. "Shit!" she said again.

Welp, she would have to write Luis the world's most spectacular thank-you note…and be careful what she mentioned being intrigued by in the future.

At least she could get rid of her lines until the cream ran out. After that, they would most likely return.

She returned the jar to its box, neatly folded the beautiful wrapping paper and ribbons, placed the note back in its envelope, and carried all of them to the closet to nest them in her empty carry-on bag.

Then she stripped off her rumpled clothing and had a long, luxurious session in the shower.

An hour later, she and Grace were wandering through the mansion, oohing and aahing at the art, the furnishings, and most especially the views. Eve had dried her hair into soft waves that flowed over the pink silk of her blouse and added Luis's lily pendant in the open neckline. She had decided on gray trousers and flat black loafers since Luis had told them life at Casa en las Nubes was casual.

Grace had paired jeans with a dark green blouse that made her auburn hair glow. She wore her Calevan dragon necklace, but with an addition. Eve looked more closely to find that the gold wings she had given Grace were strung onto the chain with the dragon. Her heart did a little dance of joy. She hadn't lost her daughter yet.

"I'm nervous about meeting Raul," Grace admitted as they stood in front of a large Picasso painting. "I know Luis says he's happy to have a new half sibling, but it must be weird."

"It has to be weirder for you than for him," Eve pointed out. "Your half brother is a prince."

"Right." Grace frowned. "I want him to like me. I also want to talk with him about his life. I hope he's willing to be honest." Grace was winding a lock of her hair tightly around her index finger, a gesture that showed Eve how anxious her daughter was.

She hooked her arm around Grace's shoulders. "Sweetheart, you are a good judge of people. You'll figure out how much Raul is willing to share with you. And there is no hurry to make a decision that will affect your whole life. You should take your time, just the way you do when you examine one of your patients."

But Eve felt the subtle pressure from Luis, so Grace must notice it too.

"It's different when it's my own future," Grace said. "I want to settle it."

Eve hugged Grace against her side. Her daughter had always been one to make decisions fast and definitively. It was both a strength and a flaw. "This is not something to rush."

She didn't add that it would affect her own life as well. That was more burden than Grace needed. Eve couldn't help wondering, though, if she could be happy living in Caleva, moving on the fringes of Grace's royal life, if that's what her daughter chose. She sighed inwardly and set the thought aside. All that mattered was making sure Grace had enough information to make a wise choice about the direction of her future.

"*Buenas tardes,*" Annamaria said, appearing from around the corner. "Do you like that painting? I am still trying to puzzle it out."

"Honestly, I'm just impressed by the size and the signature," Eve said.

The *mayordoma* laughed. "It came with the house when *el rey* purchased it. I have good news. *El rey* and *el príncipe* are almost here. I thought you would wish to meet them out on the terrace by the pool. *El rey* likes to go there first whenever he arrives. He says the sea air blows away all his worries." Annamaria gave a skeptical grimace. "It may help, but *el rey* always wears the crown, even here."

She bustled ahead of them, wending their way back to the *sala* and then through the doors onto the terrace. The late afternoon light turned the pool's surface gold while the brisk breeze ruffled it into wavelets. At the Pirates' Surprise, only one boat was still anchored at the entrance.

"May I offer you a beverage?" Annamaria asked, sweeping her hand toward an outdoor bar of stone and steel. "There are tapas on the table near the lip of the pool."

"Red wine would be lovely," Eve said.

Grace nodded in agreement.

"We have many varieties from many countries," Annamaria said. "What is your preference?"

Of course they did. This was the king's house.

"I trust you to choose," Eve said with a smile.

Eve stood entranced by the play of light on the ocean, the constant dull roar of waves slamming against the cliffs below, and the scent of salt water, *vaho* hibiscus, and something delicious wafting from the tapas table.

Annamaria brought them crystal glasses of ruby wine and then vanished into the house.

"We're not in Iowa anymore," Grace said as she swirled the wine in her glass.

"That's for sure," Eve agreed as the wine's full, rich flavor slid smoothly over her palate.

They stood a few minutes longer before Eve heard the quiet hiss of the big glass door sliding open. She turned to see Luis and his son framed in the opening, two tall, spectacularly handsome men in perfectly fitting dark suits, and her heart felt as though it would leap out of her chest.

Luis stopped in the doorway, his gaze locked on the two women bathed in sunlight, their red hair aflame and rippling in the breeze. He was overjoyed to see his daughter again, but his blood raced at the sight of Eve, a welcoming smile curving her sensuous mouth, her clothes molded to her body by the sea wind. The intensity of his reaction surprised him, but he let it flow through him with a certain pleasure. For a moment, his gaze met Eve's, and he thought he saw an answering flicker of heat there.

But he had an important introduction to make. He stepped onto the terrace with Raul by his side.

"Good evening! It is wonderful to have you here in my home," he said. "I'd like you to meet my son, Raul. Raul, this is Eve."

Eve stepped forward with a smile, and Raul met her halfway to shake hands. "A pleasure to meet you, Eve," his son said. "Pater says wonderful things about you."

Eve's smile shifted in some way that he couldn't read as she said, "He says the same about you."

"Raul, this is your half sister, Grace," Luis said and stepped back so he could watch their first encounter.

Grace put her hand out. Raul took it in his. For a moment, they stood examining each other, undoubtedly seeing what he saw. How the shape of their faces mirrored each other with the subtle differences of gender. How their eyes were nearly the same color. How the angle at which they tilted their chins was identical.

Then Raul's smile flashed, and he pulled his half sister into a hug. "*Mi hermana*, I am so happy to meet you at long last."

"Oh, thank goodness," Grace said into his shoulder. "I was afraid you wouldn't want to give up being an only child."

Relief washed through Luis as well. He had worried that Raul would not believe that Luis did not love his son any less because he also loved his daughter.

Raul laughed, and they released each other but didn't move apart. Luis understood. Finding a new family member was an occasion to be cherished. Eve was watching the encounter with an expression that mixed hope with worry. Her posture was taut, as though she were poised to jump between her daughter and his son, if necessary.

A mama bear protecting her precious cub.

He admired that. And much more.

Annamaria appeared with two glasses of wine, one of which she offered to Luis with a small curtsy. "*Gracias*, but I think we should have champagne. This is a moment to celebrate," he said, although he could not yet divulge why. He saw his *mayordoma's* glance traveling back and forth between Raul and Grace. She would draw her own shrewd conclusions. "The vintage Dom Perignon, *por favor*."

"*Por supuesto, Señor!*" Annamaria bustled away.

Eve strolled over to his side, saying in a low voice, "Raul is being so nice. I know Grace has a thousand questions for him, and it looks like she's bombarding him already."

Luis watched the two young people, who were talking and gesticulating with great animation, before he let his gaze shift to Eve. "Raul is as delighted by his new sibling as I am. Although he considers his cousin Gabriel as a brother, he welcomes another young member of the family. It is sometimes lonely to be the heir to the throne."

Eve gave him a searching look that said she understood he was speaking from experience. "Still, Raul has been the apple of his father's eye for his entire life." Her tone was light, but he heard the concern underlying it.

"He has not always appreciated that fact," Luis said with a smiling grimace. "I am grateful, though, that he has a genuine passion for serving Caleva."

Since his son had little choice.

"Do you think it comes with the genes?" Eve asked, slanting a glance up at him.

"The genes and the training from birth," Luis said. "Who knows which is more powerful?"

"I've been studying Calevan history a bit," she said. "Not every monarch was an enthusiastic ruler."

"Luckily, we have ways to remove them when that becomes apparent," Luis said. "Which no longer involves hurling them off a cliff. Although there was a certain satisfying simplicity to that."

Eve's brown eyes warmed with amusement.

"Perdon, Señor." Annamaria appeared at his elbow. "Shall I open the champagne, or would you wish to do so?"

"Ah, let me," Luis said. "I enjoy the festive sound of a cork popping."

The *mayordoma* offered him the bottle and a white towel, while Eve took his wineglass. The light brush of her fingers against his heightened the buzz in his blood. He twisted the cork until it gave a soft pop and he felt the pressure of the effervescence push it against his hand. Annamaria had returned with a silver tray of four champagne flutes, which she held while he poured the pale gold liquid into each one.

Eve had set down the wineglasses, so he handed a flute to her and kept one for himself, calling out, "Grace, Raul, let us drink a toast to this momentous day."

They seized their champagne glasses from the tray and walked over to where he and Eve stood. Their resemblance when side by side was so striking that he felt his heart squeeze with pride and amazement...and love. Yes, he loved Grace already.

"*Un brindis por la familia!* A toast to family!" Luis lifted his glass in the center of the group. "The most important thing in life."

The other three reached in to touch their flutes together in a chorus of soft, musical clinks. *"Por la familia!"* Everyone spoke in Spanish, which sent a ripple of satisfaction through him, followed by a powerful sense of completion, as though missing pieces had clicked into place. This was the family he had dreamed of having.

After they each took a sip, Raul said, "Since we're a family, I think we should have a family toast like we did when Gabriel and I were younger. Do as I do. *Arriba!*" He lifted his glass high, and everyone followed. *"Abajo!"* Raul swung his glass down low. *"Al centro!"* He thrust the glass into the center and waited for all to clink against it. *"Y pa' dentrooooooooo!"* Raul drank down the rest of his champagne in one gulp.

Grace and Eve did the same, revealing the long, graceful lines of their necks, but Luis shook his head in mock horror. "You are a barbarian, *hijo mío*. This champagne is too fine to be chugged like cheap beer."

Raul grinned as he picked up the bottle from the table and refilled the glasses before he turned to Grace. "A good celebration requires some craziness, yes?"

"Yes," she agreed. "But this is really tasty champagne, so maybe we should chug the wine instead."

"Ah, the always practical American," Raul said. "But you're not wrong. Let's take the wine and grab some tapas."

He swept the wine bottle off the bar, and he and Grace strolled to the seating area at the far end of the pool.

"Maybe we should let them get to know each other without the parents butting in," Eve said, her gaze following them.

Luis heard the bittersweet longing in her voice and recognized the pain of not being able to shield your adult child from the world.

"Then we shall go to the beach," he said, the exhilaration of having his children together bubbling through his veins along with the champagne. He wanted to shout, to dance, to release his elation in some physical way.

Eve's face lit up, and then her gaze drifted over him in a way he could almost feel before she smiled. "You're a little overdressed for beachcombing."

"That is easily remedied." He unknotted his tie and pulled it off, unbuttoning a couple of buttons on his shirt. Her eyes widened as she watched, and he slowed down his striptease to see how she would react. Shrugging out of his suit jacket, he tossed it on a chair before removing his cuff links and rolling his shirtsleeves up to just below his elbows, observing her with a sideways glance.

Yes, she was definitely breathing more quickly, and that was desire flickering across her face. An answering heat scorched through his body. He eased into a chair where she could watch as he untied his wingtips and removed his socks, relishing the warmth of the heated stone beneath his bare soles and the knowledge that Eve wanted him as he wanted her.

He stood and gestured to her loafers. "You won't need those either."

She nodded and toed off the shoes, revealing the painted toenails he had found so sexy the night before. "Oh my gosh, the terrace is warm!"

"Radiant geothermal heat," he explained. "Provided by Mother Nature."

She stared down at her toes, curling them against the stone in sensual appreciation. "Amazing."

"Bring your glass," he said. "We will savor what the young savages cannot."

CHAPTER 14

Eve felt like a teenager sneaking off to the beach to drink with her boyfriend as Luis seized another bottle of champagne from the bar and called out that they were going to the beach.

Except the champagne was vintage Dom Perignon, and Luis was a king.

She snuck a glance at the man beside her with his shirt open at the neck, his sleeves rolled up to show muscled forearms, and a glinting smile in his ice-blue eyes.

"This way," he said, waving her toward one side of the terrace where the cliff dropped away to the surf.

"How on earth do we get down there?"

"There's an elevator," he said, tipping the champagne bottle toward a stone-paved walkway she hadn't noticed.

She followed the path around an angle of the house to find a glass-and-metal structure rising from the edge of the cliff.

Luis pressed his thumb against the pad by the glass door, which slid open. "And here is our ride down."

She stepped into the glass-sided elevator car and turned to see the same view as the terrace offered. "This is...insane."

Luis laughed as the elevator glided downward. "The man who built this house was a cryptocurrency billionaire...until he wasn't. I was happy to buy it from him at less than what it cost to build, and Mikel has made it even more secure than its somewhat paranoid first owner did. It offers me a place of rest." The laughter was gone. "I can go barefoot and drink champagne out of the bottle if I choose to."

"We'll leave our glasses in the elevator, then," Eve said, understanding more about the constraints of Luis's life than she wanted to.

Heat flickered in his eyes as she took his glass and set it on the floor with hers. "Your lips will touch the same bottle as mine," he said.

Was he flirting with her? That sounded like flirting. But it couldn't be. Just because she thought he was sexy as hell didn't mean that he reciprocated the feeling.

"I figure you have a clean bill of health," Eve said.

"And you?" he asked.

"I'm up to date on my shots," she said.

His smile flashed for a moment, and the elevator eased to a stop, the door sliding open to let in the roar of surf and wind. She stepped onto the black volcanic sand, finding it slightly cool against her bare feet. She inhaled deeply to savor the exotic scent of the sea.

"Would you mind if I got my feet wet?" she asked. "Before today, I had only been to the ocean once before, so this is a treat."

"In that case, we should roll up our trousers." He put the champagne on the floor of the elevator car before bending to turn up the cuffs of his suit pants. For a moment, she just watched the play of muscles in his back under the tightly stretched cotton of his shirt.

"What do you do for exercise?" she blurted, then felt a flush rise in her cheeks.

He looked up from his bent position with a flicker of something hot in his eyes. "I fence."

"Oh, of course." She knelt to work on her own pants, a vision of him costumed as a dashing musketeer wielding a rapier dancing through her mind. "Swords are appropriate. Do you wear armor too?"

"No, I reserve that for joint sessions of the legislature." She gave a snort of laughter and rose.

"Let's go feel the Atlantic Ocean on our toes." He put his hand against the small of her back to urge her forward, and pleasure radiated outward from where he touched her to flare through her body.

He walked so close to her side that occasionally her shoulder grazed his arm, sending more flickers of sensation tingling across her skin. Even the wind blowing her clothes against her body stoked her heightened awareness of the man beside her.

"I don't know how to thank you for the Vin de Lys cream," she said. "I didn't mean for you to give it to me."

"Why shouldn't I?" he asked. "It is from my country."

"Well, because it's very expensive. Unless you get samples for free?" she asked in the hope that she could assuage her guilt.

He laughed. "I don't know how much it cost. My private assistant procured it for me."

"Trust me, it cost a lot," Eve said. "Thank you for your generous gift."

"You sound more upset than grateful," Luis said as they reached the wet sand flattened by the ebb and flow of the surf, and he dropped his hand from her back. "I hope you were not offended. I was not implying that you need it, but you mentioned you wanted to test its powers."

"I'm not offended, just overwhelmed. Honestly, I would give it back to you, except I tried it before I realized how expensive it was."

He touched her shoulder so she looked up at him, almost gasping at the blaze of intensity in his eyes. "Eve, you raised my...our daughter. A jar of face cream does not begin to balance my debt to you."

"I raised our daughter because I love her. There is no debt." Eve was fierce in her claim.

Luis waved his hand in a graceful gesture of acceptance. "I have also...disturbed your life. Consider it a compensation for that."

It would take a lot more than expensive cosmetics to fix that, but there was no putting that cork back in the bottle. She dropped the subject as a wave sent a rush of salt water lapping around her ankles. "Whoa, it's colder than the water at the other beach," she said.

"The one drawback of having a house on this coast is that no warm currents wash around this shore, as they do where you were earlier," Luis said. "Now, if we went out to the Pirates' Surprise"—he pointed to the island with the bottle—"we would be wading in warm water because of the geothermal activity beneath the caldera's floor."

"Annamaria said you liked to tell the story of how it got its name." Eve needed something to distract her from the sight of the sea breeze pressing his shirt flat over his well-defined abdominal muscles.

"I will tell you after we drink more champagne. That will improve the story." He peeled away the foil and unwound the wire cage before gently twisting the cork from the neck with a pop. The champagne frothed up to the bottle's lip, but not a drop spilled.

"You're an expert at that," Eve said.

"It is a satisfying skill. Simple and with pleasurable results." He held up the bottle so the sunlight could shine through it. "I think the foam has settled." He handed it to her.

In fact, she had never drunk champagne out of the bottle. She tried to be ladylike and just touch the opening to her lips, tilting the bottle so it would run into her mouth. She miscalculated, and it overflowed to run down her neck as she took a mouthful.

She swallowed the sparkling wine and started to brush off the runaway champagne with her fingers. "Darn! I wasted good champagne."

"Allow me," Luis said, his gaze locked on her throat. He pulled a handkerchief from his trouser pocket and wiped the champagne from her neck, stroking the fine cotton fabric slowly and gently against her skin, sending a sensual vibration over her breasts that tightened her nipples. He dabbed at one of the wet spots on her blouse, just at her clavicle, without success. "I'm afraid your blouse will have to dry on its own."

He stepped back, and a hot smile curled the corners of his mouth. Probably because he could see her hard nipples through the thin silk. Eve took another swig of champagne, closing her mouth over the entire rim this time. The cool, effervescent liquid did nothing to quench the flare of desire she felt, but it tasted fantastic.

She passed the bottle back to Luis. He kept his eyes on her face as he put the bottle to his lips. Tilting it upward, he took two swallows, the muscles in his throat working. "And now the story," he said.

The roar of an engine startled Eve, pulling her attention to the ocean. In the distance, a powerboat painted with the royal seal of Caleva cut through the waves toward another small craft, broadcasting an announcement in Spanish.

"What's all the ruckus about?" she asked.

Luis waved a dismissive hand. "Some tourists got too close, so the guards are moving them away. For security reasons, no boats are allowed within a certain perimeter around this point. The professional captains know about it, but the amateurs have to be warned."

"Has anyone ever landed on this beach?"

"Not to my knowledge, but Mikel wouldn't necessarily inform me if they had." Luis shrugged. "I have to trust my people to do their jobs, or I would never sleep soundly."

There it was, the reality of being a king. Grace would be only a princess, and not even next in line for the throne, but Gabriel was only a royal duke, and that hadn't kept him from being kidnapped and mutilated. Fear clogged Eve's throat. She reached for the bottle, taking a gulp to wash down her worries. For now.

"Come," Luis said, as if sensing her anxiety. "We'll go over to those rocks where no interlopers can see us."

He gestured to a wall of tall, jagged black boulders jutting up from the sand. As she took a step toward them, he once again brought his hand to rest on the small of her back. This time, she felt his touch like a brand, the heat of it burning into her skin and going deeper.

As the engine noise receded, Luis began his story. "Back in the days of Ricardo el Rojo, the first King of Caleva, an angry Spanish nobleman, a *duque*, came in search of the pirate who had attacked his ship carrying gold from the New World."

She had to force herself to ignore the sear of his hand and focus on his voice. But every step made his palm shift against the silk of her shirt, yanking her attention to the mad attraction racing through her body.

"The *duque* brought three heavily armed galleons to take back his gold. But Caleva protects its own. One of the ships foundered on the rocks off the harbor of San Ignacio. As the other two sailed toward the harbor, they spied El Rojo's sloop slipping away along the coastline. They gave chase, but the pirate sloop was quick, and it sailed into a fogbank when it got near this point."

They reached an alcove created by the rocks, and Luis guided her into it before lowering his hand. She wanted to grab it and return it to her back. Instead, she asked, "Is there usually fog here? Is that why it's called the House in the Clouds?"

"An excellent deduction," Luis said, taking another swig of champagne. He wiped his mouth with his sleeve. "It depends on the wind and the amount of geothermal activity. The fog comes suddenly and leaves just as suddenly. Of course, Ricardo knew the coast like the back of his hand, so he did not fear sailing into the fog. The Spanish blundered after him."

He passed her the bottle with a nod to drink more. She was developing a noticeable buzz, but she didn't hesitate to enjoy another swallow.

"Ricardo could have easily gotten away. His sloop was faster than the galleons. But he wished to send a message. He kept just far enough in front of the galleons so they could catch glimpses of his ship in the shifting fog and follow him blindly."

Luis looked out at the volcanic island. "He sailed his sloop with its shallow draft through the entrance to the caldera. The *duque* thought his enemy was trapped and didn't stop to consider that his galleons had much deeper keels than Ricardo's. The first ship grounded on the rocks that Ricardo's ship had cleared by mere inches. The second ship collided with the first. Both had their hulls ripped open by the volcano's underwater edge. *La sorpresa de los piratas.*"

"Ouch. What happened to all the sailors on the Spanish ships?" She wasn't sure she wanted to know.

"Most of them swam to shore on the island. My ancestor was always looking for new recruits, so he offered them jobs if they would swear allegiance to him. He even extended the offer to the *duque*, who turned out to be a practical man. He accepted the invitation and became one of Ricardo's councillors when the pirate declared himself king."

"I like that story. No one died," Eve said. "Well, I guess the sailors on the first ship might have." She felt guilty for forgetting about them.

"Then we will assume they also swam to shore in the harbor and received the same invitation to join the pirates." An undercurrent of amusement ran through his voice. "Do not think that Ricardo el Rojo was a benevolent man. He simply needed more people to crew his ships and settle Caleva. Had anyone refused to swear the oath to him, he would have fed them to the sharks."

"Or thrown them off the cliffs," Eve said.

"It was a queen who instituted that custom." His eyes held a wicked smile. "Ricardo's granddaughter Isabella executed several of her half siblings who tried to take the throne away from her by having them hurled off Acantilado Alto."

"I guess she was sending a message like Ricardo." Eve held out the almost empty bottle to Luis.

He took a step closer to her, so close that a lock of her wind-tossed hair snagged on his shirt. He caught the errant strands and twisted them around his fingers. "It feels as smooth and silky as it looks," he said. "I have wanted to touch it every time I have seen you."

Eve would swear her heart stuttered, but it wasn't the compliment that sent excitement and nerves skittering through her. It was the low, sultry vibration of his deep voice, the unmistakable note of seduction pulsing beneath his words.

"Thank you," she said, unable to muster anything more. The gentle tug of his grip on her hair sent sparkles of delight tingling over her scalp and down her neck to tighten her nipples even more.

In a moment of insanity, Eve lifted her hand to brush her fingertips against the silver-gray of his beard. "And I've wanted to touch this. It's softer than I expected."

Luis's eyes ignited in flames of blistering blue, standing utterly still as she ventured to feather her fingers through the gleaming curve of hair at his temple. He turned his head to press a kiss against the skin of her wrist, his lips firm and smooth.

She gasped as desire surged through her, detonated by that small touch.

"*Ay*, Eve!" His voice was a rasp of surrender to what they both knew they shouldn't do.

She rose on her tiptoes to meet him as he bent. Their mouths touched, first with a careful exploration that allowed her to savor the warmth of his lips and the slight tickle of his beard. And then he changed angles so his tongue could trace the contours of her mouth as he banded his arms around her and pulled her against him. Her sensitized breasts pressed against the hard muscles of his chest, and she gasped in pleasure. He touched the tip of his tongue to hers in a question that made her open to him so they could taste each other.

He broke the kiss to nip at her earlobe before skimming his mouth down the side of her neck. She grabbed fistfuls of his shirt as she arched back to offer him her throat. "Yes, Luis, yes!" she whispered as he licked the hollow between her collarbones before he gave her just the edge of his teeth on her neck.

She hissed in a breath at the play of pleasure against the nip of pain. And then she pulled open two of his shirt buttons so she could press her palms against the sculpture of muscles under the warm skin dusted with silver hair as springy as his beard's.

He groaned and threw his head back. "Yes, your skin against mine."

And then she realized what she had done. Her face flushed with a different kind of heat, and she pulled her hands away. "That was...unexpected," she said, trying to pretend her world hadn't just shifted on its axis.

But he was watching her with a panther's predatory gaze. "That was *muy erótico.*" He cupped her cheek with one hand and kissed her in a way that was so carnal, she shivered with renewed longing.

He broke the kiss and shifted both hands to her shoulders, while the desire that had burned in his eyes lessened. "Eve, I want you very much, but it must be your decision. If you choose, you must come to my room tonight."

"I don't know where your room is," Eve said, not understanding why that mattered. Was he worried about her suite being next to Grace's?

He made a dismissive gesture. "I will show you." He gripped her shoulders again, making sure she was looking at him before he continued. "No matter how badly I wish to, I will not come to your room. Do you understand?"

Realization dawned.

"Because you're the king," she said. "You want to make sure I don't feel pressured."

"Yes." There was a strange plea in that one word.

"You forget that Americans aren't subject to command by royalty." Eve smiled before she pulled down his head to give him a kiss. "Besides, not even a king can command someone to have an orgasm."

"Perhaps not, but I'm sure many orgasms have been faked in a palace bed."

"If it happens, I will not be faking, I promise," Eve said, her voice low and sultry.

"*Ay*, we must return to the young people to see how they are getting along." He let go of her shoulders and stepped back.

Guilt poked at Eve because she had forgotten about Grace and Raul. "Right." She winced inwardly as she thought about how much more complicated this thing between her and Luis could make the situation.

It would have to be a one-night stand. And that was only if she had the nerve to go to his room at all.

As she turned to walk beside Luis, she was surprised when he took her hand, interlacing his fingers with hers and sending a thrill up her arm.

He must have sensed her hesitation, because he said, "I can't have you in the way I want right now, but I still wish to touch you."

They waded in the surf, hand in hand, as though they were just two regular people and not a Calevan king and a vet tech from Iowa.

CHAPTER 15

"We're not telling Grace and Raul about this," Eve said to Luis, gesturing between them as they rode the elevator back up to the terrace.

"Not yet," Luis said, capturing her hand to press his lips against her palm. Delicious shivers radiated over her skin.

Or ever.

The door slid open, and Luis stepped back to let her exit first. As she headed toward the pool, he called, "Wait a moment. We can rinse the sand off our feet here."

She turned to see what she had thought was a small fountain pouring water into a bronze basin. Luis held out his hand to her. "Stand in the pool and run your feet under the water," he said. "I'll balance you."

She had never thought cleaning sand off her feet could be a sensual experience, but the water was warm, and Luis's grip was powerful. She lifted one foot at a time to let the water spray over it, leaning on Luis's strength.

"Your turn." She stepped out of the basin and tugged him into it. He had no need of her support, but he held on to her hand anyway. He had narrow feet with high arches, and when he flexed his toes in the cascade of water, the well-defined muscles in his calf bunched and shifted. It was strangely intimate to ogle his bare feet, and desire surged through her again.

Then he pivoted on one foot to run the arch of his other one up the inside of her calf. She gasped and jerked her gaze up to his. He was smiling with a roguish glint in his eyes. "I hope to explore higher tonight," he purred.

She dipped one foot in the water and flicked it upward to spatter droplets over his trousers. Surprise widened his eyes before he leaned in to say, "I could throw you in the dungeon for that...and come visit you every night."

His words rippled through her, stoking the ache between her legs. "Would I be tied up for your visits?"

He sucked in a quick breath and then threw back his head to laugh. "*Dios mío*, you beat me at my own game."

Eve grinned at him, but inside she was a roil of arousal.

"There you are!" Grace came around the corner with Raul on her heels. "Aren't you starving?"

All the sexual heat in Luis's eyes was quenched in a nanosecond. He dropped Eve's hand and stepped out of the fountain in one smooth movement without any sign of discomfort. "Have you not been eating the tapas?" he asked.

"Of course," Raul said. "But Annamaria keeps lurking at the door, which means dinner is ready."

"When one is enjoying the beach, time passes swiftly," Luis observed.

Eve almost choked at his description of what they'd been doing, but she cleared her throat to say, "I was treated to the story of how the Pirates' Surprise got its name."

"Will you tell it again at dinner?" Grace asked.

"There is nothing I like better than sharing the history of Caleva," Luis said with a smile. "Shall we go in?"

As the sexual fog cleared from Eve's brain, she looked at Grace and Raul standing side by side. This was Grace's true family, the one she was related to by blood. A pang of grief wrenched at Eve's heart. She had the unhappy sense that Grace was slipping away from her with every minute her daughter spent here in Caleva.

Being a mother meant letting go, allowing your fledgling to fly to her new destiny. But why did Grace's destiny have to be so far out of Eve's reach?

♔

Eve paced around her suite's living room, trying to sort through the hurricane of conflicting emotions roaring in her brain. She had barely been able to eat the delicious dinner, and she had probably had too much wine. But that was the only way she could manage to smile and nod and pretend everything was normal when it was so far from normal, she didn't even know what to call it.

She needed to get to know Raul, to judge whether he was really as welcoming to his new half sister as Luis claimed. He was a charmer, smooth and polished, with a flashing smile and a ready wit. He and Grace teased each other—and their father—with outward ease. Yet Eve still had no sense of who the prince truly was behind that handsome façade.

Then there was the pain and pride of watching Grace fit right into the family dynamic. Her daughter was not intimidated by the company of a king or a prince. Eve couldn't help being impressed with Grace's poise and confidence. Somehow, she seemed to have raised a young woman who could handle being a princess. But the more comfortable Grace was, the less likely it was that Eve would continue to be a large part of her life.

Eve sagged onto a chair as the truth of that lanced through her with a physical agony. It wasn't even the distance between Iowa and Caleva. It was the distance between a vet tech and a princess.

The hardest part of dinner, though, had been the sizzle of awareness that crackled between her and Luis. Eve leaped up to pace again. Every time Luis looked at her, she felt his mouth slanting against hers. The heat and arousal and ache slammed into her all over again, just from seeing the desire lighting his eyes.

If Grace and Raul had noticed the charged atmosphere, they hadn't given any sign. They must be blind. She smile-grimaced. More likely, they just couldn't imagine their parents being interested in sex, especially with each other.

After dinner, Luis had given them a tour of the house, so now Eve knew where the master suite was. Was she really going to go there?

She burned with the need to touch him again...but she had a responsibility first. Eve took three deep breaths, shoved Luis out of her mind, and went to her door, yanking it open to find Grace outside with her hand raised to knock.

"Great minds," Eve said. "I was about to knock on your door."

"I figured you would want to talk," Grace said, giving her a peck on the cheek. "*I* want to talk." She dropped onto a chair and hooked one knee over the upholstered arm.

"And I want to hear all about your conversation with Raul." Eve sat in the chair across from her daughter. "First, tell me what you think of him as a person."

Grace tilted her head back to look at the ceiling for a minute before she spoke. "He's like he was at dinner. Really nice, funny, smart, considerate, polite. He made me feel like he was genuinely happy to have a half sibling. He told me to ask him anything and he would answer it." She shook her head. "But he has such a different life that it was hard to know what to ask. And he takes things for granted that sort of freak me out."

"Like what?"

"When he's not in the palace or here, he has a bodyguard or two following him around all the time. He doesn't think it's weird when people bow to him. He spent a year in the Calevan militia and can fly a helicopter. He goes shopping either before a store opens or after it closes. He's met a ton of famous people and has some of their personal cell phone numbers." Grace shook her head again. "That doesn't even cover the official and governmental stuff he does as the future king. All of that boggles my mind, but he loves it."

Grace had the option of stepping into the royal succession after Raul. Would she want that?

"Raul is Luis's son, so I'm not surprised that he is good at what he does," Eve said with careful neutrality. "What are your thoughts about all this?"

Grace unhooked her leg from the chair and sat up. "Here's the interesting thing. Being the prince gives you a platform, and Raul can do a lot of good. His support of the charities he's passionate about has brought serious money and attention to their missions. Think about what I could do for animals with a platform like that! Not to mention having real input into the new veterinary school."

Raul was in on the seduction too. Had Luis asked him to tempt Grace, or had Raul jumped on the bandwagon on his own? Raul would want his father to be happy. Luring Grace to Caleva would accomplish that.

Eve quelled her resentment and jammed on her mom hat. Grace's eyes blazed with crusading spirit. The world needed young people like her who wanted to make a difference. Here was her daughter being offered the opportunity to have a significant impact for a cause she cared about.

"That would be really exciting," Eve said. "And you would do a terrific job."

"*We* would do a terrific job." Grace locked her gaze with Eve's. "Mom, if I move to Caleva, will you come with me? I know it's asking a lot, but I just can't see myself here without you. We're a team. And now that Nana Nelle has passed, we don't have any close family in Iowa anymore."

With the unconscious obliviousness of the young, Grace hadn't factored in Eve's network of friends built over the years. Or the fact that Eve had a job she loved ninety percent of the time and a house she had lavished loving care and sweat on to make it a home. Not to mention what Grace didn't yet realize—that Eve would not be an integral part of her daughter's new world here in Caleva. As an American commoner, Eve would always be an outsider to the royal family, no matter how cordially they might treat her.

"Of course I'll come to Caleva with you," Eve said, her heart melting that Grace would want her here so much, even as a flicker of panic rose at the thought of flinging herself into the unknown. "Does that mean you know what you want to do?" She held her breath.

"No." Grace massaged her temples. "It's such a big decision."

"You can bounce your thoughts off me, you know."

"My thoughts are still so scattered that I don't know where to start. Every time I think I have my mind wrapped around the fact that my father is a king, my brain explodes again."

"Sweetie, that's to be expected." Eve knelt in front of Grace, taking her daughter's hands in hers. "No one could be prepared for such a huge revelation. You've handled it with amazing poise."

"Things were so much simpler when it was just you and me in Iowa," Grace said, squeezing her mother's hands.

"I know." Eve sighed. "But we can't turn this ship around. You have to navigate a new course, whatever you decide it will be."

"It's a lot of pressure, but it's exciting too," Grace said.

Eve sighed again, but differently this time. She was excited for her daughter, for all that was opening up before her, but she hadn't been wrong when she'd sensed Grace slipping away from her.

They talked for another hour before Grace yawned widely. "I'm going to go enjoy that amazing bed with all its adjustments."

Eve had secretly hoped Grace would want to sleep with her, as she had back in Ames. That would take her decision about Luis out of her hands. "I love you, sweetheart," Eve said, giving Grace a hug and a kiss.

"Love you too, Mom. You're the best."

Eve closed the door behind Grace and leaned back against it, tilting her head to rest on the wooden surface. The weird thing was that she wanted to discuss Grace's dilemma with Luis. He would be brilliant at analyzing all the pros and cons and coming up with a solution. But he had his own agenda.

Which brought her back to her other quandary. She pushed away from the door just as her phone pinged with a message. She swept it off the coffee table to see that the text was from Luis.

The choice is yours, but I hope you will choose me.

So simple. So direct. Not a seduction, a plea. It was perfectly calculated to get past all her defenses.

How could she *not* choose him, this man who made her ache with the longing to touch and be touched, who made the air in any room he entered dance with electric energy, who drew her to him like a jaguar luring his prey with his lethal beauty?

This man who had suffered because he was born to be a king. The pain that lived behind his eyes tugged at her heart while his hypnotic blue gaze and long, lean muscles tempted her body.

She closed her eyes, and the memory of how her body had come alive at his touch burst through her. She hadn't felt such a sensual yearning in years. Didn't she deserve some pleasure?

She didn't answer his text because she didn't want to think. She slipped out of her suite and glided silently down the hall, alert for the sound of others stirring. Silence surrounded her as she followed the route Luis had guided them all along earlier, regaling them with stories about the artworks, the previous owner, and the technology embedded in the house. No one would have known that he was also instructing his lover on how to reach his bed.

Her steps slowed as objections raised their ugly heads. Luis was a king, a man whose behavior was scrutinized and held to high standard. Could their short fling be kept a secret? If it was revealed, how much would it damage him in the public eye? Even worse, how would Grace and Raul feel about their parents having a relationship that was based on sex? Except her attraction wasn't just about sex, and that was what made this affair dangerous.

Yet she kept going until she arrived at the floating staircase that led from Luis's office to the master bedroom. The cryptocurrency billionaire had liked to work at all hours, so he had stacked his sleeping quarters above his working quarters.

Her foot on the bottom step, she hesitated. She could turn back now and Luis would never know she had come this far.

CHAPTER 16

Luis flicked through the pages of the book on fencing strategy without reading a single word. He had brought Camacho's gift with him, thinking he might have time to enjoy a chapter or two while at Casa en las Nubes.

However, Eve had derailed his concentration the moment she had brushed her fingers over his beard at the beach, her featherlight touch streaking down to his cock like a laser. As he stared down at the open book, all he could think of was the feel of her lips against his, of her hands on his skin inside his opened shirt, and of her softly curved body pressed along the length of his.

At dinner, it had taken all his concentration to converse coherently when she sat so close that he could reach out and touch her. For a few moments, he had imagined ripping off her blouse to cup the curves of her breasts before he lowered his head to suck her nipples into peaks. He had forced himself to banish the delicious idea from his mind until now.

Now his cock hardened again as he let that picture linger in his mind.

But his phone lay stubbornly silent on the coffee table after he had allowed himself to send the one text.

A good sign or a bad one?

He slammed down the book and paced the length of the *sala* again, glancing out the wall of windows to see the lights of a large ship riding the dark sea. Probably a U.S. naval vessel since the American base lay farther along the coast.

He had tried hard not to let this happen. Eve being Grace's mother complicated the situation. Yet relationships in his life were always complicated. If he had allowed that to stop him, he would be even more alone than he already was. He had made his decision. Now it was up to Eve to make hers.

He pivoted and stalked back to where the book lay on the coffee table, hurling himself into a chair beside it. Before he could sweep up the tome again, a soft chime sounded. He went still as anticipation burned through him like a flare.

Someone was climbing the stairs to his suite. The paranoid billionaire had installed alarms within alarms in this house, and Mikel made sure they all continued to function.

Then Luis was on his feet, striding to the door to pull it open. As Eve reached the top of the staircase, she stopped, looking startled. "Luis."

Instead of racing across the landing to pull her against him and slam his mouth down on hers, he opened the door wider and stepped back. "Please come in."

She nodded and walked toward him. He tried to read her intentions, but she looked more nervous than anything else. Perhaps she had come to tell him *no*. It would be like her to do that in person because she would deem it the right way to handle a rejection.

Once she was inside the room, he closed the door. She stood in front of him, her eyes wide and unsmiling, her hands twisted together at her waist, her beautiful hair cascading over her shoulders. Not throwing herself into his arms.

"You did not answer my text," he said, keeping his voice neutral.

"It would have required that I think, and I didn't want to do that." She took a deep breath. "Luis, I made my choice."

"And what is it?" He braced himself for her answer.

"I choose you."

⚜

Eve saw the moment his control snapped, and she almost turned and ran. The desire that blazed across his face was so intense that it scared her...and sent an answering flash of wanting burning through her.

He needed only one long stride to reach her before he banded his arms around her and brought her against the hard, hot wall of his body. Her breasts were crushed against his chest, her nipples hardening to aching points, while his mouth came down on hers in a fierce claiming.

She slid her hands around his neck and into the silvery silk of his hair, trying to meld herself with him as longing slid through her. She wanted him to touch her breasts, the aching spot between her legs, and everywhere else on her body. Her craving was almost painful in its strength.

He shifted to a different angle against her lips, his tongue teasing hers. He slid his hands up to cradle her face as he explored her mouth, his lips warm and firm, the soft brush of his beard an extra fillip of sensation against her skin. The man knew how to kiss.

She slid her hands down over his shoulders, savoring the curves and valleys of his muscles until she reached the first button of his shirt and yanked it out of the hole. She wanted bare skin, so she kept going until she could tug his shirt out of his waistband and run her hands over his ribs and up his back.

He broke the kiss to let his head fall back. *"Dios mio!"* he moaned. "That feels so good."

She pushed his shirt off his shoulders and gently raked her nails over the golden skin stretched over the flexing muscles, and he moaned again. He was so beautiful in an entirely masculine way. She leaned in to lick one of his dark, flat nipples, sampling the different textures there.

"Sí, Eve!"

He didn't give her a chance to touch the other one. He sank his fingers into her hair and pulled her head back so he could lick his way down her neck and into the V of her blouse, thrusting his tongue into the valley between her breasts. The slight roughness with the heat and moisture made her shiver with longing.

He released her hair and cupped her breasts, circling his thumbs over her nipples, first gently and then harder as she pressed into his hands. Ropes of fire streaked from her nipples to flare low in her belly, and she pulsed her pelvis against his thigh as the blaze heated.

"Do not come until I am inside you," he commanded as he began to unbutton her blouse.

"Then hurry up," she said, pulling his belt buckle open. His erection pushed against the gray fabric of his trousers.

He smiled, but it was the triumphant smile of a wolf who had his prey cornered. He slipped her blouse down her arms and tossed it away before he found the catch on her bra and flicked it open.

Thank goodness she had bought new lingerie before coming to Caleva. Not because in her wildest dreams she'd thought this would happen, but because Luis had made her feel feminine again.

Of course, he wasn't paying any attention to the cream lace as he hurled it onto the chair where her blouse had landed. His gaze was locked on her bare breasts. For a moment, she worried that they were no longer perky, and then his mouth was on one and his palm on the other, and she didn't care. Pleasure zinged around inside her, lighting her up like a pinball machine.

The exquisite tension between her legs coiled tighter.

"You're going to make me come," she gasped out.

He let her nipple slide out of his mouth, grazing the tip of it with his teeth, the sensation making her buck against him. His smile was intense. "I can't allow that."

He brushed his fingers over her sensitized breasts once more, as though he didn't want to stop touching them. Then he intertwined his fingers with hers and pulled her through a door into his bedroom.

The room was lit only by the flames flickering in a modern steel fireplace, and the moonlight reflecting on the water through a wall of glass. The light glinted off the gilt decorating the spines of another wall filled with books. A brief wave of gratitude washed over her. All the flaws of her fifty-plus-year-old body would be less obvious in the dim light. At least she stayed in decent shape, because being a vet tech was a physical job.

Luis drew her to the enormous bed covered with a blue velvet duvet.

"I want to take my time with you," he said, his hands again cupping her breasts. "But I need to be inside you."

"Who says you can't do both?" she said, running her hands over the muscles in his forearms. "Just reverse the order."

"The can-do Iowan with a solution." He bent to kiss first one nipple and then the other before he shrugged out of his shirt and stripped off his shoes, socks, and trousers with swift efficiency, leaving only black boxers tented by his erection.

"Oh my goodness," she breathed as her gaze roved over the lines of defined muscles running down his abdomen, thighs, and calves.

She reached out to trace them, but he seized her wrists. "We are hurrying now so we can take time later," he reminded her, releasing her hands so he could unbutton her trousers and push them down to pool at her ankles. She toed off her shoes and stepped out of the puddle of fabric. He hooked a finger in each side of her lacy panties, but his eyes were locked on hers. "You can still say no, Eve," he said.

"Only if I want to explode from sexual frustration," she said, putting her hands on his and pushing them downward.

He laughed, a short bark of relief, before he yanked her panties to her ankles and straightened again. This time, his gaze traveled the length of her body. She would have felt self-conscious except his expression was one of pure lust. *"Hermosísima!"* he murmured, his face ablaze with his desire for her.

"My turn," she said, thrusting her thumbs into the waistband of his boxers, the fabric smooth and slippery. Silk, of course. She had to pull the front outward to clear the jut of his cock before she let them fall.

He was glorious, like a statue with planes and angles sculpted by an artist. She laid her hands on his chest to enjoy the living warmth of him, not stone at all. "I feel…a little awed," she said.

His eyebrows drew down before he stepped into her so she could feel his cock against her belly, his chest pressed against her breasts, and his fingers curling into her buttocks. He lowered his mouth to whisper beside her ear. "I am only a man desperate to make love to a beautiful, sexy woman. All I want you to feel is pleasure."

And then he backed her into the bed and lowered her gently onto the duvet before he leaned over to brace his arms on the bed as he looked down at her. "I have been dreaming about this almost since the day I met you."

He stretched one hand out to slide open a drawer in the bedside table and pull out a condom. Before she could tell him it wasn't necessary, he had rolled it onto his erection. And she understood. He was a hereditary ruler. Where he dallied could have serious consequences.

He slid one knee and then the other between her legs, spreading her thighs. "Say yes, Eve, one more time."

"Yes, Luis, yes, yes, yes!" She reached for his cock, but he was already sliding inside her, stretching her and filling the ache so completely that she felt like crying with the relief of it.

But she wanted more. She tilted her pelvis upward to bring Luis deeper. He groaned, a long drawn-out sound of pleasure. "Eve, this is so good," he said, beginning to move inside her.

"Buenísimo!" she managed to say as the friction tightened the coil of longing in her gut.

"Magnífico!" he said, withdrawing and thrusting ever more quickly.

"No. More. Words." She matched his rhythm before closing her eyes to let sensation roll through her.

Wrapping his hands under her thighs, he held her fully open so he could control every stroke. He kept shifting the angle of her pelvis so his movement sometimes pressed her clit hard, sometimes softly. She could not anticipate the exact sensation it would evoke, and the surprise pushed her up to the top, where she balanced for a long, exquisite moment, savoring what was about to happen.

He let himself loose with two hard, deep thrusts, and she exploded around his cock, the squeeze and release of her muscles sending bolts of delight crashing through her. She arched against the bed, grabbing his wrists to anchor herself as she shrieked, "Yes, Luis, yessss! Oh, yes!"

He went still, allowing her to focus on her orgasm, reveling in having him inside her as she convulsed. Her body vibrated with the delicious intensity, almost to the point of overload. Slowly, the waves of sensation eased, turning to ripples.

"Finish!" she said, tightening her muscles around him.

"*Me corro ahora!*" He drove into her once, twice, and the third time, he threw back his head to shout her name as he pulsed deep inside her.

Then she was sinking down into the gorgeous aftermath, her skin flushed with warmth, her muscles lax with release, her body humming with satiation. Luis stayed inside her, so she squeezed him again, just to tantalize them both.

"*Ay*, I have nothing left," he said with a gasping laugh.

"I don't either, but it still feels good," she said, giving a little moan of regret as he slipped out of her.

Lowering her legs gently, he grasped her knees and lifted them to turn her so she lay fully on the bed. After stripping off the condom, he stood looking down at her before he ran his palm over the curve of her hip and down the outside of her thigh. "Mmm," she said, not caring what he saw as long as he touched her.

"You are better than my dreams," he said, his voice low and caressing.

"You are a flatterer." She scooted sideways even as an embarrassed gratification surged through her. She didn't believe him, but it was nice to hear. "Come join me. I want to snuggle."

He looked surprised and oddly sad before he said, "With pleasure." He stretched out on the duvet, gathering her up against his side, her head on his chest.

"Are you comfortable?" he asked.

"Very comfortable." It felt wonderful to have his body against hers, his skin smooth and warm except where hair lightly furred his chest and thighs. The maleness of him with his long, hard muscles contrasted delectably with her softer curves. She nestled in closer with a sigh of contentment. "This is nice."

"Yes, it is." He stroked her hair in a slow, hypnotic rhythm. "Will you stay here with me until morning?"

"I, well, maybe until very early morning so no one sees me sneaking back to my bedroom." She hadn't thought about what would happen after they had sex. The debate about whether to come to his bedroom had taken up all the bandwidth in her brain. "I know we're all having breakfast together at seven thirty, but what time does Raul actually get up?"

"If you leave here at six, you should be safe." She felt his lips brush the top of her head. *"Gracias."*

He was thanking her for staying with him? "It's not a hardship, you know."

His chuckle vibrated against her cheek. "I am glad to hear that. But perhaps we should get under the covers."

She tilted her head to watch the flickering light of the fire play over the ridges of his torso. "You're keeping me warm, and I'd like to enjoy the view a little longer."

"You can still see the moon and water when you're under the duvet."

"I meant this view." She feathered her fingers over his abs, causing his muscles to contract.

"I am enjoying my view as well." He skimmed his hand over her waist and hip, a delicious shiver following his touch.

"I was putting your comfort before my happiness."

"You're a better person than I am."

"In this case, your selfishness works in my favor."

She hummed an answer as she savored the play of light over his muscled body, his heartbeat strong against her ear. Of course he would be beautiful after all those generations of kings and queens choosing the most desirable mates.

Without even thinking, she said, "Why didn't you marry again? You wanted a large family, and women must have lined up for the chance to bear your children." She realized that was very personal, even given their recent intimacy. "Never mind. It's none of my business."

His sigh ruffled her hair. "There are many answers to that question. I was very busy learning to be a monarch and father, which left me little time to seek a new queen."

She noticed he didn't argue with her that women would line up to marry him, but then why should he? He had been on every international most-eligible-bachelors list for decades.

"But once you figured all that out?" she prodded.

"I'm not sure I have figured it out even now." He paused a moment. "Once I settled into my two most important roles, I found I had no interest in anything more than...liaisons."

Liaisons. That was the category she fell into. It sounded better than a one-night stand.

"I can see that Odette Fontaine might have left a bad taste in your mouth, although you didn't know she was a psychopath back then," Eve said. "But there must have been plenty of nice, sane women you could have married."

His bark of a laugh held no humor. "Perhaps I did not trust myself to recognize which women were sane and which were not."

"You're older and wiser now. You could still have children with a younger woman."

"*Ay*, Eve, I am indeed older. Too old to want to raise babies. I am awaiting grandchildren."

He wouldn't have to raise the babies. He had staff for that, but he wouldn't want to leave a child of his to nannies, of course.

He fell silent for a long moment before saying in a harsh voice, "My wife died because she married me. I brought Odette into my family circle, and my nephew was tortured and mutilated as a result. Nothing in those experiences would incline me to attempt another serious relationship."

The raw emotion in his voice punched her in the gut. "I'm so sorry," she said. "I shouldn't have pushed you."

"Sometimes it is good to say these things out loud," he said. "We learn more when we put the feelings into words."

"Did you learn something?" she couldn't stop herself from asking.

"I have made two disastrous choices, but only two. Perhaps that is bad luck, not a pattern." His shrug shifted his chest against her cheek. "Why didn't *you* marry again? You are a beautiful, accomplished woman whom a man would be privileged to marry."

She ignored his compliment. "Maybe I didn't trust myself to recognize the wrong person either." But that was only part of it, and maybe she owed him her truth. "I felt defective," she nearly whispered. "I wasn't able to have a baby. That's why Ben left me. No one would want to marry someone defective."

His arm tightened around her as his breath hissed in. "*Qué cabrón!* That bastard! You know that is not true."

"When you're very young, and the man you love tells you the same thing over and over again, you internalize it. It's a hard thing to shake after that, no matter how much older and wiser you get."

"But now you are beyond the issue of childbearing, so what holds you back?"

"Seriously? I'm not a king with a castle, a private jet, and a yacht. No one is standing in line for a middle-aged vet tech."

"I have demonstrated that my gender can be very stupid about women. I am happy to be at the front of the line." He tilted her chin up so that he could press a kiss on her lips. She kissed him back, loving the feel of his mouth on hers.

"I'm happy that you *are* the line." She stroked the soft springiness of his beard. "This is so surreal when I stop to think about it."

"You said you did not want to think, so don't." He grazed his fingers down her shoulder to tease her nipple. Electric pleasure zinged through her. "In fact, my wiser self says that we should stop dwelling on the ugly past and focus our attention on the delightful present."

He rolled them both over so he was braced on his forearms above her while his thighs settled between hers. When he slid down her body to kiss his way along the inside of her thighs, she forgot about everything except how very good he made her feel.

♔

When Luis woke up for the second time, he was alone, and the sky was beginning to lighten. Eve had slipped out of bed while it was still dark. After he had seen her to the door, he had settled in the spot where she had lain, soaking up the lingering warmth and scent of her before he fell back to sleep.

Crossing his arms behind his head, he basked in the sense of well-being that hummed through his body. He enjoyed the feel of the smooth cotton sheets against his skin. He hadn't slept in the nude for too long. It had become routine to wear pajamas in case he had to deal with a middle-of-the-night emergency. Now he relished the sensuality of being naked.

Which led to memories of Eve touching him and of him touching her. His cock stirred agreeably at the pictures spooling through his mind. He had enough experience to be a capable lover, but Eve had responded with such joy that he had stopped thinking and just let things happen. It was freeing to forget about performing and instead be guided by pure feeling.

They had made love three times before parting, trying delicious variations on the age-old act. He should be heavy-eyed from the lack of sleep, but energy coursed through him as the sky glowed pink and gold with the sunrise. Still, he didn't get up, choosing to luxuriate a little longer in the contentment wrapped around him.

His cell phone buzzed, and he sat up with a sigh, throwing the covers back to swing his legs over the side of the bed.

He took time to stretch before he swiped up the phone to read the text. A smile tugged at the corners of his mouth.

Everything was in place for his surprise for Eve and Grace.

CHAPTER 17

"Where are we going?" Eve asked as she climbed into the black SUV to sit beside Grace. After a morning of vet school discussions and lunch with the Iowa crew, they had been driven back to Casa en las Nubes to change for the afternoon's activities. They had been told to wear jeans and bring light jackets, but nothing more.

"It's a surprise," Bridget said from the driver's seat.

Grace's face lit up. "When a king surprises you, it's bound to be good."

In fact, Eve had been surprised by almost everything about her night with Luis. First, that it had happened. That still boggled her mind. But also how much fun it had been, once she'd gotten past that first tsunami of nerves. She hadn't known what to expect from a king in bed. After all, Luis didn't have any dearth of willing lovers, so he didn't have to be good. But he was. Really good. The glow suffusing her body was proof of that.

"Mom, what are you smiling about?" Grace asked as the SUV swung onto a highway.

"Just looking forward to whatever we're going to do." Even more toward that night, because Luis had invited her back to his bed. She was just marking time until then.

"You look really happy," Grace said.

Eve turned to find her daughter watching her. "Why shouldn't I be? We're living the high life."

"More than that happy," her astute child said.

"I'm overjoyed that you are getting to know and love your new family. First Luis and now Raul. You'll understand when you're a parent." It was the truth, of course. Just not all of it.

Grace looked skeptical, but she dropped the subject as Bridget drew their attention to various points of interest along the way.

They slowed to turn through a metal gate guarded by fierce-looking stone Calevan dragons atop pillars of basalt stone.

"This is Finca de Bruma," Bridget explained. "It is the estate of *el Duque y la Duquesa* de Bruma, His Majesty's brother and sister-in-law."

They drove down a long drive lined with tall evergreen-looking trees, turning off before they reached the huge stone house Eve could see rising in front of them.

After coming around a curve, the SUV stopped outside a low building built of dark gray stone with white limestone accents. As Eve opened her door, the sound of a horse neighing rang out.

"It's a stable," Grace said as they followed Bridget around the corner and into a large courtyard bustling with grooms leading horses and hauling hay bales and buckets. On one side, two grooms stood, holding four glossy horses wearing English saddles.

"We're going riding! Just because we told Luis we wanted to. I love being a princess." Grace grinned and took off toward the waiting mounts.

Bridget joined Eve. "His Majesty and the prince will be here in a few minutes."

Eve's heart did a happy dance. Luis was coming with them! And Raul, too, of course.

"Oh, and here are your riding boots," Bridget said as a groom approached with two pairs of black leather paddock boots in his hands.

Eve took the boots and strolled to a mounting block to the side of the courtyard. Grace joined her a minute later.

"Can you believe they even figured out our shoe sizes?" Grace asked as she pulled off her sneakers.

"Annamaria just had to look in our closets." It was more the fact that someone thought to do it that amazed Eve. "Guess who's coming to ride with us."

"Luis and Raul," Grace said. "The grooms told me which horses were for whom. Luis's is the dapple gray. Raul's is the flashy chestnut. You and I get the bay mares. They're probably the boring, calm ones."

"I'm fine with that," Eve said.

Bridget approached them, dangling riding helmets from the straps hooked over her fingers. "These are adjustable. I can help you make sure they fit properly."

"Thanks, but we know how to make them tight," Grace said.

"If you don't mind, I'll check them," Bridget said with an apologetic smile. "It's my job to protect you from getting a concussion too."

"Are you riding with us?" Eve asked as Bridget helped her strap the helmet on tightly.

"No. I'm not a pro on horseback. The folks going with you are experts." Bridget moved to check Grace's helmet.

"Where are they?" Grace asked.

"Already mounted and waiting," Bridget said. "They'll stay ahead and behind so you shouldn't really notice them once you're on the trail. But don't worry, they can get to you fast."

Eve had not been worried until Bridget said that, but the strong security made sense since both the king and the crown prince would be with them.

"All set," Bridget said, rapping Grace's helmet lightly with her knuckles.

A black SUV swept up to the open side of the courtyard and stopped. Two more SUVs parked just behind it, the doors swinging open to disgorge men and women in dark suits who spread out around the stable.

One guard stepped up to the first SUV and tapped on the window before opening the back door.

Eve nearly gasped as Luis stepped out of the car dressed in tan riding breeches that outlined every muscle in his thighs, tall, shiny black boots, and a blue polo shirt. A riding helmet was tucked under his arm, and he held a pair of gloves and a riding crop.

Delicious heat rippled through Eve's body as she devoured the stretch of fabric over his wide shoulders and the long stride that carried him toward her. His gaze was locked on hers, and his smile carried all kinds of wicked messages.

Beside him walked Raul, who was dressed in similar riding kit. The two tall, powerful men with their strong family resemblance made a striking pair.

Suddenly, the activity of the stable came to a halt as everyone either bowed or curtsied to the arriving royals. Everyone except Eve and Grace…until they noticed and hurriedly bent their knees.

"*Ay*, none of that," Luis said as he came up to them. He winked. "You are Americans."

The momentary stillness ended as everyone went back to their tasks. It was weird.

"Do you even notice when all these people do it?" Grace asked with a sweep of her hand around the courtyard.

Raul shrugged. "Sometimes yes, sometimes no. It is a sign of respect to what we represent, not to us personally, so we accept it in that spirit."

Eve wasn't so sure that the respect was not personal. The Calevans she had spoken with were very enthusiastic about the royal family.

"Welcome to my surprise outing," Luis said, once again looking at Eve with that caress in his eyes. "We're going up into the mountains to see if we can find dragons for you."

"I'm excited just to go riding," Grace said.

"As am I," Luis said. "Raul and I are playing hooky."

"Oh, yeah," Raul said, grinning. "We blew off some epically boring meetings."

Eve started to feel guilty but pushed the feeling away. Luis would not shirk any important duties. Instead, she worried about staying on the horse on a mountain trail. She hadn't ridden more than half a dozen times in the last ten years, so her horseback muscles weren't in shape.

Luis said something in Spanish to the grooms holding the horses. They laughed and responded too swiftly for Eve to understand.

"You are riding Cielo," Luis said to Eve. "And Grace will ride Estrella. Sky and Star." He checked the tightness of the girth on Cielo before lacing the fingers of both hands together to provide a step for Eve to put her foot in to mount her horse.

She hesitated a moment. It seemed wrong to put her dirty boot on a king's hands.

"Eve?" He bent to lower his hands.

Praying she hadn't stepped in any manure, she gently slid her foot into his grip and grabbed the saddle. He lifted her with a surge of power that made her feel like she weighed no more than a cobweb, yet he stopped her at the right moment to swing her free leg over the horse's back. As she settled in the saddle, she looked down and found herself mesmerized by the sun illuminating the pale blue of his eyes and glinting on the silver in his hair while it painted the sharp-angled bones of his face with light and shadow. He was breathtaking, and she got to touch him again tonight.

"Are you comfortable with the length of the stirrups?" His voice woke her from her infatuated trance.

"Oh, er, um, yes, they're fine," she said before she leaned down on the pretext of checking the strap. "You set this expedition up because you know you look hot in riding clothes," she whispered.

The corners of his eyes crinkled as he flashed her a lascivious smile and murmured, "I wish to make sure you come back to me tonight."

Like there was any doubt, but it was thrilling to know that he wanted her enough to seduce her with horses.

"My muscles may be too sore for what you have in mind," she teased.

"I know several ways to relax tight muscles." He fiddled with the stirrup strap, using it for cover as he ran his hand down her thigh. A trail of searing delight followed his touch. He gave her knee a light squeeze before he went to his horse.

His foot barely touched the stirrup as he vaulted into the saddle and stroked his mount's neck, talking to him in a low voice.

"I'll lead, Pater," Raul said. "Grace, would you like to ride beside me?"

"I guess that leaves us old fogies to bring up the rear," Eve said, her heart singing at the thought of having Luis by her side for the length of the ride. It was difficult to get alone time with a king. Well, not quite alone, but as close as she could manage until night wrapped them in its concealing arms.

Raul and Grace headed toward the open side of the courtyard. Eve turned Cielo to follow with barely a touch on the reins. The mare had a mouth like silk and a smooth stride. Luis's horse was dancing with high spirits and needed a firm hand to get him moving in the right direction. Eve secretly enjoyed watching Luis's superb horsemanship as he controlled his mount. He looked every inch a king astride the high-bred creature.

"Chispa is feeling fresh today," Luis said as he came up beside Eve.

"Chispa?" Eve asked.

"It means spark," Luis explained. "He always has a devilish gleam in his eye."

As they came around the corner of the stables behind Grace and Raul, Eve spotted the four mounted guards waiting for them. All wore dark colors and windbreakers that probably covered guns slung in holsters, and none of them smiled nor spoke a word. Two broke away to move ahead of them, while the other two waited until they had passed and fell in at a respectful distance to the rear.

"Quite a cavalcade," Eve murmured, hoping that Grace understood that this would be her life, too, if she chose to become an acknowledged princess.

Luis slanted her a rueful smile. "Mikel goes into high gear when Raul and I leave campus together. But let us enjoy the scenery. This is my brother's estate until we reach the base of the mountains. Then it becomes crown land, preserved in its natural state except for the trails through it."

"Is crown land open to the public?" Eve asked.

"Yes, with strict rules against disturbing the flora and fauna. Today, this trail is closed to all but our party," Luis said.

Of course it was.

They rode along a dirt road that passed between two rolling fields enclosed by white fences. Red-gold cows grazed on the tall grass on one side while a couple of horses cantered toward them on the other. At the end of the road in front of them, a wall of trees marked the base of the mountain range that ran along the center of the island.

"It's a beautiful place," Eve said, although the mountains seemed to cut off the sky. Unlike the flatlands of Iowa, where the sky seemed almost limitless in its expanse.

"Bruma was one of the first dukedoms created by Ricardo el Rojo. My brother inherited the title because the previous duke died without offspring. It will pass to my nephew, Gabriel."

"Are you close to your brother?" Eve wanted to know all about Luis.

"Now I am," Luis said. "He is the kingdom's historian and an invaluable sounding board for preventing me from making the same mistakes my predecessors did."

"Why were you not close in the past?" Eve probed.

"The oldest fight in all of history. The woman we both loved chose Lorenzo." Luis's tone was light. Eve turned to check his expression but found it serene. Evidently, he was over whoever married his brother. "It was a shock to both of us."

That surprised a laugh out of her. "Lorenzo also thought she would marry you?"

"I was the crown prince, so yes." The glint in his eye showed he was teasing, before a cloud passed over his face. "Hélène did not want to be queen. We were all so young then. We knew very little of what life had in store for us."

Eve thought of her marriage to Ben and silently agreed.

"But what about your family?" Luis asked. "Are you close to any of them?"

Eve remembered her conversation with Grace about moving to Caleva. Was she about to give Luis more ammunition in his campaign to persuade her daughter to leave Iowa?

"I was very close to my grandmother on my father's side, but she died several years ago." Eve still missed Nana Nelle's tart good sense and twinkling blue eyes. "She was my anchor through my divorce. She watched Grace from the time she was an infant so I could work, and they had a special bond."

"And your parents?" Luis asked.

"My father had health issues, so they moved to Florida soon after I adopted Grace, and then my father died. My mother was not...supportive of Grace's adoption, so we don't speak often." In fact, when Ben filed for divorce, Eve's mother had pointed out that she had told Eve that the adoption was a bad idea. Her father had been a silent ally, sending a check every month with a sweet note commenting on the photos of Grace she would text him. But he wouldn't stand up to his wife and come visit his granddaughter. He'd said it wouldn't be worth the tongue-lashings that would result.

Now Luis knew that there were no loving family members eagerly waiting for Eve and Grace to return to Iowa.

He twisted in the saddle to look at her square on. "You raised Grace almost entirely alone. What an extraordinary woman you are!"

"Plenty of women are single mothers," Eve said, even as his words made her glow inside. "I was lucky to have a steady job and a mortgage-free house that Nana Nelle left me."

"When I think of how you and Grace struggled..." His mouth was a grim, unhappy line as he trailed off.

"Yeah, when she should have been living in a palace," Eve said, with only a touch of defensiveness.

"I did not mean that," Luis said.

"Yes, you did, just not in an unkind way." Eve sighed. "Heck, I wanted her to have more advantages than I could offer her."

Now she could have them. Opportunities neither Eve nor Grace had ever imagined in their wildest dreams.

Luis reached across the distance between their horses to clasp her shoulder, his touch sparkling through Eve's body. "Grace did not need anything more than what you gave her."

"I did my best," Eve said, reaching up to cover his gloved hand for a brief moment, finding the leather stretched over his knuckles soft and smooth.

As Luis dropped his hand, Eve realized that Grace and Raul had stopped to wait for them. The speculative look on her daughter's face meant that she had seen the touch between Eve and Luis. Not good.

"We're at the beginning of the Pico de Luto trail up the mountain," Raul said. "From here, we have to go single file. May I suggest that I lead?"

"And I will go last," Luis said. "We will keep the ladies between us."

Except there were guards in front and behind, so all of them were bracketed by protection anyway.

Raul turned his horse forward to start up the trail. Grace threw a look at Eve that said they would talk later before she followed Raul.

"Actually, I wanted to go last," Eve said to Luis.

He raised his eyebrows. "Why?"

"So I could ogle your butt in those tight breeches." She grinned at her own temerity.

The lust that blazed in his eyes almost scorched her. In a voice that vibrated with seduction, he said, "But that would deprive me of the pleasure of ogling yours."

"And the king always gets to ogle what he wants," Eve said, signaling her horse to move.

"If I could ogle what I wanted, you would be naked," Luis purred before he reined his horse in behind hers.

Everything in Eve's body went liquid as his words slid through her, setting off whirlpools of longing. She had started it, so she couldn't complain, but now she could swear she felt his gaze focused on her backside.

As they climbed through the trees, Eve tried to ignore Luis's presence and take in the beauty of the forest. Birdsong intertwined with the sound of creaking saddle leather and horseshoes clinking against the occasional rock. Sometimes, Raul's or Grace's voice drifted back. Birds fluttered between the tree branches, flashing in and out of the sunlight filtering through the leaves. She inhaled, savoring the scent of warm horse, earthy loam, and green freshness.

They rode in companionable silence for half an hour before Raul came to a halt in the middle of the trail. One of the front escorts had ridden back to speak with him. She turned to ask Luis what was going on, but when she opened her mouth, he held his finger to his lips in a shushing gesture.

Raul dismounted and came back to speak with Grace in a low voice.

Eve heard the creak of a saddle behind her and footsteps before Luis appeared at her side. "We're going through the woods from here. There might be wild creatures nearby, so we should keep quiet."

One of the guards jogged up from behind and took the reins of their horses as Luis led her up to join their children. Grace grinned and opened her eyes wide in a pantomime of *what's going on?* Eve smiled with a shrug in response.

A young woman dressed in dark green from head to toe seemed to materialize from between the trees. She echoed Luis's finger-to-lips warning before gesturing for them to follow her. Raul dropped back to let Grace and Eve go before him.

Excitement fizzed through Eve as she trod carefully behind their guide, stepping over fallen branches and dry leaves that might make noise. Grace glanced back at her with the same lit-up look of anticipation.

The guide dropped to a crouch as the trees thinned at the edge of a clearing, waving them forward to kneel beside her before she pointed to the right.

Grace gasped at the same time as Eve.

Two brilliant teal Calevan dragons sunned themselves on a large boulder. One was at least five feet long, while the other might have been a foot or so shorter. Their red-rimmed neck frills were folded back, and their eyes were mere slits as they basked in the light and warmth.

Luis knelt between Grace and Eve, and Eve turned to mouth, "Wow!" at him, her eyes wide. He nodded before he turned to admire them as well. His shoulder brushed hers, and she had to stop herself from leaning into the strength of his body.

"They're amazing!" Grace whispered.

All five of them stayed silent, gazing in awe at the rare and gorgeous creatures. This was where the dragons belonged, in the wild where their vivid color blazed against the dark gray basalt.

Eve shifted so she could watch the three Dragóns kneeling in a row, their profiles so much alike as they gazed at the creatures whose name they carried. Grace was part of this family, whether Eve wanted it or not. The Dragón blood ran strong in her veins.

"Would you like to see their frills displayed?" Luis whispered. "We will have to disturb them, so they may leave."

"One more minute, please," Grace whispered, her eyes still locked on the huge lizards.

Luis nodded. Eve jerked as she felt his warm fingers close around hers. He smiled at her surprise and kept their clasped hands hidden between their thighs. The strength of his clasp sent little vibrations of pleasure up her arm to dance in her chest. She gently squeezed his hand to let Luis know she liked it.

Movement from Grace pulled her gaze away from Luis. Her daughter slowly drew her phone from her jacket pocket and took several shots of the basking dragons. Then she nodded to Luis. "Okay, I'm ready to see frills."

He released Eve's hand, making her feel bereft, and reached forward to pick up an egg-sized stone. She almost protested until she realized he wouldn't use it to hit one of the lizards. He narrowed his eyes, intent on whatever his target was before he cocked his arm back and hurled it, hitting the side of a boulder about five feet from the huge lizards. The stone cracked when it hit, sending a rattling shower of pebbles raining onto the ground.

The bigger dragon's head reared up as its frill snapped open like a huge circular fan painted in bright bands of teal, blue, and red. It opened its mouth wide and gave a loud hissing cough almost like a lion's.

Eve's heart did a flip. It was like seeing a dinosaur come to life.

"That would make me back off for sure," Grace muttered as she took another picture.

The smaller lizard lifted its head, looking around warily, but didn't open its frill.

"Shall I try to get the other dragon to display?" Luis asked, already searching for another rock to toss.

Grace shook her head. "No, we'll leave them to their sunshine."

Eve loved that about Grace. Her daughter respected the wild creatures' right to be there more than her need for a great photo.

The bigger one kept its frill open as it swung its head back and forth a couple of times, giving them an excellent view of the huge neckpiece it sported, before folding it down again. It and its companion continued to survey their surroundings a little longer, then settled back into their sun-induced nap.

The guide led them quietly back to the horses.

"Now we will all have the luck of *el dragón* for the rest of the day," Luis said.

"That was awesome!" Grace looked like she had seen Santa Claus. "It makes me furious that people killed so many of them for their skin."

"Agreed," Raul said, his handsome face stern. "But now that we have strong laws to protect them, you can see that they are making a comeback in the wild once again."

"Thanks to your captive breeding program," Grace said. "I wonder if that big fella was born in your dragon preserve."

"If so, he's a major success story," Raul said. "Did you see the size of his frill?"

"And so brilliantly colored!" Eve said. "I was also impressed with his voice. For a herbivore, he sounded pretty fierce."

She noticed that Luis was standing slightly apart, as he so often did. Sometimes he looked very alone, and it wrung her heart. Today, though, he looked pleased and even a little self-satisfied by the success of the dragon-viewing.

"How much did you pay those guys to pose for us?" Eve asked him.

"Only their weight in *raíz dulce*, their favorite food," Luis said with a chuckle. "It was well worth it to see the reactions from you and Grace."

"Caleva is a beautiful country," Eve said, thinking of the magnificent dragons, the glorious beaches, and the fragrant *vaho* hibiscus.

"That's why I go to the wild places when I can." His head was turned as he gazed around the forest, so she could admire the sharp, strong lines of his profile. "To touch Caleva's soul."

If anyone else had said that, it would have sounded melodramatic, but Luis meant it.

"To remind yourself of why you go to all those meetings?"

"More to cleanse myself of all those meetings. Politics is a dirty business at times." He met her eyes with a sardonic look. "Gone are the days when a king could simply decree that something be done. Now I must negotiate and persuade and compromise to move my agenda forward."

Eve saw the haze of weariness cross his face. "No more talking business," she said, touching his arm for a fleeting moment. "You're still playing hooky."

"I had hoped to stay away longer, but I have some troublesome nobles trying to upset the Americans on the naval base," he said with a shrug. "We must return to the stables."

As Luis linked his hands to help her mount Cielo, Eve first surreptitiously scraped her boot sole on a tuft of grass.

He waited until she settled in the saddle before running his hand down her leg to pretend to check her stirrup leather. Once again, she nearly caught fire from the blaze in his eyes.

"I will never forget this ride," she said. "It has been pure magic."

"Caleva is an enchanted place," Luis said with a smile that invited her into his web of delights. "The longer you stay, the stronger the spell it weaves."

Grace was already ensnared in that spell.

"I think the King of Caleva is a bit of a sorcerer himself," Eve said before giving him a roguish glance. "A very wicked sorcerer at times."

He leaned in close to say in a low, seductive murmur, "And he will do sinful things to your naked body tonight." She nearly melted in the saddle.

☖

Luis and Raul had to return to the palace, so Eve and Grace rode back to Casa en las Nubes in the SUV with Bridget and Ivan. Eve sighed inwardly when Grace followed her into her suite.

"Okay, Mom, spill," Grace said as she plunked down in a chair in the living area. "What is going on between you and Luis?"

Eve tried to gauge her daughter's feelings about what might be happening, but Grace's expression held nothing more than determined curiosity. "Oh, you mean when he squeezed my shoulder today? I was talking about how much I missed Nana Nelle, and he was expressing his sympathy."

"That may be true." Grace's tone was skeptical. "But the way you two looked at each other and the body language say it's more than that."

"Oh, we're just flirting a little. Harmless stuff that leads nowhere," Eve said with a shrug. "I don't mean to gross you out, but your father is a very attractive man."

"Yeah, I get that. He's still on a lot of the most-eligible-bachelors lists, even though he's past fifty," Grace said.

"I'll put a stop to the flirting if it bothers you," Eve said, even though the thought of pushing Luis away before they could spend another night together made her want to cry.

Grace shook her head. "It's just that you haven't been on a date in, like, ten years, and now you're hooking up with Luis."

"I'm not sure what 'hooking up' means these days," Eve said.

"Going out, kissing, maybe more." Grace held up her hand. "Not that I want to know if you're doing more."

"Okay," Eve agreed with relief. "It's nothing serious. After all, he's the king."

"So? I'm the princess."

"First, Luis has been single for a long time. He isn't looking for a long-term relationship," Eve said. "Second, I'm not exactly queen material. I don't have royal blood running in my veins like you do."

"You'd be a great queen, Mom," Grace said with a grin. "At the clinic, you don't put up with crap from anyone."

"That's a little different from running a country," Eve pointed out.

"I'm just worried about you," Grace said, surprising her.

"Worried? Why?"

"You don't do casual," Grace said. "And he's the king. I think Luis is amazing, but I'm not blind to the fact that he's used to getting what he wants. He might not realize that he could hurt you."

"Trust me, my eyes are wide open," Eve said, coming over to hug her daughter. "You are a very smart cookie about people, you know."

Grace squeezed back. "I learned it from you."

CHAPTER 18

"You don't play fair," Eve said as she walked into Luis's arms late that night.

"Not if I can help it," he said, tilting her chin up and claiming her mouth in a long kiss that left her panting. "But what are you referring to?"

"This afternoon," Eve said, running her hands over his back, loving the feel of his muscles under the fine cotton of his dress shirt. He hadn't returned to the house until well after dinner, stripping off his jacket and tie before sitting down with a glass of Scotch to relax with Eve and Grace, while Raul had stayed back at the palace.

He looked surprised. "It was only a horseback ride."

"Oh, please. What about the dragons conveniently hanging around?"

He led her to the sofa where he sat and pulled her down onto his lap with a hint of a smile. "I might have sent some scouts out to see if the recent reports about a pair of large dragons were true. Perhaps those scouts located the lizards just before we started off on our ride."

"Ha! I knew it!"

"What is wrong with wanting to give you and my daughter the pleasure of seeing Caleva's most famous natives in the wild?" He nuzzled the side of her neck, nipping her earlobe as his hand traveled over her hip and down her thigh, making it hard to hold on to her thoughts.

"It's not the intention," Eve said. "It's the way you carry it out. Just a word from you, and it gets done. Flawlessly."

He lifted his head to look into her eyes. "The people who work for the crown take great pride in doing their jobs well. Not for me personally, but for the ruler of Caleva. When Raul becomes king, many of them will serve him with the same commitment to excellence."

A pang shot through her at the thought of what would happen to make Raul the king. This powerful, vital, brilliant man holding her in his arms would be gone from the world. She couldn't bear imagining it.

"You don't understand what different worlds we come from," Eve said.

"You are the chief veterinary technician at the school's clinic. You have people who support you—other vet technicians, the X-ray and MRI techs, the cleaning staff, the administrative staff. Their work frees you to do your job well," Luis said. "That is all my staff does."

"Right." She put all of her disbelief into the word.

"None of that matters at this moment." He began to unbutton her blouse, stopping to trace the lace along the edge of her bra so that her nipples tightened with anticipation. "Here and now, we are just a man and the woman whose exquisite breasts he wants to kiss."

"I'm on board with that plan." The brush of his fingertips against her skin was a delicious tickle.

He pushed out the last button and eased her blouse off her shoulders before he let his thumbs drift over her collarbone. With his index finger, he touched the lily pendant she had fastened on after her shower. "You are wearing my gift."

He leaned in to kiss her neck just above it. "I like the idea of it being the only thing you'll be wearing soon." With that, he flicked open the catch of her bra so the lace fell away from her breasts. *"Tan preciosos,"* he rasped.

He lowered his head to kiss all around one nipple, making her squirm on his lap. When he took the nipple in his mouth, surrounding it with warmth and teasing it with his tongue, arousal scorched through her. His erection was hard under her thighs, and suddenly the ache between her legs needed to be filled.

"Wait!" she said, wriggling off his lap to stand and unfasten her trousers. He watched from under heavy eyelids as she shimmied out of them and then slid her panties off as well. "I need you inside me."

"Mi querida," he murmured as he unbuckled his belt and opened his trousers, releasing his cock. He reached into his pocket to pull out a condom.

She put her hand over his before he could tear open the packet. "I can't have children, so you don't need that. I swear."

He hesitated a split second, his gaze roaming over her face before he gave an almost imperceptible nod and tossed the condom onto the couch.

She put one knee on the cushion beside his thigh, wincing as she tried to bring the other knee to the other side. The aching muscles of her inner thighs reminded her that she had been horseback riding for the first time in years.

"Are you all right?" Luis asked, wrapping his hands around her waist to steady her.

"A little sore from the horse, but that won't stop me." His strong grasp gave her the support to straddle him so that the tip of his cock brushed her clit. "Ah, Luis!" she gasped out as electric delight streaked through her.

She stared down into the searing blue of his eyes as she slowly slid downward to impale herself on his erection, moaning with pleasure at the sense of stretching and being filled.

"Now kiss my breasts," she commanded.

"*Con placer.* With pleasure." He sucked one nipple into his mouth and palmed the other, making her grab his shoulders to hold herself still through the storm of sensation rocking her body as he sucked and stroked and licked. His mouth and his hands on her skin and his cock deep within her sent waves of bliss all the way to her toes. She wanted to stay like this forever, but desire was coiling tighter and tighter in her belly.

When he tilted his hips so he pressed against her clit, she couldn't stay still any longer. Bracing her hands on his shoulders, she pushed upward, then came down, driving him deeper inside her.

His hands went back to her waist, helping her rise and fall as he matched her tempo, only in opposition so he thrust up as she sank down. "Yes, oh, please, yes!" she cried out as the delicious friction grew hotter and hotter.

"I cannot hold back for long," he said, his voice tight with effort.

"Don't try!" she said as he drove up hard. "Come with me!"

With that, he threw his head back and let loose, pumping into her with a shout of release. That sent her over the edge and into a paroxysm of contracting muscles and dissolving tension as she called out his name over and over with each exquisite convulsion.

Then they both collapsed downward, panting and hearts pounding.

"*Ay*, Eve, you are *increíble*." He skimmed one hand up and down her back as she lay bonelessly over him, her head on his shoulder.

"If that means mind-blowing, I agree." She snuggled in closer. "I've wanted to do that ever since I saw you looking like a conquistador on Chispa's back."

He huffed out a laugh. "Riding behind you on the trail, all I could think about was curling my hands around that gorgeous *culo* of yours." He illustrated by giving her buttock a squeeze.

"Great minds think alike," she said, exhaling a long sigh of satisfaction.

"Dirty minds, certainly." He shifted so that his spent cock slid out of her.

She felt the stickiness between her legs and hoped it wasn't all over his expensive suit trousers. Lifting her head, she looked around for a box of tissues. He pulled a handkerchief out of his pocket and offered it to her.

Taking the neatly ironed and folded square of fine cotton, she noticed embroidery on it. "I can't use this. It's monogrammed. With a crown!" And a stranger would be laundering it. "Don't you have tissues?"

"Those would require standing up, and I don't want to move. Nor do I want you to move." He banded his arms around her. "Consider it a self-interested gift."

She gave in and gently cleaned between her legs, trying also to blot the fabric of his trousers with little success. He took the crumpled handkerchief from her and tossed it on a nearby table.

"As much as I enjoy this position, my thigh muscles are complaining now that I'm not distracted by other things," Eve said, trying to shift within his embrace.

He immediately moved his hands to lift her off of his lap and onto the cushion beside him. "Here or the bed?" he asked.

"I like variety, so here. But you have too many clothes on," Eve said, beginning to unbutton his shirt and kissing his newly bared skin as she undid each one. She inhaled his scent of sky and water, sexually satisfied male, and a hint of starch from the shirt. "You smell so good. I want to bottle it. Eau de Luis."

He took her face between his hands to tilt it up. She expected a smile, but he looked strangely intent. "Not Eau du Roi?"

"It's *your* scent, not some generic king's," Eve said.

He leaned in to kiss her in a way that was passionate but gentle. "Eve, you are very special."

"Because I like the way you smell?"

He just shook his head before he released her and smiled. "Please don't let me keep you from your task."

She laughed and finished the unbuttoning, running her hands over the swells and valleys of his chest and abs, his muscles reacting as she touched them.

"The world's best massage," he said with a groan of pleasure, his head resting on the back of the sofa. "I confess to being a little achy myself from riding."

She trailed her fingers over his ribs, making him jump and grab her wrists. "You *are* ticklish. I wondered."

"Are you?" he asked, cuffing her wrists together with one hand.

"Nope. Not at all," she lied.

"I need to test that answer." He feathered his fingertips along her side, making her squirm and press her lips together to avoid giggling. He kissed the side of her neck before he freed her. "You are a terrible liar."

"Is that a bad thing?"

Again, the teasing look vanished. "Quite the opposite. A bad liar is to be treasured." He stood and stripped off the rest of his clothes, making her forget his strange mood swings. Before he rejoined her on the couch, he strode across the room to grab a moss-green blanket from the back of a chair, affording her a mouthwatering view of the muscles flexing in his tight butt and long legs as he moved.

"Could you just walk around the room a few more times?" she requested as he started toward her.

He looked puzzled until she licked her lips in a very suggestive way. Then he laughed, a full-throated rumble. "Are you ogling me again?"

"One hundred percent."

He stalked back to her with a predatory stride, the blanket held at his side so she had an unimpeded view of his magnificent body.

"Now I want to ogle you, only I will do it with my skin and my hands," he said, tumbling her onto her back on the cushions as he came down beside her, the length of his body pressed against hers. With a flick of his arm, the blanket unfolded in the air and settled over them like a cloud.

"You're right. Touching is better," she said, snuggling closer to feel the stretch of warm skin over hard muscle.

Luis savored the soft curves pressed against him and the ruffle of Eve's breath over his chest as she lay with her head pillowed on his arm. The sofa wasn't as comfortable as the bed—his surprisingly sore muscles reminded him of that— but it had the advantage of forcing them into close proximity.

He savored even more the fact that when they made love, Eve responded to him as a man, not a king. He had been with enough women to know when the crown was in bed with them. But Eve wanted to bottle *his* scent, not a king's. His position was a problem for her rather than a turn-on. Weirdly, he loved that.

He let his eyelids drift closed but not to sleep. He wanted to bask in Eve's feminine presence in his arms, in the physical ease that followed an explosive orgasm, and in the pleasure of having his two children with him as they had watched the dragons. It had been a good day…and it wasn't over yet.

"Grace figured out that something is going on between us," Eve said without moving.

"She knows we're sleeping together?" he asked, feeling his mellow mood slip. "Is she upset about it?"

"We didn't discuss the details. She didn't want to." Eve's voice held an undercurrent of parental amusement. "It doesn't seem to be a problem for her at the moment."

He had the sense that Eve wasn't telling him the whole story. "Is it a problem for you?"

She sighed. "Maybe a little. I don't want to complicate her decision about being a princess with our...stuff." She shifted in his embrace. "Does Raul know?"

He considered how different their relationships with their children were. "We do not discuss each other's intimate relationships."

But maybe he should discuss more personal things with his son. He had when Raul was younger, but now that they worked together, their dynamic had shifted. Subtly and gradually, so Luis hadn't noticed it until now. He took tremendous pride in his son's accomplishments, but he had slipped into treating Raul almost as a colleague. Because so many of their interactions were about governmental affairs, Raul deferred to Luis as the king. Only at family dinners when Gabriel was present did the two young men revert to their occasional respectful tweaking of Luis, a teasing he treasured.

He needed to make his conversations with his son more personal.

"He seems like a very perceptive young man," Eve said. "If Grace suspects, I imagine he does too. Do you think it would bother him?"

"Why should it?" Raul had seen him involved with other women and never seemed concerned, but Luis wasn't going to say that to Eve.

"Oh, because children can be uncomfortable about their parents having sex. Especially because they probably think we're too old to be interested." Eve sounded amused again. Then she braced her hands on his chest and pushed him far enough away that she could look into his face. "How does Raul feel about having a half sibling appear out of nowhere? He's so smooth and charming all the time that I can't gauge his real reaction."

Luis was tempted to press his lips to her beautiful mouth to stop the flow of contentment-destroying words. That would be far more pleasurable than delving into family dynamics when all he wanted was to enjoy the feel of her silky bare skin against his.

He sighed. At least he could twine the satin of her hair around his fingers while they talked.

"Since his cousin Gabriel started traveling so much to book artists for DragonFest, I think Raul has been lonely." Luis chose his words carefully. "Having a peer to talk with has been good for him. He feels comfortable sharing the life of a royal with her since he trusts her not to go to the media with any revelations." He considered some of his recent thoughts about his son. "I hope knowing Grace may even encourage him to loosen up a bit and spend less time working. I worry that he doesn't have enough fun for someone of his age."

"Grace works too hard as well, so she may not be the best influence on that front," Eve said.

He decided not to mention that he hoped Grace would share some of Raul's tasks as a royal. She would be an excellent representative for the new generation of the crown…but that was for after she graduated from vet school.

"She has a more normal life than Raul," Luis said. "I hope it will open his eyes to new possibilities."

"Huh, I never thought of it from that perspective," Eve said. "I've focused on the opening up of Grace's life."

"I am glad to hear you find it a positive." Luis brushed his lips against her forehead.

"Mostly." Eve sighed. "But back to Raul. For the first time, he's going to have to share his father with another child. That could create tension, even resentment."

"It will change the dynamic, and I don't consider that a minor matter." He had made an extra effort to show his love for Raul ever since Grace's relationship had been confirmed. "To a certain extent, he has always shared me with my nephew, Gabriel, whom I consider a son. I believe Raul is secure in my feelings for him."

"It's not the same, though. Gabriel is not your child by blood."

"Love has no limits," Luis said. "I can love Grace without loving Raul any less."

"Just be very sensitive to your son right now," Eve said, cupping Luis's cheek. "He may feel neglected with all the attention you're lavishing on Grace."

"You are right, and I will take your advice." It touched him that she was as concerned for his child as she was for her own. "There is one more reason I think Raul is glad of Grace's presence."

"What's that?"

"He wants me to be happy. He understands that Grace has been a gift to me at this stage of my life."

"You raised a good man," she said, her voice holding a slight quaver. "But that doesn't surprise me."

Her words sent a wave of pride and gratitude surging through him. To have Eve give him credit for that moved him deeply.

"I often think that Raul did more to raise himself than I did," Luis confessed. "My life is filled with so many obligations that I have never been able to spend as much time with him as I wished."

"I've watched you two together," she said, stroking his shoulder in comfort. "You have a strong connection. Raul adores you."

"I do not question his devotion. I question my part in it." And whether Raul had embraced the family business so passionately as a way to spend more time with his father.

"You inspire devotion." Her smile held a hint of sadness. "It's why you're such a great king."

He grimaced inwardly. It was better when they were speaking as two parents and his position as king didn't play into it.

"Let me go back to being a man who wants to make love to the beautiful woman in his arms, but in a bed this time." He stroked his hand down her hip before sinking his fingers into the lush curve of her buttock. He pulled her against his chest again to kiss her with lascivious intent.

When she moaned into his mouth and tilted her pelvis against his hardening cock, he stood and scooped her up in his arms, leaving the crown behind.

CHAPTER 19

Luis woke up alone the next morning and didn't like it. It had been much better during the night when he had surfaced into wakefulness with Eve's warm, naked body curled against his side. Especially since she had been happy to be roused by his hands and mouth.

He stretched his body out fully, the sheets stroking his skin as he savored the relaxation of his muscles from a night of pleasure. The aches and pains brought on by the horseback ride had eased somewhat too.

It wasn't just physical, though. Eve somehow lifted the weight of Caleva off his shoulders, allowing him to be a man, a father, a lover…all without being a king. When the weight resettled, it seemed lighter.

As usual, the chime of his cell phone impinged on his good mood. He ignored it until it chimed a second time.

Grabbing it off the nightstand, he swiped to the text message. It was from Mikel.

Su Majestad, my apologies for disturbing you. Bruno and I are on our way to you. There is an issue involving Eve that requires your immediate attention.

Luis scowled at the phone. *Eve*, not Grace. Mikel could not possibly know that he and Eve had slept together. Or maybe he could. The man had eyes everywhere.

The fact that both of his closest advisors were on their way meant the issue was serious enough that it couldn't wait until he arrived at Castillo Draconago.

He got up to shower.

Half an hour later, Luis was downstairs in his office, dressed in a pale blue shirt and gray suit trousers. He would add the tie and suit jacket in the car while en route to the palace. As he waited for Mikel and Bruno, he scanned through his meetings for the day, growling in annoyance over yet another session with the group complaining about the U.S. military base lease. The problem with many of the noble *consejeros* was that they had too much time on their hands, so they wasted Luis's.

He was surprised to notice that the newcomer, Felipe Camacho, was no longer listed as part of the delegation. Camacho seemed like a crusader, and that type didn't usually give up once they had a perceived conduit to the king's ear. At any rate, Luis would instruct Bruno to foist the group on someone else.

As though his thought had conjured him, Luis's assistant entered the office with Mikel right behind him.

"*Su Majestad.*" Bruno bowed. "My deepest regrets for impinging on your private time, but this involves your family."

Mikel slid in silently with his trademark half bow.

"What is this urgent problem?" Luis asked.

Bruno tapped at the tablet he held before placing it on the desk in front of Luis. "*La Voix* plans to run this photograph in their morning edition tomorrow."

The photo was of Eve and Luis strolling on the beach, the champagne bottle in his hand. Eve's red hair flew like a banner in the wind, and she was laughing. They looked so normal, two people enjoying each other's company in a beautiful, wild setting. Luis met Bruno's gaze. "I've been photographed with women before. What is the problem?"

"Read the caption, *Señor*," Bruno said.

"'Does the king have a new girlfriend? Who is the mysterious redhead who has our sovereign drinking champagne while walking barefoot on the beach?'" Again, Luis looked up. "We just ignore it as always. Eve will not be bothered by it since they don't name her."

"I am concerned about Odette Fontaine's possible reaction," Mikel said.

"*Joder!*" Luis swore as the import of Mikel's words hit him. "Do you think she will recognize Eve as Grace's adoptive mother? After all, the photo was taken from a distance, and it has been more than twenty-five years since Odette met Eve. *Hostia!*" Luis cursed again as a memory surfaced. "Odette traveled to Iowa three years ago to find Grace. She might have seen Eve too."

"That is my fear," Mikel said. "Not to mention that some zealous reporter will ferret out Eve's identity soon enough."

Luis was long accustomed to the public constraints of being the head of his country. However, this was one of the times when he wished his private life could be *private*.

"Can you lock down Odette's access to outside media?" Luis asked.

"Yes, but unless we put her back in solitary, other inmates may talk about it. It is almost impossible to be sure she will not find out about the photo," Mikel said.

"Bruno, persuade *La Voix* to kill the photo for now," Luis said. "We will promise them access to a much bigger story in the near future."

"Grace's story," Bruno said with a nod of understanding. "Do you have a sense of *Señorita* Howard's feelings about claiming her place in Caleva?"

Luis thumped his fist on the desk in frustration. "I wanted to let her make the choice at her own pace. She should be allowed time to sort through the implications so she never regrets her decision." He had also caused an upheaval in Eve's life, one that could change her future almost as much as her daughter's.

But Luis knew this was a ticking bomb, and they were running out of time to avoid an explosion they couldn't control.

"I need to speak with Eve," Luis said.

"*Por supuesto.* Of course," Mikel said, but he and Bruno did not move.

"I will see if she is awake," Luis said with a sigh of resignation as he picked up his phone to text Eve.

She responded almost immediately that she would be there in fifteen minutes. Luis put down his phone and looked at the tablet again.

"Send me a copy of the photo, *por favor*," he said, returning the tablet to Bruno.

His assistant sat and swiped at the tablet. "It should be on your secure phone now."

"*Su Majestad*, I offer my apologies for this invasion of your privacy at Casa en las Nubes," Mikel said. "I believe the photograph was taken from a boat that never should have gotten that close. I have added an additional patrol to prevent this from happening again."

Luis waved away the apology. "It's only a photograph and not even a scandalous one. It happens to be a problem only because we are trying to keep a secret."

They had not even kissed when the photo was taken, but Luis had wondered how her lips would taste many times before that. It showed in his body language. Mostly, though, he had felt a quiet joy in sauntering barefoot on the sand beside a woman he found intriguing...and sexy.

Then Eve walked into the office, dressed in jeans and a long-sleeved green T-shirt. Her glorious red hair—that he had tangled his hands in last night—was still wet from a shower and tamed into a thick braid.

"*Buenos días*, Luis!" Her smile was brilliant with happiness, and an answering joy bloomed in his chest as he stood. Then her glance fell on Bruno and Mikel standing by the desk. The smile shifted into wariness. She was a smart woman.

⛫

Eve's stomach lurched as she took in the three imposing men who faced her. Luis was smiling, but Bruno and Mikel had solemn expressions.

"*Buenos días*, Eve," Luis said. "You look lovely this morning."

A lie. She had just gotten out of the shower when his text arrived. Hoping that he was inviting her for a quickie in his office, she had twisted her wet hair into a braid and thrown on the first clothes she dragged out of the closet. But Luis's gaze was as warm as his smile, so maybe he was blinded by lust.

"Good morning, *señora*," Bruno said, while Mikel gave her a respectful nod.

"This looks ominous," Eve said.

250

"More of a nuisance." Luis came around the desk to put his hand on the small of her back and guide her to the seating area. "Please, let us sit."

Luis took the chair next to hers and held out his hand for Bruno's tablet. "One of our media outlets plans to run this tomorrow."

He tapped the screen before he passed it to Eve. Her heart sank as she looked at the photo and read the caption, but then she remembered that they hadn't even kissed each other at the point the photo had been taken. "It's just two people enjoying the beach. We're not doing anything shocking."

Well, there was the flirtatious tilt of her head and the intent focus of Luis's gaze. Their bodies seemed angled toward each other, too, but it was all subtle.

"It doesn't matter what we were doing," Luis said. "You and I were together. If it is published, Odette could see it and recognize you."

"But I haven't seen her for more than twenty-five years," Eve protested.

"Yes, but she may have seen you," Luis said. "About three years ago, Odette traveled to Iowa to see Grace."

"That makes no sense. Grace didn't know who her birth mother was until you told her!" Eve said, trying to absorb the information.

"Odette did not reveal her presence to Grace. She simply observed her. Which means she might have observed you too," Luis said.

"Oh, crap!" Eve looked at the photo again. Although the picture had obviously been taken with a telephoto lens, her red hair stood out, and her face was probably clear enough to be recognizable. If Odette had seen Eve three years ago, she might be able to identify her.

"Bruno will be able to get *La Voix* to postpone publication of the photo, but now that we've been seen together like this, this paparazzo, or someone from the paper, will be trailing you for another opportunity. And they will track down your name." Luis took the tablet from her and set it aside before he grasped her hands, his grip warm and strong, an anchor she craved. "We need to get ahead of this so that Odette is not provoked into releasing her version of the story before we can introduce Grace to Caleva on our terms."

"Get ahead of it how?" Eve was still reeling from the idea that Odette had been near her daughter three years before.

"We need Grace's decision," Luis said. "I wished to give her more time, but events have overtaken us."

No, not *events*, but her stupid attraction to him had triggered this mess. Her self-indulgence was going to rush Grace into making a decision before she was ready. Guilt wrung her chest, and Eve pulled her hands out of Luis's grasp.

"We'll go back to Iowa," Eve said. "Then no one will take pictures of me or Grace here, and Odette will never know."

"That would be a mistake," Mikel said. "Here, we have some influence with the media, but in the U.S., we have almost none. It will be much more difficult to protect Grace there."

"'Protect Grace.'" Dread ripped through Eve. Cocooned in the protective net woven around Luis, she had almost forgotten to worry about Grace's safety. Mikel's words burst that bubble of innocence with a single pinprick.

Some of her panic must have shown on her face, because Luis leaned in to say in a soothing tone, "Eve, Grace will be fine, no matter where she is." He swept his gaze between Mikel and Bruno. "If you would give us some privacy," he said.

They turned and left the office, closing the door behind them.

♕

"I am so sorry, Eve." Luis wanted to touch her, but she looked ready to explode. "I didn't wish to pressure Grace, but we cannot wait much longer to make an announcement."

He wasn't surprised that the timetable had been taken out of their hands. It was partially his fault. He had been so focused on getting to know his daughter and her getting to know him that he had pushed the limits of secrecy.

Eve stood abruptly. "I knew I shouldn't get involved with you. It was irresponsible and selfish. Now I've put Grace in a terrible position."

Her words slashed at him like daggers. If she felt irresponsible and selfish, how could he feel less so? Even worse, he could see the direction of her thinking, and it led directly away from him. Worry twisted in his gut as he stood too.

"Eve, it was not your fault. It was mine. I know too well how voracious the paparazzi are. I should have been more careful about exposing you."

He took a step toward her, but she held up her hand to stop him.

"No, we're done now," she said, crossing her arms over her chest as her tone grew hard. "Before you force Grace to make a decision about what her role will be in Caleva, you have to sit down with her and tell her every bad thing there is about being a member of the royal family. No more of this fantasy stuff with castles and dragons and...and founding veterinary colleges. You give her the gritty, ugly reality." She gulped in a breath that was almost a sob. "Like your nephew getting kidnapped and having his ear cut off."

That slammed into Luis like a runaway train. "You want me to remind Grace that her mother is a psychopath?"

Eve's shoulders sagged. "No. No, you shouldn't bring that up again. She knows it all too well." She shot an enraged look at him. "Did you ever think that it might have been better for you to stay away from Grace? Then she wouldn't be burdened by that terrible heritage."

That was a bullet tearing through his flesh. "Yes, but she also has a glorious heritage as a princess of Caleva. Should I have deprived her of that?"

Eve looked stricken, and he couldn't help himself. He wound his arms around her, feeling the shudder of her body as she gave way to tears. "Eve, *querida mía*, our daughter is a strong, smart woman. You raised her to be that way. She will make the right decision."

"I'm afraid for her," Eve said into his shoulder. "Can you promise she will be safe?"

"I can promise that I employ some of the best, most loyal people in the world who will do everything they can to keep her safe. None of us can do more than that. Not even you. Not even in Iowa before anyone knew she was my daughter." He rubbed gentle circles on her back.

For a long moment, she remained rigid in his arms, and then her body softened, and she leaned into him.

"I'm not ready for this," she said. "I expected to have more time too."

"More time for what?" But he understood. His appearance in Grace's life would change Eve's future as well. He was arrogant enough to feel it would be for the better, but Eve might not agree—yet.

"More time to be Grace's mom." A sob wrenched from her throat.

"*Cariño*, what are you talking about? You will always be Grace's mother. That will never change." Her misery clawed at him. How could she believe he would take Grace away from her?

She moved restlessly in his arms. "Forget it. I'm being selfish again." She pushed at his chest, and he reluctantly let her go. Pulling a clean handkerchief from his pocket, he held it out.

She gave an odd little huff of a laugh before taking the square of cotton and blotting her tear-streaked face. So she had thought of last night's handkerchief.

"Grace needs to finish vet school before she starts princessing," Eve said, spearing him with a direct gaze. "That's nonnegotiable."

"Of course." Not that he was happy about waiting that long. "And I will speak with her today about the negatives of being a royal. *Te prometo.* I promise you."

"And you will protect her while she's at school in Iowa." Eve continued to glare at him. "Mikel said that would be hard."

"Mikel holds himself to almost impossible standards. Believe me, Grace—and you—will be secure, even in the U.S."

She waved a hand in dismissal of her own safety. He grasped her shoulders. "Eve, you must be protected as well. You are Grace's mother and important to her."

"Like your nephew, right? You love Gabriel, so he became a target." She drew in a ragged breath. "I hate this paranoia."

He did not remind her that Raul had been the real target. That would strike too close to home.

"Eve, do I seem paranoid to you?" He waited for her to shake her head. "I am careful. I listen to Mikel's advice...most of the time. But I do not live in fear. Nor do Raul or Gabriel, despite his terrible ordeal. The truth is that any of us could die tomorrow for reasons that have nothing to do with being members of the royal family. We embrace our lives wholeheartedly. Otherwise, we are not really alive."

"But you're used to this craziness. Grace isn't."

"Do you not think the advantages outweigh the disadvantages?" he asked.

"Probably. Maybe. I don't know." She shrugged his grasp off her shoulders and stepped back, wrapping her arms around her waist. "This thing, whatever it is, between us—it's over now."

A dark void opened at his feet, and he balanced on the edge. "Eve, no! The damage is done." *No, that is the wrong thing to say.* "We won't need to keep our secret much longer. We can be together in public without any concern."

"No. I need to be Grace's mother now." Her voice was like stone. "You need to be Grace's father. The only contact we will have is in looking out for her best interests."

Her expression said she wasn't convinced he could be trusted with the latter.

"We cannot pretend that there is nothing between us." He reached for her, but she flinched a step backward. He dropped his hands, clenching them into fists against his thighs.

"It was only a…a liaison. Isn't that what you call your relationships?" she said. "It wasn't meant to be long term anyway."

But he wasn't ready for it to end. He had just discovered the delight of her. "It was not meant to be only two nights," he said.

"It shouldn't have been even one," she said. "Look at what a mess we made."

"No, not a mess. Remember what pleasure we gave each other, what joy we found together, what we can look forward to as we grow closer." His words held a desperation he couldn't suppress. "Eve, don't punish yourself for finding happiness or for giving it to me."

"It's not punishment. It's reality," she said, taking another step away from him, her posture rigid.

He had not felt this helpless since had gotten the news that Gabriel had been kidnapped. What words could he use to bring Eve back to him?

A quiet knock sounded on the office door. He wanted to curse and tell whoever it was to go away, but Eve went over to open it.

"*Lo siento, Su Majestad*, but you have a meeting at the palace in one hour," Bruno said.

"Cancel it," Luis said.

"It is with the U.S. ambassador," Bruno insisted.

"*Joder!*" They had a sensitive matter to discuss that couldn't wait. He turned to Eve. "You and Grace will come to the palace at…?" He looked at Bruno.

His assistant checked his tablet. "The two o'clock meeting can be canceled."

"Before two, then," Luis said. "We will talk. About everything."

She nodded, her braid moving against her shoulder. God, he wanted to sink his fingers into the thickness of it and use it to tilt back her head so he could feast on her mouth.

"I'll tell Grace what's happened," she said, her eyes unhappy.

He held her gaze. "Eve, she will be fine."

But would *he*?

CHAPTER 20

Eve stood in front of the door to Grace's suite, trying to pull her thoughts together. Fury, guilt, fear, and a yawning loneliness spiraled inside her. This conversation with her daughter would determine the trajectory of their lives, and Eve wasn't nearly prepared enough.

She squared her shoulders and knocked. "Grace, it's Mom."

"Hey!" Grace swung the door open, wearing one of the teal terry cloth bathrobes they'd found in the suites' closets. "I thought we weren't having breakfast until eight."

Eve stepped inside and hugged Grace, reveling in the smell of her daughter's freshly shampooed hair and the feel of her young, strong body.

Grace returned the hug before she leaned away to examine Eve's face. "Mom, are you okay?"

"Yes, but we have a situation." Eve tucked a strand of hair behind Grace's ear before she let her go. "We need to talk."

Eve sat on the sofa while Grace plunked down in a chair beside it. "What's going on?"

"A paparazzo took a photograph of your father and me on the beach two nights ago." Eve fiddled with her braid. "We were just walking, but Luis was holding a bottle of champagne, and we were laughing. The media outlet that bought the picture has decided I'm the king's new girlfriend...and they're going to identify me as such when the photo is published."

"I knew there was something going on between you two," Grace said with satisfaction. "But what's the big deal about the photo?"

Eve winced at what she would have to say next. "There is concern that Odette Fontaine might see the photo and recognize me, which would lead her to the conclusion that you are in Caleva as well. Evidently, she came to Iowa a few years ago to see you, and she might have seen me too."

"She was in Iowa?" Grace looked stunned.

"No one knows why she didn't contact you." Or they weren't telling, which was fine with Eve. "Something must have scared her away."

"Oh." Grace's voice was very small.

"Sweetie, be glad she didn't drag you into her madness." Eve's heart was breaking for her daughter.

"I just... It's strange to think she was there, and I didn't know it." Grace gave a little shiver. "Like she was stalking me."

"Or maybe she was just checking on you. She wanted to see how you had grown up." Eve took Grace's hand, twining their fingers together. "But that leads us to now. Your father is afraid that the photograph will trigger Odette into revealing your identity before you're ready. He believes they can get the photo suppressed for a few days, but that's the best we can hope for. He wants to make sure your story is told the right way in the media."

"I understand. They want to make the announcement about me before she can," Grace said.

"That means you need to decide what you want to be in relation to Luis and Caleva," Eve said, the weight of her daughter's choice bowing her shoulders. "But Luis wants to speak with you first…about the realities of being a royal."

"Raul has given me a pretty good idea," Grace said.

"He's told you about the media and lack of privacy? About the possible danger to you, like what happened to his cousin?" Eve nearly choked on the last one.

"Not so much about his cousin. I get the feeling that's sort of classified," Grace said. "But I asked him about the other issues. He was pretty honest that it's not all castles and tiaras."

Grace sounded so…adult. Having her student daughter living with her sometimes made her forget that Grace was nearly thirty and quite savvy. "That's good."

"But there are so many wonderful things about it." Grace's face lit up. "I could help the animals of an entire *country*, not just my vet practice. Maybe I could even influence more countries to follow Caleva's lead in fighting cruelty to animals. How amazing would that be?"

"I'm proud of you for being so passionate about it," Eve said with sincerity. But also with inward sorrow. She had lost Grace to the Dragóns. And she could no longer protect her from the dangers that might lie ahead.

Eve paced through all three rooms in their suite at Castillo Draconago, occasionally stopping to stare out a window at the view of the lushly flowering palace gardens dotted with statues and cascading fountains. She was waiting while Luis had his promised heart-to-heart discussion with Grace about the downsides of being a princess.

All those neatly raked gravel paths and artfully pruned shrubs shone a spotlight on the differences between Grace's future life in Caleva and her former life in the modest old farmhouse in Iowa. Eve already knew what Grace's choice would be. Her daughter wouldn't be scared away by anything Luis told her. Eve just wanted Grace to step into her new position with her eyes wide open.

Eve sighed.

She was going to miss Nana Nelle's house and all the memories she and Grace had made there. Tromping through drifts of snow to haul in the Christmas tree they had cut down themselves. Grace racing around the backyard with whatever dogs were in residence at that time. Sitting on the wicker porch swing, drinking iced tea and eating Scotcheroos. Grace bringing her a baby robin that had fallen out of its nest, the tiny creature so gently cupped in her daughter's young hands. Sitting on the braided rug in front of a roaring fire, playing Scrabble and sipping hot chocolate.

She swiped her palms across her cheeks to keep the tears from falling and spotting her silk blouse. She would make a new life here in Caleva amid the fragrant *vaho* hibiscus and giant green lizards. Maybe she could find a house by the ocean. That would be a dramatic change for her landlocked Iowan soul. As long as it was far enough away from Luis that she didn't get constantly reminded of what they had shared so briefly.

A knock sounded on the door, and she called, "Come in."

Bridget stepped in and closed the door behind her. "*Señora, Su Majestad* requests that you join him now."

Eve followed the bodyguard through the corridors of the palace until they entered a sitting room and stopped at a large oak door. Bridget rapped on it twice before opening it and gesturing Eve through. As the door clicked closed behind her, Eve had a blurred impression of a huge ornate desk on one side of the large paneled space and a small dining table in another corner before her gaze settled on Grace and Luis. They sat across from each other in two leather armchairs in a seating area that also held a couch and coffee table. Luis stood as she came into the room. His tailored gray suit showed off his broad shoulders and long legs, making her picture the swells and valleys of muscle underneath the fabric all too vividly.

Their gazes caught and held, an electric current of emotions crackling between them.

"I told her the truth," Luis said, his voice deep and raw.

"Thank you," Eve said before she tore her attention away from him to gauge how her daughter had weathered Luis's revelations. "Sweetheart, how are you feeling?" she asked as she sat on the sofa and leaned in to search her daughter's face. She found no fear, just a touch of shock.

"A little overwhelmed," Grace said before she lifted her chin. "But I've made my choice. After graduation, I want to return to Caleva and be a full-fledged princess, in line for the throne after Raul. That will give me the strongest platform to work from."

Then her shoulders sagged, and she scooted onto the couch beside Eve, winding her arms around her. "It's a lot, Mom, and I'm sorry to drag you away from home, but you'll come with me, right?"

"You know I will," Eve reassured her with a squeeze, even as she fought back tears. She had expected Grace's decision—had thought she was braced for it—but the reality of it still hit her like a mule's kick in the gut.

Her little Grace would be a princess. It was surreal.

"I'm so proud of you, sweetheart," Eve choked out. "You'll do great things."

Then she couldn't stop the tears, which made Grace cry too. They simply held each other for a long moment before Grace sat back, her mascara smudged, her face glistening with tear tracks. Without thinking, Eve looked around and found Luis leaning forward, a tooled leather box of tissues in his hand.

Not a handkerchief this time.

Grace yanked a couple tissues out of the box and handed one to Eve.

Eve mopped her face and then grabbed another tissue to clean up Grace's smudged mascara. Her daughter smiled as Eve dabbed at the black streaks.

Eve balled up the soggy paper in her fist and snuck a glance at Luis. He sat on the edge of his chair, his face taut with concern.

He had gotten what he wanted. She had known he would the minute she'd realized who he was back in the lawyer's office in Ames. He could offer Grace an entire country. Her daughter would be crazy to turn it down.

"I would give you more time to digest this, but we have further decisions to make." His voice was gentle.

"I'm fine," Grace said. "What else do we need to talk about?"

His lips thinned to a grim line before he said, "Bruno will schedule a press conference as soon as I tell him when, but we need to decide on what we will say about your background, *hija mía*."

"You mean about Odette Fontaine," Grace said.

"I do not want your introduction to Caleva to be tarnished by Odette's ugliness," Luis said, his voice low.

"I don't see how we get around that," Grace said. "All our friends in Ames know I'm adopted, so we can't say that Mom is my birth mother."

"Not to mention that there's adoption paperwork on record," Eve pointed out.

"No, we cannot use that subterfuge," Luis said, "but we might be able to arrange another one. We will say that your birth mother is deceased and that we will not reveal her name to protect her family's privacy." He grimaced. "Of course, there are certain members of the media who feel that no one is entitled to privacy, so they will go digging. We will need to mislead them. Mikel can find a deceased Calevan woman who fits the parameters, and Quinn can lay a false electronic trail that connects her to your adoption records."

"That's real spy stuff." Grace sounded impressed.

"But what about Odette? What would stop her from insisting that she's Grace's birth mother?" Eve asked. "Won't the DNA in that databank be a problem?"

"That DNA record has been permanently erased," Luis said. "We would say that Odette's claim is that of a criminal convicted of kidnapping and attempted murder. With our false trail, her claim should not receive much credence."

"But she could still stir up that ugliness you were trying to avoid," Eve said, dreading that for her daughter.

"I'll talk to her," Grace said, sitting up straight. "I can persuade her."

"No!" Luis's voice was sharp. "I don't want her to feel she has any power over you."

"I'm not afraid of her," Grace said. "Which means that she has no power."

"*Ay, mi cielito*, you do not know her," Luis said, gentling his tone. "She does not think like a normal person."

Eve wanted to agree with Luis in order to protect their daughter from a monster, but she knew Grace better than that.

"I need to meet her," Grace said, her chin lifted. "Maybe I can solve our problem at the same time."

Luis turned to Eve with a plea in his eyes, but she shook her head. Before she had adopted Grace, Eve had read as much as she could on how an adopted child felt. She had learned that no matter how loving the adoptive mother was, a child still carried the wound of abandonment deep inside. Grace had the chance to confront the woman who had chosen to give her away. It was important to let her do it.

"I want to go with you to the prison," Eve said, putting her arm around Grace and feeling the tension in her shoulders. "I'll wait outside while you meet Odette, but I'll be there when you are done."

Maybe she was a coward, but she did not want to watch Grace face the monster who was her biological mother while being powerless to help her daughter through the ordeal.

"Of course," Luis said. "I will accompany you as well."

Grace took a deep breath. "Okay, how soon can we do it?"

"Tomorrow," Luis said. "Tonight, I want you to meet the rest of my family."

✠

At seven in the evening, Luis walked into the Sala de los Enebros, the juniper-wood-paneled sitting room where the family always gathered before dinner. His assembled relatives all turned to fix their gazes on him.

"What is this urgent news you have for us?" Lorenzo asked, his forehead furrowed with concern. "You are not ill?"

"Not at all," Luis said, touched by Lorenzo's worry. His brother was not generally demonstrative. "I have good news."

"Do not keep us in suspense," Hélène, Lorenzo's wife, said from where she perched gracefully on a velvet-and-gilt chair, her blond hair gleaming.

Luis swept his gaze around the people in the room, the inner circle of his family. He nodded to Raul, leaning casually against the arm of a sofa, and smiled at Quinn and Gabriel, who sat close beside each other on a green love seat.

"I am happy to announce that our family is about to expand. I have a daughter, a half sister to Raul." He watched surprise and shock ripple over their faces.

"You have done a DNA test?" Lorenzo asked as the implications sank in. "Of course you have."

"Yes, there is no doubt that she is mine," Luis said.

"May we inquire who her mother is?" Hélène asked.

"I will get to that," Luis said. "But I wish to tell you more about Grace first. Her mother gave birth to her and immediately gave her up for adoption. A young couple from Iowa became her parents. Unfortunately, they divorced soon thereafter, and her mother, Eve Howard, raised her as a single mother, with courage, resourcefulness, and strength. Grace is an impressive young woman because of that upbringing. She is in her last year of veterinary school."

"*That's* why the American vet students came here," Gabriel exclaimed.

Luis smiled, mentally giving Quinn full marks for her discretion. She had not even told her fiancé about the potential veterinary school. "Precisely."

"Ah, she is here in Caleva," Hélène said. "Will we be meeting her this evening?"

"Both Grace and her adoptive mother will be joining us," Luis said. "But I wished to give you time to absorb the news."

Gabriel stood and approached Luis, his face alight. "I am very happy for you, *Tío*. You have always wanted a larger family." He ignored protocol and laid his hands on Luis's shoulders to give them an affectionate squeeze. "That's why you made me feel as though I were Raul's brother, not a mere cousin."

"You're just relieved to get moved down the line of succession, Gabri," Raul joked.

"Well, yes, that too," Gabriel said with his brilliant smile.

"*Gracias, sobrino mío,*" Luis said, matching Gabriel's grasp of his shoulders. Now that his nephew had found the love of his life, Gabriel had become the emotional lodestone of the family. He did not hesitate to express what others might not. Luis cherished his openness.

"We are all delighted to welcome a new member to the family," Hélène said smoothly. "Especially a young one to liven us up."

"Raul, when did you know?" Lorenzo asked. "About your *media hermana*, your half sister."

"As soon as Pater first found out about the possibility," Raul said, avoiding the touchy part of the situation.

Lorenzo turned to Luis. "How long ago was that?"

Now for the ugly part. "The day Raul gave the opening speech for the joint *consejos*."

"When you were supposed to give the address," Lorenzo said. "But why?"

"Because Odette Fontaine blackmailed me into canceling my appearance. She forgot that I had a worthy substitute, who handled the speech superbly." Luis let his proud gaze rest on his son.

"Odette?" Hélène frowned. "What did she—?" Horror dawned on her elegant face. "*Mon Dieu, non!* It cannot be! Odette is the mother?"

Luis understood Hélène's reaction, but anger still flared.

"Odette is Grace's biological mother, but do not visit the sins of the mother on the child," Luis admonished with all the authority of his position. "When you meet Grace, you will see that she is nothing like her birth mother."

"Why didn't Odette tell you about the child back then?" Hélène asked. "She wanted you to marry her. That would have forced your hand."

"She claims she didn't know she was pregnant when I broke off the relationship," Luis said, the anger fading to pain. "When she discovered her condition, she decided to punish me by giving our child away."

"She could not have chosen a crueler revenge," Lorenzo said, his eyes dark with sorrow. "I am so sorry."

"*Gracias, mi hermano,*" Luis said, touched by his brother's understanding. "But at least our story has a happy ending. Grace will join our family as the princess she should have always been."

"Does Grace know who her biological mother is?" Gabriel asked, touching the ear that had been reconstructed after his kidnapping. "That is a heavy burden to shoulder."

"She knows," Luis said. "She is troubled by it, but she was raised by a woman who overflows with goodness and decency. That gives Grace the confidence to repudiate the ugly legacy of her birth mother."

Raul spoke up. "I have spent enough time with Grace to be certain that she shares nothing of Odette's insanity. She is caring and empathetic. She intends to use her position as princess to advocate against cruelty to animals."

Luis nodded to his son with gratitude.

"What about her adoptive mother?" Hélène asked. "How does she feel about her daughter's new position?"

Eve's tears from that morning haunted him. "It is perhaps harder for her than for Grace," he admitted. "But she plans to move to Caleva after Grace graduates from veterinary school." He looked at Quinn. "I hope you can help your fellow Americans acclimate to Caleva."

"Honestly, it isn't hard to love it here, but I'll be happy to do whatever I can," Quinn said.

"Thank you," Luis said with a smile at the young woman. He added an undertone of steel when he scanned the assembled group and said, "Are you ready to welcome my daughter into the family?"

"Of course we will welcome her," Hélène said. As always, she was aware of the nuances of a difficult situation. "She is your child."

Hélène had more reason than anyone but Gabriel to hate Odette. Luis admired her generosity in setting aside the terrible half of Grace's parentage.

Luis nodded and pulled out his phone to tap the button notifying Bridget that Grace and Eve should join them.

Eve was concerned when Grace reached for her hand as they followed Bridget through the corridors of the palace.

"It will be fine," Eve said, giving her daughter's fingers a reassuring squeeze. "If they don't behave, your father will throw them in the dungeon."

Grace gave a choked-off laugh. "It's handy to have a king for a father."

Sometimes. Eve wished with all her heart that Luis had been someone *less.* Less prominent. Less constrained by tradition. Less devastatingly attractive.

But then he wouldn't be Luis.

As they rounded a corner, Eve nearly gasped. Luis stood waiting in the hallway, looking like all the things she wished he wasn't—regal, commanding, and sexy as hell in his pale blue shirt and charcoal gray trousers. Even worse, when he saw them, his eyes lit with warmth and excitement.

"Buenas noches," he said, smiling. "My family eagerly awaits you. Please come in." He opened the door and gestured them through.

Eve hung back so that Grace could go first. Unfortunately, that allowed Luis to place his hand on the small of Eve's back to usher her in. His touch scorched through the fabric of her dress like a brand, the heat radiating across her skin to settle deep inside her. She broke the contact as soon as she could, stepping away from him so that he could be beside his daughter.

Of course, all the people in the room had turned to face them, and she felt caught in a spotlight. Then everyone stood as Luis escorted Grace into the room.

"Lorenzo, my daughter, Grace, and her mother, Eve," Luis said, stopping in front of a man who was nearly his twin. Lorenzo lacked Luis's air of command, though, and a shadow of sadness enfolded him. "My brother, Lorenzo, *el Duque de Bruma.*"

Lorenzo took Grace's proffered hand in both of his. "I am delighted to meet you. Welcome to the family. We are very happy to have you here." His smile seemed sincere if subdued.

"A pleasure to meet you too," Grace said.

Lorenzo then turned to Eve with his hand held out. "An honor. My brother speaks highly of you and what an excellent mother you are."

Eve murmured something polite as she flushed at the praise from Luis. But of course he would tell them that to counteract the taint of Odette Fontaine.

It went on that way as they were introduced to the others. Everyone spoke words of welcome and joy at having a new addition to the family. They seemed sincere, but it was a relief to greet Quinn, who said in a low voice as Luis moved on, "I know what it's like to meet them all at once. You're doing great."

It was overwhelming. These people—even Quinn as Gabriel's fiancée—knew exactly where they belonged in the world. They weren't arrogant or condescending or overbearing. There was no need to be. They were royal dukes and duchesses and princes and kings. Their place in the hierarchy was crystal clear, and it was at the very top.

Grace was holding up well, but Eve could see the tension in her shoulders. Yet when her daughter faced each of the Dragóns, her features were reflected there. It was clear that Grace belonged in this room.

Eve did not.

From now on, she would be a visitor in her daughter's world. Eve had to hold on to her smile as her lips threatened to tremble.

As Grace was drawn into conversation with the younger generation, Luis stopped beside Eve. "Our daughter is amazing," he said, love ringing in his voice.

That nearly tipped Eve into weeping. She swallowed and managed to choke out, "Yes, she is."

He must have heard her struggle, because he lowered his head to speak with soft concern. "I hope you are glad to meet my family. I want you to know and like them."

She nodded, not trusting her voice.

Somehow, he guessed her feelings. "Eve, you are a part of this family as well. You are Grace's mother, and that secures you a place of great respect here."

"I...I appreciate that," she said.

Hélène approached them, rescuing Eve from Luis's kindness. She took a deep breath to fight back the tears.

"I know that Luis has enlisted Quinn's assistance," the blond duchess said. "But I wish to offer you mine as well. I have spent a fair amount of time in the U.S., so I am aware of the cultural differences." Her smile softened the perfect angles of her face.

"Thank you," Eve said, understanding that Hélène also offered the experience of someone closer to her own age. "I look forward to learning about Caleva from your perspective."

A woman dressed in black trousers, a white shirt, and a Calevan green tie approached and bowed silently to Luis. He nodded before offering one arm to Eve and the other to Hélène. "Let us go into dinner. I am fortunate to be able to escort two beautiful women to the table."

Eve slid her hand around his elbow and braced herself for the unwanted thrill of touching the firm muscles of his forearm under the fabric of his shirt. How long would it take to stop reacting to him this way?

As they approached the table, the same woman who had signaled Luis about dinner pulled out the chair to the left of the head of the table. Luis smoothly handed Hélène into the proffered seat before bringing Eve around to the right-hand chair, which he pulled out himself. When she was seated, he went to the head of the table and sat without ceremony, although she caught him wincing slightly. At least she wasn't the only one still feeling the aftereffects of their riding expedition.

She glanced down the table to see Raul holding a chair for Grace. Gabriel and then Quinn sat on the same side as Eve, facing the prince and her daughter, while Lorenzo sat at the foot of the table. In between, the glow of candles in silver candlesticks reflected off crystal, silver flatware, and the gilt dragons painted on the chargers at each place setting. Not exactly casual.

As soon as everyone was settled, Luis surprised her by saying a brief prayer of thanks. He must have seen her puzzlement, because he leaned over to say, "It is a tradition within the palace to always say grace."

She nodded as servers placed small plates of something that looked similar to Iowa ham balls in front of each diner.

"Chef Marta thanks you for the recipe," Luis said, a smile lighting his eyes. "Although she says that she has given it a Calevan twist. I'm not sure what that means."

"Ham balls!" Raul exclaimed. "I dream of these!"

As Hélène looked confused, Eve said, "They're a specialty from our home state of Iowa." She turned to Luis. "It was kind of you to ask your chef to make them for us."

"It was Raul's request, not mine," Luis said, spearing a ham ball with his silver fork. "Not that I'm complaining."

Everyone politely complimented the Iowan cuisine. Eve would have laughed if she hadn't felt so out of her depth. Even the so-called informal dining room seemed calculated to overwhelm her, with its green silk-covered walls, gilt-framed paintings, and tall windows hung with yards and yards of matching silk.

She mentally squared her shoulders. She was here to support Grace and to make sure no one made her daughter feel in any way unwelcome.

As dinner progressed, it became apparent that she need not have worried. Luis firmly steered the conversation to topics that Grace would enjoy or was knowledgeable about. He made sure their daughter shone in front of his family.

His family reciprocated, drawing Grace out and paying flattering attention to her words. Of course, Eve was included, both by Luis's skill and by the fact that Iowa and veterinary matters were prominent in the discussion.

By the end of the main course, Eve was glowing with pride at how brilliantly Grace was handling the situation. Even more, she might admit to liking Luis's family members.

She turned to tell Luis and found his gaze resting on Grace, his face filled with the same pride she felt. A sudden lightness floated through her, as though a weight had slid away. For a moment, she couldn't figure out why, and then it hit her.

She would no longer be a single parent. Luis would share her responsibility for supporting and protecting Grace from now on. For all that it made her sad to loosen the close bond she and Grace shared, it was also a relief to know that there was another person in the world who would always be there for their daughter. Not to mention that Grace's other parent could wield his considerable power and influence on her behalf.

Before she thought about it, Eve leaned in to touch Luis's hand where it rested on the linen tablecloth. "Thank you," she said. "You are a good father."

He turned his hand to grasp hers before she could withdraw it, his fingers strong and warm around hers. "It is easy to be a father to Grace. You have raised an exceptional young woman."

He tightened his grip a moment before releasing her hand, and she mourned the loss of the connection.

She couldn't stop herself from thinking of the secret passage that led from the king's chambers to where she would sleep tonight.

Luis felt the imprint of Eve's hand against his skin after he reluctantly let go. Her unexpected touch had sent a sear of desire through him, even as her words made his heart swell. She had acknowledged him as their daughter's father with a look of happiness. No longer was he the interloper, the bringer of danger, the disruptive influence. A tension he hadn't recognized he carried eased.

Now he wanted to pull Eve into his arms and kiss her until she agreed to come to his bed again.

Instead, he sat back and watched his family embrace his daughter and her mother. Contentment flowed through him like a warm, buoyant river. Somehow, he had sensed that he was missing a piece for all the years of Grace's life. Now he had found her, and his family was complete.

His pleasure faltered as he realized that Eve's presence was part of his feeling of well-being. If she were not at the table, he would not be experiencing the same delight in the gathering. Yes, he wanted to tear off her clothes and taste every inch of her skin, but he also wanted her laughter, her strength, her good sense, and her bone-deep decency. She was an anchor that he could trust.

"What is it?" Eve asked in a low voice, and he realized he was frowning.

He couldn't lie to her. "I was thinking about how important you are to this." He swept one hand around to indicate the people at the table.

And to me. But he couldn't say that yet.

She shook her head. "Grace will do fine. Your family is being lovely. I'm surprised to say this, but I like them."

"Surprised? Why?" Yet gratification warmed him.

"Oh, gee, I don't know. Maybe because they're royalty, and their lives are as different from mine as…as a Martian's." She spoke lightly, but he heard the conviction in her words.

"What is the saying? 'We still put our pants on one leg at a time.'" He matched her tone.

"No, you have a valet to hold your pants while you leap into them with both feet," she said.

And there it was…the laughter he treasured.

Hélène was watching them with a speculative expression, so Luis included her in the conversation to keep her from drawing too many conclusions.

Conclusions he wasn't sure of himself.

CHAPTER 21

The next morning, Luis once again sat at the head warden's desk at CárcelMax, waiting for Odette to be brought to him. Mikel had used the same methodology as the last time Luis had faced his ex-lover, so only the most trusted bodyguards knew of this visit.

Grace and Eve would follow an hour later in another nondescript vehicle, but Luis intended to threaten Odette into behaving herself when she met their daughter. However, he would let Grace try to persuade her birth mother to keep their connection a secret. If he were to ask Odette to keep it secret, she would broadcast the news to the world out of pure spite.

The door opened, and he stiffened as Odette was led into the office, the chains of her shackles clinking softly. She looked thinner, her skin even more pasty against the yellow prison clothes.

When she saw him, a cruel smile curved her lips. "Well, well, a second visit from the king. I am honored." She dipped into a curtsy made awkward by the guards holding her arms. She straightened and examined him for a long moment. "You look hale and healthy. You're feeling well these days?"

"Sit." The anger at her insolence ignited inside him, but it burned cold today.

The guards released her as she sank onto the wooden chair in front of the desk. "Leave us," Luis told them, waiting until the door was closed behind them.

He sat silent, searching for a resemblance between the woman in front of him and his daughter. The red hair, of course, although Odette's lacked the healthy shine of Grace's. He continued to examine the shape of her face, her ears, even her hands. With a surge of relief, he found nothing else to demonstrate they were related.

"Did you have something to say to me?" she prodded.

Luis smiled inwardly. Speaking first showed weakness.

"I found our daughter," he said.

Interest flared in her eyes. "I assumed you would."

"If you had bothered to talk with her, you would have learned she is a very impressive young woman," Luis said.

"Have you acknowledged her as yours?"

"In private, yes." Luis was not going to discuss that matter further with Odette. "She wishes to meet you."

Odette's head snapped back as though he had slapped her, but she recovered. "Of course she does. I am her mother."

"No, you merely gave birth to her. The woman who raised Grace is her mother." Luis let his control slip enough to show Odette his steel. "At least you chose well on that front."

"You approve of...Eve, isn't it? How does she feel about her adopted daughter suddenly acquiring a rather overwhelming father?"

Luis couldn't stop the tiny curve at the corners of his lips as he thought of Eve's initial reaction to his identity. "She is coming to terms with it."

"What choice does she have?" Odette's voice was pure acid. "Your wish is a command."

"You have never understood what it means to be king," Luis said. "Today, I am here as a father first."

"Then tell me why Grace is so eager to meet me." Odette lifted her cuffed hands. "I am a criminal, after all."

"Perhaps she will tell you herself," Luis said before he leaned forward and locked gazes with Odette. "But whatever she says, you will treat her with respect. You will not deliberately inflict any emotional pain on her. You will pretend to be a normal human being with some semblance of human decency. You fooled all of us for years, so you can fool your daughter for an hour."

"Are you going to sit in on our heartfelt reunion and censor my every word?" Odette asked, but he saw a flicker of uncertainty in her face.

He *wanted* to be there in the room, ready to shield his daughter from the monster in front of him, but Grace needed to face Odette on her own. "Grace is a strong young woman. I trust her to deal with you." He lowered his voice to a snarl. "But I will be watching every second of your meeting. If you say or do anything to traumatize her, I will end your encounter immediately and make your life here a living hell. If you damage Grace in any way, you will be on your knees, pleading for an end to your suffering."

Panic flashed across her face before she pasted on a smile. "You used to be softer," she said. "But you've been king a long time. And kings develop a ruthless streak because they wield the power to make and break people's lives. You've broken me, *querida*. Are you happy now?"

Revulsion roiled through him at the endearment, but he didn't let her see it. "You were broken long ago." He pushed the button to call the guards.

As the door opened, Odette said, "Don't you want me to swear I will be good?"

"Your promises are worth nothing." Luis beckoned the guards forward. "I'm counting on your self-interest."

Luis stood at the barred window in the warden's office, his gaze on the nondescript brown car that had carried Eve and Grace to this grim, unhappy place. As he waited for Grace to be escorted through the layers of steel doors, he tried to think of a way to dissuade her from meeting with Odette. For all of his threats, he felt powerless to stop his former lover from hurting his daughter. Odette could spew too much poison before Luis would be able to stop her.

Luis did not like feeling powerless. Especially when he had promised Eve that he would be here to protect their daughter. If he failed, he would be failing the two most important women in his world right now.

The private door to the warden's office swung open, and Mikel escorted Grace inside before leaving again. She had already shed the bulky coat and hat used to disguise her and was wearing a green blouse and tailored gray trousers. She looked pale but calm.

"Hija mía," he said, going over to kiss her on both cheeks. "You can still change your mind about this meeting. I *wish* you would change your mind."

"If I don't face Odette, I will always have questions," Grace said, her chin lifted and her eyes clear with resolve.

"I fear you will have yet more questions after you meet her," Luis said, resignation in his voice.

"That will be her fault, not mine," Grace said. "I will have done my best."

"If only more people understood that concept," Luis said, admiring her mature wisdom.

He led her to the warden's large leather chair. "You will remain behind this desk at all times for your own protection." He pointed to the red button bolted to the top of the desk. "This is the panic button. Do not hesitate to push it if you are at all concerned...about anything. Mikel and I will be in the next room." He gestured to the door she had entered through. "We will come immediately."

"Mikel said that Odette will be in shackles, so I don't see how she could hurt me," Grace said.

"There are many ways to hurt someone without physical contact," Luis said, his heart twisting at the terrible potential. "We will also be watching and listening through the cameras in here. If I feel the conversation needs to be stopped, I will do so."

She met his gaze straight on. "I know you and Mom believe that's necessary, but it isn't. Please do not interrupt us unless my life is in danger."

She was strong, his daughter, but she had never dealt with someone like Odette. He would not hesitate to shut down the meeting if he judged it was going in a dangerous direction.

He held the chair while Grace seated herself. "Are you ready?"

Grace nodded without hesitation, but her knuckles were white where she held the chair arms.

He bent to kiss her. "Your courage will carry you through."

That earned him a strained smile of gratitude. With reluctance, he left his daughter alone to face her monster of a birth mother.

In the adjoining room, Mikel had set up four monitors to display feeds from the four cameras in the warden's office.

"We will be able to surveille Odette from multiple angles to ensure that she doesn't have some hidden weapon or tool to unlock her restraints," his security chief explained as Luis seated himself in front of the array of screens.

Mikel spoke into his cell phone. "Bring the prisoner into the warden's office now."

On the screens, Odette entered the room, looking slumped and hopeless as she shuffled between the two large guards.

Grace rose from her chair, watching as her birth mother sat and one guard fastened the chain to two clamps on the floor.

"Is that really necessary?" Grace asked, a note of distress in her voice.

"It is by order of *el rey*," the guard said.

Luis blew out a breath of relief when Grace did not try to countermand his order.

Odette's head had been bowed throughout the exchange, but when the guard refused to unchain her, she raised her gaze, and Luis saw the scorching anger in her eyes. Grace must have seen it, too, because she sat abruptly and pushed the chair back as though to put more distance between them.

The anger dissipated as swiftly as it appeared, and Odette surveyed Grace without concealing her examination. "So, Luis found you."

"Yes," Grace said, staring back at her birth mother with the same open curiosity.

"How do you like being a princess?" Odette asked. "Is it all you dreamed of?"

"I never dreamed of being a princess. I wanted to be a vet."

"Ah, yes, helping our fellow creatures. A noble profession." Odette's voice held an undercurrent of mockery.

"Being a princess will allow me to help more of them," Grace said.

"Even nobler." Odette sat back in the chair with a rattle of chains.

Grace remained silent, refusing to engage. Luis admired his daughter's toughness in the face of Odette's derision. After a beat, his daughter said, "Why did you put me up for adoption?"

Luis heard the tension in Grace's voice and braced himself for whatever twisted reason Odette would give.

Odette sighed. "I was young and stupid and angry with your father for rejecting me. In retrospect, I should have told him I was pregnant. I think he would have married me, and I would have been queen. Instead…" She lifted her chained hands with a shrug. Then the anger blazed again. "He didn't deserve me. Or you."

"Why didn't you raise me yourself without telling Luis I was his?" Grace asked.

"I had plans, ambitious plans. A child would have gotten in the way of those. I wouldn't have climbed to be CEO of Archambeau if I had been held back by worrying about you. Does that hurt your feelings?"

"You never knew me, so how could it hurt my feelings?" But Luis saw the pain in Grace's stiff posture.

"Because you'll always feel abandoned by your real mother," Odette said, twisting the knife. "I've read the studies about adopted children."

"I feel grateful that you gave me to my mother. She's an amazing person," Grace said. "And she has never ordered the kidnapping or mutilation of an innocent man."

Luis wanted to stand and applaud his daughter's refusal to be intimidated.

Odette, though, smiled at the attack. "You're wondering if, deep down inside, you're like me."

"No, because I was raised by a woman of decency and honor. I also have a father who is a fine human being," Grace said. "Nurture beats nature in my case."

"You think Luis is a good person?" Odette gave a sneering laugh. "He's a king. He has to be ruthless to make the necessary decisions on a daily basis. With every choice he makes, someone loses. He is unperturbed by that, believe me."

Anger burned in Luis's throat. Odette's insinuation was persuasive because it held a kernel of truth.

"That doesn't make him a psychopath." The word hung in the air.

"That's what they told you I am?" Fury blazed in Odette's eyes again. "I'm perfectly sane. I have excellent reasons for everything I've done."

And that made her a psychopath.

Grace looked sick to her stomach, but she didn't push the panic button. "Why did you come to Iowa three years ago?" she asked.

"Curiosity. I wanted to see how you had turned out."

"Why didn't you talk to me?" Luis heard the hurt again and hoped Odette would not.

"Because once I saw you, I couldn't. You have my hair, but those fucking Dragón genes wiped out everything else about me. You look just like *him*." Odette practically spat the word before she calmed down and examined Grace again dispassionately. "You're not beautiful, but you are striking. You look like Raul and Gabriel."

Luis half rose in fury at the cruel insult to his daughter's beauty. He wanted to smash the words back down Odette's throat as Grace looked stricken.

"And then I heard you speak." Odette shuddered. "You sound like an uneducated peasant."

"I sound like I'm from Iowa." Now Grace's voice was rock steady.

Luis subsided back into his chair with a surge of satisfaction at his daughter's courage.

"Exactly."

"You gave me to people who lived in Iowa, so what did you expect?" Grace pointed out.

"I suppose I thought your breeding would overcome your environment." Odette shrugged.

"You have no right to criticize my environment or my upbringing," Grace said. "You lost that right when you put me up for adoption."

"Ah, the young one has teeth. Perhaps you *are* my daughter." Odette laughed. "Don't look so horrified."

"I'm only horrified that you would ever approve of anything I do."

Odette suddenly looked bored. "Do you have any other questions? Because I am ready to go back to my cell."

"Yes. I want your promise that you won't tell the media that you're my mother." Grace's voice held no plea, no desperation. "That is the least you can do for me."

"I gave you to a good mother, didn't I? That is where my obligation ends."

"I think you have one more obligation to me. Since you refused to do the hard work of being my mother, you cannot now claim that I am your daughter. I want your promise that you will not do so." Now his daughter put a touch of command in her tone.

Brava, hija mía!

"If I'm a psychopath, your logic won't work on me, will it?" Odette bared her teeth in a grimace of a smile.

Grace just waited, her gaze never faltering.

Odette stared back at her. Finally, the older woman shrugged. "All right. I won't claim you as my daughter. For now."

"Is that a promise?"

"You can call it that, if it makes you happy," Odette said.

Grace nodded, and Luis waited for the signal that she was ready to end the meeting.

It did not come, and he clenched his fists on the desk in front of him.

"That's why you dragged me in here?" Odette asked after a moment's silence. "Not to finally meet your real mother? I'm a little offended."

"You're not my real mother," Grace said. "I did want to meet you, though. I needed to see if there was any of you in me. I'm relieved that there is not." She said it with confidence.

"Time will tell, won't it?" Odette said. "Now, let me go back to my cell where I don't have to deal with needy children."

"I don't need you," Grace said. "I have a mother and a father. Unlike you, I am loved."

"Being loved is overrated." Odette shifted to stare directly into the camera above Grace's head for a long moment. Then she leaned forward to focus a malevolent glare on Grace. "Tell your father that I'm remaining silent about being your mother for your sake, not his." Once again, she flicked a glance at the camera before she sat back. "Also, I plan to stick around to see how you manage as a princess."

"With the support network I have, I'll manage just fine," Grace said as she pushed the button to indicate she was finished with the meeting.

Mikel sent in the two guards. After they unlocked Odette's shackles from the floor clamps and Odette rose from her chair, Grace also stood.

"Will you come see me again?" Odette asked, her voice curious rather than pleading.

Grace thought a minute. "I don't think so."

Relief cascaded through Luis.

"In that case, farewell," Odette said. "Maybe you'll come to my funeral."

Grace shook her head.

The moment the door closed behind Odette, Luis raced into the warden's office. He examined Grace's face, finding tears welling in her eyes. "Are you all right, *hija mía?*" he asked in a gentle voice.

She blinked a few times. "She says she won't tell the media I'm her daughter 'right now.' It's not worth much, but I think she meant it for the present."

He touched her arm. "That was well done. But I am concerned with how you felt about meeting her."

"She was brutally honest. She could have lied and pretended to regret her actions, but maybe this way is better for me. I felt no connection with her at all." One tear tracked down her cheek.

"I'm so sorry." He enveloped her in his arms, and she leaned into him with a little sob. He stroked his palm over her hair and murmured words of comfort in Spanish and English.

After a few moments, she pushed away. "I think I should go to Mom. She'll want to know what happened."

"Of course," he said, releasing her with reluctance. He wanted to soothe away all the ugliness of her encounter, but he understood that she needed to see her real mother. The one who loved her and had cared for her all her life.

Eve sat in the back of a bland brown SUV parked in a small, concealed lot beside Caleva's maximum security prison. The prison looked like a modern corporate headquarters except for the two perimeters of high, electrified fences surrounding it, with access via heavy steel gates staffed by uniformed guards with serious-looking guns. Cameras were everywhere as well. Mikel had told her that no one had ever escaped from CárcelMax, and she believed it. It had given her cold chills to watch Grace disappear into the place through a blank steel door, even though she'd been escorted by four large, scary-looking bodyguards.

Her chills turned icy at the thought of Grace facing her psychopath of a birth mother. Eve wanted to be there so badly, but Grace needed to do this on her own. If Eve had listened in, it would have changed the dynamic of the meeting. Grace had to be able to say what she wanted to without worrying about hurting Eve's feelings.

Luis and Mikel were monitoring the encounter, so she would have to trust them to take care of her daughter.

But the waiting was killing her. Her fingers cramped, and she unknotted the tense tangle of her hands in her lap to stretch them. Glancing at her watch, she couldn't believe that only fifteen minutes had passed.

Luis had limited Grace's meeting with Odette to an hour, but so much damage could be done in that stretch of time. Grace was a strong person, but she had no experience with the kind of horror someone like Odette could inflict. Even worse, Grace would be wondering if she had inherited any of her birth mother's insanity.

Eve buried her face in her hands with a moan of helplessness.

"Are you all right, *señora?*" her driver, Enrique, asked.

Eve lifted her head. "Do you have children?"

"Only nieces and nephews, but many of them," he said.

"Imagine your favorite niece going into this terrible place to face a woman who committed a hideous crime. A woman your niece shares genes with."

After a moment of silence, Enrique said, "How may I help you?"

"Tell me about your nieces and nephews. All of them."

Eve lost count of Enrique's relatives and began to wonder if he was making some of them up to keep her distracted. Then he went silent, and Eve realized he was listening to his earpiece.

Another glance at her watch told her that thirty more minutes had passed. After a moment, he said, "They're on their way out."

"Oh, thank God!" she said. "And bless you, Enrique, for keeping me sane."

Eve locked her gaze on the steel door, restraining herself from jumping out of the car as it swung open. She could barely see Grace because she was surrounded by bodyguards. Enrique remained inside the car—guarding Eve, as he had explained earlier. It was strange to need guarding.

And then Grace's guards were hustling her into the car before one climbed in beside Enrique, and the others piled into their escort car.

Grace pulled off the knitted cap that had concealed her hair and threw her arms around Eve. "I'm so glad Odette gave me to you," she said, her voice muffled in Eve's shoulder.

"Oh, sweetie, what happened?" Eve wanted to strangle Odette with her bare hands.

After a long moment, Grace slid out of Eve's grasp. "Do you have any hand sanitizer?" she asked. "I need to get the feel of that place off me."

"Of course." Eve dug in her purse for the small bottle she always carried.

Grace poured a generous pool of the liquid into one palm, handed the bottle back to Eve, and rubbed her hands together long and hard. Then she took a deep breath.

"She looked horrible, slumped and sickly and sad. And she was in chains. They even locked the chains into brackets on the floor, as though this pathetic-looking creature was going to attack me. I felt sorry for her until she looked at me." Grace gave a little shiver. "The anger in her eyes was terrifying, and then I was glad she was locked down."

"She didn't try to get to you, did she?" Eve took Grace's hand because she needed to touch her daughter.

Grace shook her head. "She wasn't physically violent." She turned to look at Eve, and her face was pale. "I think she did me a favor. She could have manipulated me by saying she regretted putting me up for adoption, but she was brutally honest. She didn't want a child. I would have gotten in the way of her career plans." Grace's voice was edged with pain.

Eve realized she was gripping Grace's hand too tightly and loosened her hold. "Oh, sweetheart. I'm so lucky she gave you to me."

"I wanted to know the truth, and now I do. It's a relief not having to feel regret that my biological mother is in prison for the rest of her life. She belongs there."

Eve had no idea how to respond to that, so she made a sympathetic sound.

Grace looked down at where their hands were joined. "I thought I might feel *something*, since she gave birth to me, but there was no sense of recognition, no internal voice saying, 'This is your mother.' She was a complete stranger."

"Maybe that's a good thing," Eve offered.

"You're the only mother I need or want," Grace said, tears streaking down her cheeks.

"You'll always have me, sweetheart." Eve felt answering tears gather in her eyes. "And Luis."

"Odette hates him," Grace said. "Because he rejected her."

"A long time ago," Eve pointed out. "A normal person would have moved on."

"I wonder what Luis was like back then," Grace said. "I can't imagine him young and reckless enough to have an affair with Odette. He's so controlled."

Eve couldn't help thinking of Luis in bed. He was not controlled there.

"It was a tough time for him," Eve said. "He had lost his father and his wife and was learning to be king. All that pressure needed an outlet."

"I suppose I should be glad since I wouldn't be here if he hadn't had the fling with Odette," Grace said with a grimace. "The good news is that she promised not to claim me as her daughter, for the time being. I realize she could change her mind, but she believes she makes rational decisions, so maybe she'll stick to it."

Grace appeared to understand a fair amount about Odette, which was impressive.

"At least it will buy time for Luis to make the announcement about you and for Mikel to set up the false trail for the media," Eve said. "Once those things are done, Odette will find it much harder to get the legitimate media to believe her."

"She could still make an ugly stir, though," Grace said.

"Did you speak with Luis after you saw Odette?" Eve asked.

"Yes." Grace looked down again. "He was very sweet and kind, but I couldn't deal with all the baggage between him and Odette. I wanted to talk to you."

An unworthy flash of triumph zinged through Eve. Grace had chosen to share her feelings with Eve, not her father. Eve quashed the petty thought. "You don't need to apologize for taking care of yourself in this situation, sweetheart. Your father won't have a problem with that."

Grace slumped back against the seat. "I'm so glad that's over."

"Are you sorry you met her?"

"No." Two more tears traced down Grace's cheeks. "I had to know if I was like her. But I'm not. I don't even look like her, thank God!" Grace's voice was fierce.

"Of course you're not like her." Eve used her thumb to gently wipe away the tears. "I told you that already. I would know if my daughter was a psychopath."

"You're biased," Grace said with an exhausted smile.

"Not *that* biased."

"I love you, Mom."

"Right back at you, honey." Eve leaned over to give her a kiss on the cheek.

"Odette said being loved is overrated."

"Only because she doesn't know how to love someone, so she can't feel loved in return. It's a two-way street."

"That's how I know for sure I'm not like her. Because I always feel your love."

Eve swallowed hard.

"I'm starting to love Luis too," Grace said.

"That's a good thing," Eve said and meant it, but she felt the pain of her own separation from him.

"You know how you insisted that he tell me about the downside to being a princess?" Grace said. "I feel like I haven't seen *his* downside. Odette said something about a king having to be ruthless."

"Don't let Odette poison your relationship with your father. That would play right into her hands," Eve warned. "Luis has done nothing but draw you into the embrace of his family." Eve let her mouth slant into a wry smile. "Perhaps a little high-handedly, but only because he was overjoyed to have found you."

"He definitely pulled some major strings to get me to Caleva for the vet school meetings," Grace admitted.

"Think of how Raul and Gabriel interact with him," Eve said, considering the deep ties of affection she had seen among the three men. "There is no fear there. Respect, yes, but they clearly feel secure with Luis."

Grace nodded before she looked at Eve. "And if he ever tries to steamroll me, I've got you on my side. Not even a king could stand up to you when you get riled up."

Grace gave her far too much credit. Eve had let Luis distract her from her responsibilities to her daughter. "As long as he doesn't throw me off the cliff."

Grace's laugh was shaky, but it was a laugh. Her daughter would be fine.

Two hours later, Luis paced across his office yet again. He had attempted to read a report, but he could think only about Grace and how she had come through her meeting with Odette. He knew Eve would support their daughter through whatever emotions were buffeting her, but he wanted to help Grace too.

When the door opened, he spun on his heel to see Bruno gesture Grace inside. A slash of disappointment cut through him as the door closed without also admitting Eve.

"Grace, *hija mía!*" In three strides, he was across the room and embracing her. His heart stuttered when she laid her head against his chest and hugged him in return. "Are you all right?"

She nodded against him and then slipped out of his arms to lift her head. "It's behind me, and I'll be fine. But thank you for worrying."

He wanted to push her to tell him how she was feeling, but she would share if she wished to. He was impressed by her composure after such a gut-roiling encounter.

"Do you feel up to talking about what we need to do next?" he asked, watching her face for any sign of distress.

"That's why I'm here," she said. "I figured we should make the announcement as soon as possible."

"Are you sure you're ready to face the media spotlight?" he asked. "It will be quite a commotion at the outset."

"It's part of my job now," she said with a ghost of a smile.

"Indeed, and you will have the support of the palace PR staff as well as my own and the family's. They can coach you on what to say and what not to say." Luis gestured toward the seating area. "Let's sit and talk through the schedule."

Grace seated herself in an armchair, her back straight, her legs crossed at the ankles. The PR people would not need to teach her proper posture.

"If you are prepared, I wish to call the senior palace staff together this afternoon to introduce you," he said as he took the chair across from hers. "They should hear the news before the general public does, and they can be trusted not to leak it."

Her face lost a little color, but she nodded.

"We will set up the public announcement for tomorrow afternoon," he continued. "Select media representatives will be invited. If you wish, you may make a short, prepared speech, but there will be no questions." He would not let the ravening wolves of the press loose on her. Once the frenzy died down a bit, the palace would orchestrate an interview or two.

"I can do that," she said, squaring her shoulders.

"There will be legal documents to sign, securing your place in the royal family and in the succession to the throne. The lawyers are working on them as we speak," Luis said. "We will also have a ceremony crowning you a princess of the realm, but that will take some time to plan, so you don't have to deal with that right now."

"Do I have an official name as princess?" she asked.

"As my second child, your title is *la Princessa del Vaho*, Princess of the Mist," he said. "There are other lesser titles— some with landholdings—that become yours as well."

"Who has them now?"

"They reverted to the crown, so they're in my safekeeping."

"Oh, good. I wouldn't want to take anything away from another royal." She took a deep breath. "You said there's land with the titles. I assume you have managers for that?"

"Very good ones, although you will be free to fire them and hire new ones, if you choose." Her expression of horror made him smile.

"Is there anything else I need to know right now?" she asked.

"Nothing pressing." In truth, there was so much she would need to learn, but he did not doubt her capacity to handle it. It would just take time.

"Enough of the logistics." He leaned forward. "It will be my great joy to tell the world you are my daughter." He injected every ounce of the pride and love he felt into his voice.

A glint of tears shone in her eyes. "And I am honored to be claimed as your daughter." She swallowed. "I've been thinking about what to call you. Would it be all right to call you Dad? I know it's not Spanish or very formal, but I always wanted a dad."

Luis thought his heart would explode out of his chest. "Nothing would make me happier. I will strive always to deserve the title."

"No striving is necessary," she said. "We just have to love each other." She smiled shyly. "Dad."

CHAPTER 22

Later that night, Luis sat on the sofa in his palace suite, once again paging through the book of fencing strategy without being able to absorb any knowledge from it. Occasionally, an illustration would catch his attention for a few seconds, but mostly he thought about Eve and Grace. Were they back from the veterinary group's farewell dinner?

Eve said she would tell the Iowans that she and Grace would not be on the plane returning with them to the U.S. tomorrow, giving a vague excuse about being asked to stay and further develop the fear-free aspects of the future vet school. Bruno had already contacted the veterinary college in Iowa to clear Grace's absence with those in charge of her academic career there, while substitute vet techs had been arranged for Eve at the clinic.

Luis would have them here with him for a few more days following the announcement in the morning. It would crack a hole in his chest when they left, but he already had plans for a visit to Iowa in a few weeks. There was also Grace's graduation ceremony in about six months. The winter holidays in between he planned to negotiate with Eve and Grace. It would not be enough, but his schedule did not allow for much more, and Grace was uncomfortable about taking additional time off from her rotations.

He felt a sudden roil of nausea and a stab of pain in his gut, a powerful reaction to the upcoming separation.

His gaze drifted to the panel that opened into the secret passageway between his suite and Eve's. The temptation to follow in his ancestors' footsteps and sneak into Eve's bedroom was almost overpowering. But he had told her that she must come to him. That was a salve to his own conscience rather than a belief that Eve would feel any pressure because he was the king. She did not fear his power. Or curry it.

He closed the book and tossed it onto the coffee table before he stood, a wave of fatigue making him catch the back of the chair for balance. He needed to sleep because tomorrow would be a day of speech writing, and he had to be mentally sharp. He wished to use his own heartfelt words to introduce Grace to Caleva as their princess. Starting toward his bedroom, he slipped the dragonhead cuff links out of his shirtsleeves as he walked.

The familiar soft click of a latch and a draft of air made him turn to see Eve step out of the secret passage. As she closed the panel behind her, he took in the waves of her glorious hair, the curves of her body beneath the simple blue dress she wore, and the clean, beautiful lines of her profile.

In a few strides, he reached her and gathered her in his arms, seeking her soft lips in a kiss that sent fire licking through his veins. She leaned into him, her breasts pillowing against his chest, and wound her hands around his neck and into his hair. He slid his hands downward to cup her lush bottom and press her closer against him. She gave a little moan that opened her mouth so he could tease her tongue with his.

His cock hardened as he tasted the heat and silk of her. Elation flooded his body.

She had changed her mind and come to him.

As he shifted to ease his thigh between hers, she slid her hands down over his shoulders to flatten her palms against his chest. The friction and warmth were so delicious that it took him several moments to realize she was pushing him away.

He released her mouth and lifted his head. "What is it, *querida?*"

"I came to say goodbye, not to—" She took a step back, so he reluctantly let his arms drop from around her.

"Why can we not do both?" he asked.

She shook her head. "I just wanted to…to say thank you for…well, for being you, I suppose." Her smile had an edge of sadness. "It was fun, but now we have to go back to our real-life roles. You're the king, and I am the adoptive mother of your daughter. We need to keep it that way for Grace's sake. I will find a house away from San Ignacio so I'm not in the public eye. However, I will need to be able to join the royal family for special occasions without any awkwardness. If we continue our…liaison, that might become a problem."

She was making rational sense, but he did not feel rational about her. "You will be *part* of the royal family because Grace is." He could not stop himself from taking her strong, capable hands in his. He had to touch her. "She will need you here as she navigates her new life. You are her anchor, her place of comfort and security."

His place of comfort and security too. He wanted Eve here, where he could listen to the music of her laugh, relish her sharp observations, and persuade her into his bed.

She pulled her hands from his grip and banded her arms around her waist. "No!" She looked toward the windows. "I'm going back to Iowa, and you're staying in Caleva. We will continue on with our lives, and this little interlude will fade into a pleasant memory."

This little interlude. He did not like to hear what had happened between them being dismissed that way. Anger flared like a kerosene-soaked torch, and his stomach clenched again. But something nagged at him, so he forced himself to take a mental step back and think. It was her body language. Despite her words, she was not projecting rejection.

She was protecting herself.

He wanted to fold his arms around her, to melt the stiffness from her posture so she once again was warm and pliant against him. He shoved his hands into his trouser pockets, the cuff links clinking against his signet ring.

"You will not fade in my memory," he said, pushing so much intensity into his voice that it became a growl. "You will burn like a flame. You going back to Iowa will not quench that, especially when I will see you again in a few weeks and then again at Grace's graduation."

Even though there were several feet of air between them, she unwound her arms to make a pushing motion with her hands. "I'm just a novelty, a stranger, an American."

The anger sparked again. "You think I am that easily enthralled?" he snapped.

"Enthralled?" she said. "No. I think you were intrigued. And possibly grateful to me for raising your daughter."

"Madre de Dios!" He clenched his fists in his pockets. "You are a beautiful, sensual woman of great intelligence and honor. Your spirit glows with compassion and decency and kindness. Perhaps all those things make you a novelty, because you are so unique, but it is not the trivial novelty you speak of."

Her eyes widened in a look of disbelief as he spoke.

God, he wanted to kiss her.

"You're projecting onto me what you want Grace's mother to be like," she said. "You don't really know me."

Now he wanted to shake her. He took a deep breath. "Over many years and meetings with thousands of people, I have learned to take the measure of a person quickly. By now, I am rarely wrong. *I know you.* I know I want you in my life."

She had her arms curled around her waist again, yet he saw her sway toward him, an unconscious movement that told him so much. She looked away. "I'm not queen material."

His breath seemed to evaporate from his lungs. *Queen material.* He hadn't considered the possibility that she could be his queen, a partner by his side for the rest of their lives.

As he examined the idea, she turned back to him with a dry look. "Yeah, that's what I figured, but I can't invest in this relationship and then walk away without a backward glance."

He started to tell her that she was wrong about his moment of hesitation, but agony slashed through his gut like a rusty sword.

♛

Luis began to speak, but before he could agree that she wasn't cut out to be a queen, he doubled over with a groan that sounded like it was wrenched up from his toes. "Luis! What is it?" She dashed to his side as he sank to the floor, his arms clutched around his abdomen. "What do you need?"

"*Basura,*" he said through clenched teeth.

"Trash can?" she translated to confirm.

He nodded, the tendons in his neck standing out with strain.

She desperately scanned the room and saw a leather trash can sitting beside a desk. Racing to grab it and return to his side, she knelt and placed it in front of him. He vomited into the receptacle so violently that it seemed like his stomach might come up his throat.

He dry-heaved a few more times before he let go of the trash can and braced his hands on the floor on either side of it. Lifting his head, he said, "I'm never ill."

She remembered his comment about eating a lot of strange things in his travels. "I know."

"Call Mikel," he said and then vomited again.

Panic welled up in her throat at the implications. "I don't have my phone."

He swallowed hard and ground out, "Panic button. Beside door."

She pushed to her feet and raced for the main door. A red button was mounted on the wall. She pressed it several times before running back to kneel at Luis's side.

She was a medical professional, even if it was for non-human patients. She needed to focus. "Luis, tell me what you're feeling beside the nausea."

"Pain in my abdomen. In my thighs." He paused to inhale deeply. "Tingling in my feet."

"When did it start?" She laid her hand gently on his back to offer comfort.

"Just now. No, I felt the nausea earlier. Ignored it." He wrapped his hands around his stomach with another groan. "Not food poisoning. Ate here all—"

He collapsed, his head striking the trash can, which she grabbed before it could spill its contents.

"Luis!" She rolled him onto his side to keep him from aspirating in case he vomited again. But his body lolled in a way that said he was unconscious. "Shit!" She yanked a pillow off a nearby chair and wedged it under his head before she checked his pulse. Weak and fast but there.

The door flew open, and Mikel rushed in, followed by two men with guns drawn. Mikel took in the scene with a sharp glance and turned to his men. "Get a gurney and the ambulance."

"What happened?" he barked at Eve, kneeling beside Luis to pick up the same wrist she had.

"We were talking, and he suddenly doubled over," Eve said. "He threw up twice before he collapsed. He said his thighs hurt, his feet are tingling, and he was nauseated earlier."

Mikel nodded in acknowledgment of Eve's summary as he checked Luis's breathing. The two men raced back through the door, wheeling a gurney between them.

"Help me," Mikel commanded them.

The three of them lifted Luis onto the stretcher with exquisite gentleness, tilting the back up so he didn't risk choking on vomit. One took a basin from a shelf beneath it and placed it on Luis's legs before gently strapping him securely to the gurney.

Eve wanted to reach out to him, but the men were in her way, standing on either side of Luis.

She tore her gaze away from his white, slack face when no one moved toward the door. "Shouldn't you go to the hospital now?"

Mikel nodded, his face like granite. "The moment the corridor is clear. We don't want anyone seeing the king on a stretcher." He went still in that way his men did when listening to their earpiece. "Let's go!" he commanded.

Something nagged at Eve's brain. If Luis hadn't ingested poison through something he had eaten, how could he have gotten so sick?

"Rat poison!" she said, jogging behind the swiftly moving gurney. "Tell the doctors to check for thallium poisoning."

Mikel threw her a skeptical glance. "How could he have eaten rat poison?"

"You can absorb it through the skin," she said. "He has weakness and pain in his thighs. That can be a symptom of thallium poisoning. I've seen dogs collapse like that."

Mikel nodded, his gaze focused and sharp. "I'll make sure to tell them."

Luis's escort threw open a small door, and they entered a garage of some sort. A white van waited with its doors ajar to reveal an impressively equipped mobile medical unit manned by two men in white lab coats. Luis's gurney was lifted inside, and Mikel vaulted in after it.

As soon as the van's doors were closed, the garage door clanked open, and the van sped away.

Eve stared after it, her stomach in knots as she replayed the violence of Luis's breakdown and remembered the poor, dying dogs who had been brought into the clinic too late to save from the poison.

"*Señora*, I'll take you back to your room," one of the men said, holding the door open for her.

"I...thank you," she said, stepping into the corridor as she tried to recall everything she could about thallium poisoning. That particular type of rat poison had been outlawed in the U.S. because of its deadliness for humans. In fact, it had been used to commit a spate of murders in Australia in the 1950s. Still, old packages were sometimes forgotten in barns or basements until an animal got into it.

The antidote was Prussian blue. Hemodialysis was used to clear the thallium from the bloodstream. But the doctors here should know that, shouldn't they? Or should she text Mikel to tell him?

As she debated, they arrived at her suite. *"Buenas noches, señora,"* her escort said, ushering her through her door before departing. She closed the door and leaned against it, her eyes closed as fear squeezed its fingers around her heart.

Luis would be all right. He had the best doctors in the country treating him. Still...

She raced into her bedroom to grab her phone and text Mikel the information about thallium poisoning. He didn't respond. She sat on the bed and slumped forward, elbows on knees, head in hands.

He'll be fine.

She lifted her head. Should she tell Grace? Or Raul? They would just worry along with her, but they had the right to know, because Luis was their father.

She shoved up from the bed and crossed through the suite's living room to knock on Grace's door. "Sweetie? It's Mom."

"Come in," her daughter called.

Eve opened the door to find Grace propped up in bed with her laptop on her knees. She set it aside when she saw Eve's face.

"What is it?" Grace asked. "What's wrong?"

Eve sat on the bed and took one of Grace's hands in hers. "Your father was just taken to the hospital, unconscious and with severe intestinal distress. Mikel is with him, and he has the best doctors in the country, but I thought you should know."

"I want to go to the hospital." Grace tugged her hand away and threw off the covers.

"I don't know if we're allowed to," Eve said. "Mikel said they don't want people to know that the king is ill."

"Shit!" Grace said. "There has to be a way. I'm calling Raul."

"I don't know if he's aware of the situation," Eve said. "I was going to talk with him next."

"Why are you the one telling us?" Grace asked with sudden focus. "Were you with him when he got sick?"

"Yes. I went to talk to him in his apartment, and he collapsed."

"What do you think is going on?" Grace was pulling on jeans and a T-shirt as she talked.

Eve hesitated. "I'm not a doctor—not even a vet like you—so I don't know."

"You have an idea, though, I can tell," Grace said, shoving her feet into her sneakers.

"It might be thallium poisoning," Eve said. "I told Mikel to have the doctors test for it."

Grace's cheeks lost all their color. "Rat poison? No!" she whispered, going still. "That's ugly stuff. Even if he survives, there could be permanent damage…"

"He's strong, and he's the king. He'll have every medical advantage it's possible to give him," Eve reassured her…and tried to reassure herself.

"I'm calling Raul," Grace said, grabbing her phone from the nightstand.. "He'll get us to the hospital."

Eve thought about stopping her, but she wanted to be at the hospital as badly as Grace did. "Tell him gently," she said as she heard the phone ringing through Grace's speaker.

"I just heard Pater went to the hospital." Raul's voice was tight with concern. "Do you know what happened?"

"Mom was with him, and she's here, so she can tell you." Grace nodded to Eve.

Eve repeated her abbreviated version of the night's events, leaving out her theory about thallium poisoning. She had no qualifications for diagnosing Luis's illness, so she wouldn't share it with the prince.

"We need to get to the hospital," Grace said as soon as Eve finished. "Mom says Mikel doesn't want anyone else to know that the king is sick, but you must know how we can sneak in."

"Come to my apartment, and we'll leave from here." He disconnected.

"Do you know where Raul's apartment is?" Eve asked.

"Just beyond Dad's," Grace said, pulling on a hoodie.

Dad's. She'd said the word so naturally. Something about that made Eve's heart clench. "Let me get a sweater," she said, dashing out the bedroom door.

Grace led the way down the hallway. A guard stood in front of the door to Luis's apartment, nodding as they passed.

"Why are they guarding it *now*?" Eve murmured.

"Maybe to keep anyone else from getting poisoned," her daughter said.

A cold realization hit Eve. It was a crime scene. Mikel and his personnel would be going through the rooms with a fine-tooth comb.

Grace stopped in front of a door and knocked. Raul opened it and waved them inside. He was dressed like Grace, in jeans and a T-shirt. "We're going out the same way Pater did. There's a car waiting for us in the garage." He hesitated for a moment before saying, "When my father is…incapacitated, I become acting head of Caleva. I don't want to invoke that provision yet, so let's keep this very quiet."

"Of course," Eve said, understanding that Raul hoped his father would recover before any announcement needed to be made.

She prayed he was right.

A knock sounded on a different door, and Raul called, "Come in."

A powerfully built man dressed in dark trousers and a long-sleeved shirt stepped inside. "We are ready, *Señor.*"

"Let's go," Raul said, waving Grace and Eve in front of him.

The man led them swiftly through narrow corridors with rough stone walls and worn stone floors. Eve wondered if these had been built for servants or soldiers defending the castle, or both. After several twists and turns, they arrived at the same garage where the van had whisked Luis away. Now a beige minivan stood in the dim light, its side door open.

After they had climbed in, their guide slid the door shut and jumped into the front passenger seat. As soon as he had settled, the driver headed for the now-opening garage door.

"How long to the hospital?" Grace asked Raul.

"About fifteen minutes at normal speed," Raul said. "The medical van would have gone faster."

"And there were doctors in the van with him," Eve said, to comfort her daughter. "They would have started diagnostics and treatment right away."

Grace was silent a moment before she gave a choked sob. "Dad and I just found each other."

"Are you aware of something about my father's condition that I'm not?" Raul asked, his voice sharp.

"We don't have any more information than you do," Eve assured him.

"You seem very concerned, though," Raul said. "Why?"

Raul was far too astute. Eve sighed inwardly. "Based on my very brief observations of your father's symptoms, I had one idea about what might have caused them, which I passed on to Mikel. Remember, I am not a doctor, and it is just one of many possibilities."

"And your idea is?" he prodded.

"It might be thallium poisoning," Eve said reluctantly. "In the U.S., thallium was once used for rodent control, so I've seen the symptoms in animals. Remember that I don't work with human patients, so I'm speculating."

"And thallium poisoning is bad?" he asked.

"Only if it doesn't get treated right away," Eve said with partial truth. It also depended on how much thallium Luis had absorbed. "Which isn't the situation here."

"You believe someone tried to kill him." Anger hardened his voice.

Eve turned to look Raul in the eye. "All I know is that your father said he is never sick. Tonight, he vomited violently before he blacked out. That made me consider causes other than natural ones."

"But he ate at the palace for every meal today," Raul said. "It would be virtually impossible to get poison into his food."

"Thallium can also be inhaled or absorbed through the skin. It's a heavy metal," Grace explained.

"Joder!" Raul swore. "Mikel will find whoever did this, and they will be locked up for the rest of their life."

That wouldn't help Luis survive, though. Eve hated the fact that the last words she had said to him before he'd collapsed had been harsh ones. Why hadn't she admitted that she loved him and that was why she had to walk away?

Because if he knew, he would have persuaded her to stay. She still had enough of a sense of self-preservation to be sure of that.

Still, she wished she had been...nicer.

At least she had been there to call for help immediately. What if he had been alone? Could he have reached the panic button before he had passed out? A vision of Luis dying on the floor, alone, in a pool of vomit, made her heart twist in horror.

"We're almost there," Raul said. "We'll go in a back entrance to get to the private floor of the wing where the royal family is treated." He had donned a sweatshirt and now pulled the hood up over his head. "Grace, you should cover your hair too," he said. "Eve, do you have a hat?"

She hadn't thought about a disguise when she'd grabbed her sweater. When she shook her head, Raul said, "Dario, can you give *Señora* Howard a hat of some kind?"

Their guide opened the glove compartment and pulled out a black baseball cap, which he handed to Eve. She gathered up her hair into a ponytail and threaded it through the back of the cap before she pulled the bill low over her face.

The minivan came to a stop in front of a metal door with a single light over it. Dario escorted them through a series of utility hallways, all empty of people, into a foyer with a marble floor and a giant flower arrangement on a round wooden table. Two guards in dark suits stood by the outside door.

Dario nodded to them before hitting the button for the elevator.

Brass doors slid open to reveal a large car, its walls embellished with beautiful glass tiles. This must be the private wing Raul had mentioned. The elevator whooshed upward multiple floors to the penthouse level and disgorged them into a plush reception area with a wooden desk graced by another flower arrangement and manned by a pleasant-looking young man dressed in teal-green scrubs.

"Buenas noches, Su Alteza Real," the man said, rising to bow to Raul and smile at Grace and Eve. His name tag said he was Jacobo. *"Señor* Silva will be here in just a moment. Please make yourselves comfortable." He gestured behind the desk.

Beyond their greeter, a large Calevan coat of arms was mounted on one wall above a cushy-looking sofa that anchored a whole seating arrangement of upholstered chairs and tables...with more flowers, of course. There was nothing clinical about the royal family's waiting room.

"May I offer you a beverage?" Jacobo asked.

"We can help ourselves, *gracias,*" Raul said, coming into the seating area. He went to a wall of cabinets and opened one door to reveal a well-stocked refrigerator. "Who would like a bottle of water?"

Eve figured it would give her something to do with her hands, so she joined him to accept what turned out to be a glass bottle with a Calevan dragon on the label. As she twisted off the cap, Mikel came through a set of double doors on the other side of the room.

He gave a half bow to Raul and nodded to Eve and Grace. Eve got the distinct feeling that if the Crown Prince of

Caleva had not been their companion, Mikel would have told them both to go home.

"Mikel, how is he?" Raul asked, his voice intense.

Mikel gave Eve a look she couldn't decipher. "*Señora* Howard was correct in her suspicion of thallium poisoning. They have given him the antidote and are flushing his system now."

"But *how is he*? What is the prognosis?" Raul asked again.

"The doctors are optimistic," Mikel said, his tone soothing. "They will know more after the antidote has had more time to clean out the poison."

"I want to see him," Raul said.

Grace moved to stand beside the prince. "I want to as well."

Eve was desperate to see Luis, but she was low man on this particular totem pole, so she remained silent.

"The doctors will bring you in as soon as possible," Mikel said. "Right now, he is still unconscious, and they are working hard to eliminate the effects of the poison."

Fear and worry slashed through Eve, making her stomach roil. Thallium could do severe damage to various systems and organs if the dosage was high.

Raul spun on his heel and went over to stand in front of a plate-glass window, his arms crossed tightly. Eve wanted to put her arm around him in comfort, but she didn't know how the prince would feel about it coming from her.

Instead, she leaned over to whisper in Grace's ear. "Go be with Raul. He needs someone to talk to right now. Try to reassure him that thallium poisoning can be treated effectively." Talking to her half brother would also give Grace something to do other than worry about her father.

Grace nodded but turned to hug Eve, murmuring in her ear, "You may have saved Dad's life." She gave a tiny sob and let go, wiping the back of her hand across her cheek before joining Raul.

Eve watched until Raul let his arms drop to his sides and shifted to look at Grace as they conversed in low tones.

"May I speak with you privately?"

Eve jumped as Mikel spoke from right behind her. "Of course."

Mikel gestured toward an open door across the room, his expression bland.

She accompanied him into a small conference room containing a long wooden table on which were arrayed several laptops. Mikel held a rolling leather chair for her to sit in. After closing the door, he sat across from her.

"What do the doctors really say?" she asked, since Raul and Grace couldn't hear them.

"What doctors always say," Mikel said with a grimace. "That they won't know until the treatment has had more time to work."

Eve nodded, but panic tightened its fist around her heart.

"I know you are worried about His Majesty, but I need to ask you some questions," Mikel said. "My apologies."

Puzzled, she nodded.

"Have you had any digestive issues since you came to Caleva?" he asked.

"Digestive issues? No."

"Has Grace complained of any health problems?"

The truth dawned on her. Mikel was already trying to track down Luis's poisoner.

"No, she's been fine."

"You have spent some time alone with His Majesty," Mikel said. "Did he eat or drink anything during those...encounters?"

Eve felt heat rising in her cheeks. Of course Mikel would know there was something going on between them. After all, she had been alone with Luis tonight when he'd collapsed. "I... Let me think." She reviewed the times they had been together and shook her head. "He didn't eat anything that I saw."

"And you didn't give him any food or beverage that came from outside either the palace or Casa en las Nubes? Perhaps as a gift?"

"That would be like bringing gold to King Midas," Eve said before she stiffened in outrage. "You can't think that *I* poisoned Luis!"

"It is my job to explore all possibilities." Mikel's voice held no inflection.

"Why would I tell you what I thought the poison was if I wanted to kill him?" She was furious and baffled.

"You regretted your action when you saw the effect. You wanted to be the hero who saved your daughter's father and the king. One never knows how a murderer will justify their crime," Mikel said.

"Seriously?" She couldn't believe he would think that. "How would I get my hands on thallium? Thallium-based rat poison has been illegal in the U.S. for decades."

"You said you have seen its symptoms in dogs, so clearly it can still be found there."

"Leftover in some random farmer's barn! I wouldn't know how to find any myself," she protested. "And I would have had to carry it all the way to Caleva with me. Why would I even think to do that?"

He looked at her in a way that said he was picturing her as a murderer. "Perhaps you resented having the king sweep into your daughter's life and take her away from you. Did you give him anything at all, perhaps a gift of some kind?"

"No!" Now she was terrified. The relentless Mikel would not hesitate to lock her up in the CárcelMax prison, with psychopaths like Odette. She fought down her fear and tried to think rationally. She couldn't tell Mikel that she wouldn't poison Luis because she was crazy in love with him. She hadn't even told Luis that.

The simplest truth fought its way through her panic. "I could never harm Luis, because of Grace, whom I love more than anyone in the world. To take Luis away from her would hurt her deeply." She looked directly at Mikel. "You have a daughter. Wouldn't you do almost anything to protect her from pain?"

The silence stretched as Mikel's gaze rested on her face. When he finally spoke, it was in a low voice. "What I have done to protect my daughter is beyond anything you can imagine, so I accept your reasoning."

Relief flooded Eve, and she let out a shaky sigh.

Mikel did not stop asking questions, though. "Did you notice His Majesty handling any objects more than once?"

"Objects?" The change in subject threw her off-balance again.

"Something that might have carried the thallium," Mikel said. "We are going through the registry of gifts he has received recently, but you could help narrow down the search."

As she considered his question, Eve's cheeks flushed again. Mostly, Luis had been touching *her* when they'd been together in private. She banished that from her mind and closed her eyes, trying to conjure up her memories of each time she'd seen him alone. "I can't think of any—wait! I never saw him pick it up, but he had the same book at Casa en las Nubes and in his room at the palace. It caught my eye because it had a picture of fencers on the cover, and Luis said he likes to fence for exercise."

Mikel pulled out his phone and scrolled for a moment. "*Fencing Strategies Through the Ages?*"

"I didn't read the title." She had been focused on more important things…like Luis looking at her as though he wanted to tear her clothes off and taste every inch of her body. The memory sent a flicker of heat through her veins.

Mikel tapped at his phone for a few moments before he looked up. "We know who presented him with the book. If the thallium came from that…"

Eve shivered at Mikel's malevolent expression. She hoped he never looked at her that way.

"*Gracias, señora,*" he said. "Your help has been invaluable."

Eve had whiplash. First, he accused her of trying to murder Luis, and now he was praising her?

He must have seen something in her expression because he said, "I had to ask. It is my job."

And he made no apology for it.

"I will need to speak with Grace as well," he said.

The mother bear in her rose up. "If you accuse her of trying to murder her father, I don't care how scary you are, I will make your life hell." She didn't know how, but she would find a way.

He considered her for a moment. "I believe you."

"So you won't accuse her?" Grace was upset enough about her father. Eve didn't want her daughter to go through the same wringer Mikel had just put her through.

"I will do my job." He stood. "But I have no reason to believe your daughter was involved in the attempt on His Majesty's life."

Relief swept through Eve, and she blew out a breath. "Thank you."

Mikel went to the door, opened it, and waited until she followed him. "To be clear, I would not hesitate to accuse even the prince if I thought it was necessary to the investigation," he said, waving her into the reception room.

Luis had said he trusted Mikel with his life. There was a reason for that.

CHAPTER 23

Eve sat on the edge of the sofa in the waiting area, staring at the door to what she thought of as Mikel's interrogation room. When Grace emerged, she looked concerned and upset, but she didn't have the shattered look of a daughter who had just been accused of murdering her own father. The security chief remained in the conference room.

"No word from the doctors?" Grace asked as she sat beside Eve.

"Not yet," Raul said before he resumed pacing between the reception desk and the windows.

Eve did not attempt to soothe him with empty words. They all knew that Luis was receiving the best, most focused care available in the country of Caleva. They knew he was healthy and strong. But none of them knew how much poison he had absorbed.

Eve considered Mikel's suspicion that Luis might have come into contact with the thallium via the fencing book. She worried that Luis had possibly been handling the book over several days, which could mean that the thallium had been building up in his organs and causing them damage, even before today.

She tried again to remember if she had seen Luis touch the darned book but couldn't.

"He's going to be okay, Mom," Grace said, taking her hand.

Eve realized she had been staring straight ahead without seeing anything.

"Of course he is," Eve said with hope rather than conviction. "I just want him to be okay right now."

"We all do," Grace said as they exchanged worried glances. As a vet student, Grace knew all too well the deadly effects of thallium poisoning. "Hey, Raul, are you trying to get in your steps for the day or something?"

Raul halted in the middle of the room. "I feel better moving."

"Maybe we could play a game," Grace said. "I'll bet someone could find us a deck of cards."

Jacobo leaped out of his chair at the reception desk. "I will get them for you." He jogged over to one of the wooden cabinets and pulled out a square storage basket. "How many decks would you like?"

"Two. We'll play Oh, Heck!" Grace said.

"I'm not familiar with that game," Raul said. "Please play without me."

"It doesn't work with just two people," Eve said, supporting Grace's attempt to distract Raul. "We'll teach you."

Raul hesitated, but his good manners overcame his reluctance. As the receptionist placed two brand-new decks of cards on the coffee table, the prince sat in one of the chairs.

Eve let Grace explain the basic rules of the game to her half brother. Although he kept casting glances at the door to the medical wing, Raul caught on quickly and was on track to win the game when the door finally opened.

Raul was out of his chair before the woman in the white coat had taken two steps into the room. *"Su Alteza Real,"* she said with a small dip of a curtsy.

"Dr. Ibarra, how is he?" Raul asked.

"Su Majestad is receiving hemodialysis to flush the poison from his system. He has also received the antidote. He is responding to both right now," she said.

"That means he's not going to die?" Raul asked.

"No," the doctor said gravely. "He is very strong, and we began treatment quickly."

"Oh, thank God!" Grace said, her voice cracking. She and Eve had come to stand beside Raul. The doctor looked confused by their presence.

"My apologies," Raul said. "Dr. Ibarra, may I present Eve and Grace Howard. *Señora* Howard was with my father when he collapsed. She is the person who suggested you test for thallium poisoning."

Dr. Ibarra shook Eve's and Grace's hands before turning to Eve. "Your suggestion was very helpful. Without it, we might have taken longer to look at thallium as a possible cause for *Su Majestad's* symptoms. You are a doctor?"

"A veterinary technician," Eve said in a dry tone. "I've seen the symptoms in dogs who ingested old rat poison."

To her credit, Dr. Ibarra did not bat an eye. "Sometimes experience is more valuable than a degree."

"We would like to see my father," Raul said in a tone that made it clear he was a prince.

Dr. Ibarra hesitated before she said, "Of course, *Señor.* Keep in mind that he is medicated for the pain. He is also exhausted from both the poison and the treatment. He may be sleeping, and it would be best if you did not wake him."

"We will not disturb him," Raul said, making it clear that he would not be dissuaded.

Eve almost volunteered not to go, thinking that would make the doctor happier. After all, she was neither Luis's child nor his wife. When the doctor turned to lead them through the door, though, Eve followed.

She needed to see Luis, even for just a moment.

As they walked into a wide, well-lit corridor, a security guard in a dark suit stepped in front of them. Seeing Raul, he gave a bow and went back to his post. Eve knew immediately which room Luis was in, because two more security guards stood outside the door. She could see another one at the far end of the hallway.

Dr. Ibarra ushered them down the corridor, which was eerily quiet for a hospital. Luis must be the only patient in the royal wing. Since he was the king and he needed to sleep, everyone near his room spoke in hushed voices or not at all.

It brought home yet again the vast gulf that separated her life from his.

The doctor opened the door silently and waved them through. The room was large and dim. It took a moment for her eyes to adjust enough to focus on the figure lying in the bed, surrounded by blinking monitors and seemingly held captive by a web of wires and intravenous lines running to his body.

His eyes were closed, and his face was drawn, the angles of his strong bones painfully sharp. More shocking was his terrible stillness. All his charisma and power and life force had been stripped away by the poison. He looked not like a king, but like a very sick man.

Eve had to swallow a gasp as fear seared through her. The doctor had said Luis would survive, but his appearance made that hard to believe.

Grace lifted her hand to cover her mouth, tears gleaming in her eyes. Eve pushed her own distress aside and squeezed her daughter's shoulder in reassurance before checking on Raul.

The prince's face had lost all color. He looked as though someone had walloped him in the gut. She reached for his hand, folding her fingers around his, not caring if she was being presumptuous. He looked startled and then gripped her hand almost convulsively.

Eve could almost feel all of them sending their hearts toward the man lying motionless on the white sheets. If a person could be healed by the force of love, Luis should be rising from his bed at any moment.

Unfortunately, it didn't work that way.

No one moved for several minutes as they hoped Luis would open his eyes or at least stir to demonstrate that he was alive.

Dr. Ibarra finally stepped between them and the bed, gesturing that they should leave the room.

Raul released Eve's hand when they turned to exit. The moment the door closed behind the doctor, he said, "I wish to stay in the room with him tonight."

"I do too," Grace said. "I'll sit in one of the recliners."

Eve had noticed the two overstuffed chairs at one side of the room.

"I…" Dr. Ibarra hesitated as her gaze traveled between Raul's and Grace's faces.

"I want to be with him when he wakes up," Raul said, his voice carrying a snap of command.

Dr. Ibarra gave in with a nod. "But you must not attempt to wake him. His body is in a battle to recover from the effects of the poison. He needs all the rest he can get."

Grace turned to Eve. "Mom, you'll stay here, too, won't you? There's that sofa in the waiting room."

"Of course I'll stay," Eve said, although she once again felt the pang of having no official reason even to be in the waiting room in the royal wing of the hospital. But Grace would need her if Luis took a turn for the worse.

"I'll text you when he wakes up." Grace hugged her and headed for the door with Raul and the doctor.

Eve returned to the waiting room and sank into the closest chair. Doubling over, she gave way to a long, wrenching sob. She had expected Luis to look ill, but not so inert that he seemed lifeless. She felt like she had been kicked in the stomach. Another sob twisted itself from her throat.

Mikel had said that the doctors refused to make a commitment about Luis's full recovery. After seeing Luis, Eve discounted Dr. Ibarra's reassurances to Raul that his father would be fine. She feared that the doctor had just been offering comfort to a worried son.

She hoped like hell that Mikel was hot on the trail of whoever had done this. The poisoner deserved to rot in CárcelMax along with Odette Fontaine.

"*Señora*, may I get you anything?"

Eve straightened to find Jacobo kneeling beside her, offering a box of tissues. The gesture reminded her of Luis's handkerchief, and a fresh wave of tears coursed down her cheeks. "Thank you," she said, accepting the tissues. "I…"

There was nothing he could get her that would cure this anguish.

"I can show you to a bedroom where you can rest. It will be more comfortable."

She felt like she shouldn't have the luxury of a bed when Grace and Raul were keeping vigil in chairs. Big, comfortable chairs, but still not beds. Her rational self reasserted itself. "That would be great."

The receptionist led her to a carpeted hallway that looked like it belonged in a hotel. Opening one of several doors, he gestured her into a small but plush bedroom. "The bathroom is equipped with toiletries," he said. "You'll find the Wi-Fi password on the credenza. *Buenas noches.*"

He closed the door with a soft click, and Eve went to the bed to touch the soft cream-colored blanket folded at its foot. The coat of arms of Caleva was embroidered in teal green in one corner. She rubbed her fingers against the fabric, guessing by the texture that it was cashmere.

She didn't belong here. In this room. In this wing. Anywhere near Luis. It didn't matter how much she loved him, he was the king. She was not a queen.

She used the bathroom to splash cold water on her tear-streaked face. Before she turned on the spigot, she stared at herself in the mirror, noting every line at the corners of her eyes, every laugh line around her mouth, the slight sag of the skin under her chin, and the dark circles under her eyes. The dark circles could be attributed to her worry and the fact that it was the middle of the night, but the rest of it? Definitely not queen material.

And she couldn't handle being a *liaison*, with all the brevity that implied. Luis hadn't asked for it, but she had given her heart into his keeping. She couldn't bear to have him toss it back to her when he got bored.

As soon as Grace's identity had been announced publicly, Eve would be on a plane back to Iowa. Time away from Luis—and the spell of seduction he had woven around her—would help her get her mind right before she returned to Caleva permanently.

In the meantime, she closed her eyes and prayed for his life.

CHAPTER 24

Luis surfaced into wakefulness and wished he hadn't. It felt like someone had swung a wrecking ball into his abdomen while every other part of his body throbbed with pain of varying degrees. He would swear that even his hair hurt.

He opened his eyes to find himself in a hospital room, connected to an alarming number of blinking machines.

And then memory flooded back.

Eve telling him goodbye. The overwhelming urge to vomit. His legs so painful he couldn't stand. Eve calling for help before he blacked out.

What the hell had happened to him?

Judging by the number of wires and tubes attached to him, it was something serious. Or they were being extra careful because he was the king. Since he was never ill, it was hard for him to judge.

He glanced around the room to find Raul and Grace asleep in recliners. His heart contracted. If they were in the room, his situation must be worse than he thought. Yet warmth flowed through him to see both his children sitting vigil over him.

Eve was not there, though.

Loss hollowed him out. Had she abandoned him already?

He closed his eyes. A single tear seeped out and trickled into his hair, a sign of weakness he despised, but he couldn't stop it. He didn't want to put on a reassuring face for the benefit of his children or a strong, regal mask for the benefit of the medical professionals.

He wanted Eve so he could be just a man who felt like he had been dragged to hell and back.

No, she wouldn't leave him when he was seriously ill. She must be nearby.

His glance swept over his children again, taking in their sweatshirts and rumpled hair and the blankets they had wrapped around themselves. They had been here for some time.

The lack of light around the edges of the shade covering the window indicated it was night. But which night?

He closed his eyes, trying to conjure a memory of what happened after he arrived at the hospital.

Mikel's voice drifted through his mind. What had he been saying?

Poison.

Luis's eyelids snapped open. He wasn't ill. He had been poisoned. But how? He had eaten only food prepared by his own staff. He started to shake his head, but it hurt too badly to move. Mikel must be wrong.

On the other hand, Raul and Grace were sleeping in the room with him.

"Raul." His voice came out as a raspy whisper. He worked some saliva into his mouth and tried again, pushing this time. "Raul!"

Grace stirred, sliding out of the chair to tiptoe up to his bedside, her gaze focused on his face. "Dad?" she whispered. "Are you awake?"

"Yes," he croaked, his heart swelling with the joy of being called *Dad*.

Relief lit her face as a tear snaked down her cheek. "Oh, thank God!" She turned and spoke in a low but carrying voice. "Raul! He's awake!"

His son bolted out of his chair to the bedside, brushing Luis's fingers ever so gently. Raul's careful touch told Luis more than Raul had meant it to. "Pater! *Gracias a Dios!* We should call the doctor."

"Not yet," Luis said. "I need to hear from you what happened, what is wrong with me."

Raul and Grace exchanged worried glances across his bed, but Raul said, "You were poisoned with thallium. It's a heavy metal that was once used in rat poison. But you're responding well to the treatment."

He *had* been poisoned. "How?"

"Mikel is working on that," Raul said. "It can be absorbed through the skin, though."

"How long have I been here?" Luis asked.

"You collapsed while talking to Eve about four hours ago," Raul said. "No one outside this wing knows other than Mikel and your security detail."

"*Muy bien,*" Luis said, closing his eyes in gratitude that the country was not aware of his condition…yet. Hopefully, he would recover swiftly enough to inform them after the fact.

"Do you want to go back to sleep?" Grace asked.

He opened his eyes again. "Is your mother here?"

"Yes," Grace said. "I promised I would text her when you woke up. Is that all right?"

Longing made his heart clench. "Please ask her to come in," he said.

"Eve may have saved your life," Raul said, his expression intense. "She recognized the symptoms of thallium poisoning from her work with animals. She told Mikel to have the doctors test for it right away."

"I owe her so much," he murmured, blinking hard to fight back another damned tear. He was so weak that his emotions were controlling his body.

"She's on her way," Grace said before shoving her phone back into her jeans pocket. "Would you like some water?"

At her mention of a drink, his thirst rose up like a demon. "Yes, very much," he said.

Grace picked up a cup with a handle and a straw. "Shall I hold it for you?" she asked.

Luis considered the pain it would inflict to lift his arm and decided to rely on his daughter's help. There was a strange pleasure in that. "Please."

She leaned in to bring the straw to his lips, taking care not to tangle with any of the lines attached to his body. The ice water tasted better than the finest champagne, refreshing the inside of his mouth and soothing his parched throat. He drank several sips before releasing the straw. "Thank you, *hija mía*. I needed that more than I knew."

As Grace set the cup back on the bedside table, the door eased open.

When Eve glided quietly into the room, peace flowed through Luis like a warm tide. Her face was bare of makeup, her hair was yanked back in a messy ponytail, and she still wore the same blue dress as when she had come to his room. Now it was wrinkled and partly covered by a sweater.

She had never looked more beautiful.

"Querida!" he said.

Raul made a startled movement, and Luis realized what he had revealed to his son.

Eve did not acknowledge the endearment, but the worry on her lovely face eased. "I'm so glad you're awake," she said. "We were very concerned."

He wanted to grab her hand and pull her onto the bed with him, to feel the warmth and softness of her body against his. "I understand that you saved my life by realizing that I had been poisoned by thallium. There are no adequate words to express my gratitude."

Tears gleamed in her eyes but did not fall. "I only sped up the testing process. The doctors would have figured it out on their own." She swallowed. "How do you feel?"

"I have had better days." He did not want to worry Raul and Grace. "But I will recover."

"Do the doctors know you're awake?" Eve asked.

"I would prefer not to inform them yet," Luis said. "Being with my family is curing my aches and pains."

"Are you in pain? Where?" she asked, her gaze skimming over his body with renewed anxiety.

He managed a rueful smile to cover the truth in his humor. "Everywhere. Even my hair. But it is bearable."

She did not return his smile. "What about Mikel? He should know," she pointed out.

Mikel's name brought darkness into the room. His head of security would be digging into the ugliness of who had done this to Luis, and how and why. Luis did not wish to face that yet, not when he was basking in the company of three people he loved with all his being.

The thought snapped his gaze to Eve's face. Yes, he loved her. It seemed impossible in such a short time, but he knew his own heart. Before she had come into the room, he had felt incomplete.

He needed to tell her that…when he could stand up and take her in his arms and kiss her objections away.

"Raul, please let Mikel know I am awake," Luis said with an inward sigh as the weight of being king settled onto his shoulders again.

Raul nodded and tapped at his phone, waiting a moment before saying, "He is on his way from the conference room."

"*Gracias, hijo mío,*" Luis said, wishing Mikel had been somewhere farther away and feeling guilty for it. He should be grateful for Mikel's devotion.

"If I might have some more water, please?" he said to Grace, wanting to savor a few extra moments of her solicitude before the world intruded.

He had time for three sips before the door opened to admit Mikel.

"*Señor!*" The word seemed to burst from his usually imperturbable security chief. Mikel approached Luis's bed and bowed low. "I rejoice to see you awake. How do you feel?"

"Better now that I am surrounded by my friends and family," Luis said in a non-answer. He had caught the combination of relief and guilt on Mikel's face and did not wish to add to the man's concerns. "Thank you for getting me to the hospital so quickly, my friend."

"Do not thank me," Mikel said, his face stark with regret. "*Señora* Howard called for help and also suggested that the doctors test for thallium poisoning. She is to be credited for your swift treatment."

Luis caught the look that Eve cast at Mikel, a quizzical lift of her eyebrows and a sardonic smile. He would ask her about it later.

"I am fortunate to have an entire team of protectors," Luis said before he forced himself to ask, "How is your investigation progressing?"

"I would not wish to trouble you with that now," Mikel said, skimming his gaze over the others.

Luis half lifted one hand to wave a dismissal of Mikel's discretion but laid it on the blanket again when he realized it was attached to an IV line. "If you have any answers, we would *all* like to hear them."

"Of course, *Su Majestad*," Mike said, his eyes blazing with ruthless determination. "We found the delivery mechanism for the poison. It was the book about fencing strategy that was given to you by Felipe Camacho."

"Camacho was one of the group complaining about the military base," Raul said, his voice hard.

Luis dredged up his encounters with the man but could remember nothing intense enough to incite murder. "He wanted to return to the imaginary good old days of Caleva, when honor and decency reigned. I don't know why that would cause him to want to kill his king, especially in a way that would be so easy to connect to him." Luis shook his head. "How did the book poison me?"

"Thallium poisoning can transpire through the skin," Mikel said. "Random pages in the book are infused with thallium, so when you touched them, it transferred to your fingers and worked its way into your tissues and bloodstream."

"I paged through it a couple of times before tonight." He hadn't actually read it since he had been distracted by thoughts of Eve. "I didn't become ill until now."

"The doctors can explain it more thoroughly, but evidently it built up in your system gradually," Mikel said.

"It's a heavy metal," Grace added. "It gets more concentrated over time with additional exposure."

Luis nodded to her. "That brings us to the question of Camacho's motive. Surely neither the military lease nor the minor incidents Camacho complained about are reasons for murder."

"When we find him, we will ask him." Mikel's face was like granite. "He left the country two days ago, but we are on his trail. I will let you know when he is in custody."

Luis nodded. Mikel would be relentless in his pursuit of Camacho. The man didn't stand a chance of escaping.

Suddenly, exhaustion swept over Luis like a wave.

"Perhaps you should call the doctor now," he said, letting his heavy eyelids drift closed.

Eve saw panic cross Raul's face as he pushed the call button.

"Don't worry," she said. "He'll slip in and out of sleep as his body sloughs off the poison."

In truth, she hated to see Luis's eyes closed. When Grace had texted her that Luis was awake, Eve had cried tears of relief that she had quickly washed away before racing down the hall to his room. While Luis still looked too frail and weak, his ice-blue eyes held their usual blazing intelligence and focus, and his smooth baritone grew stronger every time he spoke.

Now the vitality seemed to drain from him again.

Dr. Ibarra and three more medical personnel hurried into the room. "Is there a problem?" Dr. Ibarra asked.

"No," Luis said, his voice a low rasp. "I thought you should know that I am awake." His eyelids fluttered open. "I am just not sure how long I can stay that way."

Dr. Ibarra turned to Luis's visitors. "Would you please step outside so we may examine our patient?"

"I would like to speak with you as soon as you are finished," Raul said, in what was clearly a command.

"Of course, *Su Alteza Real*," the doctor said with a nod.

Mikel held the door as they filed out into the hallway. Eve was glad she had insisted that he be called into the room. She had caught the intense relief on the face of the usually unflappable security chief. He had needed to see that Luis was recovering.

"Let's go to the waiting area," Eve said, taking in the drawn faces of Grace and Raul. "The doctor will find us there."

Once again, Mikel ushered them through the door before he disappeared into the conference room.

Raul sank onto one of the sofas while Grace curled into an armchair beside him.

Eve was about to perch on the arm of Grace's chair when the prince dropped his head into his hands. His shoulders shook silently, and Eve realized he was sobbing. She changed directions to sit beside him.

"Raul, your father is going to be fine. You saw how alert and strong he was. He just needs more rest." If she said it firmly enough, it would be true.

Raul nodded into his hands but didn't lift his head. His voice was muffled as he said, "It's the relief. Before, he looked so..." His shoulders shook again.

"I know," Eve said soothingly. And she did. "But when he was awake, he was entirely himself."

"As long as there's no long-term damage." Raul raised his head and rubbed his hands over his cheeks. Grace held out a box of tissues, which he accepted. "Dr. Ibarra feels the thallium concentration wasn't high enough for that, but she said we have to wait and see."

"Doctors are always cautious about a prognosis," Eve said.

"I feel more confident of that after seeing him awake," Raul said.

Eve gave his shoulders a quick squeeze and shifted sideways a couple of feet to allow him his space.

But Grace moved to sit beside her half brother, leaning her head on his shoulder. "Mom's right. He just needs rest."

Raul put his arm around Grace. Her daughter was so smart. The prince was now focused on comforting his little sister instead of worrying about his father.

That allowed Eve to give in to her fear that Luis would die, even though he seemed to be fighting off the poison's effects with the help of the treatments he was getting. She felt herself begin to shake as the iron grip she had clenched around her feelings disintegrated. She leaped off the sofa and staggered over to the refrigerator, hoping the young people didn't notice her wavering gait. For a long moment, she clung to the door handle and leaned her forehead against the stainless steel.

Luis wasn't a dog or cat that had ingested the poison in an isolated barn. He was a human king who had merely brushed his fingers over it and who had the best medical care in the country.

Luis wouldn't suffer nerve damage. His kidneys wouldn't fail. He wouldn't even lose his glorious silver mane of hair. He would rise from his hospital bed with his chin tilted at its normal regal angle, dress in one of his custom-tailored suits, and stride out of the hospital as though nothing had happened.

She closed her eyes to imprint that rosy image on her terrified brain.

"Mom? Are you all right?" Grace's voice came from across the room.

Eve lifted her head and pulled open the refrigerator door. "Just debating what I want to drink." She took a deep breath before she turned. Grace and Raul still sat side by side on the couch. "Can I get you something?"

"A double shot of tequila?" Grace's voice held a sardonic note.

"Sounds good to me," Eve said. "But the best I can offer is Calevan beer."

"There's a full bar in the cabinet to your right," Raul said.

"If I drink anything alcoholic, I will fall over asleep," Grace said. "Just water, please."

Eve pulled three bottles of water from the fridge and brought them back to the seating area. The three of them sipped their water, too keyed up and exhausted to chitchat as they waited for news from Dr. Ibarra. Every once in a while, Mikel's voice would penetrate the closed door of the conference room, too muffled to distinguish any words but snapping with authority, impatience, or anger.

Eve tilted her head to rest against the back of the armchair, her eyelids drifting closed. Instead of her invented picture of Luis fully dressed and walking, she saw him lying in the hospital room, still as death. She jerked her head up to banish the image.

The door from the hospital corridor swung open, and Dr. Ibarra came through. All three of them jumped to their feet. Raul met the doctor halfway across the room. "What did your examination show?"

"We are very encouraged," Dr. Ibarra began. "*Su Majestad's* vital signs are moving back toward normal."

Eve had to grab the back of her chair to keep her knees from buckling in relief.

"He still needs rest, but we are confident he will make a full recovery," Dr. Ibarra continued.

"Oh, thank God!" Grace said, her voice half a sob.

Raul ran his hand over his face, his shoulders sagging inward before he straightened again. "What would you guess the time frame will be?" he asked. "I do not wish my father to return to work until you say he is ready, but we must decide what and when to tell the media."

Of course. Now that Luis was out of the woods, the fact that he was the head of the country became a pressing concern. Eve looked at Raul with respect.

The doctor grimaced. "*Su Majestad* wishes *Señores* Sanz and Vargas to come to the hospital later today. I advised against it, but..." Her shrug said that one could not override the king's commands.

Raul made a wordless sound of frustration. "One moment," he said to the doctor before going to the conference room door to knock and then open it. "Mikel, the doctor and I need your assistance."

Mikel emerged from the conference room immediately. "How may I help?"

"Dr. Ibarra, would you please repeat what you told me about my father's condition?" Raul asked.

As the doctor went through her report again, Eve saw a mixture of profound relief and searing guilt on Mikel's normally inscrutable face. The man must be exhausted to let so much emotion show. When Dr. Ibarra mentioned Luis's requested visitors, Mikel's mouth tightened into a grim line.

"You have to help me convince Pater to rest another day," Raul said to Mikel.

Mikel nodded but swung his gaze to Eve. "Perhaps you would add your voice to our efforts," he said. "His Majesty might give your words more weight."

Mikel did not elaborate on why, but Eve felt a warm flush climbing her cheeks. He didn't know that her relationship with Luis was over, but that didn't stop her from wanting Luis to give himself time to recover.

"I'll try," she said before turning to the doctor. "Is he still awake?"

"He was when I left him," she said.

Eve raised her eyebrows in a query to Raul. The prince nodded. "We'll see him now, Doctor."

Eve started to beckon for Grace to join them, when Raul—bless him!—said, "Grace, perhaps the newest member of our family can talk some sense into Pater."

All four of them trooped into Luis's room together. He opened his eyes as they approached his bed. "Ah, my favorite people have returned. I fear I won't be good company since the doctor tells me I should sleep."

"Exactly," Raul said. "Which is why Bruno and Francisco should not come to the hospital later today. It's Sunday. You have no official meetings scheduled. You must give yourself time to heal."

"*Ay, hijo mío*, we have arrangements to make for introducing Grace to Caleva," Luis said, his voice stronger than before.

"How do you think I will feel if you make yourself worse because of me?" Grace asked, her voice fierce. "*I* know I'm your daughter. That's all that matters right now."

"You are ganging up on me, I see," Luis said with a ghost of a smile. "Well, Mikel, what is your argument for keeping me away from my advisors?"

Mikel did not smile. "If you die, I will never forgive myself."

His words sliced the air with their stark truth. He was responsible for the king's security, so he blamed himself for not preventing Luis from being poisoned. Eve wanted to tell him not to be so hard on himself.

"That is blackmail, *mi amigo*," Luis said, his faint smile vanishing. "You will not shoulder the blame for this." He swept his gaze around the monitors surrounding him. "No one could have anticipated rat poison in the pages of a book."

"I must anticipate *everything*," Mikel said, his voice vibrating with intensity.

"You are not God. You cannot control the entire world," Luis said with the authority of a king. "Catch the man who did this, and you have done all that could be expected from any human being."

"He has already been located in Spain. My people are on their way to take him into custody." Mikel's face held a grim satisfaction.

"*Muy bien*," Luis said. "Congratulations on a job well done. I mean that." He sighed. "I will not summon Bruno and Francisco. Instead, I will call them to explain what has happened and where I am."

"I will do that, Pater," Raul said. "Once you start talking to them, you won't stop."

Amusement glinted in Luis's eyes. "You know me too well, *hijo mío*. All right, you speak with them. I will remain a useless lump in this bed for the rest of the day."

Relief rolled through Eve. She didn't have to contribute her two cents to the discussion.

"Eve, I would like to speak with you privately," Luis said, ruining her reprieve. "The rest of you need to go get some real sleep. The doctors will alert you if I show signs of expiring."

Raul and Grace looked cheered by their father's sardonic humor, even though they both cast inquiring looks at Eve.

As they bid Luis good night, Eve twisted her hands into a knot of tension. What did Luis want to talk with her about in the middle of the night in his hospital room? She was so wrung out that she could barely think straight…but maybe he was counting on that.

When the door closed behind the others, Luis held out the hand that was free of IV lines. "Eve!" His voice held such a combination of longing and exhaustion that her heart clenched.

She came to his bedside and took his hand, savoring the feel of his warm, strong fingers closing around hers. How was she going to leave this man when just the barest touch made her want to throw herself on the bed to curl up against his poor, abused body?

"How do you *really* feel?" she asked, searching his beloved face to find dark circles under his eyes and his skin still drawn harshly over his bones.

His grip tightened. "Like death warmed over, which is perhaps accurate." He brought her hand to his lips, pressing them against her palm in a kiss that reverberated down to her toes. "Thank you for saving my life."

"I didn't save your life." She couldn't stop herself from brushing the fingers of her free hand over the silk of his hair. "I don't know why people keep saying that."

He turned his head into her touch with a tiny moan of pleasure, and she stroked down his cheek.

"Dr. Ibarra is a highly qualified physician who is not prone to giving credit to others," Luis said. "Yet she says that your suggestion about thallium allowed them to begin treating the poison much faster than they otherwise would have done. If you did not save my life, you prevented any lasting aftereffects."

The thought of his beautiful, sculpted body damaged in any way made her flinch.

"I'm glad I guessed right," she said, waving her free hand in dismissal. "Please don't keep thanking me."

"I will not mention it again, but know that my profound gratitude to you remains in my heart." He frowned and brought their clasped hands up to rest on his chest. "We must talk, *querida*, but not here while I am weak and confined to this bed."

Thank God! She wouldn't be able to hold on to her resolution when he looked so in need of comfort, and especially not when he called her *darling* in Spanish in that deep velvet voice of his.

"Promise me that you won't leave Caleva until we've spoken alone," he said, his ice-blue eyes burning with the intensity of his request.

Her intention to sneak away to Iowa the moment the announcement about Grace was over went up in smoke. She had planned to put thousands of miles between them so she could reclaim her practical Midwestern good sense.

"I think we said all that was necessary last night," she evaded.

"I have so much more to say to you, *mi corazón*," he disagreed. "But this is not the place or the time. Please give me the chance."

Now he was calling her *his heart*. Hope swelled, but she smacked it down. He was just feeling overblown gratitude for her part in diagnosing the poison.

"I'll wait until we've talked," she said in a rush.

"Muy bien." His voice held relief as he squeezed her hand lightly. "I have another favor to ask of you."

Nothing could be worse than knowing she would have to say no to him yet again. "Of course," she said. "What can I do to help?"

"Would you stay with me until I fall asleep?" he asked. "With you, I do not have to be strong. I can just be a man who feels like shit."

He had just shot holes in her hard-won resistance, but at least he didn't know that.

"Let me pull up a chair," she said, glancing around.

"No, here." He patted the bed beside him with their clasped hands. "Next to me."

Just a few minutes before, she had fought off the desire to lie down beside him. "I don't know…"

"Please. Allow me that comfort." It was part command, part plea.

His naked need destroyed her already disintegrating defenses.

"Okay, but I have to be careful not to disconnect anything," she said, letting go of his hand to ease herself through the network of tubes and wires until she could stretch out on the bed.

He shifted so that he could drape his arm around her shoulders. "Come closer and rest your head on my chest. I want to see your beautiful, fiery hair."

She carefully scooted until she was pressed against his side from shoulder to knee. Even through the sheets, the heat and solidity of his body felt so exquisite that she nearly cried. When he stroked his other hand over her hair, murmuring, "So smooth, like silk," delicious shivers raced across her skin.

She felt his lips against the top of her head, the merest whisper of a touch, but her whole being was so sensitized to him that she could feel every tiny movement. His breath ruffling her hair, his pulse beating against her arm, the rhythm of his heart.

"*Ay*, Eve, I need this," he said. "I need *you*."

For now. He was weak and ill. He wanted a simple, easy kind of comfort. She could give him that. She snuggled closer, trying to weave her love around him like a cocoon of healing.

After a couple of minutes, the hand stroking her hair went still. His breathing deepened, but it wasn't until the powerful band of his arm went slack that she was certain he slept.

Yet she didn't move. It was too wonderful to be in bed one more time with this complex, demanding, brilliant man. Just as a man, not a king. She tried to memorize the masculine scent of him under the hospital smells and the way every part of him felt pressed against her.

Because this would be the last time.

CHAPTER 25

By Sunday evening, Luis had recovered enough to be thoroughly bored.

He had awakened in the morning without Eve in his arms, which he had expected but not approved of. Falling asleep with her soft, curving body pressed against his had been the only pleasure he had known since he had collapsed. He closed his eyes to remember the silk of her hair against his palm and his lips.

And then he snapped his eyelids open again so Raul wouldn't think he had gone back to sleep. All day long, Grace and Raul had taken turns sitting in the recliners to make sure he did nothing but sleep, eat, and be examined by the doctors. Grace had even chased Mikel out after he had made the bald announcement that Felipe Camacho had been captured and brought back to Caleva. Of course, Mikel followed Grace's command only because he also believed Luis should rest.

Luis had dubbed his children the royal tyrants, and his heart swelled at the delight of them caring for him.

In truth, sleeping most of the day had probably been the wisest course, but he would never admit that out loud.

Now he wanted Eve. He had not seen her since the delight of having her curled against him last night.

"Raul, I'm tired of sleeping. I want some conversation," he said. "Can you ask Grace and Eve to come in? And Mikel, if he's here."

That would camouflage his real target.

Raul glanced at his watch. "Only for half an hour or so."

"Who is the king here?" Luis said.

"You are the invalid king. As the healthy prince, I take precedence." Raul grinned. "Let me get you some entertainment, Pater."

Luis mock-huffed at his son's presumption. As soon as Raul closed the door, Luis raised the top of the bed so he was in a sitting position, then straightened the sheets to appear less rumpled. He glanced down at the V-necked teal T-shirt that he wore and decided it looked respectable, even though he had been wearing it since that morning. Not that he could change it anyway. Although he was attached to fewer monitors now, he still needed assistance to unleash himself.

He chuckled inwardly. If he was worried about how he looked for Eve, he was nearly recovered.

As the door opened, he squared his shoulders and lifted his chin to project his return to health. "Good evening," he said, his eyes on Eve as she followed her daughter into his room.

She had changed her clothes and was now wearing navy trousers and an emerald green blouse with white flowers scattered over it. His fingers itched to unbutton it to reveal the curves of her breasts.

Yes, he was definitely feeling better.

A delicious blush climbed Eve's cheeks as she said, "You look much better." And he knew she was remembering last night. *Good.*

"I feel my strength has returned, thanks to the excellent care I have received here." He let his gaze rest on the three of them.

The door opened again, and Mikel slipped in.

"*Señor.*" Mikel bowed after he had spent several seconds examining Luis's face. "I am glad to see you improved."

"Much improved, Mikel," Luis said. "I will be leaving the hospital tomorrow."

A chorus of protest arose. He silenced it with a wave of his hand. Or thought he had.

"Pater," Raul said, undeterred. "Bruno has already canceled all but the most pressing meetings tomorrow, and I will be handling those."

"Excellent. That will free me up to focus on the press conference announcing Grace as my daughter. I wish to hold it on Tuesday," Luis said.

"Dad, there's no rush," Grace said. "I don't want you to have a relapse because you've overtaxed yourself."

But the clock was ticking for many reasons. If Luis went back to the palace tomorrow, no one but Luis's closest circle needed to know about the poisoning. Mikel had kept even Lorenzo and Gabriel away from the hospital, despite their vociferous protests. His security chief had made the strong argument that the more members of the royal family who visited, the more likely someone would be spotted, bringing the media down on them. Luis had spoken with his family members by phone to assure them that he was not about to depart this mortal coil yet.

In addition, the editor at *La Voix* might become impatient at being put off and decide to run the photograph of Eve and him on the beach. The photo he now cherished. Odette's reaction was not such a concern now—although who could predict a madwoman's response?—but he wished to protect Eve from any distasteful speculation.

"I will do all my work sitting down," Luis said in a tone that brooked no argument. "Mikel, I expect a full briefing on Camacho tomorrow."

"Of course, *Señor.*" Mikel's face offered no clue as to how the investigation was progressing.

"Sit, everyone," Luis said, cutting off any further objections. "Talk to me. As Raul said, I need entertainment."

Eve snorted. "Are you calling us court jesters?"

He let his gaze run down her body as he thought about how he would prefer to entertain himself with her. She frowned at him with a warning glance at the others, who were finding places to sit. He gave her a lascivious smile that turned her frown into a scowl. She turned away as Mikel brought up a chair for her.

"Does anyone know a good joke?" Grace asked. "Jesters are supposed to make the king laugh, right?"

"When is a king like a piece of wood?" Eve asked with a slight edge in her voice as she threw him a challenging look.

"That's a riddle, not a joke," Grace said.

"I believe your mother may be referring to my stubbornness on the subject of my health," Luis said. "The correct answer is when he's a ruler."

His audience gave him a mocking cheer, while Eve rolled her eyes at him.

"What is the most frustrating thing for a dragon at its birthday party?" Raul chimed in.

They all looked at Luis. He thought for a moment before he shrugged.

"Wait, I know!" Grace held up her hand like a student in class. "Blowing out the candles."

Mikel surprised him by speaking. "What person is strong enough to move a king's castle?"

"You know riddles?" Eve asked, looking startled.

"I have a teenage daughter," Mikel said.

"I think I know the answer," Raul said. "Pater?"

"By all means," Luis said.

"A chess player." Raul looked triumphant.

"Nice!" Grace said. "Who designed King Arthur's round table?"

Eve gave a little choke of laughter. When no one else spoke, she blurted, "Sir Cumference."

Luis groaned along with the rest of them, but his heart was dancing. Eve and Grace had brought this lightness to his family and his life.

There was a long silence as everyone waited for him to contribute his own offering. He racked his brain, but all he could think of was the riddle of the Sphinx, and they would all know the answer to that. How could he not know a single other riddle? "Why are you looking at me? I'm the patient."

"We were hoping you could come up with something better than Grace's horrible pun," Raul said.

"Oh, I can do worse," Grace said. "What do you call the king's tax collector?"

"I don't want to know," Raul said.

"Sir Charge!" Grace crowed.

"No, no more!" Raul groaned, burying his face in his hands.

Luis chuckled and looked at Eve. Her face was alight with laughter as she watched Grace and Raul behaving like the siblings they were, finding the same joy in their banter that he did. Their gazes met. A shadow of regret dimmed her soft brown eyes, and he wanted to pull her into his arms to tell her there was no need for that.

Instead, he balled up a handful of hospital blanket in one fist and squeezed in frustration.

A chime sounded from Raul's phone. "Time's up," his son said, standing. "Pater needs to rest."

"*Ay, hijo mío*, do not consign me to boredom again," Luis objected. What he meant was that he wanted to cling to the happiness brightening his room. Even Mikel was sprawled casually in his chair.

But everyone else stood as well.

"What is happening here? It is treason to disobey your king's commands," Luis said in mock outrage.

"Not when the king refuses to listen to his doctors," Eve said. "Treason becomes good sense."

"That's what all traitors say," Luis grumbled.

He was somewhat mollified when Grace kissed him on the cheek and said, "I'm so glad you're feeling better, Dad."

The sound of *Dad* spoken in her delightful Midwestern accent sent a wave of warmth through him.

Mikel bowed, and Raul squeezed Luis's shoulder as he said good night, his love and worry written on his face.

Luis waited to see what Eve would do. She nodded to him. "Get a good night's sleep."

He opened his hand, palm up, on the blanket, but she flushed and gave a tiny shake of her head. He did not mean to ask her to stay. That could not happen again. But he craved her touch.

She backed away from his bed, and he closed his fingers around empty air.

Patience was a virtue he had learned to cultivate.

CHAPTER 26

"Lunchtime! Yes!" Grace said as she and Eve were ushered into a sitting room in the palace the next day. A buffet table held a platter of finger sandwiches, a tray of artfully arranged tapas, and an assortment of cookies and miniature cakes. When they had returned from the hospital that morning, they had been introduced to Carmen Molano, a stern, older woman with black hair and a black dress, who was in charge of preparing them for the announcement about Grace the next day. She had inspected their meager wardrobe and put together what she deemed appropriate outfits for them. The dark plum dress that Grace had worn for her first meeting with Luis passed muster, while Eve once again would wear her blue silk sheath. The royal photographer had been called in to approve the clothing and discuss hair and makeup. Then they had practiced waving because Grace would be presented in person to her new subjects on El Balcón de la Verdad, the Balcony of Truth, called that because the ruler was sworn always to speak the truth when he addressed his people from there.

Throughout it all, Eve worried about Luis. He had walked with a firm stride to the hospital elevator that morning, dressed in navy trousers and a light blue shirt, flanked by three bodyguards and Mikel. Yet the angles of his strong facial bones had jutted sharply under his drawn skin, and his face had held a gray pallor. He'd smiled as he lifted a hand in farewell, but it had seemed strained.

She desperately wanted to check on how he was doing, but Carmen had informed them that *Su Majestad* was working in his office and not to be disturbed. Not that Eve would have dared to insist on seeing him, but Grace was concerned about her father as well.

Grace piled food on a plate and plunked down in an armchair. "I'm surprised Carmen isn't here instructing us on how to eat a sandwich."

"I suspect it would involve a knife and fork," Eve said, adding paper-thin *jamón* to her own plate.

"Being a brand-new princess is exhausting, but the food is good," Grace said, wolfing down a finger sandwich in two bites.

Eve sat beside her daughter and put her plate on the side table between them. "Sweetheart, things are moving very fast now. I want you to stop for a moment and really think. Are you one hundred percent sure that you wish to be acknowledged as Luis's daughter? Because once the announcement is made, your life will never be the same."

Nor would Eve's, but that was secondary to her child's happiness.

"You mean because I might be poisoned?" Grace asked. "Or kidnapped? I know you're worried about that."

"I won't lie. I am concerned about your safety," Eve said.

"Mikel caught the man who poisoned Dad," Grace pointed out.

"But not before your father almost died," Eve said, the terror twisting her heart again.

"I'm not the king or even the crown prince, so I think I'll be less of a target," Grace said.

Eve winced at the last word, feeling the jab of it in her gut.

Grace must have seen it because she leaned over to touch Eve's forearm. "Dad told me that Gabriel and Raul were extremely drunk when Gabriel got kidnapped, and they had stupidly ditched their bodyguards. I will be more careful, I promise." She gave Eve's arm a little squeeze. "Besides, I could just as easily get trampled by a crazed horse at vet school. Or bitten by a rabid fox."

"I know, sweetie," Eve said with a sigh. Grace was still young enough not to believe in her own mortality. "But what about the other issues? You've now seen firsthand how careful your father has to be about his private life." Guilt about the photo on the beach poked at her again. "You can't even see a doctor without having it be news."

And that was why Luis was not allowing himself to recuperate as his body needed to.

"It's going to be a big change, and some of it isn't so great." Grace ate another bite of sandwich as she considered. "But I balance it against the good I can do for animals. As a vet, I could help maybe a couple of hundred animals. As a princess, I can help thousands, maybe even millions, if I can get international attention. How amazing is that?"

"Amazing indeed." Eve hated to follow that with another ugly topic, but she needed to know how Grace was handling it. "There's another concern, though. No matter what false trails Mikel lays, or how many denials Luis issues, someone, sometime will find out that Odette is your biological mother."

"Probably Odette herself will tell them," Grace said, a flicker of disgust in her voice. "She is fine with kidnapping and mutilation—so I'm sure she would have no qualms about ignoring her promise to me."

"I'm so sorry." Eve hated that Grace would carry the knowledge of her birth mother's sins for the rest of her life. "You should not allow her crimes to cast shadows over your own life."

Grace made a pushing motion with her hand. "That's not it." She turned a face of misery to Eve. "I tell myself I should be grateful that Odette didn't raise me herself. What kind of person would I be if she had? But it's hard to be rejected by your criminal psychopath of a biological mother. Not even such a damaged person wanted me as her child."

Eve's heart nearly ripped in two. She leaped out of her chair and knelt in front of Grace. "She didn't reject you because *you* were damaged. She did it because *she* is so damaged that she is incapable of loving anyone, not even the most amazing daughter in the world." Grace choked out a sob. Eve gave her hands a gentle squeeze. "Do you know how often I have blessed your birth mother for giving you to me? Every single day! How ironic that I am so profoundly grateful to a terrible person, but she did at least one good deed in her life."

Eve drew back to lock her gaze on Grace's tear-streaked face. "I've never told anyone else this, but the first time I held you in my arms, I felt more than just gratitude and love. I felt a profound connection with you. I felt that you were meant to be my child, but my body couldn't carry you, so you borrowed Odette's, just to get you onto this earth. She was only a vessel. I was always your real mother." Eve stroked Grace's damp cheek. "Sorry if that sounds a little crazy, but I believed it then, and I still do."

"Mom, you're the sanest person I know," Grace said. "I like your story better than mine because it *feels* true here." She touched her chest over her heart. "If anyone tries to claim that Odette is my mother, I will tell them how wrong they are. My one and only mother is Eve Howard from Ames, Iowa."

Eve used her napkin to blot the tears as Grace's words wound around her own heart. "Never forget that, sweetheart. You have strong roots."

Grace mopped her face and took a deep breath. "I needed to get that straight in my head. And that's why I need you here in Caleva with me."

Which required that Eve uproot her life and move it to a foreign country. Hadn't she longed for adventure when she was a teenager? Here it was, and she was terrified. Her worry for Grace might be so pressing because it was intertwined with her own anxieties.

"Okay, you've convinced me that you know what you're getting into," Eve said, knowing when she was beaten. "From now on, it's full speed ahead into your future."

"And yours." Grace's face was solemn.

If only her daughter knew how hard it was going to be for Eve to see Luis and not be able to touch him. Eve curled her fingers into fists on her lap.

Grace gestured to Eve's untouched plate. "You should eat. Who knows when they'll allow us a meal break again since this afternoon is about rehearsing for our official appearance."

It was useful to have young people around. They focused on the necessities of life.

⚜

Luis leaned back in his desk chair and closed his eyes. His speech was complete. Grace's shorter speech was ready for her approval. Bruno had set up the press conference, and Mikel was organizing security for the royal family's appearance on the balcony.

Now that events were well under way, exhaustion dragged at every inch of his body, and he longed to collapse on the soft, comfortable couch beckoning to him from just across the room.

Someone knocked on the door. Luis forced his eyes open and sat up straight. "Come in."

His brother came through the door. "Luis, *hermano*, I just heard that you were here." Lorenzo stopped in front of the desk while he scanned Luis. "You don't look well. Why are you not still in the hospital?"

"Because I felt recovered enough to be bored." Luis tried to brush off his brother's concern with levity, but he was touched nonetheless. "And I couldn't take the chance that the media would find out where I was."

"*Ay, imbécil!* You are going to end up back there, only worse," his brother said, glaring at him. "At least go lie down in your *habitación*."

"I can't," Luis said, not bothering to try to keep the fatigue out of his voice. "I have run out of time and must announce my daughter's existence to Caleva. That's why I've called the whole family to the palace tonight. The announcement will be made tomorrow."

Lorenzo sat. "At least it is a happy occasion that drags you out of bed. But what about your poisoner?"

"I want that kept quiet for now. Such ugliness should not cast a shadow on the joy of Grace's presence." Luis let his head rest against the chair's back. "Mikel has brought the perpetrator back here and has questioned him. I expect his report soon."

"I want to be present to hear why this madman tried to murder you." Lorenzo's voice held anger.

"You are welcome to join the briefing." Luis would have put it off himself until he had the energy to muster some of the same fury, but Mikel's hard work deserved a prompt hearing.

"Have you eaten?" Lorenzo asked, his gaze on the plate of tapas sitting on Luis's desk.

"My stomach still feels like it got kicked by a mule," Luis admitted.

Lorenzo winced in sympathy.

There was a knock before the door opened to admit Raul and Mikel.

"*Señores.*" Mikel's bow acknowledged both Luis and his brother.

"*Pater, Tío.*" Raul lowered his head in a respectful greeting before he took the chair next to Lorenzo's. He waited a beat and asked, "Shouldn't Grace and Eve be here?"

Luis had considered that. "They have enough on their plate preparing for the announcement tomorrow. Once that is over, we will bring them into the loop." With a carefully edited version of the facts, if necessary. Eve was already worried enough about Grace's safety.

Mikel remained standing, a laptop and a folder tucked under his arm.

"What have you found out?" Luis asked him.

Mikel placed the folder on the desk. "If I may summarize?"

Luis nodded.

"Felipe Camacho's twenty-two-year-old daughter began dating a U.S. sailor from the military base. She became pregnant, and the two decided to marry. Camacho is very conservative. He found it shameful that his daughter was pregnant without being married."

"Ah, that's why he felt the need for a return to decency and morality," Luis said, the man's words coming back to him.

Mikel continued. "He blamed the sailor for seducing her and refused to allow the young man in his home. At the same time, he attempted to confine his daughter to the house so she could not see her lover and so that no one would know she was pregnant."

"That's not conservative," Raul muttered. "That's medieval."

Luis thought of Grace. Never would he treat her in such a cruel way.

"Not surprisingly," Mikel continued, "the sailor assisted Camacho's daughter in escaping, they married, and the daughter moved to the United States to be near the sailor's family, where the baby was born. She has refused to let her father visit his grandson."

"Who can blame her?" Lorenzo said.

"Unfortunately, her refusal drove Camacho off the deep end," Mikel said. "He developed a deep hatred of the U.S. military presence in Caleva, and he holds *Su Majestad* responsible for it. That led him to concoct an elaborate plan to poison you, *Señor*." Mikel paused for a moment. "I believe it was a way to sublimate his anguish at losing his daughter and grandson."

"Which he brought on himself," Raul said without sympathy.

Luis understood the man's agony at being separated from his child and grandchild, but he felt no sympathy for him.

"First, he got elected to the Consejo de los Ciudadanos because he felt that would be the best way to gain access to the palace," Mikel said. "He attached himself to the group of malcontents who would be most likely to meet with you, in this case about the naval base's lease since it's in his district. He is a professor of mathematics at the university, which allowed him to use the school's chemistry laboratory. There, he created the poisoned pages in the book, using thallium rat poison that he obtained from Eastern Europe."

"A book?" Lorenzo asked.

"He presented me with a recently published volume about fencing history and strategy," Luis said. "He even recommended particular chapters to read. I wonder if those pages held the most poison."

"It was inspected via the usual security measures, including testing random pages for harmful substances," Mikel said, his voice without inflection, but Luis saw the hollowness of failure in his eyes. "The poisoned pages were not among those tested in the initial inspection."

"An elaborate plan indeed," Lorenzo said. "The man must be highly intelligent in a twisted way."

"I'm almost flattered," Luis murmured. "And a little surprised." Camacho didn't seem like a criminal mastermind.

Mikel's lips tightened. "Camacho claims he did not wish you to die, so he infused only scattered pages with the thallium. He just wished you to suffer some of the pain that he felt."

"His intention is unimportant," Lorenzo snapped. "He poisoned the king."

"He will be tried and sentenced, Lorenzo," Luis said. "With the full force of the law. But not until after we have introduced Grace to Caleva. Let joy reign first."

"That completes the summary of my report," Mikel said. "I would be happy to answer any questions."

"Questions can wait until I've read the report," Luis said, eyeing the couch again.

Lorenzo and Raul understood the meeting was at an end and stood.

"May I speak with you privately, *Señor?*" Mikel asked.

Luis swallowed a groan. "Of course."

His son and brother said their farewells.

Mikel set his laptop on the desk and flipped it open. "I would like to play you part of the recording of the interrogation."

"By all means," Luis said as Mikel swiped at the laptop's screen.

"This is taken from the camera that records the prisoner head-on so that facial expressions and body language can be analyzed later," Mikel explained as he started the video.

Felipe Camacho sat in a cone of light with dimness surrounding him. His mane of white hair hung limply around his face, and he sat slumped in a metal chair, his handcuffed hands resting on a metal table.

Mikel's voice came from off-camera. "You call yourself a patriot, wanting Caleva to be only for Calevans. Yet you attempted to murder your king, which is not the act of a loyal Calevan. Why?"

Camacho's head snapped up. "No! I did not try to murder him! I only wanted him to feel the daily pain that I feel. He would not die. She promised me that."

"*She?*" Mikel asked. "Who is *she?*"

Luis's fatigue vanished as his attention was riveted on the man in the chair.

Camacho shook his head, his lips pressed together.

"Who is *she?*" Mikel's voice was implacable. "She caused you to nearly commit regicide. You owe her no loyalty. Who is she?"

But Luis knew. And it explained the complexity of the scheme to poison him.

"I don't know," the prisoner said. "I never met her. She never told me her real name."

"How did she contact you?" Mikel asked.

"I met with a group of people who were looking for candidates for the *consejo*. Candidates who want change in Caleva. I told them my daughter's story so they would understand my commitment." Camacho's handcuffs rattled on the tabletop in his agitation. "Several days after my interview with them, I received an email at my university address. It was signed just Isabella."

Isabella. The name of the infamous Queen of Caleva who had hurled her half siblings off the heights of Acantilado Alto. Odette and her mind games.

"You conspired to murder your king via email?" Mikel's question dripped with incredulity.

"Of course not. I am not stupid." Camacho was insulted. "We used a dead drop and handwrote our communications."

"And how did she persuade you to poison the king?"

"She knew about my daughter. How I have suffered. She, too, has lost a daughter, so she understood my need to exact payment."

Such a lying, manipulative *bruja*. Rage boiled in Luis's chest.

"Whose idea was the thallium?" Mikel asked.

"Isabella's. She knew where to obtain it and that it could be absorbed through the skin, since poisoning Luis's food would be nearly impossible. She suggested using a book, and I found exactly the right title to pique the king's interest." Satisfaction vibrated in Camacho's voice.

"I also made the calculations about where to place the poisoned pages in the book," Camacho continued. "Even if he read two chapters at a time, he would only receive enough poison to create discomfort, not death."

"How did you know he would read only a chapter or two at a time?" Mikel asked.

"He is the king, a very busy man," Camacho said. "He would not have the leisure time to read the entire book at once."

"Did you not consider that he might page through it, rather than reading it chapter by chapter?" Mikel prodded.

"He would receive no benefit from glancing through it," Camacho said. "*Su Majestad* is an expert fencer. He would wish to learn from the book, not just look at the pictures."

Luis shifted in his chair. He had paged through the volume repeatedly because he had been distracted by his feelings for Eve. How ironic that he had nearly killed himself that way.

Mikel stopped the recording. "The rest is more of the same."

"It was Odette," Luis said, fear and fury spinning through his brain. "She has her tentacles deep in that group of malcontents in the *consejos*. We have to find and shut down her conduit to them."

Mikel nodded stiffly.

"You did the right thing in not sharing this with the others," Luis said, drumming his fingers on the desk as he considered the implications of a public trial. "We must tread very carefully."

"Thus far we have no proof of Odette's involvement," Mikel pointed out.

"I do not doubt your ability to unearth it," Luis said. "I'm just not yet sure how I wish to use it."

Mikel cleared his throat and pulled an envelope from his breast pocket but did not offer it to Luis. "*Señor*, I wish to apologize for the breach in security, both at the prison and here," he said, his voice tight. "This is my letter of resignation. My hope is that you will not accept it. Not because I deserve another chance, but because I will redouble my efforts to prevent such a terrible event from occurring again."

Luis waved Mikel's apology and letter away. "I don't want your resignation."

"Why not? It is my job to prevent harm from coming to you." Mikel's eyes burned with regret.

"A crazed intruder once got into the Queen of England's bedroom. U.S. presidents occasionally get shot," Luis said. "We are targets, and sometimes a madman or madwoman will get through even the most rigorous defenses." He held out his hand. "The letter, please."

Mikel frowned as he gave the envelope to Luis. His security chief's expression lightened when Luis tore the envelope in half and then in quarters before dropping it into the shredding bin.

"I need to pay another visit to Odette," Luis said. "We must come to an understanding. Set it up for early tomorrow morning and keep the visit between the two of us." The anger-fueled adrenaline was draining away, leaving him aching and exhausted.

Mikel bowed, picked up his laptop, and exited without a word.

Luis pressed a button on his desk that signaled he should not be disturbed. Then he went to the couch, arranged a couple of pillows at one end, and stretched out on the cushions with a groan.

CHAPTER 27

With a huff of relief, Luis seated himself in the warden's leather chair. His legs were still shaky and painful from the thallium, and he was eating only the blandest of foods. He could not show weakness now, though.

He braced his forearms on the desk and nodded to one of the cameras, signaling his security chief next door that he was ready.

A few minutes later, the outer door opened, and Odette shuffled into the room with her escort of guards. She did not raise her head to look at Luis until the guards had fastened her chains to the floor clamps and left the two of them alone.

"Another visit from His Majesty the King," she said, her voice laced with sarcasm.

"We have Camacho in custody," Luis said.

Odette's gaze flickered for a split second, but she covered it with a blank look. "Who is Camacho, and why should I care?"

"Don't bother," Luis said, too tired to spar with her. "I came to tell you that we are shutting down your computer privileges permanently. The only person you will meet with from now on is your lawyer, and those meetings will be monitored via camera and by a guard. All of your assets have been frozen and put in escrow for your heirs, to be released only on the occasion of your death." As Luis recited each item, he found satisfaction in seeing a flash of panic in her eyes.

"You have no grounds on which to base your withdrawal of my protected rights as a prisoner. I will file a formal protest," Odette said with a snarl.

Luis leaned forward. "You conspired with Felipe Camacho to commit regicide, the only crime in Caleva that carries a death sentence."

Instead of flinching, she made an insolent appraisal of him. "I would applaud this Felipe Camacho, except that you do not look dead to me. I confess to being disappointed in him." Then she gave him a knowing smile. "Even if you could prove I was involved, you wouldn't invoke the death sentence because that would cause our daughter pain."

She put the slightest emphasis on *our*, which made Luis's vision go red with anger. "She is not your daughter," he said.

"Her DNA says otherwise," Odette said.

And then it clicked into place. Grace was Odette's insurance policy. Odette had told Luis about his child because she had set in motion her plan to poison him. If she failed and got caught, Grace's existence would save Odette's life.

"In fact, you don't dare put me on trial," Odette said with a smug lift of her eyebrows. "I might be provoked into saying something you would regret. In fact, you won't try even this Camacho person because I might somehow get dragged into it. It's a delicate situation."

She was enjoying what she perceived as her position of power.

"Did you promise him immunity?" Luis asked, amazed at her arrogance. "You were wrong. He will be tried and convicted."

Rage blazed in her face. "You wouldn't risk that."

"Camacho committed the highest treason against the King of Caleva, and it is my duty to protect the crown from any and all threats," Luis said, although it was going to be the most carefully staged trial ever to take place during his reign. He winced inwardly at the sensation it would cause in the media.

"Then I will tell the world that Grace is my daughter," Odette said, her chains rattling as she shifted in her chair.

"How?" Luis asked. "You will have no communication with the outside world that isn't censored. Not to mention that now no one will take you seriously because you have no evidence. I have made sure of that."

Odette tensed as though she would leap at him despite her shackles, but then she settled back. "We are at an impasse. I will remain silent about being Grace's biological parent, and you won't try me for treason because it would hurt Grace to have her birth mother executed."

"I don't intend to invoke the death sentence for Camacho because he was just a tool that you manipulated," Luis said. "But he will spend the rest of his life in prison."

"Perhaps we can share a cell," Odette mocked.

Luis leaned forward on the desk and put all the ferocity and power of his position in his voice. "If you attempt to harm anyone in my family, I will not hesitate to put you on trial for attempted regicide and carry out the death sentence. If you had bothered to speak with my daughter on your visit to Iowa, you would have learned that Grace is a strong young woman whose integrity is bone-deep. She would understand the necessity of bringing you to justice."

"She doesn't know about my alleged role in your poisoning?" Odette asked in surprise. "Why wouldn't you use that as a weapon against me?"

"Because I am capable of making someone else's needs a priority over my own. It's not a mentality you could comprehend." Luis bared his teeth in a non-smile. "Although you will understand that I hold the information about your crime in reserve in case of future need. Keep that in mind."

"You should keep in mind that I am not done with you," Odette said with a hiss. "I will make you pay."

Without another word, Luis pushed the button that summoned the guards, stood up from the warden's chair, and walked out of the office, leaving Odette chained to the floor.

That afternoon, the royal family and Eve gathered in the original throne room in the most ancient part of Castillo Draconago. The rough-hewn stone walls were hung with huge tapestries depicting ships at sea, Calevan dragons cavorting on rocks, and deep-red lilies blooming amid mists and cliffs. In the middle of the outside wall were the huge oak double doors that led to El Balcón de la Verdad, where the kings and queens of Caleva had appeared to their subjects over the centuries.

Eve stood apart from the royals, her hands knotted together in front of her to stop their trembling. Then the shakiness migrated to her knees. As she looked around at the faces marked by the unmistakable Dragón features, all she wanted to do was slink away through a side door. Only her love for Grace kept her in this room where she did not belong.

The press conference had been sensational, the reporters beside themselves with excitement at the story of the unknown princess. Eve had watched it on a video monitor in a private room. The conference had also been broadcast to giant screens set up on the plaza outside the palace. The clamor of the crowd had penetrated even the three-foot-thick castle walls.

Luis looked every inch a modern-day monarch in his dark gray suit, pale blue shirt, and lily-red tie. On camera, he radiated power, strength, and authority. Only Eve, Grace, and Raul knew how much makeup it had taken to give Luis's skin that healthy glow.

When Grace had given her prepared speech from memory in a bell-clear voice without a tremor, Eve had nearly burst with pride in her daughter. Grace was more than worthy to be *la Princessa del Vaho*.

Now her daughter stood with her father and Raul, the three of them forming a unit that excluded Eve.

She had known this would happen, but it still sank fangs of sharp jealousy and aching loneliness into her soul.

The king's assistant, Bruno, went to the balcony doors. "*Su Majestad*, would you like to greet your people now?" he asked in a formal tone.

Luis looked at Grace, who took a deep breath and nodded. Luis stepped toward the door, Raul on his right side and Grace on his left. The rest of the family arrayed themselves in the places they had rehearsed the day before. Eve found her assigned position beside Gabriel. He flashed a reassuring smile at her. When she tried to return it, the muscles of her mouth wouldn't cooperate.

"Just smile and wave," he said in a low voice. "That's all that is required."

In fact, she and Grace had been warned not to say anything—unless it was totally innocuous—because the media employed lip-readers.

Bruno and another staff member pulled open the doors, and the roar of the crowd surged into the room like a tidal wave. Eve tried to will her knees not to buckle as she stepped onto the balcony a pace behind the king and his two children.

The huge plaza was packed with people, some waving Calevan flags of teal, red, and gold. The spectators clung to lampposts, filled balconies, perched on roofs, and overflowed onto the streets that fed into the plaza.

As Grace lifted her hand in the wave they had been taught by Carmen, the crowd began to chant, *"La Princessa! La Princessa!"*

Eve's quaking terror got shoved aside for a moment as she reveled in her daughter's triumph. Grace was not just being acknowledged by her father. She was being embraced by an entire country.

When Luis put his arm around Grace's shoulders, the chant changed to, *"El Rey Luis! La Princessa!"*

As Gabriel raised his hand, the roar grew louder. He was considered a hero in Caleva, not to mention a famous musician, so he was tremendously popular. Happy to stand in his shadow, Eve locked her knees and put up her hand as well, even though she was sure no one knew or cared who she was.

Then her own daughter betrayed her by turning, holding out her hand, and nearly shouting to be heard. "Mom! Come up here with me!"

For Grace, she would do anything, so she forced herself forward to stand beside her daughter and wave again, the thousands of voices nearly deafening her. Behind the balustrade, Grace found Eve's free hand and gave it a quick squeeze, tossing her mother a brief look that said, *Can you believe this?*

Eve somehow smiled back.

As she did, she glanced sideways at Luis. His silver hair gleamed in the sunlight, and his smile blazed with joy. Standing with his chin and hand lifted, he seemed to grow taller, as though he drew strength from the respect and devotion of his people.

Maybe that deep connection explained why he was such a great king.

Eve kept smiling and waving and wishing she could sink through the stone floor of the balcony until she had no idea of how much time had passed.

At last, Bruno's voice came from behind them, saying, "You may return to the Antiguo Salón del Trono."

No one moved until Luis gave a final wave and turned. Then the group parted like the sea to let the king, Raul, and Grace pass through before trailing them back into the room. Eve knew the doors had closed by the sudden muffling of the cheers.

As Eve tried to regain her equilibrium, the members of the royal family chatted as though nothing special had happened, discussing their plans for the next day's dinner, asking about a political matter, or even cracking a joke. As though being greeted by cheering crowds was an everyday occurrence.

It probably was. Not every day, but often enough to be treated as no big deal. Soon, Grace would come to feel this way, too, taking it in her stride as though it was just another meeting in her busy royal life.

The distance between Eve and Grace yawned wider and wider, like the rift between tectonic plates pulling apart.

For a moment, Eve could barely breathe as the impact of it slammed into her chest.

She gulped in air as she watched her daughter accept a hug from Lorenzo's elegant wife, Hélène. Luis stepped back to give his brother room to offer Grace his congratulations as well. Eve caught the moment Luis staggered for a step and grasped the carved back of a medieval wooden chair with one hand to steady himself.

The man had nearly died of thallium poisoning three days before, and now he was pretending that he was fine.

Eve might not be part of the royal family, but she wasn't going to allow their stubborn idiot of a king to exhaust himself to the point of collapse. She loved him too much for that.

She marched across the antique carpet and fetched up beside Luis. He gave her a smile that had a strained quality to it, and he did not let go of the chair. "Eve, our daughter is handling herself with amazing poise and dignity."

A spurt of pride made Eve pause her mission for a moment as she watched Grace laughing with Gabriel and Quinn. "She's quite an impressive princess," she agreed. "But you and I need to talk."

Luis's smile vanished. "What is the problem?"

Eve moved in front of him so her back was to the group of royals. "I saw you nearly fall a moment ago. You need to go back to your apartment and rest. Now."

"I cannot," Luis said. "Grace and I have an interview with *La Voix*. It is their reward for killing the photo of us on the beach." His smile was slightly wicked this time. "I treasure that picture myself."

Eve's traitorous body answered his smile with a liquid slide of heat. "Have Bruno cancel it, or I will. If you don't go to bed now, I will sic Dr. Ibarra on you."

"Dr. Ibarra cannot order me to bed." His voice held all the arrogance of his position.

"She can tell your family that you require several days of bed rest. I'm pretty sure they can apply enough pressure to put you back in the hospital."

"*Ay*, Eve, you don't know what you ask," Luis said.

She stepped closer to him and locked her gaze on his face. "I know that everyone in this room cares deeply about you. If you don't make an exit in the next five minutes, I will tell them what I saw."

And then she waited with her fingers mentally crossed. If he refused, no one could actually make him go to bed.

His sigh seemed to come from his toes. "*Bien*. But you will accompany me to my *habitación*...as my crutch. I do not wish to stumble on the way."

He must feel like crap to have agreed so quickly, but not for a second did she think he needed her assistance. However, if she could get him into his bed faster that way, she would do it.

"Please continue to welcome Grace into the family," Luis said, changing the timbre of his voice so everyone turned to listen. "I must speak with Eve and Bruno privately."

There was a chorus of goodbyes. Raul met his father's eye, and Luis gave a small shake of his head. Luis gestured Eve toward a door that Bruno hurried to open for them.

"Bruno, I regret to ask this of you, but I must cancel the interview with *La Voix* today," Luis said, striding down a passage lined with suits of armor. "Tell them they still have the exclusive but reschedule it for tomorrow."

The king's assistant didn't blink. "Of course, *Señor*."

"That is all I require now," Luis said, continuing to walk.

"Yes, *Señor*." Bruno peeled off at an intersecting corridor.

As soon as his assistant was gone, Luis slowed his pace. "We need to be deep in conversation so no one approaches us."

"Okay. Um, will Grace have a Bruno equivalent?" Eve asked, matching her stride to Luis's. Should she take his arm to support him?

"Yes, she may choose from our palace staff, or she may hire from the outside, as long as Mikel has vetted the candidate," Luis said.

"I could use a Bruno myself," Eve said. "He's pretty handy."

"He would be flattered to hear you say that," Luis said.

As they made a turn, the corridor became wider and less medieval. It also had people bustling through it. Luis picked up his pace, and people stepped to the side with respectful half bows in a ripple of movement as he passed. Every now and then, someone murmured, *"Felicidades,"* which Eve assumed was meant as congratulations to Luis on his newly discovered daughter.

One man started to approach them, but Luis looked down his nose while giving a minuscule shake of his head. The man practically doubled over in a bow as he backed away.

"What should we talk about?" Eve asked, remembering that they should be conversing.

"Grace, because she is an extraordinary young woman." His voice held both wonder and pride. "And you are an extraordinary mother. She is who she is because of you. *Gracias a Dios* that Odette chose you to raise our child."

Eve stumbled as his words tore through her, leaving a confusion of emotions in their wake. Gratification at his tremendous compliment was a brilliant glow, but resentment at the way he had taken her daughter away from her seared like acid. Overshadowing it all was the loneliness that hollowed her out.

"Thank you," she choked out.

"Are you all right, *querida?*" he asked in a low voice.

"Please don't call me that," she said as the endearment slashed at her heart.

His mouth tightened with displeasure. People moved out of their way with speed now.

They made another turn into a hallway where two guards in dark suits stood in front of closed double doors. She recognized it as the entrance to the private quarters of the palace.

One guard leaped to open the doors. *"Su Majestad. Señora."* He bowed them through.

The doors closed behind them, and Luis slowed again. "That was a long hike," he said.

Eve put her arm around his waist. "Lean against me, and I'll help you."

He wrapped his arm over her shoulders and surprised her by shifting so she was carrying some of his weight. "You must feel worse than I thought."

"I'm just tired," he said. "The emotions have been powerful these last few days."

They passed the door to Eve and Grace's suite and continued toward the end of the hallway where Luis pressed his thumb against the electronic pad, and the latch clicked open.

"Come in with me," he said. *"Por favor."*

She nodded because he still leaned on her. They went through the wide doorway and into the sitting room where Luis had collapsed. Now, everything was neat as a pin, and the air held the faint clean scent of citrus. There was even a new leather trash can.

He headed for a door across the room, where she could see a large ornately carved bed. She would get him in there and then clear out.

He was leaning on her more heavily now. Why did the rooms in his *habitación* have to be so darn huge?

But they made it into his bedroom, where he sagged onto the giant bed, which had wooden frilled dragons winding up and down the bedposts. The carvings would give Eve nightmares.

Eve knelt at his feet to untie his polished wingtips.

"You do not need to do that," Luis said. "I can manage."

She glanced up at his drawn face. Even the makeup couldn't hide his pallor now. "You take care of your necktie."

She heard the rustle of silk as she slipped off his shoes. When she stood again, the necktie lay tossed on the other side of the bed, and he was unbuttoning the top buttons of his shirt.

God, she wanted to comb her fingers through his silvery hair and kiss his deliciously sculpted lips. He would pull her down with him as he fell back onto the green velvet duvet, and they would strip off each other's clothes...

"Eve." Whatever he saw in her face had lit a hot blue flame in his eyes.

She took a step backward. "Right. Do you want to change into pajamas?" she said in her cheerful, no-nonsense, vet tech-to-pet owner voice. "Tell me where to find them."

"I do not need pajamas." His voice was a low purr. "But perhaps you will help me with my clothes."

"Nope. You're on your own with that." She backed up another two steps. "I'm going to go sit in your living room to make sure you stay in this bed for the next three hours."

"I will not be able to sleep knowing you are almost within my reach. Stay here with me, as you did in the hospital," he said, holding out his hand, those long, elegant fingers beckoning her to give in to temptation.

Remembering how they had touched her sent a rush of heat between her legs.

"Once your head hits that pillow, you won't be able to keep your eyes open," she said. "Now lie down before you fall over."

He gave a ghost of a laugh. "You would be safe with me for that very reason."

Pulling back the covers, he lifted his long legs and slid between the sheets, making her ache to slide in with him.

"Promise you will be here when I wake up," he murmured as he closed his eyes.

She couldn't stop herself from coming back to his bedside. Leaning over, she smoothed her hand over his gleaming hair and laid a gentle kiss on the smooth skin of his temple.

The gladness in his smile almost broke her heart.

Luis woke up slowly and with some confusion, opening his eyes to find himself in his bedroom in the dimness of dusk. A line of bright light from the barely open door traced across the Persian rug, but no voices came from beyond it.

He pushed himself upright as memory returned. Eve had forced him into bed but had refused to join him. It would have been so much better to wake with her lovely body curled against his side.

But she had promised to stay outside the door to keep his sleep from being interrupted. That prodded him to throw off the covers, scrub his hands over his face a couple of times, and cross the room to push open the door.

Raul sat at Luis's desk, typing away on a laptop. Grace perched cross-legged on the sofa with a tome of Calevan history open on her lap, earbuds in her ears.

And Eve was curled in an armchair by the fireplace, reading on a tablet. Someone must have brought her a change of clothes, because she wore jeans and a pale green shirt. The sight of her bare feet with their bright red nail polish sent a flicker of lust through him.

She looked up even though he swore he hadn't made a sound. "Luis!" Her tablet slid out of her hand to thud onto the floor as she stood. "How are you feeling?"

He felt her gaze roam over his face and body as though she touched him, but her inspection was clinical. A doctor examining a patient.

"I hate to admit it, but better," he said, raking his fingers through his hair as he realized he must look disheveled.

Raul leaped up from his chair, while Grace pulled out her earbuds, both of them calling out their chosen names for him. *Pater. Dad.* He grabbed the doorframe as his heart twisted in his chest.

This! This was what he wanted his life to be. No more of the solitary ruler knocking around in his lonely *habitación*. He wanted to be greeted by a woman who stood up to him for his own good and his two children who worried about their father's well-being. This was what it felt like to be loved.

Grace bolted across the room to give him a quick hug before she stepped back to survey him with a critical gaze reminiscent of her mother's. "Are you sure you feel better?"

Raul followed his half sister but contented himself with giving Luis's shoulder a firm squeeze. "You slept for over five hours, Pater."

"Ah, that explains the darkness in my room," Luis said, but he was looking at the woman across the room. The woman who kept this distance between them.

That had to stop.

Tomorrow, he *must* convince her how wrong she was about him.

CHAPTER 28

Eve and Grace sat in the back of a black SUV, escorted by two other black SUVs, on their way to Casa en las Nubes. Eve leaned her head against the leather seatback with gratitude. The last three days had drained her.

After the morning's interview with *La Voix*—which Grace had handled like a champion—Luis had called the royal family together to brief them on the identity of his poisoner. While the mood was solemn, no one seemed overly shocked that a crazed math professor had nearly murdered Luis. It made Eve wonder how often such things happened but were covered up. Which made her worry about Grace's safety even more.

As soon as Luis had answered all the family's questions, he had left the room, saying that Dr. Ibarra was waiting to examine him, which sent a ripple of relief through Eve. He was pushing himself too hard after his brush with death.

Then Bruno had informed Eve and Grace that Luis thought they would be better off at his private home, away from the media frenzy that the announcement about Grace had stirred up. Their belongings had already been packed and awaited them in the SUV.

Grace had surprised Eve by not objecting to being removed from the hubbub at the palace. Her daughter was lit up with energy and purpose, the way she had been when she was applying to vet school.

Eve snuck a glance at Grace and found her frowning. "What is it, sweetie?"

"I was just thinking about Felipe Camacho," Grace said. "What an asshole!"

"Er, that seems mild, considering he tried to kill your father," Eve said. The memory of Luis's too-still body in the hospital bed socked her in the gut.

"He'll be punished for that," Grace said, sounding a lot like Luis in that moment. "I was thinking about how he treated his daughter. When she needed him the most, he behaved like crap." She turned to Eve. "If I had gotten pregnant, you would have been there with me every step of the way, no matter who the father was."

"I'm glad you know that," Eve said, counting her blessings that she hadn't had to deal with that particular situation.

"Of course I do," Grace said without a moment's hesitation. "I don't blame his daughter for leaving Caleva. Felipe Camacho doesn't deserve to know his grandson."

"Keep in mind that he's an older man with a rigid set of religious beliefs. Maybe if his wife had still been alive, she might have softened his reaction," Eve said.

"Well, I'm glad he's not my father," Grace said before she brightened. "I got lucky. I've got the best parents in the world."

It hurt a little not to be the only parent any longer. At the same time, it eased some of the heavy responsibility.

Eve's head spun. Her emotions were in such a turmoil these days. She couldn't wait to get back to Iowa, where she would be able to get her mind right.

"Dad seems a lot better today, don't you think?" Grace asked.

Eve nearly groaned. When they had met before the *La Voix* interview, Luis's perfectly tailored navy suit had highlighted the glinting silver of his hair and the glacial blue of his eyes. What had really made her insides go liquid, though, had been the return of his electric charisma that blazed into every corner of the room.

"Only because we forced him to stay in bed for the rest of yesterday," Eve said. "He'll probably overdo things again and have a relapse tomorrow."

"Maybe you can persuade him to rest this afternoon," Grace said with a sideways glance.

"If he comes to the house, I'll try." Luis had offered no information about when they would see him again. She assumed sometime in the evening, since she and Grace were leaving for Iowa the next morning. On the royal jet.

That would be an experience.

Eve winced in anticipation of the hullabaloo in Ames. Mikel had already sent a security team to their house. Grace had texted her closest friends about the news after the announcement yesterday, so word would be out at the vet school. Dealing with all the questions was going to be a pain.

Even worse, Eve would have to live with Luis's absence. The prospect of it sent a jab of agony through her. At least she would not have to see him every day, to be reminded of how his hands felt on her skin and how the icy blue of his eyes could blaze hot when he looked at her. Of how her body melted with pleasure when he made love to her.

No, it was more than that. He made her feel like she was important to him. Important to a magnificent man who also happened to be a king. No wonder she had been stupid enough to fall in love with him.

The SUV slowed, and Eve glanced out the window to see the huge gates swinging open. But instead of heading straight toward the house, Ivan turned onto a different road that wound down toward the water.

Eve was too tired to ask questions, so she just sat back and let the car take her wherever Ivan had been directed to go. Soon enough, she would be on her own again, so she might as well enjoy her last day of being chauffeured around.

As they descended, the trees became fewer so the deep blue of the ocean was visible, the sun sparkling off the wavetops. She would miss the water when she returned to land-locked Iowa.

"Are you okay, Mom?" Grace asked, leaning forward. "You seem down."

"Well, we're leaving tomorrow, and I'll miss things like this view," Eve said, forcing herself to smile.

"We'll be back as soon as I graduate, so you won't have to do without it for long." With the buoyancy of youth, Grace was already looking forward to her new life.

While Eve was dreading hers.

The SUV glided to a stop, and Ivan leaped out to open Eve's door. Eve obediently exited the car, but turned back when she realized Grace was still seated. Her daughter grinned and gave her a wave before Ivan shut the door again.

"Eve!" Luis's voice came from the direction of the water.

She pivoted to see him standing on a pier where a sleek white speedboat was docked. Instead of his usual suit, he was wearing a loose white linen shirt over jeans. His smile was dazzling as he held out his hand, palm up. "Please join me."

"I…" She looked back to see the SUV making a smooth three-point turn before it headed back up the cliff road.

Well, shit! She wasn't going to be able to avoid this conversation with Luis.

On a boat. What was with that?

When she swiveled toward Luis again, he was closer, and his smile had dimmed, but he still reached for her. "I want to show you something beautiful. Will you come with me?"

She put her hand in his, the feel of his long fingers closing around hers sending a streak of longing through her. He pulled her to his side by threading her hand around his elbow.

And she understood. This was going to be a seduction, which she would have to resist with everything in her. It would be hard enough to survive without him as things were. If she spent more time in his arms, her heart would shatter when they were done.

"Do you suffer from seasickness?" Luis asked as they approached the boat.

"I don't know. I'm from Iowa," she said, trying to undercut her feelings with humor. "Not a lot of giant bodies of water there."

He nodded. "The sea is not rough today, so you should be fine." He released her hand. "Wait here a moment."

With a fluid motion, he stepped from the dock onto the craft's side and then onto the deck. Then he turned and held out both hands to her.

She suddenly realized she was still wearing her overused blue dress and high-heeled pumps. "I'm not really dressed for a sea voyage."

"*Ay*, of course." Luis made a sound of apology. "There are clothes for you in the cabin. For now, perhaps you could remove your shoes? I will make sure you do not slip and fall."

She hesitated. "Are you sure you should be exerting yourself like this?"

"Dr. Ibarra has cleared me, I swear." His expression was mock solemn as he drew a cross over his heart with one finger. "I knew you would not come if I did not consult with the good doctor."

She would believe him because he didn't lie to her, although he didn't specify what precisely the doctor had cleared him *for*.

Eve slipped off her heels and handed them to Luis to place on the boat's deck. When he turned back, she took his hands and stepped carefully onto the side of the boat. As she balanced there, he shifted forward, supporting her with all his strength. When she took the next step onto the deck, her body slid down the front of his with enough friction to fan the heat already flickering through her at his nearness.

When he did not move back, she looked up to find his face taut with the same desire that seared through her. For a moment, they stood, just barely touching, their gazes ensnared.

And then he surprised her by releasing her hands and turning. "The cabin is this way," he said, placing a hand on the small of her back to bring her in front of him.

As they went forward into the cockpit, she was startled to see a large blond man in a white shirt and teal shorts standing at the wheel.

"Our captain, Gervais," Luis said.

Gervais nodded. "Welcome aboard, *madame*."

"And here are the stairs to the cabin," Luis said, gesturing to a low door beside the helm. "Your bag is in the large bedroom."

He stepped away so she could duck through the hatch and descend the stairs. The interior of the boat was as sleek as the exterior, with highly varnished wooden built-ins. The bedroom held a king-sized platform bed tightly made up with snow-white linens. Her carry-on bag rested on top.

Who had packed it? Given Grace's complicit wave as the car door had closed, Eve suspected her daughter. She closed her eyes for a moment in sorrow. Of course Grace would like to see Luis and Eve together, but she didn't understand that it wouldn't be a lifetime commitment.

Shoving the thought aside, she unzipped the bag and spilled the contents onto the bed. Her toilet kit and hairbrush. Pink rubber-soled sandals that were actually Grace's. Her sundress and her bathing suit. No shorts or shirt. What had Grace been thinking?

Well, she couldn't wear the silk sheath on a boat, so she yanked down the back zipper and shimmied out of it. She wasn't going to wear the bathing suit, though, so she pulled on the sundress, a gauzy cream-colored sleeveless affair with a split neck held together by tasseled ties. Grace had talked her into buying it at a store in San Ignacio, even though Eve had thought it was a bit too young and Bohemian for her middle-aged Iowan style. She ran the brush through her hair and slipped on the sandals.

When she emerged from the hatch, Luis was still standing in the same place. The moment he saw her, his gaze focused like a laser. She could feel the intensity of it. "You look breathtaking, *querida*. The embodiment of summer."

His voice vibrated down into her bones like the deep purr of a big cat. She shivered at the endearment. "I bought the dress in San Ignacio. Grace picked it out for me."

"Our daughter has excellent taste," he said, his eyes crinkling with a father's affection.

Our daughter. He drew Eve in with every word.

"Let us sit on the front sundeck so you can see our destination as we approach it," Luis said. "Gervais will go slowly so we don't get wet."

He led her to a narrow walkway alongside the cockpit. Once they passed it, the deck opened up all the way to the bow of the cruiser with silver-gray sectional seating lining the space. The boat's engine rumbled to life, and a dockhand jogged up and down the pier, casting off the ropes.

Luis waited as Eve surveyed the seating options and chose the end of the sectional facing forward. He frowned a little at her message that she wasn't looking to sit beside him but settled in the corner, stretching out his long legs diagonally. She was surprised that he wore boat shoes with no socks. In fact, she had never seen him dressed so casually. He spread his arms across the back of the cushions and tilted his head back to bask in the sun, looking as though he hadn't a care in the world.

He didn't fool her. Kings always had cares.

The boat's engines changed timbre, and the cruiser eased away from the dock. When they motored out of the inlet and into open water, a chorus of engines rose as a small armada of motor craft moved into position around them. Not too close, but clearly in a defensive formation.

Their security escort.

Luis did not pay them any attention. In fact, he closed his eyes, although his posture did not indicate exhaustion, but rather enjoyment of being on the water in the sun with the breeze ruffling his silver-and-gray hair.

Since his eyes were closed, Eve savored the muscles of his forearms displayed by his rolled-up sleeves. Her gaze drifted across his powerful shoulders to skim down to the swell of his thigh muscles, those thighs that had pushed her own open so he could slide his cock inside her. She jerked her attention back up to his face and started when she found his blue eyes fastened on her.

She gave him a tight smile and shifted to stare forward as they rounded a rocky point. Ahead, a volcanic island rose out of the water, its rocky cliffs dotted with brilliant green shrubs. La Sorpresa de los Piratas.

Where Ricardo el Rojo had lured the Spanish galleons onto the rocks. Where Luis was luring her to what? Continuing their affair? She couldn't, but saying no was going to be hell.

She glanced back at him to find he still watched her. She tilted her head toward the island and mouthed, "La Sorpresa," because between the sea wind and the boat's engines, it was too loud to shout across the space between them.

His smile flashed as he nodded.

The wind picked up, whipping her hair across her face until she collected it in a ponytail within her fist. The boat danced a bit on the waves, occasionally sending a spray of water upward so a few droplets landed on Eve. In the bright sunshine, it was refreshing.

And then they were at the entrance to the island's sheltered bay, idling slowly between the stone walls that rose from the sea and into the perfect circle of turquoise water. Their escort boats did not accompany them, probably peeling off to patrol the exterior of the island.

"How stunning!" Eve gasped as they were embraced by the ancient volcano's sloping crater. A crescent of sand lay before them, but the cruiser veered toward a dock that jutted out into the blindingly blue water.

As they came alongside the pier, Luis grabbed a rope and leaped from the boat onto the wooden planks. With an expert's ease, he wrapped the line around a cleat in a figure eight. Gervais did the same at the boat's stern.

"Come ashore," Luis said, bending down to reach for her.

Supported by Luis's rock-solid grip, she stepped onto the gunwale and then the dock.

"Oh, my bag," she said. "It has my bathing suit." She wasn't going to miss the opportunity to swim in this incredible water.

Gervais disappeared down the hatch and returned to set her bag on the dock.

"Everything else we need is already here," Luis said, giving her hand a squeeze before he let go to cast off the rope.

Gervais swung the cruiser away from the dock and headed for the break in the volcano's wall.

"Now, we are here alone," Luis said. "Just a man and a woman. Nothing more and nothing less."

"You're telling me that Mikel has no bodyguards anywhere on this island," Eve said, doing her best to puncture the spell Luis was weaving around her.

Luis grinned. "I cannot fool you. There are guards, but they are on the outside walls, facing out to sea. No one is within this caldera. It is ours." He swept his arm around the circle. "I'm starving. Let's eat." He took her hand and picked up her overnight bag.

"There's food?" Eve walked beside him off the dock and onto a boardwalk that wound over the rocks toward the beach.

"I told you we have everything we need," he said.

"You might have a different idea of what we need than I do," Eve said, looking around at the incredible scenery as they strolled.

"At this moment, all I truly need is you. Beside me."

That yanked her attention back to Luis. He was looking down at her with that solemn intensity that made her insides dissolve into a delicious, warm goo.

"I, uh, right. Thank you." Why the hell was he torturing her like this?

His solemnity shifted to faint amusement, but he didn't comment on her lack of appropriate response.

They came over a slight rise in the rocks to find a teal-and-white-striped pavilion set up on the beach. Inside the canvas shelter, a table and two chairs rested on top of a large raffia rug. An array of teal-green coolers stood next to the dining area. Outside on the beach were two luxurious lounge chairs with stacks of white towels neatly folded on their cushions. A couple of closed beach umbrellas were staked into the sand next to them.

"Good Lord!" Eve said. "I feel like I've stumbled into the *Arabian Nights*."

Pleasure glowed in Luis's eyes. "Come into my tent with me."

"As long as I don't have to entertain you with stories." But she allowed him to seat her at the table.

He began flipping open cooler lids and pulling out containers of food, some warm, some cold, which he set on the table. Eve pried them open to find an array of seafood, fresh fruits and vegetables, and still-warm bread.

Luis rooted around in another cooler and triumphantly pulled out a bottle of Dom Perignon. Eve started to protest, but he had already popped the cork. He poured it into the two champagne flutes on the table and sat. "No picnic is complete without champagne." He tilted his glass toward her. "To our daughter!"

That was a safe toast, so she clinked her glass against his.

"Try the *percebes*—barnacles—and *lapas*—limpets." He held out a beautifully arranged platter of shellfish. "They were plucked from the sea this morning."

He didn't wait for her but placed a couple of each on her plate before he chose several for himself. Picking up a limpet shell, he sucked the meat off it like it was an oyster. "And that is how you eat it."

Eve examined the conical shell before lifting it to her lips. When she started to suck it into her mouth, Luis's gaze locked on her with a fiery intensity. Maybe that was why oysters were considered an aphrodisiac.

She put the shell down and used the tiny fork set beside her plate to eat the next one.

"The fork is for the *percebes*," Luis said, picking up what looked like a mossy rock with a hole in the top. He jabbed his fork inside the hole and pulled out a chunk of mostly white meat, which he held out to her across the table. "It tastes like the ocean."

His eyes were scorching as she took the shellfish into her mouth where the taste of the salt sea burst on her tongue. "This must be what mermaids eat," she said, dropping her eyes to stop the wave of heat searing through her just from his gaze. She took a gulp of champagne to cool off.

"How appropriate! The sirens of the sea," he said, his voice deep and smooth. "Have another."

She glanced up to see him holding out another chunk of barnacle to her. She bit it off the fork as quickly as possible before picking up her own fork. "I think I've got the hang of it now."

Instead of looking disappointed, he ate his shellfish while a satisfied smile curled his lips.

She was just as bad as he was, watching that sensual mouth of his slurping up limpets and remembering how those lips had felt against... Nope, not going there. Except she couldn't banish the thought, and she felt herself grow wet.

"Um, I'm not that hungry," she said. "You go ahead and eat while I go stick my feet in the water."

"I will go with you." He put his fork down and stood. "I want to see your face when you feel the temperature."

Oh, shit. She couldn't escape him.

"Let me get my sandals off," she said, reaching down to tug down the back strap. By the time she had slid out of both shoes, Luis was beside her, his own feet bare and his jeans rolled partway up his calves.

She stood, and he rested his hand on the small of her back as they strolled across the sand. She felt like her skin would be branded with his handprint as the warmth sank into her.

He stopped when they reached the water's edge. "I haven't been here in too many years," he said as he scanned the ancient volcano. "I had forgotten how beautiful it is."

His voice held awe, pride, and regret. Then he turned to her with a glinting smile. "Now you must feel the water." A light pressure from his hand moved her into the clear, sandy-bottomed shallows.

"Oh my gosh, it's like bathwater." She looked down at her warm, wet feet in astonishment.

He chuckled and stepped in himself. "It would be hotter if the ocean wasn't constantly swirling cold water into the caldera. There's a thermal vent somewhere far below here that spews forth enough heat to warm the whole harbor."

She wanted to go swimming in the beckoning water, but Luis would go too. The sight of his well-muscled body glistening with rivulets of water would make it impossible not to touch him.

She drew in a shaky breath and wiggled her toes in the sand. "Are there fish in here, or is it too hot for them?"

He didn't answer her, so she lifted her gaze to meet his. He was no longer smiling.

"Eve, *querida*, I don't wish to talk about fish." A few strands of her hair got caught in the breeze and whipped across her cheek. Before she could tame them, Luis tucked the strands behind her ear. Then he ran the back of his hand over her cheek. She forced herself not to lean into the delight of his skin against hers. "Perhaps we could sit," he said, gesturing toward the lounge chairs.

"Look, you don't have to apologize for how you reacted the other night," she said before the memory of him crumpling onto his knees made her heart twist all over again. "I never expected anything more than some…" *What?* "Some sex and fun." That sounded awful enough to put him off.

He ignored her speech, merely gesturing that she should go in front of him to the lounge chairs.

She moved the towels and perched on the foot of one. Luis did the same, sitting sideways so he was facing her. He started to reach for her hands but changed his mind, letting his wrists drape over his knees as he looked straight at her.

"Eve, when you said you weren't cut out to be a queen, I did not hesitate because I thought you were right." His eyes clouded with guilt. "And I hate that you have believed that all this time."

Eve opened her mouth, trying to think of something to say to stop him from making this worse, but he held up his hand. "Please, let me explain."

She knotted her hands together on her lap and waited.

He looked away for a moment before returning his gaze to her face. "I have made such terrible choices in the women I have loved. Long ago, I made a decision never to marry again because I could not bear to make another mistake. It seemed better to go through life alone than to destroy the life of another woman."

She couldn't bear for him to think that about himself. "You didn't des—"

He shook his head to stop her, his lips in a tight line. "It's how I felt. So I put the hope for a relationship built on love out of my mind. Very successfully." He gave a self-mocking grimace. "As it happens, it is surprisingly difficult to come to know a woman well when one is a king."

"I can imagine." She thought of the number of people surrounding him most of his waking hours. Of the constant claims on his time and attention. Of the schemers and syco-phants who cared about him only because of his position. Her heart ached for his strange loneliness.

"But I had the good fortune to find not only a daughter, but her mother, a woman I came to know well," he said, his face softening. "Eve, I didn't hesitate because I don't believe you are queen material. I hesitated because my mind had been closed to the idea for so long that I needed time to process the astonishing possibility. I was stunned that I had been so blind as not to see you in that light before."

"And then you collapsed," Eve said flatly. But her heart was banging against the walls of her chest in an unsettled way.

"The timing could not have been worse," he said, his tone grim. "For that alone, I will never forgive Camacho."

Eve would never forgive Camacho for nearly killing the man she loved.

Luis reached for her hands now, holding them gently in his, the touch sending sparks up her arms to race through her body.

"*Mi querida*, what I ask of you I do not ask lightly. Being queen is not something you want, I know. All I can say is that you can do much good in the country and even in the world from that position. That might balance the burden somewhat." His sigh came from deep in his lungs.

He clasped her hands more tightly. Eve was grateful for that because she was beginning to shake with nerves. What was Luis leading to?

"I think you would make a spectacular queen, but that does not matter." His face was luminous with emotion. "I brought you here, away from all the trappings of my position, because I wanted to speak to you as just a man. Because I want you as a man wants a woman. I want your face to be the one I see first every morning and last every night. I want to worship your body and give you the pleasure you deserve. I want to cherish and protect you."

His gaze traveled over her face as though he was trying to will her to say something, but Eve could not make her tongue move. She could barely get any oxygen into her lungs.

He changed tack. "We would be a family. Raul, Grace, you, and me. It would be incomplete without you. You are the glue, the final piece. Without you, there would always be an empty space."

Tears welled in her eyes at the haze of sadness over his face.

As he leaned forward, his tone became urgent. "Please do not shut me out of your life. Allow me the chance to change your mind."

Hope was doing a tap dance in her chest, but she couldn't give in to it yet. "To change my mind about what, exactly?"

"*Ay*, Eve, I am offering you my battered, rusty heart. No, it is already yours. I love you, *cariño mío!* With everything in me." His grip on her hands was so tight it almost hurt. "I want the chance to make you feel the same way about me."

She thought her heart would explode with joy. "Oh, you clueless man, I love you too. That's why I tried to leave you."

His eyes burned with a luminous exhilaration. "I don't entirely understand, but I don't care." He released her hands to cup her face and kiss her with desperate hunger, his lips questing and yet tender. She hung on to his broad shoulders as she answered him by opening to him and teasing his tongue.

He pulled away an inch to say, "You love me," with a look of amazement before he kissed her again, his hands sliding into her hair to tilt her head to the angle he wanted. Once again, he stopped, his face a study in relief. "I thought I was going to lose you."

"I thought I was going to lose *you* Saturday night," Eve said. "That was much worse."

"I had no intention of dying when I had just found a daughter and the love of my life." He yanked at the ties holding her neckline closed so he could lick the hollow at the bottom of her throat.

Desire raced through her like a wildfire, and she moaned as she let her head fall back. He skimmed his lips lower to the swell of her breast. Heat liquified between her legs, and she ached to have him inside her.

"Wait!" She threaded her fingers into his hair to lift his head away from her. "Did Dr. Ibarra clear you for...*this?*"

"She told me to listen to my body." He cupped Eve's breasts, his gaze a scorch of wanting. "And this is what it is telling me to do."

The pressure on her aroused nipples ripped electric sensation through her. "I don't think that's what the doctor meant." But Eve's body agreed with his, so she gave in.

Sliding her hands inside the open collar of his shirt, she traced her thumbs over the sharp lines of his collarbones. The buttons slipped from the buttonholes as she pushed the linen aside so she could brush her palms against the light furring over the hard planes of his chest. She found the raised circles of his nipples and danced her fingers over them.

He groaned and sat still as she jerked his shirt all the way open. "You are so gorgeous," she said, running her hands over the sculpted muscles of his abs before she skimmed them down to rub the hard bulge of his erection.

"*Madre de Dios*, yes!" He hissed through his teeth as she stroked him again. "I cannot go slowly."

He glanced around before grabbing the terry cloth sheet tucked over the lounge cushion. Standing, he flicked it open like a tablecloth and let it settle on the sand.

He took her hands and drew her to her feet before he touched the hem of her dress. "May I?"

"Oh, please, yes!" She would have ripped it off herself, but it was far better to have him drag it up until she lifted her arms so he could pull it off and fling it away. Then his hands were all over her body, unhooking her bra and tossing it, skimming her panties to her ankles so she would step out of them while using his strong, chiseled shoulder to balance herself.

He wrapped his hands around her hips, his fingers stroking the curves of her bottom, while she unbuckled his belt and unzipped his jeans. He let go of her to shove his jeans and briefs onto the sand.

They stood for a long moment, simply savoring the sight of each other naked in this beautiful place. Then Luis reached for her, and their bodies slammed together in a whirlwind of heat and touch.

When he slid his hand between them to glide a finger against her clit, Eve's knees nearly buckled at the explosion of sensation.

"Now! Please, now!" she gasped out as she arched into his hand. "Make love to me!"

Without releasing her, he moved them both to the spread cloth and sank onto it. Eve lay down, arching her back and spreading her legs in a blatant invitation. She thought she might die of frustration if he wasn't inside her in the next few seconds.

But he knelt between her legs and did nothing more than stare down at her, although his face was tight with barely restrained lust. "I wish to worship your body, to wrap you in pleasure."

Eve lifted her hips, knowing that he could see the glistening of her arousal on the insides of her thighs. "I want you inside me *now!*"

He seized her hips, lifting them even higher before he plunged into her, seating himself deeply, filling the ache while driving her hunger higher. She covered his hands with hers and rolled her pelvis against him.

Then he was moving, fast and hard, and the delicious tension wound tighter and tighter in her belly, building with every thrust. "Yes, yes, yes, yes!" she panted.

"Eve, *cariño mío, mi corazón, mi amor!*" he answered her.

An exquisite moment of stillness held her on the edge, the world contracting to the place where they were joined. And then she convulsed in an orgasm so intense she shrieked and arched and dug her fingernails into his hands.

As her muscles clamped around him, he threw back his head and shouted in Spanish, his release pumping inside her and triggering another climax of her own.

Closing her eyes, she savored the ripples of afterglow, but even more the feel of Luis inside her, his grip on her hips easing to almost a caress.

"*Mi corazón,*" he said, his voice a husky whisper.

She pried her eyelids open to see him gazing down at her, the angles of his face soft with tenderness. He slid out of her and stretched out on the towel, rolling her halfway onto his chest. "I adore you," he said, stroking his hand over her hair and down her back.

"I'm glad," she said. "I adore you too." She couldn't stop a few tears that trickled down her cheeks and onto his chest.

"Why are you crying?" He shifted abruptly to lift her chin, frowning as he ran his thumb over the wet tear tracks.

"Because I'm so happy. And because we just had amazing sex," she said.

"It *was* amazing." He smirked a little before the frown returned. "But that should not make you weep."

"It's a normal thing when you're madly in love," she said, cupping his cheek. "It even has a scientific name, but you've fried my brain so I can't remember it."

"Say that you are madly in love again," he commanded.

"I'm madly, crazily, insanely in love with you," she said, tilting her face to receive his kiss. "Now tell me you love me too."

He whispered it against her lips. "I love you. *Je t'aime. Te adoro.* In every language I speak, my heart belongs to you."

His words licked over her skin, into her veins, and curled themselves into her heart.

Luis lay on the towel, cushioned by the soft sand, the sun warm on his face, and thanked God that he was alive. Not because he had nearly died only three days ago, but because of the incredible woman whose body was pressed against his chest and ribs and thighs. He tangled his fingers in her glorious, shining hair and heaved a sigh of pure contentment.

She stirred a moment before going still again, and he smiled. They were both lax with satisfaction.

Happiness soaked into the marrow of his bones. He had not thought he would ever feel this way again… No, he had never felt like this before. Had never known this solid sense of rightness in his world.

He was accustomed to being alone, had accepted that it was how he would live the rest of his life. He had come to believe that being king meant he must be apart and solitary. After his past experiences, he had not dared to seek more. He could still feel the aching emptiness of his isolation.

Yet now he had not one, but two children who filled him with love and delight. His beloved, damaged nephew had found joy again. His country was peaceful and prosperous.

But his profound happiness came from this extraordinary woman, who was more than a friend, more than a lover.

She was the partner of his soul.

As his heart swelled with the immensity of his emotions, he understood why she had cried.

EPILOGUE

Seven Months Later

Eve heard the crunch of tires on gravel and then car doors opening and closing. Voices drifted through the open window of the small stone-walled room where she stood, fidgeting with the bouquet of Calevan lilies clutched in her trembling hands.

Grace's question wafted in first. "Is this some kind of a church?"

"It's a chapel." The response came from Gabriel, since they were on his parents' estate.

"Oh my God!" Grace had figured out what was about to happen. "I can't believe she didn't tell me."

Luis had proposed to Eve only three days before. On La Sorpresa de los Piratas. And they had made love floating in the warm blue water afterward. Her skin flushed with delicious heat at the memory.

She had not hesitated to say yes, because there on the island, they were just a man and a woman who adored each other. More all the time.

But now the weight of what she was marrying into sent the butterflies in her stomach into a frenzy.

She pulled her right hand away from the bouquet to look at the engagement ring. She had moved it to leave her left ring finger bare for the ceremony. The ring sported a large oval ruby of the same deep red as the lilies in her bouquet, set off by a frame of diamonds set in deep yellow gold. It had been made for Queen Isabella, a gift from her husband, the grandson of a kidnapped English nobleman. Now it was Eve's.

Because she would be the Queen of Caleva.

The stomach butterflies started turning somersaults. She took a deep breath and brought up the image of Luis emerging from the turquoise harbor of the caldera, naked, the water sparkling as it ran down along the curves and valleys of his muscles. That was who she was marrying today. A man who happened to come with a crown.

A man who had agreed to her request for a small, private wedding with only family and very close friends, even though he wanted to shout their love to the world. She had asked for this because she figured it would be the last private ceremony for the rest of her life.

The ancient wooden door to her little sanctuary creaked open, and Carmen, leader of the infamous Protocol Squad, slipped inside. "It is almost time, *señora*," she said.

When it was decided to hold the wedding as soon as possible, Carmen had proven to be an invaluable ally and general. She had conjured up musicians, flowers, and a custom-made dress. Luis had taken on the job of enlisting the Archbishop of San Ignacio, sworn to secrecy, to conduct the ceremony.

Carmen fussed around Eve, fluffing the pale rose-colored lace skirt of the tea-length dress. "May I say that you look very beautiful."

"*Muchas gracias.* For everything." Eve smiled at the intimidating woman before she turned to the mirror, a modern touch in the medieval space.

Her hair was swept up in elegant waves to support a diamond tiara, pulled from the vault under the palace. A fingertip-length veil of fragile rose silk tulle with beading along the edges fell over Eve's shoulders and back. The dress's bodice was fitted, with a sheer lace overlay across her shoulders and down to her elbows, while the skirt billowed out over several layers of tulle. Her rose satin pumps were beaded in swirling designs of lilies and *vaho* hibiscus.

Her only other pieces of jewelry were the gold earrings Grace had given her and the lily pendant Luis had gifted her with on her arrival in Caleva. She touched it now, amazed at how far she had come from that day.

Old, Queen Isabella's ring. New, the dress. Borrowed, the tiara. Blue, her toenails. She had painted them pale blue because Luis thought her polished toenails were sexy.

The music from the small orchestra ceased, and she heard a stir from the chapel's nave. Luis must have emerged from his own waiting room to stand at the altar. Carmen cracked the door open so they could listen.

"My family. My friends. *Bienvenido!*" His deep, smooth voice carried without apparent effort all the way into their room by the chapel's entrance. Eve felt it vibrate inside her.

"You have undoubtedly guessed that you are here to attend the marriage of my adored Eve and myself. We wished it to be a private declaration of our commitment to each other, with only our most beloved in attendance. Thank you for doing us the honor of being our witnesses."

There was an excited murmur of voices, and then the orchestra began to play the bright, brassy "Hornpipe" from

Handel's *Water Music*, chosen in honor of Caleva's island identity...and Luis's proposal site.

Carmen opened the door wide with an encouraging nod, and Eve stepped out onto the red carpet overlaying the mosaic aisle of Finca de Bruma's medieval chapel. Stone arches soared over her head, and stained-glass windows threw brilliant colors across the pews and the guests.

Eve took a deep breath and started forward, smiling tremulously as she scanned the faces turned toward her. Mikel, in a dark suit as always, but accompanied by his teenage daughter, the irrepressible Serena. Luis's right-hand man, Bruno, with his lovely blond wife. Grace's two best friends from college and vet school, who had spent many a night studying at Eve's dining room table. Eve's closest friend from the clinic, Dr. Pam Baker. The Iowans had been lured to Caleva on the pretext of a post-graduation vacation, all expenses paid.

There were Luis's brother, Lorenzo, and his wife, Hélène. The brilliantly talented Gabriel and his fiancée, Quinn, who had helped Grace and Eve with their induction into the royal family.

Handsome, hardworking Raul, whom she was coming to love as a son. Darling, wonderful Grace, now officially Dr. Grace Howard Dragón, her face beaming with delight.

Beyond them, in front of the altar, stood two men. The archbishop, dressed in sweeping ceremonial robes and pointed hat.

But Eve's focus locked on Luis, standing tall, straight, and magnificent in his dark red uniform jacket loaded with medals and gold braid over his teal-green trousers with their red stripes. The window above him threw a splash of bright gold over his face and hair so he appeared to glow from within.

The aisle seemed so long when she just wanted to be beside him, but she forced herself to process slowly, as a queen-to-be should. She would enjoy unfastening all his gold buttons later.

As she reached the apse, Luis stepped forward to take her right hand. His expression was solemn, but his ice-blue eyes were brimming with his love. It washed through her like the warm water of the caldera. She hoped he could see the same emotion in her face.

He smiled and tucked her hand into his elbow, turning them both toward the priest. As the archbishop intoned the beautiful words of the marriage service, Eve felt every tiny shift in Luis's body. Even the air brushing her skin was permeated with his presence.

Luis spoke the simple, formal vows first. She had expected him to do his magic voice-projection trick, but instead he stated them in a low, intimate timbre that was almost a caress, his eyes blazing down at her. When he came to the phrase "until death do us part," they held each other's gazes at the memory of what might have happened.

It was her turn, and she made sure every wedding guest could hear what she said. It took a couple of hard swallows before she could begin, but once she got going, the words rang out loud and clear.

"The rings, if you please," the priest said.

Eve placed her bouquet on the small table Carmen had positioned for this purpose. She slipped Luis's simple gold wedding band off her thumb and placed it on the velvet cushion held by the archbishop.

After he blessed the rings, the archbishop offered the cushion to Eve. Picking up the ring and taking Luis's left hand, she said, "With this ring, I thee wed and pledge you my love, now and forever." Such simple words to contain a promise for the rest of their lives.

She slid the ring down his long, elegant finger and squeezed his hand before letting go.

Luis picked up her matching gold band and took her hand, repeating the same vow. He lifted the ring to his lips for a kiss before easing it onto her finger.

They turned back to the archbishop, who solemnly pronounced them husband and wife before breaking into a smile. "You may kiss each other."

Luis wrapped his arm around her waist and pulled her against him from shoulder to knee before he bent to kiss her, long and with carnal intensity, while she clung to his shoulders to keep her knees from buckling.

The church erupted into whistles and hoots.

Eve pulled back a few inches from Luis's marauding mouth. "You're not supposed to kiss like that in church."

"I'm the king," he said, those gorgeous, sculpted lips curving in a wicked smile. "I can kiss my bride any way I want to."

And he did.

ACKNOWLEDGMENTS

A book like this does not get produced in a vacuum. It takes the support and input of an incredible cast of brilliant people who lend their expertise to various parts of the process. I am so grateful to this amazing team who have helped to bring *Royal Caleva: Luis* into the world.

Huge thanks to:

My critique group, Miriam Allenson, Lisa Verge Higgins, and Jennifer Wilck, who not only make my books so much better, but who keep me sane. Of course, they are writers too, so they may not be the best arbiters of sanity. That's why I love them so much.

My developmental editor (and audio agent), Andrea Hurst, who is always right about what needs fixing, no matter how much I wish she wasn't. Truly, she makes every story I write stronger by whole orders of magnitude. She also made it possible for my audio fans to listen to the Royal Caleva novels.

My copy editor, Joyce Lamb, who is spectacular at catching my many, many mistakes...and I'm not just talking grammar. She prevented me from changing Mikel's eye color, caught my foul-up of Luis's backstory timeline, and corrected a myriad of other details that I botched. I am in awe of her attention to the smallest issues. (By the way, Joyce did not copy edit these acknowledgments because I had not written them yet, so don't blame her if there are mistakes in them.)

My cold reader, Jessica Poore, who made sure I included enough information about Caleva and its denizens so a reader of this book wouldn't be confused if she/he hadn't read the first book in the series. Jessica's smart suggestions were invaluable.

My proofreader, Kimberly Dawn, whose eagle eye catches all the errors I inserted while trying to fix the problems my copy editor, Joyce, found. I feel so much more confident about publishing my book after Kimberly has run her fine-tooth comb through it.

My cover designer, Eileen Carey, who somehow just *knows* what I want the cover to look like—I think she and I are linked psychically—and produces something even better than my original concept.

My formatter, Lisa Verge Higgins, who sweats every single tiny detail of both digital and print editions, so they look beautiful and clear for my readers. Yes, this is my second mention of her because she does it all. Lisa is a marvel!

My marketing guru, Laurie Cooper of Pub-Craft, who keeps me organized and moving forward through a long list of tasks, so the world will know about the release of *Royal Caleva: Luis*. She is a joy to work with and is another one of those people who keep me sane.

The New Jersey Romance Writers, a wonderful community of fellow writers who cheer me on and share my madness. It's good to know other folks who hear voices in their heads.

My children and children-of-the-heart, Rebecca, Loukas, Emily, and a new addition to the family, Sal, all of whom remind me that there is a life outside my fictional world and draw me into it with love and laughter. I'm so proud of all of them!

My sister Damon and her family, who daily demonstrate the meaning of courage and love.

Mobi and Skoda, my tabby cat brothers who have brought so much love, delight, and purring into my home. I even named my publishing imprint after them.

The members of my Review Crew, the fabulous folks who read my books before all the typos get fixed and who post stellar—but always honest!—reviews on the day the book releases. They are so important to the success of my stories. I honor their commitment and hard work.

My readers, who close the circle for me as an author and whose support allows me to keep publishing more of the stories that I love to write and that they—thank goodness!—love to read. You are the wind beneath my wings!

ALSO BY NANCY HERKNESS

To find out more about my books and to buy them,
go to my website: www.NancyHerkness.com.
While you're there, sign up for my newsletter
and receive free novellas.

Royal Caleva series
Royal Caleva: Gabriel
How to Plan a Royal Wedding: A Novella

The Consultants series
The Money Man
The Hacker
The Agent

Second Glances series
Second to None: A Novella
Second Time Around
Second Act

Wager of Hearts series
The CEO Buys In
The All-Star Antes Up
The VIP Doubles Down
The Irishman's Christmas Gamble: A Novella

Whisper Horse novels
Take Me Home
Country Roads
The Place I Belong
A Down-Home Country Christmas: A Novella

Stand-Alone novels
A Bridge to Love
Shower of Stars
Music of the Night

ABOUT NANCY

Nancy Herkness is the award-winning, best-selling author of contemporary romance for readers who love richly developed characters and an immersive reading experience. If you want to savor the thrill of falling in love, dive into one of Nancy's books.

Author of the Royal Caleva, Consultants, Wager of Hearts, and Whisper Horse series, as well as several other contemporary romance novels, Nancy has sold over a million books. She is also a two-time nominee for the Romance Writers of America's RITA® award.

Nancy has received many honors for her work, including the American Fiction Award for Romance, the Booksellers' Best Award, and the National Excellence in Romance Fiction Award. She graduated from Princeton University with a degree in English literature and creative writing.

A native of West Virginia, Nancy now lives twelve miles west of the Lincoln Tunnel in suburban New Jersey with two tabby cats.

For more information about Nancy and her books, visit www.NancyHerkness.com. While you're there, sign up for her monthly newsletter—and get a free novella or two.

Made in the USA
Monee, IL
13 June 2024